Love you to DEATH

Published in the UK by Scholastic, 2023
1 London Bridge, London, SE1 9BG
Scholastic Ireland, 89E Lagan Road, Dublin Industrial Estate,
Glasnevin, Dublin, D11 HP5F

ISBN 978 0702 32543 4

A CIP catalogue record for this book
is available from the British Library.

Printed by CPI Group (UK) Ltd, Croydon, CR0 4YY
Paper made from wood grown in sustainable forests
and other controlled sources.

1 3 5 7 9 10 8 6 4 2

www.scholastic.co.uk

GINA BLAXILL

Love you to DEATH

SCHOLASTIC

To the Kalettes, Melanie and Nina —
all the best things come in threes.

Sunday 26 February

Sunday dawns with foreboding clouds that swiftly blacken. It's like the weather gods know my mood.

The seafront draws me to it like a magnet. There's something so atmospheric about the crashing waves and poor light when I feel low.

Aaron hasn't messaged. I really thought he would have by now. I'm usually the one who compromises when we fight, but I can't bring myself to apologize after how he behaved last night.

I'm halfway up the pier when some activity by the cliffs catches my eye. There's a cordon flapping in the wind and a growing crowd. Are those … police officers? There are figures in scrubs too, shielding whatever's happened.

Wait. That's not just any patch of beach. It's the nook.

Our nook. The secret place Aaron and I share.

I feel the air frost over. The only sound is the deafening thump of my heart, growing louder and louder. My feet fly down the wonky wooden slats. By the time I hit the beach I'm panting, my chest tearing in two, but I push on until I reach the nook.

Someone in uniform steps into my path, telling me in a low, firm voice that this is a crime scene and to please move away. Other voices echo around me. One word cuts through the hubbub.

Body.

It can't be.

Surely Aaron wouldn't jump. *Get a hold of yourself, Mia.* Yes, he was finding school tough, he talked about being under pressure, he was still struggling with grief, but he was getting better. Our argument wasn't catastrophic. I would know if things were that bad, right?

I pull out my phone.

WhatsApp: no messages from Aaron Mercer.

Aaron Mercer, last seen online yesterday at 19.38.

Aaron Mercer's voicemail, his familiar cheery voice asking me to leave a message.

Bleep.

A social media notification pops up on my screen.

Followed by another.

And another.

My feed's *exploding*.

In a daze I read the messages.

RIP mia, wish id known you better, you didn't deserve to die
Heaven's gained another angel, I hope you're at peace, fly

high Mia
Can't believe you're gone. So tragic. RIP xxx

What the hell?

More comments spring up. I feel like I'm in the grip of a nightmare, like I've gatecrashed my own funeral. Is this some sick, elaborate joke? But why—

Oh. *Oh.*

Further down the feed is another thread:

What happened??
Go to the beach. Police are everywhere. There's a body. It's definitely Mia.

But it isn't me. I'm here on the wet shingle surrounded by excited chatter and the crash of the waves.

If the body isn't mine … it must be *hers.*

Eight days earlier

"Crazy bitch!"

The man is right up in my face. I'm too startled to react at first. I've waited for friends at the end of this residential street dozens of times with no problem. It's early afternoon – broad daylight. Not the time for trouble.

Hoping he'll lose interest, I avert my eyes and back away, bumping into the postbox. Something sharp snags my tights.

The man leers close. He reeks of booze, his eyes wild and bloodshot. "What's with the frilly doll dress?" he slurs. "It's the twenty-first century, love."

A fleck of spittle lands on my cheek.

"Please leave me alone." It doesn't come out sounding very assertive.

This man's big, unpredictable. I'm aware of everything. How tiny I am in comparison. The empty street. *Run*. My boots have heels, but he's drunk. Surely I can outpace him. I slide around the postbox, but the man's arm shoots out, stopping me.

"Know what I think?" His face is close enough for me to see the crumbs in his beard. My heart lurches into my mouth. "I think—"

"Is there a problem here?" The voice is my boyfriend Aaron's. Over the man's shoulder I spy him jogging towards us.

Drunk guy instantly withdraws. "All right, all right, mate. Just a bit of banter."

Aaron reaches us, sliding his arm around me protectively. "Lay off her, all right? Go. Now."

And, like magic, the man legs it, zigzagging across the pavement.

Aaron turns to me, face flushed from running and full of concern. His eyes have a wild spark in them. "Are you OK, Mia?"

Did the last minute just happen? "I … don't know. He was suddenly there, insulting me. If you hadn't come—"

I stop. Horrible and all-too-common stories about what happens to girls who have the misfortune to be in the wrong place at the wrong time flit through my mind. My legs go putty-like and I lean into the safety of his arms.

"You're safe now," Aaron says. "It's OK. Just a random drunk man." His voice catches as he squeezes me tight. It sounds like he's reassuring himself as much as me.

Aaron isn't usually intense like this. I lean back so I can meet his eyes. "I'm fine, Aaron. It's over now."

He gives me a weak version of the usual wide, shy smile I love. "Just as well he backed off. I'm not sure what I'd have done if he hadn't. I'm a lover, not a fighter." He cranes his neck in the direction the man stumbled. "Do you still want to go into town? I don't mind if you'd rather not."

"No, let's go. We can't stand Leyla up. I might need one of those hideously expensive brownies, though. You know, as a pick-me-up. You look like you could use one too."

"I'll treat you." Aaron lets go of my shoulder but takes my hand. He's looking sheepish now.

My own shock is fading too. Part of me is ashamed. Was I pathetic back there? Should I have handled it myself? Been firm, instead of defaulting to being nice? Ugh, I even said *please*.

I glance up at Aaron, wondering what it's like to never feel physically vulnerable. He's skinny and all arms and legs, with floppy ginger hair and big glasses, but his shoulders are broad, and at over six feet tall, people think twice before messing with him.

He catches me looking. "What was this 'banter' about, anyway?"

"My clothes, obviously." I look down at my flouncy moss-green dress, hemmed with a white frill. I've layered it with a roomy crocheted lace cardigan, a new Etsy steal which makes me feel cute and comfortable. Ten minutes ago, I'd been excited about showing the outfit off. If I'd zipped my parka up, the man probably wouldn't have picked on me at all. "It's too much, isn't it?"

"No! You look great. Is that the hairband you made with the stuff from the market?"

How lucky am I to have a guy who notices things like this? Aaron's into aesthetic details – he's designed some incredible original characters for the manga he's been sharing online. Without his encouragement, I'd never have had the confidence to go full-on Mori Girl, a look I fell in love with after reading *Honey and Clover*. The idea is you dress like you live in the forest, in natural fabrics and draping layers, all neutral shades and earth tones.

Buoyed up, I squeeze his hand. We chat about Aaron's manga as we wind through streets of tall, Edwardian terraced housing. Aaron warns me not to look at a lamp post with a missing pet poster; he knows I can't deal with anything bad happening to animals.

Soon we're in the town centre. It's heaving, just like it has been all half-term. A lively warren of winding lanes with independent shops selling everything from beads to books to artisan sandwiches, Southaven is colour and buzz all year round.

The Green Leaf, my favourite coffee shop, is tucked

down a quieter lane between a vintage clothing boutique and a bubble-tea parlour. A rainbow flag flutters from the first-floor window. The bell jangles as I push the door open.

Behind the till is the owner, Cale. He raises his eyebrows. "Oh, hey, Mia. Did you forget something?"

I frown as I loosen my scarf. "Um, no? We've only just arrived."

"Huh. You weren't here ten minutes ago?"

I shake my head, bemused.

Cale peers at me more closely. "A girl I could swear was you just left. Ayo saw her too. Didn't you, hon?"

"Sure did," Cale's husband calls from the kitchen.

"Really? How much did she look like me?"

"Enough that I didn't question it. There was a queue so we didn't chat – I guess I wasn't paying enough attention. She must've thought I'd lost it, handing over your usual latte without even asking what she wanted! Are you sure you're not messing with me?"

Cale carries on joking as he brews our coffees. This girl must have been quite convincing for both him and Ayo to make a mistake – I pop into The Green Leaf all the time. So I have a lookalike. One who accepted my oat milk latte, then vanished into the chilly February afternoon.

I'm already forming a suspicion of who she might be…

"Don't," I say to Aaron, who is struggling not to grin. "It's not funny."

"It is a bit though, Mia."

9

I roll my eyes and go to join Leyla, who's nabbed the table by the window with the big sofas. My best friend's wearing an oversized tee with a spaceship motif, loose jeans and a jacket nicked from her brother Riyad's wardrobe. Her curly black bob is tucked behind her ears, her glasses slightly steamed up.

"Did you hear that?" I ask.

"Nuh-uh, Mimi." Leyla picks up her phone. "We don't talk until you get a question right. Let's see… How many of Henry VIII's wives were called Catherine?"

"Ugh, Ley. Give it a break."

"You know the rules."

This "rule" is a new one, ever since my form tutor Mr Ellison selected me for the school Quiz Challenge team, along with Riyad and our friend Oliver. Hardly cool, but I'm secretly thrilled – I've never been chosen for anything before. My GCSE results were what our head of year politely described as "variable".

I take a wild stab. "Three?"

"Correct." Leyla grins. "And yeah, I heard. You know what this means, don't you?"

I groan. "It means you were right."

A month ago, Leyla and I were in the indie bookshop, trying to decide which of the thrillers in the window display would be best for Mum's birthday present. Leyla had nudged me and pointed out the year eleven girl at the bus stop outside, long hair in the same half-up half-down style I often wear, with a big white bow just like one I own.

On her shoulder swung a Studio Ghibli tote bag identical to mine.

"This must have been her," says Leyla. "She's been copying your style for weeks. Every time we see her, there's something new. Her coat's a lot like yours. For all we know, she dresses the same as you outside of school too. We've never seen her in anything other than the violet horror, have we?"

For the billionth time, I'm grateful that sixth formers don't have to wear the school uniform that somehow managed to be equally unflattering for my pale freckled skin and Leyla's light brown.

"It can't have been her, though. She's blonde." I swivel around. "Hey, Cale? What colour was that girl's hair?"

"Same as yours," says Cale.

I turn back to Leyla. "See? It was someone else."

She looks at me knowingly. "Or year eleven girl has dyed her hair."

"Oh my God. Do you think so?" I let out a low whistle. "A lot of girls would kill for corn-blonde hair. Why would she dye it mousy brown?"

Aaron arrives, balancing our coffees on a wooden tray. "Is this such a big deal? Maybe she's just into the same look as you?"

I doubt that. Mori Girl is way past its peak of popularity and these days it's niche even in Japan. But I push the thought away. "Yeah, maybe. We don't *know* she's dyed her hair." Embarrassed, I search for a new topic. "Hey, you know what happened on my way here, Ley? Aaron saved me…"

As soon as I've said it, I wish I hadn't. *Leyla* wouldn't need to be saved. She'd have sorted it out herself. Drunk guy probably wouldn't have challenged her at all. I'm the one who's polite and likes to please. Until now, I thought that was the best way to get by, to not make myself into a target.

Leyla gives Aaron side-eye. "Is this story going to make me want to vomit? You guys are too much sometimes."

Aaron clasps his coffee cup, his expression clouding over. "Some drunk guy was hassling Mia. He was pretty aggressive, and I thought— Well. It was good timing that I showed up. I didn't do much, though."

Cale interrupts by delivering a warm vegan brownie which is oozing chocolatey goodness.

"I know you two share everything," he says, placing it between me and Aaron with two forks. "Oh, are you coordinating today?"

I glance at Aaron's pale green T-shirt. "Not intentionally."

"Too cute," says Cale. "Could you be any better matched?"

I secretly love it when people tease us, even though it's cheesy as anything. "I mean … Aaron *could* stop eating meat and dairy," I say, waggling my eyebrows, and Aaron pulls a face.

"Well, nobody's perfect," says Cale. "Ask your friend Oliver which film that's a quote from, he'll know. Is he not coming today? You guys are normally the fabulous foursome."

"He's working, I think."

"Shame. Remember, I want an invitation to the wedding when it happens, lovebirds." Then the doorbell tinkles, and Cale goes to welcome two guys carrying a cute French bulldog.

Leyla slides her phone across the table. "Your doppelgänger's name is Jade," she says. "I've seen her with Camille Bailey – turns out Camille's her year thirteen mentor. Feel free to compliment my brilliant detective work."

The screen shows a WhatsApp chat between Leyla and Camille. Camille's shared a link to a photo on the school website. I zoom in on one of the girls in the shot. This is the first decent look I've had at Jade's face, and *whoa*. It's like looking in a mirror. Well, not quite – her chin's sharper than mine, her nose less upturned, and her hair's nowhere near as long. I can almost sit on mine. But we both have the doll-like faces with big eyes that often have people assuming you're younger than you are. Jade even has freckles too, and she looks pretty petite.

With *brown* hair…

No wonder Cale and Ayo mistook Jade for me! I can't write off the similarities any longer. This isn't coincidental, or someone taking a bit of style inspiration. A girl I have never even spoken to is copying my look, right down to very specific details.

We discuss Jade as we finish our drinks. According to Camille, Jade hasn't made herself very popular since she started, loudly complaining about what a dump Southaven High is, and how she'd rather be at her old school. Normally I'd have sympathy – it can't be easy moving with GCSEs looming – but this whole thing has set me on edge. Jade and I could easily exist never crossing paths. Sixth form teaching happens in an entirely different building to the rest of the school. But she must be watching me, taking an interest in me – to the extent of copying all my accessories and dyeing her hair to match mine...

It feels too odd. Almost violating.

Sinister, even.

"Are we going to talk about this all afternoon?" Aaron asks playfully, after the conversation has circled several times. "If it bothers you, ask her. It's probably just a compliment." He lays down his fork. As usual he's gobbled up most of the brownie. "Be right back."

Leyla waits for Aaron to vanish to the toilets before saying what I knew she would. "He seems in a good mood today."

I scoop up the last wedge of brownie. "Maybe he's starting to feel normal again."

"If I didn't know better, I'd ask if you set up that playing-hero thing. Let's hope his mood doesn't crash when school restarts. Sooner or later he's going to get into trouble for skiving. How dare his parents make him do A levels. Outrageous."

Leyla's so super-academic that she doesn't get why

Aaron's sore that his parents insisted he stay on at sixth form rather than going to the art college in nearby Brighton. I feel I have to defend him. "Aaron's been dealing with a lot. Watching his granddad dying really messed with his head."

"Has he stopped the early hours phone calls?"

I nod, feeling a bit guilty for being glad. I tried my best but often didn't know what to say when Aaron rang up all sad and angry. "Thanks for saying it was OK for him to come today. I know you don't like Aaron gate-crashing."

"As long as it's not all the time, and it's not PDA central. I accept you're deeply in *lurve*."

Leyla thinks the way I am with Aaron is "extra". She's far more interested in chemistry and her violin than dating, and she's pretty certain she's not into boys anyway. It's been nice to see her and Aaron getting along today – sometimes there's friction.

"Want to hear something funny?" she says. "Yesterday Riyad and I were clearing out the old junk from the garage." She grins. "We found Cowboy!"

"No!" I gasp.

"Yes! An age-old mystery, solved."

I start to laugh. Riyad, who's a year older than me and Leyla, won the stuffed blue cow at a funfair when we were small, and became very attached to it. When Cowboy went missing, he accused me and Leyla of hiding it. That was back in the days when Riyad used to hang out with us, before he got in with the popular crowd. "Poor Cowboy! Riyad's far too cool for him now."

Aaron returns, and we chat for a while before Leyla has to leave to pick up a few things from Boots.

"See you tomorrow, Ley," I say.

"Two o'clock sharp!" She waves.

The Electric Palace, the cinema where Oliver works, is holding a special screening for teenagers, which Leyla and I have been roped into helping with. It's not paid, but neither of us minds. I occasionally cover shifts anyway as a favour to my twenty-three-year-old cousin Ivy, who's one of the cinema managers.

After Leyla leaves, Aaron gives me a big smile.

"D'you want to see what I've been drawing? I know it bores the hell out of Leyla, so I waited."

Aaron digs around in his rucksack. Then he freezes. I follow his gaze, but all I can see is his usual pencil case, bottle of water, sketchpad and an unopened envelope.

Aaron snaps the rucksack closed. "Let's get out of here."

"Didn't you want to— Hey!"

He's nearly at the door. I grab my parka and race after him. Outside, Aaron takes a deep gulp of air. His pale skin has gone several shades whiter. I take his arm. It feels tense. Have Leyla and I jinxed things by agreeing he seemed in good spirits? I've seen Aaron in a lot of low moods, but he's not normally anxious. "Are you OK?"

"Fine… Just feel a bit sick. Maybe I had too much brownie." For a second he's motionless. Then he spins round, grasping my hands. "Hey, shall we go to the nook? It's been ages."

I blink, thrown by the suggestion. Before winter set in, we often used to walk along the beach after dark and kiss in the secluded nook by the cliffs. Aaron thought it was hilarious when I said it was romantic, pointing out the discarded beer cans and strong smell of chips wafting from the pier. "What, now? It's freezing. The wind chill will be killer."

"Oh, yeah, true." He drops my hands. "Just trying to cheer you up – you know, after your weird afternoon. Let's go back to yours."

Confused, I let him propel me away. Aaron glances over his shoulder several times then relaxes as we leave the lanes behind.

Back at mine, we get out Exploding Kittens, but abandon the card game when my five-year-old brother Felix starts pestering us. Aaron comes to the rescue again, drawing dinosaurs with manga eyes for Felix to colour and humouring him as he reels off obscure facts about the Triassic Period.

"Sorry," I whisper when Felix runs off to show Mum and Dad his colouring.

Aaron grins. He seems himself again now we're inside. "I don't mind. We'll get plenty of alone time next weekend."

At this, my cheeks colour. Aaron's parents are away next Saturday night. He's made it very clear what he would like to happen then, but I'm not sure, and I don't really know why. It's not that I doubt us. Wasn't Cale saying just hours ago how perfect we are for each other?

Mum calls us for dinner. Aaron's so much a part of the furniture that whenever he's here she lobs another portion in without asking. It feels cosy and comfortable, the five of us huddled round the table with Dotty the cat winding through our legs, and Dad and Aaron discussing how the local football team is doing. It's so normal, as though Aaron's funny behaviour never happened.

Life is good. Really good. I'm lucky.

After dinner I go out on to the street with Aaron to say goodbye. I balance on next door's low front wall so I'm a better height for a goodnight kiss. Aaron leans in, our noses bumping lightly as our lips connect. I smile into the kiss.

"I'll see you tomorrow at the cinema," Aaron says, drawing back. "You'd better go inside now, Mia. It's not safe to be out here in the dark."

I frown at this. Bad stuff rarely happens in Southaven. Although… There is something about the silent, sparsely lit street that suddenly unsettles me. It was only hours ago that I was approached by the drunk guy.

I shudder. Maybe Aaron has a point.

"Look at you getting all protective." I lean in to kiss him again.

As our lips meet, there's a flash.

Once, twice, a third time. Something clatters.

I pull back. A silhouetted figure streaks off into the darkness.

"What on— Did you see that flash? Was someone ... taking photos of us?" I cry.

Aaron grabs my arm, saying something about getting inside, but I'm already dragging him over the road to where the noise came from. An overturned recycling bin lies on the pavement, plastic packaging spilling across the uneven slabs. I didn't notice anyone here when we stepped outside. Did they come out of a house? Or were they hiding? There's a plasterer's van parked nearby. Easy to duck behind...

"Was someone *spying* on us?" I whisper.

"Course not." But Aaron's voice sounds thin, as though he's fighting to keep it level. "No one would do that. Why would they? They were probably photographing something else."

"Like what?" The pitch of my voice rises. "Next door's hedge? Why run away?"

"I don't know. Maybe it wasn't even a camera, I didn't see."

"What else could it have been?"

"Forget it, Mia. I'm sure it's nothing." But Aaron's pale face tells me he doesn't believe that any more than I do.

Coldness sweeps over me. Someone *was* watching us.

As soon as I wake the next morning, anxiety slithers into my belly. *Last night.* Someone spied on us.

Aaron practically dragged me back inside – and kept messaging to check I was OK once he got home. Clearly he only made out it was nothing to protect me. He's like that – last year he went to ridiculous lengths to hide that his neighbour's lovely tuxedo cat had been hit by a car.

A message pops up on my screen: my friend Oliver.

Hey. WhatsApp says you're online. I'm taking
Jimmy for a walk on the beach. Fancy coming?

Maybe fresh air will clear my head.

On my way to the beach, I glance over my shoulder a

couple of times, but the road is silent. The air feels heavy and clouds sit low in the sky. A storm brewing, maybe? We don't get tons of rain here on the south coast, but when it really chucks it down, it's dramatic – waves lashing the seafront and cliffs and exploding on to the pier.

As soon as I arrive, excited barking cuts through the air. A bundle of golden fur hurls itself at me. I kneel down to give Jimmy a good fuss, giggling as his wet nose glances my ear.

"Someone's pleased I'm here! Oh, you are such a handsome boy."

"Thanks, the dog's not bad either." Oliver appears. I snort-laugh, and he grins. "Just joking. Come on, Jimmy. Leave Mia alone. I know she's your favourite person, but she doesn't want your drool in her hair."

I gently push the golden retriever back. "Jimmy only has eyes for you really. You're adorable together."

"I'll take adorable." As usual, Oliver's smartly dressed in jeans and a striped knit jumper over a shirt: a cool nerd look that could come across as try-hard but suits him. His dark hair is mussed by the drizzle. "Sorry I couldn't join you yesterday. I had to cover a shift. Speaking of work, exciting news! We've started offering vegan cake options, supplied by none other than The Green Leaf. I stole you a brownie. *Voila.*"

Out of his messenger bag comes a paper-wrapped brownie. After eating a brownie yesterday, I don't fancy another, but I don't want to hurt Oliver's feelings so I split it in half and nibble away as I catch him up on our discovery about Jade.

"Hmm, I'm with Aaron," he says. "As a boy, hair dye is not my area of expertise, but I'm sure it's nothing. What does Ley think?"

I shrug. "That it's kind of funny and cringe-worthy." The feeling that Jade's behaviour is somehow sinister is hard to shake, but Leyla and Oliver are the ones with the smarts. If they think it's no big deal, maybe it isn't. Perhaps I'm just extra shaken by what happened on the street last night.

Oozy chocolate wedges in my throat. I fill Oliver in. "Am I being dramatic?" I ask, glancing up at him. Olly's not quite as tall as Aaron but he still makes my neck ache. "The only thing I can think of is that someone was trying to catch their partner cheating, and it was mistaken identity. You occasionally hear about stuff like that, right?" Ugh, I probably sound delusional. I shake my head and lighten my tone. "Or maybe they were photographing Sue and Fiona's hedge. I mean, as hedges go, it's pretty nice?"

"Oh, a nine out of ten, definitely," says Oliver. "I don't think you're being dramatic. It seems unlikely you were photographed, though."

Aaron said the same. But Aaron also said it wasn't safe out there. And despite trying to brush off the camera flashes, he was creeped out – I know he was. "Olly… Has Aaron seemed OK to you recently? Yesterday he was … I don't know. Jumpy. Strange. Very up and down."

"I hadn't noticed. I'm sure he's fine. Perhaps" – Oliver

smiles as he tosses Jimmy his ball – "spies are active in Southaven and have their eye on you. Under all the buzz and glamour, great evil lurks…"

"You watch too many films, bro."

"No such thing as too many films, Mia. If any shady characters do jump us, you run, and I'll threaten to suck their blood." I burst out laughing and Oliver smiles more widely – I often joke that with his pale skin, dark hair and black coat Olly could pass for the world's nicest vampire.

We pass an hour playing with Jimmy, dodging every time he streaks past, spraying us with seawater. Oliver tells me about an obscure 1950s movie he's discovered that he thinks I'd like. His encyclopaedic knowledge of classic films never fails to amaze me.

As we chat, Aaron sends me a good morning text and cute GIFs of baby animals "to cheer me up". Normally I'm the one messaging him constantly. More proof that last night rattled him.

Oliver walks me home, which I'm secretly grateful for. There, I play schools with Felix and his cuddly toys, then spend an hour with Mum on the sewing machine unpicking the mistakes I've made on the pocketed skirt I've been running up. It's so nice to clear my mind of suspicions and focus on something normal.

After lunch I head out to the Electric Palace. I busy myself shovelling popcorn into striped paper bags while, across the blingy red and gold foyer, Oliver and Leyla assemble naff life-size cardboard cut-outs of James Stewart and Kim Novak to link with today's film, *Vertigo*. The Electric dates back to the age of silent movies and almost exclusively screens films that fit with its old-school image. To Oliver it's basically heaven.

Hands cover my eyes. "Guess who," a voice says in my ear.

I pretend to think. "Oh, I don't know. Is it the Loch Ness Monster?"

"What? That's random as hell." Aaron laughs, removing his hands. I turn around and he gives me a hug.

"I know I'm early," he says. "Just wanted to check you were OK."

"Since you messaged this morning?" I tease.

Aaron rubs his jaw, looking sheepish. He gives me a quick kiss on the cheek before hastening away to join his mates.

Fifteen minutes later the event is open and the foyer is flooded with people. Leyla and I are soon busy restocking popcorn and mopping up spilled Coke while Oliver moves around the foyer snapping photographs for promotional material on what looks like the school camera. My cousin Ivy greets people at the door, all red lipstick and 1940s glamour. Heat pumps out from the radiators. The laughter and chatter grow loud. Familiar, telltale pressure builds at my temples.

Please don't let this be the beginning of one of my migraines. I push my hair away from my hot face, leaning against one of the pillars.

A hand brushes my shoulder: Oliver. "Are you OK?"

"Just a headache. I'll be fine." I don't want to make a fuss.

Oliver disappears, returning a few minutes later with a glass of water and a couple of blister packs.

"Paracetamol or ibuprofen," he says, ignoring the queue growing by the ice-cream counter. "Take your pick."

Gratefully, I gulp down two ibuprofen with the water. The coolness is immediately soothing. "You're amazing. Thanks, Olly."

"I knew you weren't 'fine'. Take a seat, OK? We're opening the screen in ten anyway. Oh, wait a sec. There's popcorn in your hair."

He leans in close. His fingers are gentle as they comb the tangle of my ponytail. Out of nowhere, my cheeks redden.

"There." Oliver extracts a tiny kernel. There's colour in his cheeks too.

I tell myself it's just the radiators and settle down on the closest unoccupied sofa. All the same, I sweep the foyer for Aaron. These days, Aaron's cool with our friendship, but it was a different story when Oliver started at our sixth form in September. Maybe me forming a close friendship with another guy made Aaron feel insecure – we'd only just got together then. He's actually known Olly for ever. Their parents are old uni mates.

I can't pick Aaron out in the crowd. But then I see *her*.

And she's staring straight at me.

Jade stands by the window, clutching a paper cup. She

25

wears an oversized cardigan over an earth-green smock dress, lace socks poking above round-toed ankle boots. A Mori Girl outfit – exactly the kind I'd put together. What really draws my attention, though, is her scarf: sage green, polka dots, strips of lace. I own the exact same one.

And I made it myself. It's unique. There's no way she could have made her own version – I've never even posted a picture of it online, and I've not worn it for months. It's been stuffed in the back of my locker since a weirdly humid week we had in October when I fainted in the canteen. Jade had only been at our school for a few weeks.

Is it possible she's *stolen* my scarf?

We stare at each other, motionless. Jade's body is rigid. The colour has drained from her face. Then her face contorts. Her eyes become hard and angry, and her hand tightens around the cup, scrunching it up. She starts walking forward. A gaggle of sixth formers passes between us. By the time they've gone, Jade's turned away, head bowed. The unfamiliar girl she's with has an arm around her.

How long was Jade watching me before I noticed? I tear my eyes away and stand up, squeezing through the crowds. Aaron's nowhere to be seen, but Leyla and Oliver are chatting by one of the pillars.

"You guys." My voice is squeaky. "Look."

When Leyla sees Jade her eyes pop.

"Whoa," she exclaims. "This goes beyond liking your look."

"Exactly. She's stolen my scarf!"

26

Oliver glances between us, his eyes lingering on Jade. "Couldn't she own the same one?"

"No. It's unique – I made it."

Oliver frowns. "Is yours missing?"

"I don't know," I admit. "But I can soon find out. It should be in my locker."

"So … Jade snuck into the sixth form block and broke into your locker?" Leyla sounds sceptical.

"What other explanation is there?"

"Hey, you three." Ivy appears. "Time we herded this rabble into the screen."

We break apart.

The ache in my head has eased – it wasn't a migraine after all – but I feel sick and dizzy. There's a new suspicion building that I don't want to face. If Jade is obsessed enough to make herself into my double, maybe even steal my belongings … might she also follow me? Photograph me, even? Was that her last night?

I need to find Aaron.

I fight my way to the screen, scanning the rows of battered velvet chairs. No Aaron, but his laddish mates are at the back, and there's an empty seat next to Riyad. They're throwing popcorn in the air and laughing too loudly. I wish Aaron didn't hang around with Riyad's group – he got close with them playing football over the summer. What he sees in them other than protection from being picked on, I have no idea.

Either Aaron's in the toilets, or he's hopped to his car,

which his mates use as a dumping ground for their crap. I can't very well bang into the gents so I hurry down the back staircase to the exit. As I push the heavy door open, I hear raised voices outside and freeze. One is hard and rough sounding. The other is Aaron's.

I peep through the gap. My boyfriend is pinned to the wall by the bins. Looming over him is someone I'd know anywhere: Quin Farrell, the angry guy from the year above us who used to throw chairs at teachers before school chucked him out. Alias, Psycho Quin. I hate that nickname, but whoever gave it to him clearly intended it to be offensive.

"I don't know anything." Aaron sounds like he's struggling to breathe. I spot his car keys lying on the tarmac. "Honest."

"Like hell you don't." Quin snarls. "I'm gonna ask you again. What's your game with Jade?"

Jade. Her name sends a jolt through me.

"You've got the wrong person," says Aaron. "I don't know who Jade is."

"Yeah? Her suddenly dressing in Victorian dolls' clothes like your girlfriend doesn't ring any bells?"

"I thought she just liked Mia's look," mumbles Aaron.

Quin grabs the collar of his jacket, and my heart leaps into my mouth. "So you *do* know who she is."

"OK, yes!" Aaron cries. "But only because Mia mentioned her. We've never spoken."

Quin shoves Aaron against the wall. He's average height and isn't obviously strong-looking, but somehow he seems to tower over Aaron – his body is like a coiled spring about to be released. One eyebrow is pierced, something that would never be allowed if he was still at Southaven High.

"I'll count to ten," he says. "You're gonna tell me the truth, without bullshitting. I'm assuming you don't want your pretty face messed up."

Aaron lashes out, pushing Quin against one of the bins. Aaron makes a break for it, but Quin recovers quickly and grabs his arm. In a flash, he has Aaron pinned again. Does Quin have a knife? Those jeans are skintight, but there's space in his hoodie…

Before I can think better of it, I step outside. The door bangs behind me.

Quin whirls round, letting go of Aaron. Aaron shakes his head at me frantically.

I draw a deep breath. "Leave him alone."

It sounds pathetic. I'm barely five feet, and Quin didn't get that nickname for nothing. He narrows his eyes. His thin face is all angles and cheekbones, the half-ugly half-handsome kind of look an artsy photographer might enjoy shooting. He wears his brown hair swept back, and right now his fair skin is flushed.

"It's rude to interrupt," he says, but he sounds more sarcastic than aggressive.

"I'm not leaving." And now my voice is wobbling – perfect. "Aaron already said he doesn't know anything."

"I wouldn't be so sure about that. I think your boyfriend's been playing you."

My heartbeat quickens. "What does that mean?"

"Work it out." Quin glares at Aaron. "If you lied, you'll fucking regret it."

He pulls up his hood and stomps away through the car park.

"That was a really bad idea, Mia." Aaron is massaging his shoulder. "He's dangerous! You saw the mess he made of Riyad last summer. Broken ribs, missing teeth, the works! He could've done that to you, easy-peasy. Worse, even."

"What was I supposed to do?" I demand. "Watch him beat you up? You protected me from that drunk guy. I have your back too."

"It's not the same. You shouldn't have put yourself in danger." Aaron pulls me into a hug. He's trembling. After a moment, I realize I am too. Protecting Aaron or not, I can't believe how reckless I was. Everyone has heard the Quin horror stories. Explosive anger issues, attacking people over nothing; there are even rumours he's done time.

"Why was Quin even asking you about Jade?" I ask.

"Dunno. Maybe they're together or something. I didn't even think Psycho Quin knew who we were."

He certainly does now. I draw back. "She's in there, Aaron, dressed exactly like me. Not a bag, or hairstyle. Identical. And she's wearing one of my scarves."

Aaron blinks, as though he doesn't have the bandwidth to process all this. "I was telling the truth, Mia. I was shitting myself when he grabbed me." He hesitates. "If she really looks that much like you … maybe Quin thinks there's something going on with me and her? Like, she copied your look because that's what I'm into? There isn't, obviously. Anything going on, I mean. You're the only girl I want."

And now *your boyfriend's been playing you* makes sense. Aaron actually looks worried – like I'd doubt him, even for a second.

I squeeze his hand. "I know there isn't. I get why Quin might think it, though."

"This isn't about me." Aaron pauses. "The one Jade's interested in is you."

Aaron's words play on my mind as I hoover the foyer carpet later. The event's over, and there's half an hour to clear up before the cinema opens its doors for the early evening screening. We're out of food and Oliver's heaved four huge bin bags of empty cartons and wrappers outside, so I guess that means the event went well. I wouldn't know. Everything after the incident in the car park is a blur. *Vertigo* might as well not have been on for all the attention I paid to it.

I'm desperate for space to think, but first I have to fetch Felix from his friend's house. I wish Aaron hadn't left straight after the film. He had to pick his parents up; their car tyres were slashed on Friday night and the replacements haven't yet arrived at the garage. A few days ago I wouldn't have thought twice about walking down a few well-lit streets after nightfall by myself, but the world no longer feels quite so safe.

To my relief, I barely pass anyone on the ten-minute journey, and Felix doesn't kick up a fuss about going home. He skips beside me, chattering to his imaginary friend on the defunct phone Mum lets him take out. I wish I could get on to his level, totally carefree.

The one Jade's interested in is you.

I grasp Felix's hand as we cross the road. From the corner of my eye, I catch a movement: a figure in a bulky coat with a cap drawn low, ten metres back. They cross over, too.

A chill creeps up my spine.

I'm being jumpy. Whoever's behind us probably just happens to be walking our way. Even so, I quicken my step, hurrying Felix along beside me. Thirty metres further, we cross again. Seconds later the other person does the same. When we turn left, so do they.

It's not my imagination.

They're following us.

3

Blood pounds in my ears. Wild thoughts spiral through my mind. What do they want? Is this *Jade*?

I clutch Felix's hand tighter, picking up the pace again. Jade – if it is her – drops back. Does she know she's been spotted? These back roads are so quiet! Even with houses either side of us and lights blazing, I feel vulnerable and horribly conscious of needing to protect Felix.

Walk walk walk. We'll be home in two minutes. Felix is still engrossed in his 'phone call'. I mustn't let on I'm scared.

Home looms into view. Twenty metres, ten. Five. I risk

a glance back. The figure has stopped under a dead street light. Waiting.

They already know where I live.

Inside, I slam the door, dizzy with relief. I dash upstairs, open the bathroom window and look out, scanning the street.

They've gone.

I slam the window closed, shutting out the night. Despite the comforting warmth of the radiator, my skin erupts in goose pimples. Was it Jade? I didn't get a proper look, and that coat was bulky, the cap drawn low. But the girl is…

Well. *Obsessed with me.* Even thinking it makes me feel wrong, but what other explanation is there for all of this?

"Mia?" I jump. Felix stands in the bathroom doorway, still in his coat and shoes. He looks little and lost. "Where are Mummy and Daddy?"

I hug him. "Oh, Fe! Sorry. I didn't mean to forget you. Mum and Dad are out. Come on, it's sleepy time. We can read a story in bed if you like. I'll do the silly voices."

Felix brightens. Half an hour later, he's in pyjamas, under his PAW Patrol duvet – we barely made it to the end of *Mr Strong* before his eyelids started drooping. Downstairs, I triple-check the doors and windows are locked, even though Jade's hardly going to break in. This is paranoia. She's fifteen, almost as petite as I am. It's not like she could really hurt me.

Yet the hatred in her eyes earlier said otherwise… I don't know what this girl's capable of. Following me – *stalking*, even – is extreme and she's done that more than once. Taken covert photos, too.

A desire to know who this girl is seizes me. I run upstairs, settle on my bed beneath my fairy lights and open Instagram. I don't know Jade's surname but chances are she's been all over my page, studying what I wear.

Dotty makes herself cosy on my lap. Her warmth and familiar purr comfort me a little. I click *Followers*. Jade might not be this blatant, but— *Oh my God*. My most recent follower jumps out at me: pizza_quest. The moody black and white profile picture is slightly unfocused but there's no doubt.

It's Quin Farrell.

Crap.

Quin's page is pretty bare. Two of his three photos are of food. The other is some baby wearing a baseball cap. But when I tap on the photos that he's been tagged in, pictures flood the screen. They all have one thing in common.

Jade.

I tap a picture from last September. Jade – or lyricaljazzgirl12, as she's known on here – kisses Quin's cheek. She's pressed up close, all perfectly tousled hair – still blonde here – and falsies that would make me look like a drag queen, wearing a top that's basically a bra. He pulls a face but doesn't really look annoyed. The caption says "MY FAVE", with the fire emoji.

So they *are* a couple. Wait, no – someone's commented "is your stepbro single, haha". Below that Quin tells Jade to eff off, and Jade replies: "mwah you'll never get rid of me! Xx"

So Jade's related to the local hard guy. Great.

I scroll through Jade's life – or rather, the life she wants the world to see. Insta-Jade is nothing like the sulky girl I've spied mooching around town alone, or the one who looked like she wanted to kill me. This Jade is the kind of mainstream girl who intimidates me, always giggling with a gang of similar-looking friends. She shares endless pouty selfies and reels of her Lycra-clad body bending into impossible dance positions. I envy that effortless confidence. Sometimes I wonder if I use the Mori Girl thing to hide.

There are no pictures of her new look. Jade hasn't posted for three months. Weird. It's like she's had a personality transplant. Why make yourself into someone who is your total opposite? Her hair's shorter in the photo with Quin – she must be growing it out now to be more like mine.

I carry on tapping, searching for clues. Jade and her friends with ice creams. Jade waving a freshly manicured hand alongside a smiley woman I assume is her mum. Jade and Quin on the beach. Motivational quotes about friendship and believing in yourself. Standard social media stuff, basically.

Except, just before she stopped posting altogether, darker stuff appears in her captions.

Sometimes the worst place you can be is in your own head.

I want a boyfriend who makes me feel wanted even when I'm hard to love.

Lonely is not being alone, it's the feeling that no one cares.

These captions accompany black and white selfies – Jade made up but not looking at the camera. I frown. Is this a reaction to switching schools, or something deeper?

"Mia?"

I jump. Mum gives me a funny look from my bedroom doorway.

"Everything all right? I called hello but you didn't answer."

I glance at my watch. Nine? Have I really been online-stalking Jade for over an hour?

"I'll come down in a sec. I've not eaten yet."

Mum tuts. "Sometimes I think you'd forget your own head if it wasn't attached to your body."

As I sneak one last look at my phone, I wonder if Jade's at home too, looking at photos of me.

School starts again the next day. The first thing I do is search my locker. There's all kinds of junk inside, including a wrinkled, stinky apple, but I was right: no scarf. The padlock looks fine. But now I'm running through a mental list of things that I haven't been able to find recently, some of which might also have been in my locker… That hair bow. My silver pendant. The cute cat-print umbrella. I need to fully sort through my room at home and work out what's missing.

"*Why* obsess about me?" I ask my friends as we eat lunch in the quadrangle. Aaron is off playing football. Next to my falafel salad is half-term's sociology homework, which I'm trying to speed-finish. All the Jade stuff wiped it from my mind. I've been trying so hard to pull my grades up, too. "As far as I can tell, the only thing Jade and I have in common is we love our mums. Jade stopped posting pictures with her mum a year ago. Maybe something bad happened?"

"Did you seriously go the whole way through her account?" asks Leyla.

I blush, feeling grubby. "She probably did the same to me."

"The part I don't like is that she lives with Psycho Quin," says Leyla. "That's deep-level shit, Mia. He's bad news. Mum and Dad should've pressed GBH charges for what he did to Riyad. I can't believe you actually used to fancy him."

"Jesus! Only for, like, *five minutes*." Trust Ley to remember. Catching Oliver blink, I say quickly, "It was a silly bad boys phase."

He pulls a face as he fishes a limp cucumber wheel out of his sandwich. "Don't get the appeal, but OK. Please will you just copy my homework? You'll get an earful otherwise."

"From Ellison?" Leyla snorts. "Unlikely. Mia can do no wrong for him."

I roll my eyes at Leyla, then cave. "Just this once, Olly. Thanks."

Oliver hands me his exercise book. I pick up my biro, then put it down. I can't even concentrate on Oliver's precise sloping handwriting.

"This Jade thing is out of control," I say. "I don't know what to do."

After a moment Leyla asks, "Do you think she might be dangerous?"

A weird emptiness opens up inside me. "I think she could be."

My last lesson is sociology. At the end of class, Mr Ellison calls, "Mia, Oliver? Wait a moment, please."

Oh, crap. Mr Ellison was marking while we were doing group work – he must have noticed our homework was similar. I join Oliver by the teacher's desk and open my mouth to admit what I did, but Mr Ellison speaks first.

"How's the prep for Quiz Challenge going?"

My muscles relax. "Fine thanks, sir," I say, and Oliver nods.

"Great." Mr Ellison smiles. He's fresh-out-of-uni young, with geek glasses, springy brown hair and stubble, his skin still a warm tan from spending Christmas hiking in the Australian outback. Today's tie, from what Oliver and I call "the quirky collection", features giraffes wearing sunglasses. "I spoke to Riyad earlier and he's been swotting too. From next week, I'd like to schedule meetings after school. I'll let you know about those later."

Relieved I'm not in trouble, I speed over to the canteen where Aaron's waiting. We'd agreed to go to the board game cafe, but I don't fancy it with this Jade stuff hanging over me. When I tell him where I want to go instead, he makes a huffing noise.

"Could've sent me a message earlier," he grumbles as we

walk there. "Riyad and the gang are going to the climbing centre, but I said no because I thought this was our time. Now I'm missing out."

I fidget with the unicorn charm that dangles from my keys, a gift from Aaron. "Sorry. Go and catch them up if you like."

"No point. You know, you're getting as obsessed with this girl as she is with you, Mia." He sighs. "At least we'll have Saturday night. I want that to be about us, OK? Not Jade."

"Yeah, of course," I say quickly, not wanting to admit that Saturday is another thing that's fallen off my radar. "Has something happened, Aaron? You seem kind of…"

"Grumpy?" He gives me a tighter version of his usual smile. "Loads of homework, that's all. Half of it I don't even understand." He pauses. "It wouldn't be like this at art college."

I bite my lip. Whenever Aaron brings up art college, it makes me twitchy. A few weeks ago I checked something on his laptop and he had loads of tabs open on college websites – not only the one in Brighton, but places in London and Manchester too. Is he secretly making applications to colleges that would mean moving away? If that's his plan, I wish he'd confide in me, but now isn't the time to bring it up. Relieved that he isn't really annoyed at me, I give Aaron's hand a quick squeeze.

He waits outside the school library as I sneak in.

This place wasn't somewhere I ever saw myself returning to. I've spent too many hours here swotting unsuccessfully and trying to find the right words for essays I somehow never did well on however hard I tried.

Sixth formers aren't allowed on site unless they're library monitors or help run school clubs. My luck's in. Camille Bailey, Jade's year thirteen mentor, is here, arranging paper and pencils for the creative writing club with the help of a couple of younger girls. Camille was happy to message Leyla about Jade the other day, and I know her better than the year elevens, so I approach and give her a wave.

"Hey, Camille. Can we chat a moment?"

"Sure." Camille straightens, smiling. She's a tall, pretty Black girl with dreadlocks she wears tied back. "How can I help?"

"I wanted to ask about Jade. You know, your mentee."

"I noticed what Jade was wearing at the cinema," Camille says. Of course she did – Camille works as an usher with Olly. "I assumed you were friends?"

"Hardly. We've never spoken. Any idea why Jade's paying so much attention to me?"

One of the girls nearby hoots with laughter, then covers her mouth, glancing round. Luckily, the fierce librarian is too far away to hear.

"Sorry," the girl says. "But you're talking about Jade Turner, right? The idea of Jade paying attention to anyone other than her precious boyfriend is hilarious. He's all she ever talks about."

I frown. There wasn't a boyfriend on Instagram – although

she seemed to want one badly. He must be recent, from the past three months. "Really? What does she say about him?"

"Nothing interesting," says the girl. "Endlessly going on about how perfect he is, and how *seen* she feels, and how she's *sooo* in love."

"Who is he?"

"She won't say."

"What, a *secret* boyfriend?"

"Ellie asked if he was hot and Jade wouldn't even show her a picture. She's vague about where they go and what they do, too. We've seen love letters but they were typed. I think she's made him up."

The girl returns to setting up. I look at Camille. "It doesn't sound like Jade's made many friends here."

Camille guides me towards a quieter corner. "I think that's on purpose," she murmurs. "Jade didn't want to switch schools. I've heard she acts up with teachers, too. Maybe the plan is to get chucked out, or she's seeking attention. There's trouble at home as well."

"What kind of trouble?"

"I don't know much, only what her stepbrother told me. He's worried about her."

Camille's on speaking terms with Quin? I struggle to hide my surprise. They'd have been in the same year, but I'd never have imagined they'd have anything in common – Camille's one of the popular crowd, and really into school. "So you don't know why she's copying me?"

"Sorry, no." Camille checks her watch. "I'd better go, Mia. I need to get the club started, then dash to the labs. Ms Abdullahi tutors me on Mondays."

It takes me a second to realize Camille means catch-up tutoring. She missed a month of school last year – some mystery illness. Rumours circulated about that, none of them kind. I hover, debating what else to ask. Then the door bangs open again.

It's Jade. She's scowling, tie loose, shirt untucked and top buttons undone. I duck between the bookshelves.

"Hi, Jade," Camille calls. "Are you here for creative writing club?"

"Not my thing." It's the first time I've heard Jade's voice and it sends an electric shock through me. "I just need to kill half an hour and it's freezing outside. I was supposed to get a lift home, only the baby has to go to the doctor's because she has a temperature. Like, fine, I get it, but Mum didn't tell me until the *last* minute, and I've missed my bus. It only comes once an hour."

Camille makes a sympathetic noise. "Could your boyfriend help? He has a car, right?"

Jade wets her lips, her eyes downcast. "He won't."

"Won't?"

"I mean can't. He would if he could, totally. Meeting up … it's complicated."

A few of the girls titter, and one nudges another.

Jade's head snaps up. "He wrote the sweetest message earlier." She sounds defiant now. "'You are my dream girl and I never get tired of looking at you'... He loves me. We're really good together."

Wow. I'd love it if Aaron sent me sweet stuff like that, but he's visual, not wordy. Although ... it does sound a little like Jade is making excuses for her boyfriend. Is the relationship less perfect than she's making out? Could that have something to do with why she photographed me with Aaron?

There are more giggles. Camille says something about being kind to each other.

Through the gaps in the bookshelves I glimpse Jade smack her bag down on a table in the corner. She rubs her eyes, sniffing, then swears and fishes for a mirror to inspect her make-up. Were those ... tears? But when Jade turns, her face is the picture of I-don't-care. She opens a chocolate bar and tears into it while scrolling through her phone, in blatant defiance of both the "no food" and "no phones" library policy. The phone is pretty basic-looking. Not what I'd expect from a girl who until recently was addicted to selfies. Although ... is that a second phone peeping out of the top of her bag?

I'm sure Jade must feel my eyes boring into her, but she doesn't glance up. My heartbeat races. I could confront her. Demand to know what her problem is. Would that make things worse?

"Sure you don't want to discuss poems with us?" one of the girls calls. "They're about love."

Jade flips her the finger without looking up.

"I saw that, Jade." Miss Dawson, the librarian, stalks over. "If you can't respect the library rules, leave. And I know for a fact you were instructed to remove that make-up already today."

"Whatever," growls Jade. She grabs her bag.

"Don't think I haven't spotted you, Mia Hawkins," Miss Dawson calls, and I freeze. "Why you feel the need to spy on the creative writing club I have no idea, but you have your own library in the sixth-form centre. Kindly depart."

I've no choice but to come out into the open, hanging my head. Jade stares, her eyes big.

Miss Dawson waves towards the door. "Both of you, out."

My pulse quickens. Not only does Jade know I was watching her, but now we have to exit the library – together.

Seconds later, we're out in the murky corridor. Hundreds of faces stare down at us from the class photos mounted on the walls.

Ignoring Aaron blinking at us from a couple of metres away, Jade shoots me a look of pure venom. Slowly and deliberately, she reaches into her pocket. Out comes a packet of chewing gum. Jade slips a wad into her mouth and chews, her eyes never leaving mine. Then she spits it into her hand and rams it on to one of the class photos.

She stalks away. I back against the wall. It's a long time before I can bring myself to step towards the photo she smeared.

The chewing gum is stuck fast. And the face it obscures is mine.

My walk home passes in a daze. Aaron puts his arm around me and says comforting things, but the words don't sink in. I keep looking back. I can't see Jade. But that doesn't mean she isn't there.

At home, I tear through my wardrobe. Dresses hit the carpet and shirts slip from hangers. A linen smock falls over Dotty, who shoots off with an outraged yowl. A pile grows at my feet. Crap, why do I have so many clothes?

Here are scarves, in a box at the back. Stripes, checks, florals – but no polka dots with lace. There are other pieces missing too. That hair bow. My silver pendant. The cute cat print umbrella. The barely-used clutch handbag I found on eBay, too. Is it possible Jade has somehow stolen them? I don't remember taking these things into school, but I must have. She can't have been in my room, can she?

I flop down on my bed, blowing out a long breath. The more I discover about this girl, the further I feel from understanding her. She transforms herself into me, and yet she hates me. She follows and photographs me with Aaron, and yet she has a boyfriend of her own, who for some reason is secret.

None of it adds up. I FaceTime Leyla. She frowns as I fill her in on what happened earlier, flipping a biro one way up, then the other.

"Mimi…" she says slowly. "Don't bite my head off – but are you sure Jade's secret boyfriend isn't Aaron? It *would* explain why she's obsessed with you."

Even though I've thought it myself, I still flinch. "You're only saying that because you don't like him."

Leyla immediately looks frustrated, and I wish I hadn't spoken – this is an old wound. "Aaron takes you for granted. What about those times he cancelled on you? I know he said it was because he was feeling down, but … he could have been meeting her instead."

I'd forgotten that. I go quiet, mulling it over. Then I shake my head. "I trust him. Even if I didn't, Jade didn't even register Aaron's presence earlier. This is about me, not him."

"Quin thought the boyfriend might be Aaron. And he knows Jade much better than we do."

"Ley, Aaron wouldn't cheat. I'm confident, OK?"

"I wish I trusted him as much as you do," Leyla mutters.

That evening I sit glued to my window, but the road is still. I google stalking. The results fill me with dread. Unless your stalker causes harm, there's not much the police can do to protect you. Jade's scary and wild. Dangerous, even. And stalking is a crime. But we're teenage girls. I simply can't believe that the police will take this seriously. People in authority see me in my frills and cutesy dresses and immediately think "airhead". And, to lots of people, teenage girl automatically equals silly anyway.

Tears of frustration well in my eyes.

What do I do?

Saturday crawls round. I wake up with a tight ball of anxiety clustered in my belly.

Aaron's messaged.

> Hey beautiful how is 6.15 tonight
>
> I thought we could see that film you were talking about at the electric
>
> By the time it finishes my parents will have gone :-)

I bite my lip. Tonight is supposed to be The Night. Aaron brought it up several times this week. I went along with it, made out I was excited too because I know he is, but I barely gave it any head space.

I know Jade has been a distraction, but could it be that I

don't actually want this yet? I love Aaron. He's everything I want in a boyfriend. He's even agreed to cosplay as Tuxedo Mask to match my Sailor Moon for the anime con we're going to this summer, despite groaning that he'll look like a pretentious dickhead. I couldn't be luckier. We've been together six months. He keeps saying that's a long time, and I guess it is. So why wouldn't I want to take this next step with him? It's true that the idea of having sex for the first time in Aaron's dark boy-cave bedroom is off-putting, but Aaron's seventeen. He can't exactly whisk me away for a romantic mini break in a grand hotel.

"You're ridiculous," I mutter to myself.

Oh God. I can't say no now. Aaron will be really disappointed. The next time we get a house to ourselves could be months away.

This is *Jade's* fault. If her creepy stalking hadn't cast a shadow over my life I could have got myself in the mood this week. Well, screw Jade. She's ruined enough for me already. She's not going to ruin this.

When the time to leave approaches, I pick out my nicest bra and pants and a floral-print dress that's really for summer but I know Aaron likes. I apply eyeliner, then remove it. Aaron doesn't like the made-up look anyway.

Calling goodbye to my parents, I step outside. A street lamp flickers, then goes black. The hairs on my nape prick up. The only sound is my pumps padding along the pavement. Not even the distant purr of traffic, or someone's telly. All the houses have their curtains closed.

Fewer seem to have lights on than usual. Or is that my imagination?

I told Aaron I'd meet him at the Electric because I didn't want Mum to clock that my "sleepover at Leyla's" isn't real, but I wish I wasn't walking alone. The lie doesn't feel great either, but Mum isn't cool about this kind of thing.

I quicken my step. *Think about Aaron; loosen up.* Yet suddenly my head is crowded by the idea of Jade, tailing me and Felix down this very street. Jade, photographing me from the shadows. Jade, ruining tonight, which should be exciting and romantic and wonderful.

Footsteps.

I whirl round. A dark figure looms up from behind.

Fear seizes me. I run.

I make it to the end of the road, then turn left, under the railway bridge—

A hand seizes my shoulder.

"I want to speak to you." Jade's face is inches from mine, her eyes big and fierce. Her nails dig into my flesh.

I pull back. "Get away from me!"

"No, listen. I need to tell you something."

Heart pounding, I squirm out of her grip and bolt.

Jade makes a noise that's half sigh, half snarl. Her chunky heels clatter behind me. Seconds later her fingers close around my wrist. Jade drags me back and pushes me against the slimy wall of the railway bridge, exactly like Quin did with Aaron.

"Don't you dare run away," she hisses.

"I know you're stalking me," I hiss back. "And stealing my stuff—"

"You know shit about me, Mia Louise Hawkins. But I know all about you now." Jade's right hand balls into a fist. There's an intensity in her gaze – anger and hate, maybe even pain. "This is all your fault! If you didn't exist—"

"I've never done anything to you!" I cry. "I know you're jealous, but you can't blame that on me."

Her face contorts. Tears gleam at the corners of her eyes. "Oh, shut up, Little Miss Perfect. You're clueless! Now, I'm going to tell you something, and you're going to listen, because you need to know—"

Before she can finish her threat, I shove her. The heel of Jade's boot catches on the kerb. She falls, her palms smacking the asphalt.

"Leave me alone, else I'll call the police," I snarl. Then I run, as fast as I can.

"Come back!" Jade shouts. "It's important."

This time, her feet don't pound after mine. At the top of the street I glance back. Jade's sitting in the road with her head in her hands. She looks little and lost, but I'm not fooled.

I don't stop running until I reach the Electric Palace. I double over, gasping for breath.

Aaron's there already, wearing his smart jeans. Under his arm is a small bouquet of flowers. His leg jiggles, as though he can't bear to keep still. The street light behind him blinks, flicking his rangy shadow on and off like a switch. He's frowning over a sheet of paper. A letter?

Aaron glances up and spots me. He quickly folds the paper and shoves it into his pocket. "Hey, beautiful," he calls. "I wasn't expecting you to be early. Did you actually run? I didn't know you were that keen."

The pitch of his voice doesn't sound right. The big smile he plasters on his face as he hastens over isn't convincing either. Has something happened?

Aaron thrusts the flowers at me. "For you. See, I can be romantic sometimes. Look, do you want to blow off this film and go straight to mine? Mum and Dad left early, so—"

"Aaron, she threatened me," I say without taking the flowers.

Aaron's smile vanishes. "What?"

"Jade. Just now. She pinned me up against a wall. I think she's dangerous, and—"

"Wait, Mia, please," Aaron interrupts. "Do we have to do this here, now?"

I stare at him. This wasn't the response I was expecting.

Aaron takes a deep breath. "I'm sorry this girl is bothering you and it's not nice. Believe me, I've got plenty on my mind too, but we can't let anything ruin our evening. I think we should get out of here and go back to mine."

"Aaron! Are you serious? Why are you brushing this off? I was chased – threatened!"

I wait for him to clock that this is important and fold me into his arms. Aaron tries another smile, but all I can see is exasperation.

"Nothing's going to happen to you with me here, promise," he says. "Come on, let's go home. You'll calm down on the walk. Then we can enjoy ourselves. Please don't worry about Jade. I don't know what her deal is, but it's nothing, I'm sure of it."

I have to bite my lip to stop myself shouting. "It's not nothing! It got physical. I had to run away from her. She's not going to back off. If anything, she'll get worse. Should I go to the police?"

"We'll work that out later." He pauses. "Mia, come on, you promised tonight was about us."

"I can't believe all you can think about right now is getting me to go home with you! I'm not coming. I'm not in the mood."

"I'll get you in the mood."

He takes my arm. Something explodes inside me, and suddenly I'm shouting.

"I'm scared! I don't know how I can make that any clearer. I need help, not you downplaying it because me being upset isn't convenient right now. You're acting like a dick!"

Aaron recoils, his eyes big. I'm shocked at myself too. The main doors of the Electric Palace open. People trickle out. Aaron grabs my shoulder, pulling me away.

The pressure of his fingers feels like they're burning my skin. I jerk away. "Get off. You're hurting me."

He lets go.

"I was there for you when you needed me." I'm shaking now. "It wasn't easy and most of the time I felt useless, but

I did it because I cared. Does that only go one way? Or does sex matter more?"

"Jesus, Mia!" Aaron cries in frustration. "You're twisting everything. Don't you dare say I don't care. You have *no* idea how much I care, how much I've put into us – even when it would be far smarter to walk away. No idea!"

Aaron doesn't look like my boyfriend any more. He's towering over me, his eyes wild and the hand that isn't holding the flowers raised. I try to back away. Aaron steps forward. Then he stops and takes a deep breath. He rakes his raised hand through his hair.

"Sorry." His voice cracks. "I don't want a fight. I'm under a lot of pressure at the moment. Making out I don't care was literally the worst thing you could have said. I love you. I know I don't say it often enough but it's true. Maybe we should just watch that film instead."

The olive branch dangles in front of me. It would be so easy to take it. I usually do when we disagree.

"No," I whisper. "I don't want to be around you right now."

He stares at me. I stare back. Aaron curses. Then he storms off, hurling the flowers into the gutter.

It's a long time before I can coax my wobbly limbs into moving. Part of me is pulled towards the Electric. The urge to spew everything out to Oliver is overpowering. I actually thought for a second that Aaron was going to hurt me! Oliver will know the right thing to say. He always

54

does. But no – the entrance is buzzing, he'll be busy. If he's even working tonight – I have no idea.

I stumble home. Ivy sticks her head round the sitting-room door, phone in hand and looking surprised.

"Weren't you out, squirt? Hey, what's up?"

I forgot Ivy was babysitting Felix while Mum and Dad go to their friends' anniversary dinner. At least I won't have to face them.

Ivy says a hurried goodbye to whoever she was video-calling and guides me to the sofa. She's still wearing her Electric Palace lanyard and a wiggle dress with a low neckline Mum would call "unprofessional". Her dyed blue hair is pinned up in victory rolls.

I gulp, and the tears come hard. Ivy's face swims with sympathy as I choke out that Aaron and I have had a fight. I keep Jade out of it, focusing instead on him being pushy.

"Ah, crap," she says. "I'm sorry. You two get along so well! I can't even imagine you arguing."

"Was I out of order?" I ask anxiously. "I know I'm high maintenance sometimes, but—"

"Who said you were high maintenance?"

"No one. I just think I am. I get emotional and wound up about things and Aaron doesn't know how to deal with it. Ivy, I cry over *missing pet posters*."

"Oh, sweetie! That's you wearing your heart on your sleeve. It's not a bad thing. He'll come around." She winks. "Making up can be fun. Then you can get back to doing what you do best: being adorable."

I rub my eyes. Suddenly I have no energy. "I don't understand why he got so angry. I never thought he'd be pushy like that. It's not OK, even if he was disappointed."

"I bet he realizes that, now he's had a chance to cool down. There might be another reason he was on edge, nothing to do with you."

Ivy wasn't this laid-back two years ago when the guy she met backpacking dumped her in a particularly messy and hurtful way. Auntie Lou had to fly out to pick Ivy up from a hostel in Thailand she was so distraught. Evil Tom's name is still dirt in our family. I honestly think if he reappeared Uncle Ben would deck him. So would Auntie Lou, probably.

Weirdly, reliving Ivy's big break-up has cleared my head. Tonight wasn't my fault. Aaron didn't listen. He's the one who blew up.

I think more carefully about what he said. All that talk of being under pressure, and saying that he's stuck by me when it would be smarter to walk away… What did he mean by that? Up until now, everything in our relationship's been good, so why would Aaron be conflicted? Perhaps he really has been secretly applying for art colleges. Maybe that's what those letters I keep seeing are – acceptances. Could that be it? Or is there something I'm missing?

"We can patch things up." I try to believe it. "Tonight is a blip."

Ivy gives me a thumbs up. "Wait for him to come to you. Absolutely no messaging."

I'm not sure I have that level of chill, but I promise anyway. Dotty wanders in and rubs herself against my legs, purring. I scoop her up and bury my nose in her familiar-smelling fur, feeling small and hurt.

Ivy pops a singing show on the TV, but my mind can't focus. It slides back past the argument to Jade, and her angry eyes, and the way she spat my full name. Without her, Aaron and I would never have shouted at each other. Would she smile, if she could see me here in tears?

There's a bigger question, too. One that chills me. What will she do next?

But, as I find out the next morning, Jade will never do anything again.

Because her body, a body at first mistaken for my own, is found by the cliffs.

5

I stand on the wet shingle clutching my phone. It's still pinging, the *RIP Mia* messages mounting. Around me, waves crash, and when I exhale deeply, my breath clouds in the crisp Sunday morning air. I squint against the late February sunshine. I can just about see the crime scene through the chattering crowd, though Jade's body is shielded from view.

Relief floods me. Aaron hasn't walked off the cliff. That this has happened by our nook is a coincidence.

Then shame smacks, hard. A fifteen-year-old girl is dead, and I'm *relieved*? How gross am I? Somehow death fills Jade with innocence, even though she stalked and threatened me.

No one ever says bad things about dead people, especially not when they're so young. They're angels taken too soon, loved by everyone, promising futures cut short.

Crap. How *can* Jade be dead? Only yesterday she had her face shoved right up in mine, burning with vital anger. I could smell her shampoo!

I need to tell you something. It's important.

Whatever she was so desperate to share, it's too late to find out now.

I retreat to the promenade and crash on to the closest bench, the distant jingle of the arcades replacing the hubbub of the crowd.

Leyla picks up my call immediately. I blurt everything out, then tell her to look at the posts on Instagram and call me back. While I'm waiting I message Oliver. The idea of him seeing those tributes and believing them, even for a moment, is unthinkable. I text Aaron too. He needs to know I'm OK, fight or no fight.

Someone taps me on the shoulder. It's Leyla, on her roller skates. She gives me a humourless kind of grin.

"Before you think I've discovered teleportation, I was close by," she says. "This is so effed up. Are you OK? Hey, careful."

She teeters on her skates as I leap up and crush her in a hug. Over her shoulder, I can see more and more people gathering. I can't remember a buzz like this since the summer carnival. That makes me feel a little sick.

We sit down. Leyla drops her voice. "You think it's her?"

"Who else can it be?" I say. "I haven't told you about last night yet."

I explain my encounter with Jade under the railway bridge, and the ensuing argument with Aaron. "… I was so afraid I wasn't thinking clearly. Jade was angry, but now I think about it, there was something else too, bubbling beneath the surface. She was … disturbed. Hurting, even. Do you think she jumped?"

Leyla removes her helmet, frowning as she runs a hand through her curls. "She could've fallen. The fences at the top of those cliffs are hardly robust."

Or … could she have been walking along the beach and something terrible had happened? No, this is Southaven: solid and safe. Who was it who said the simplest explanation is often true? Some philosopher I read about for Quiz Challenge, I think. And the simplest explanation here is that her death was an accident.

"You could've come to me last night, you know," Leyla says quietly. "Bestie, remember? I wasn't doing anything special. Reading the *New Scientist* could've waited."

I feel small. Before Aaron came along, Leyla and I used to do stuff on Saturday nights. She and Oliver hang out by themselves instead sometimes, but he's often at the Electric. "I felt ashamed, I guess."

"Why? Because for the first time ever, you guys weren't" – she air quotes – "perfect? I wouldn't rub that in your face, silly."

"Sorry."

"It doesn't matter." Leyla squeezes my arm.

"Should I tell the police about last night?" I ask. "Whatever Jade wanted to tell me was eating her up. It might be relevant."

"I'd wait. We don't even know for sure the body's her, do we?"

"I guess not. And hearing about last night might upset her family. Hey – do they even know yet?"

Leyla goes pale. Without meaning to, we look again towards the beach. *Jade's family.* To them she was probably the happy, confident girl who joked around with her stepbrother and danced so gracefully, whose feed sparkled with life.

With effort, I say, "I'd better post something. No one needs fake news spiralling."

"Do you want me to do it?" asks Leyla. "I'm sure I could compose a pissy 'Mia's not dead, thanks' message."

"Oh God, would you?"

"Sure. You don't need to see that crap. It's basically like a computer game, right? Shooting down sick tribute messages instead of zombies."

My laugh is shaky. "I love you."

"Love you too, Mimi."

Leyla taps away on her phone. More police have arrived at the nook and they're moving the crowds along. The horrible moment I thought Aaron was dead feels like a lifetime ago.

Aaron. Suddenly all I want is to see him and patch up the argument that no longer feels so big or so final.

By the time we arrive at Aaron's house I'm clutching a stitch, out of breath from jogging alongside Leyla on her skates while answering a call from a confused Oliver. It bothers me that Aaron hasn't called or even messaged, but it's still early – he's probably asleep.

The brand-new estate he lives on is an upmarket one, with identical, detached modern houses that don't quite fit with the colourful, kooky vibe of the town. Oliver lives here too, just over the road.

No one answers when I ring the bell. I call Aaron while Leyla rattles the letter box. Nothing. He must not be home.

Hang on. From under the garage door, a soapy trail trickles across the pavement.

Leyla notices too. "Is he seriously washing his car?"

"Must be. His parents aren't around." Hurt opens up inside me. "He's actually blanking us. Blanking me. At a time like this. No, stop." I catch Leyla's arm as she moves to bang on the garage door. "I don't want to speak to him any more."

Leyla purses her lips. I sense she wants to criticize Aaron, but instead she shrugs and turns away – then her eyes widen in recognition. I follow her gaze. A familiar car is pulling up on the kerb: Riyad's.

"Hey, Riyad!" I call. "Have you spoken to Aaron today?"

Riyad spots me out of the car window and freezes.

His expression flips from neutral to alarmed. The next second, the car's screeching away again. Leyla and I watch open-mouthed.

"What the hell?" says Leyla.

"He really stepped on it. Why would Riyad avoid us like that?"

"I don't think he even saw me. It was you he was looking at." Leyla chews her lip. "At least I know he's OK. Ri didn't come home last night. I was getting worried."

"Oh! You should have said."

"It's all right now. He was probably with a girl. Boy owes me for covering with Mum and Dad. I'll corner him later and ask what's going on."

"Good luck," I mutter. Riyad is the king of evasive answers, one reason why I avoid him. "I should get home. I don't want the fake news getting back to Mum and Dad."

Leyla and I part ways, promising to chat later. I trail home, my heart heavy, and my mind still spinning over the shock of the last few hours.

Mum and Dad are reading the Sunday papers with the coffee they brew fresh at weekends, and Felix is building a Lego fortress for his plastic army men. I watch the cosy little scene, feeling far, far away. Mum glances up. Wordlessly I hold out my phone.

At first both my parents are bewildered. Then, when I explain Jade's been mistaken for me, they cotton on.

Mum's hand flies to her mouth. "Oh, Mia. What a tragic accident! Did you know each other?"

"Not well." I can't bring myself to say *she stalked me*. Jade can hardly threaten me again.

I picture her motionless body, blood seeping into the sand, crushed beer cans and other rubbish around her – the shell of the girl who sneered that I knew nothing.

There's very little news by the time early evening crawls round. People from school have got the message that I'm OK, but that doesn't stop the flurry of rumours. Aaron is still giving me the silent treatment. I can't believe how childish he's being. Sometimes Aaron closes off but he's never sulky. Yeah, I rejected him yesterday, but we're *alive*. That seems an enormous privilege. I bet Jade's boyfriend would give anything for her to message him.

The doorbell rings. *Maybe that's Aaron!* I fly down the hallway and fling the door open.

Outside are two unfamiliar women. The taller one is about forty, mixed-race with close-cropped hair and a plain looking suit. She projects calm authority. Even before she flashes her ID I know she's police.

"It's Mia, isn't it?" she says. "I'm Detective Sergeant Forster, and this is Detective Constable West. Are your parents in? I'd like a quick word."

We assemble around the kitchen table: me, Mum and Dad on one side, the detectives on the other, like some bizarre job interview. The theme tune of the TV show Felix has been parked in front of trails through from the sitting room.

64

DC West lays a notebook and a file on the table. She's younger than her colleague, with keen eyes and a ponytail.

"I know you're aware that a body was discovered this morning." DS Forster doesn't waste time with small talk. "We want to ask you a few questions."

"Is it Jade?" I ask.

If DS Forster's surprised, she doesn't show it. "I need you to keep this confidential until we make an announcement, but yes, Jade Turner's family have identified the body. They reported her missing when she didn't come home yesterday."

Even though I knew, the words hit me like a heavy weight. DC West slides out a photograph from the file on the table. It's a CCTV image of Jade in the parka identical to mine at the bus stop outside Tesco Metro, an oversized bow in her hair. Under the coat she wears a flouncy cream skirt and ankle boots with a low heel. With a lurch of my stomach, I recognize it as yesterday's outfit.

"Jade was last seen here at 17.45," says DS Forster. "She'd taken the 39 bus from Wrabney, where she lived."

Wrabney's five miles down the coast — Southaven's poorer, sadder, rougher cousin.

Mum and Dad peer at the photo, then exchange glances. They're clocking the resemblance.

I study my nails. Pastel-yellow varnish, slightly chipped. The colour's called Lemon Sorbet. Perhaps Jade's wearing it too, in the mortuary. "If you're going to ask why Jade suddenly changed her image, I don't know," I mutter. "We weren't friends. We spoke once."

"What about online? Did you chat there at all?"

"No, never."

"Did you see her last night?"

She knows? I shift on my chair, deeply uncomfortable now. I have a sneaking suspicion that DS Forster has a bombshell she's about to drop. There must be a reason why speaking to me is a priority. I take a deep breath and explain what happened – my fears that Jade had been following me, stealing from me, and then what happened when she cornered me under the railway bridge. I focus on the detectives, not Mum and Dad, painfully aware they're hearing all of this for the first time.

A deep crease appears between DS Forster's eyebrows. She glances at DC West, who gives a tiny shrug. "And you don't know what Jade was referring to, when she said she needed to tell you something?"

I shake my head. I'm sweating, and I feel sure I must look guilty even though I haven't done anything wrong. I can't tell from their poker faces if I'm in trouble or not.

DC West reaches inside the file. More photos come out, this time sheathed in protective plastic.

Every single one is of me.

My breath catches. Dad inhales sharply, and Mum gives a start.

"Jade's stepbrother found these hidden in her room," says DS Forster. "They're only a sample. There were hundreds of photos in total."

Some I recognize: my own, lifted from social media.

Others have been taken covertly – me pushing Felix on a park swing, buying bread in the corner shop, even looking very serious at the local climate change protest last month. And there are a ton of me and Aaron. My eyes fix on one enlarged picture of us kissing. His T-shirt, my earrings… That's from the other night! I *knew* Jade was spying on us.

She's been watching me for *months*.

"Are you sure you have no idea why she was so interested in you?" asks DS Forster.

"Absolutely none," I croak.

Mum clears her throat. "Obviously, these photos are … extremely disturbing, but … can I ask why you're here? Jade is no longer a threat to Mia. Do you think this has something to do with why Jade… I mean, I assume her death was an accident, or… It wasn't suicide?"

DS Forster is still looking at me. "Where were you the rest of yesterday evening, Mia?"

What? Is this … an alibi she's asking for?

"Detective, I really don't think—" Dad starts, but one glance from DS Forster silences him.

The kitchen has gone deadly quiet.

"I met my boyfriend at the Electric Palace at six fifteen, about ten minutes after seeing Jade." I find myself fumbling my words, even though my parents discovering I lied hardly matters now. "We couldn't, uh, agree which film to see, so I came home. My cousin Ivy and I watched that new singing show. She … she can confirm that."

"Right. And your boyfriend is?"

"You don't need to speak to him, do you?"

"I can't share that."

That means yes. So they're interested in Aaron too. "His name's Aaron Mercer. Is Jade… I mean, did someone…"

Gently, DS Forster says, "We're treating Jade's death as suspicious."

Suspicious.

I zone out for a moment, gripping the table to keep myself upright. Dad grasps my shoulder, his face full of concern.

"Are you all right, Mia?"

"Yes, I…" I gulp. "That's… It's awful."

"I'm sorry." I wonder how many times DS Forster has said those words in her career. She asks a few more questions about my interactions with Jade, but stops after I repeat several times that I know nothing.

"All right," she says. "If you think of anything else, Mia, however minor, please get straight in touch. We may want to speak to you later."

Alarm bells ring in my head.

DC West speaks for the first time. "Here's a card with our contact details. If you ever worry you're being followed again, please report it."

I don't say the obvious – that it's not likely, given my stalker is dead.

"And, like I said," DS Forster adds, "please keep what we've shared with you confidential until it's public knowledge tomorrow. In the meantime, I'd also ask you to be careful whenever you're not at home or school, and don't go out alone. Especially in the dark."

My mouth falls open. "Am I in danger?"

"I'm sure DS Forster doesn't mean you specifically," Mum says quickly. "Everyone needs to be careful, until whoever did this is caught. Right, detective?"

There's a long pause – longer than I like – before DS Forster says, "We have no reason to believe Mia is in specific danger at the moment. However, given her resemblance to Jade, there's a chance that seeing her could startle or provoke the attacker. So like I said – be extra careful."

I feel the colour drain from my face. Her meaning is very clear: my stalker might be dead – but her killer is very much alive.

After the police leave, Dad makes tea and we sit around the kitchen table again. I clutch my mug, barely registering the heat burning my palms.

Mum breaks the silence. "You were being threatened and followed, Mia. Why on earth didn't you tell us?"

Mum's tone isn't chiding, but I can tell she's hurt. I stare at my tea. I think about how Mum made a big thing about sixth form being a new start, a chance for me to turn things around after my disappointing GCSE results. About how I overheard her complaining to Auntie Lou about my "attention-seeking clothes" and "nightmare food choices". About how wary she was of me having a boyfriend. Being stalked feels like yet another failure, further evidence that I'm difficult and make my parents' lives hard. I'm supposed to be changing all that.

"I guess I wanted to sort it out myself," I mutter. "I'm sorry you found out like this."

Dad sighs. "This isn't what we mean when we encourage you to be more independent."

"I'm sorry I lied about meeting Aaron, too. We, er..."

Mum presses her lips together: she's worked it out. "You need to be careful with boys, Mia. Even the nice ones. You're only sixteen. You've loads of time for all this later."

"All this" means sex. I squirm, shame welling up inside me. She's disappointed. Again.

Dad looks like he's squirming too; he leaves this stuff to Mum. "Maybe you should talk about this another time, when Mia isn't in shock."

"All right. Please don't lie to us again, though, Mia." Mum pauses. "You didn't see the film? You came straight home?"

"Yes, Mum," I say flatly. "Ask Ivy. And before you bring

it up, I don't want to talk about arguing with Aaron. It doesn't have anything to do with this."

"The police want to speak to him, though."

"Because of those photos, I assume," Dad says. "He's in them too. We know Aaron wouldn't do anything wrong."

Mum's suspicious expression clears, and she nods.

Felix wanders in, asking for a drink. I leap up, relieved to be off the hook. As I hand him a juice, I check my phone: nothing.

Have the police gone to Aaron's house? Will they ask for his alibi, too?

I wish he'd speak to me.

The next day I slip out of the house early. My sleep was choppy, with surreal, disturbing dreams. The girl that I thought wanted to destroy me is dead – *and someone killed her.*

Someone who might harm me.

It can't be real. But it is. Southaven looks the same as it did yesterday, yet the world I know has gone.

Until the police find out more, I have to be careful. I probably shouldn't even be out right now, but for some reason I really need to see the beach again.

I quicken my step. When I get there, I lean on the railing and gaze over the cliff. Through the murky morning mist I can make out a white tent at the nook, cordoned off by tape. What will the police be doing today? Dusting for prints? Searching for clues? Tracking the killer?

A shiver creeps up my spine.

My phone buzzes: Oliver, asking if I want him to walk me to school. That's sweet – my house is totally out of his way. I feel bad for being disappointed that it was his name on the screen, not Aaron's.

Aaron finally messaged last night, while I was taking the bubble bath Mum insisted would relax me.

> sorry ive not been around. I need some
> space. Hope youre ok

What am I supposed to assume from that? Is Aaron simply hurt and angry? What about how hurt and angry I am?

Or … is it possible that I've missed something? Aaron insisted we weren't safe the night Jade spied on us by my house – but he also played down the threat Jade posed. Twice now I've seen him reading letters. He shouted that he was under pressure. He hasn't been acting like the Aaron I know.

I turn to go – then stop. A couple of metres away someone else is leaning on the railings. A boy. His hood is up but his body is angled towards the tent. And his shoulders are shaking with sobs. A jolt goes through my body. Instinctively, I call, "Are you OK?"

The boy goes still, and I immediately regret speaking. I should have let him be. For many people – especially boys – crying is a private thing. Before I can do anything else, he takes off, trainers pounding as he disappears down the closest side street. I only catch a flash of his face, but that's enough.

It was Quin Farrell. And he was crying his eyes out.

Oliver and Leyla flank me protectively as I scurry into

school. I filled them in about the police visit last night, stressing that it needed to be kept secret. This morning they were waiting by the gates, dressed in black and wearing shades, "embracing our bodyguard badassery", as Leyla put it. We laughed in that hysterical way you do when something's so far from funny it's absolutely hilarious. I feel a fierce burn of love for them for propping me up.

People fall silent as I pass. There are nervous titters, long glances. No one says a thing. The last time I saw Jade runs on a loop in my head. *I'm going to tell you something, and you're going to listen, because you need to know.* I assumed it was a threat. Now it seems possible I got that wrong. Could what Jade knew even be the reason she's dead?

"Don't take this as definitive." Leyla is leaning against the locker next to mine, her arms folded. "But I've been scouring the cesspit that is the online grapevine – purely for research purposes, because it's sick as – and people are saying Jade was hit round the head."

So that's the cause of death. "Are they saying anything else? She wasn't..." I take a deep breath. "You know. Assaulted. In the other way."

"I read the police statement, and there's nothing like that," says Oliver. He shows us the link on his phone. Apart from naming Jade there's little new information, but the police confirm there's no evidence of sexual assault. That's something, I guess.

I pass back the phone, thinking of all the reports you see about dead women and girls, and the awful things that have been done to them. These news stories are so frequent and familiar that it's easy not to feel the horror and outrage we should. Or to block the stories out entirely, as I've been guilty of doing in the past, because I'm safe in my own bubble. Today, it strikes me that we should be angrier. How have we got used to living in a world where we're numb to things that are completely and utterly not OK?

I wish Aaron was here. I could use one of his comforting hugs, but it looks like he's skipping school again. That feels personal, and it bites.

"I wonder who did it," I say. "Someone she knew, or a random sicko?"

"If murder mysteries are to be believed," says Oliver, "people kill with complicated motives, often involving inheritance and wills and revenge plots spanning decades. In real life, well." He shrugs. "We didn't know her, did we?"

I hoick up my shoulder bag, frowning. "No ... but she's not a total stranger. We know she has a mysterious boyfriend. I'm not convinced everything was as great with him as she made out. Jade must have kept him secret for a reason. That's pretty shady. If I were the police, he'd be my prime suspect."

The three of us go quiet. You don't have to pay much attention to the news to know how horribly common it is for women to be killed by their partners.

Leyla breaks the silence. "What about Aaron? Did the police speak to him in the end?"

She doesn't say out loud that she thinks their interest in

him is suspicious. I sigh.

"I told you earlier: he wanted space. But I think I know why they asked about him now." I wait for a group of girls to pass by, then say, "Quin probably told them he thought Aaron was the boyfriend."

Leyla nods. "That figures."

Oliver speaks up. "Quin's pretty violent, isn't he? If he has self-control issues … what's to say he didn't hurt her?"

I shake my head. "Quin was really protective of Jade when he threatened Aaron. And…"

"And what?" Leyla prompts.

"Nothing." For some reason, it feels wrong to share that I saw Quin crying.

"I wonder why she went to the beach that night," says Oliver. "It was cold and dark. If the last sighting of her was on the Tesco CCTV, she probably headed over after confronting you. She can't have gone anywhere public, else she'd have been picked up by another camera."

My frown deepens. "Yes. And why go to mine and Aaron's nook?"

Yesterday that felt coincidental. Today it feels anything but. My sense that whatever happened to Jade must have been connected to her obsession with me deepens. I kick the locker softly with my heel. There's a link. I just can't see it.

The day crawls along. Officially, it's business as usual for the sixth form, though barely anyone's focusing on learning. It's already been decided that our school will still participate in the town's teen Talent Showcase tomorrow. I'd barely given the event any thought. I'll be attending – not because I have any talents to display, chance would be a fine thing – but because Mr Ellison wants to say a few words with the Quiz Challenge team on stage. Normally that would be nice, a proud moment.

Across the road, in the main school, the vibe today must be very different – especially for Jade's year. Yet I find myself wondering how much they care, beyond agreeing it's a terrible, shocking thing to have happened. Jade was only at Southaven High for five months and doesn't seem to have made any friends.

They've added a photo to the police statement now. Seeing it on the police Twitter appeal brings home a whole new level of horror. Jade wears the same clothes she did when confronting me and in the CCTV. Her last ever photo. It's not a selfie – her mum or Quin or someone must've taken it. She's carefully made up, her glossy hair beautifully styled. Maybe it's my imagination, but the way she glares down at the camera looks defiant. Like a girl on a mission.

By the time I'm due to head to the Talent Showcase after school the next day – early, to help with set up – it's raining so relentlessly I'm worried the bathroom skylights might shatter. Mum and Dad are still at work, Felix is with a friend. Normally when I need a lift, I ask Aaron. He was so proud when he passed his driving test first time and usually leaps at the chance to play chauffeur. He'll be there tonight if his parents have anything to do with it – several of his art pieces are on display.

This could be our chance to talk. I open WhatsApp. I hesitate, my finger hovering over his name. Then I message Leyla instead.

Half an hour later, I'm in the back seat of Riyad's Corsa, sandwiched between Leyla and Tyler from year thirteen. In the passenger seat is Tyler's cousin Brooke, who goes to another school. I've only met Brooke once before and she got under my skin by flirting with Aaron in that low-key kind of way girls notice and boys don't. At least she's absorbed in her phone so we don't have to chat.

We slow down at some lights. Riyad glances over his shoulder at me. He's good-looking if you're into *Love Island* type guys, all pretentious sweeping fringe and glowing light brown skin. Tonight he's dressed smartly, but normally he wears blingy accessories and tight patterned tees with fake Ray-Bans propped on his head. Like he even needs them in winter.

"I wouldn't have thought I was your first choice for knight in shining armour," he says. "Very happy to give you a lift, though. Always space for a little one, Squidge."

I cringe at the use of my childhood nickname. Leyla rolls her eyes. "Are you ever going to let 'Squidge' go?" she asks. "Stop winding Mia up."

When Ley and I were younger, Riyad used to look out for us all the time. I thought he was great. I can pinpoint the exact moment that changed: two years ago, when we kissed during a game of spin the bottle. Riyad made it a full-on snog, a bit heavy for a light-hearted game. I felt weird afterwards, and not only because your first kiss being with your best friend's brother is so cliché, but because Riyad made out it was a non-event, saying douchey things like "glad to give you a bit of practice, Squidge".

"I'm not winding her up," says Riyad now. "Mia is little. It's a fact. Where's lover boy then, Squidge? Don't tell me you've had a…" He mimes horror. "Tiff?"

"You sound like something out of an old-fashioned drama," I say. "Aaron and I are fine."

Brooke bursts out laughing. Catching Leyla glare daggers in the interior mirror, she says, "Sorry. Just read something funny. Not laughing at you, Squidge."

She giggles again and turns back to her phone. I dig my nails into my palms to stop myself snapping back.

The lights flick to green. Tyler complains about the music Riyad has playing from his phone, and Riyad laughs that Tyler has no taste. The attention is off me, but I can't help asking, "Have you spoken to Aaron since the weekend, Riyad? You went to his place on Sunday. We saw you."

"Is that right?" says Riyad.

"Yes. Why did you clear off so quickly?"

"Because I saw you, Squidge, sensed danger, and decided to leave before your lovers' tiff went nuclear. Such a shame. I enjoy watching your chaste little romance."

Dick. I hope Aaron hasn't mentioned what we were planning to do on Saturday night. I should've known better than to ask Riyad a question and expect a straight answer.

Leyla pats my hand and whispers that Riyad had somewhere else he needed to be. This screams "lie" but I don't pull her up on it. For someone with such a sharply honed bullshit detector, Leyla has one blind spot – her brother.

"As for Aaron…" Riyad is indicating to pull into the car park behind the town hall. "Yeah, we've spoken. He needs a break. He's got a lot going on, you know."

"What did he say to you? Is he OK?"

"You're his girlfriend. You ask him."

"I'm asking you."

"And I'm not answering."

Riyad definitely knows something, but I know better than to carry on bugging him. We park. Brooke breezes away with a spring in her step, not even bothering to collapse the passenger seat so Tyler, Leyla and I can clamber out.

The moment we're out of the car, Leyla and I dash for shelter, holding our coats over our heads.

"Where's an umbrella when you need one?" Leyla mutters. That makes me think of my missing umbrella – the one Jade presumably stole. How much stuff belonging to me will the police find in her room?

Without meaning to, I glance over my shoulder. I just

had the weirdest sensation of being watched.

Inside the town hall, helpers line up chairs in what was once the ballroom of some rich person's home. Catering students from the vocational college roll in chiller trolleys of canapés.

Mr Ellison is on the stage fiddling with a laptop at the podium. He's wearing a tailored maroon suit and hipster shoes. The outfit makes him look weirdly hot. For a teacher, obviously.

"Mia, good evening!" he calls. "You're looking very sophisticated. I've tweaked the quiz slide, come and see."

Leyla takes my coat, saying she'll hang it in the cloakroom. My face goes hot as I climb up beside Mr Ellison. My embroidered blouse and sweeping plaid skirt are already making me sweat, even with my hair braided and pinned up. "Um, looks great."

"Are we expecting your family tonight? I'm looking forward to meeting them."

"Mum's coming," I say. "My dad's staying home with my brother. He's not big on small talk. Dad, that is, not Felix."

Mr Ellison laughs. I give him a half-smile and join my friends on the other side of the hall. Leyla's wearing a checked waistcoat and matching super-wide-legged trousers that suit her tall, slim build. She looks a bit like a gender-bent Sherlock Holmes. Oliver's classic tux wouldn't look out of place at a wedding. He smiles nervously when he sees me.

"Hey, Mia. Am I OK? Ley's been taking the mick. Says

I'm overdressed."

He is a bit, but I don't want to dent his confidence. "You look cool." I nod at the school camera around his neck. "I see you're student photographer again. Unpaid labour. Not so cool." I pause. "Have either of you seen Aaron?"

"Olly has," says Leyla. "He made Aaron give him a lift over."

"I didn't make Aaron do anything, but he has a car and I didn't fancy getting drenched." Oliver glances at me. "He didn't want to come."

Surely this can't all be about avoiding me? I always question my instincts, but the sense that something bigger is wrong with Aaron is growing now.

"I need to find him," I say. "He is here, right, Olly? He didn't drive off?"

Oliver nods. Leyla asks if I want backup, but I shake my head.

"I'll have better luck alone. Thanks, though."

A quick sweep of the foyer confirms Aaron isn't here, but a girl from his art class tells me he's in the conference room which is being used as a gallery. The old-fashioned lift is out of order so I take the grand staircase, my heels clicking on the cool marble.

Up on the third floor it's silent apart from the flicker of a broken light. The dark red carpet and low chandeliers remind me of a hotel.

Aaron's pieces jump out at me from the gallery doorway. One is a recent blown-up page from the superhero manga he's been working on. Sadness stabs me. Without my input, the Red Fox would still be a big-boobed Wonder Woman knock-off instead of a kickass CEO with a dark past and a genius IQ. Her story feels as much mine as Aaron's. We spent hours plotting it.

I step into the room. Aaron is alone and whirls around from where he was standing by the window. In his hand is a sheet of paper and a torn envelope – another letter? Our eyes lock. Aaron's hair looks unwashed, his cheeks faintly pink. He stuffs the letter into his pocket and stands there, looking at me. The expression in his eyes is haunted.

"Aaron, what's going on?" I ask.

Aaron clears his throat. "I'm needed downstairs."

He tries to step around me. I block him, then wish I hadn't. Being close enough to see the mole by his ear and smell his familiar deodorant gives me a rush, an unhelpful reminder of the fuzzy feelings I couldn't get enough of when we first got together.

I grasp his hands. "Are you OK? You can tell me anything. I know the police have spoken to you – and you're applying for far-away art colleges too, aren't you? It didn't need to be a secret. That letter's an acceptance, isn't it?"

Aaron looks completely blank. "Art colleges? I haven't… I can't talk now, Mia." He pulls away, swallowing. "I know I'm being a shit boyfriend, but everything… I just… Sorry."

Aaron pushes past me into the corridor. A gaggle of students are climbing the staircase so he makes for the nearby fire escape. A kick and the door's open. I catch it before it can swing shut. Through the gaps in the railings I catch a flash of his grey blazer.

"Aaron!" I yell, but he ignores me.

Downstairs, the foyer and reception rooms are flooding with visitors – parents, students and nosy old people already tucking into the buffet and marvelling at the high, painted ceilings. I watch from the staircase, my nerves tingling.

I find Oliver and Leyla where I left them, heads close as they peer at a phone. Then Leyla backs away, shaking her head.

Crap. What now?

"What's happened?" I ask.

"Nothing," says Oliver, at the same time Leyla says, "You should see this."

She shoves the phone at me. On the screen is a report about Jade's death.

"It says the police believe her body was moved." Leyla can barely contain her impatience. "She wasn't killed at your nook. Maybe I'm being ridiculous, but—"

"No, Ley," Oliver says. "You can't say this to Mia!"

This is making as much sense as if they were talking another language. "Say what? Why are you looking so spooked?"

"Did you find Aaron?" asks Leyla. "Would he speak to you?"

"No. He was acting weird. He ran away, he— Wait.

What does Aaron have to do with Jade's body being moved?"

Leyla draws a deep, shuddering breath. "I… I'm going to come out and say this, and you can tell me it's ridiculous. What if Aaron did this, Mia?"

I step back, staring at her. Leyla quickly continues, "I'm not saying he's a cold-blooded killer. It could have been … an accident. Aaron never liked you talking about Jade. He told you it was nothing, yet he was freaked out the night she photographed you. He could have met her after you argued on Saturday. All the copying, and Jade hating on you – the simplest explanation is that Aaron was the secret boyfriend. I've thought that all along—"

"I've told you, Jade wasn't interested in Aaron!" I cry. I can feel my face flooding with colour. "And I don't see what this has to do with her body being moved!"

"Aaron has a car." Leyla pauses. "A car he was washing inside his closed garage the morning Jade's body was discovered, Mia. A car he didn't want to use tonight, and Olly says reeked of *bleach*. Why the hell would you bleach the inside of your car unless you were desperate to get rid of something? Like blood? And" – Leyla's talking rapidly now, words running into each other – "how do you explain Jade's body turning up at your nook? I don't know *why* he'd take her there, but out of all the places in Southaven? It's a huge coincidence."

"Coincidences happen!" I hiss. "There are loads of things that contradict your theory."

"Like what?" Leyla's face is flushed too. "I don't want it

to be him, Mimi, don't think that… It's suspicious, though. Isn't it?"

"Aaron did not do this." Yet, to my horror, doubt creeps into my voice. Something *is* wrong with Aaron. His erratic behaviour, his nerviness, the way he's been avoiding me since Jade's death. DS Forster asked for his name. Was that out of suspicion, or routine? Has she questioned him?

Leyla can't be right, surely. Aaron wouldn't. He couldn't. He's always been so gentle…

I squeeze my eyes shut, willing this to go away, but when I open them, I'm still here, surrounded by canapés and laughing parents.

Oliver grasps my hand. "It's OK, Mia," he says. "I don't think Leyla's right, even if something strange is going on… Are you going to pass out? You've gone pale. Do I need to fetch the smelling salts?"

He's trying a joke, but his eyes are full of concern – and uncertainty. His hand feels firm and solid. That drags me back into the present.

"This is ridiculous," I snap, dropping Oliver's hand. "We need to find Aaron and get him to tell us the truth."

"How? If he isn't talking to you, he sure as hell won't talk to me." Leyla looks at Oliver. "Aaron's not blanking you, though."

Oliver chews his lip. Then he says, "We could … search his car?"

"What?" I yelp. "No!"

"Hear me out. If there's no trace of anything there, that

proves Leyla's theory is wrong."

"Not if he bleached it!" Leyla cries.

"Bleach wouldn't necessarily remove blood," I find myself saying. "Felix cut his foot and bled all over the carpet once. Mum tried everything, but it still stained."

I'm suddenly hit by the absurdity of discussing cleaning products and murder while finely dressed people mill around us for what is supposed to be an evening of celebration. Why am I even entertaining this plan?

Leyla drops her voice. "We could at least look. Aaron will never know."

"I can get the key easily enough," says Oliver. "My coat's in his car. I could pretend I've left something in the pocket."

"No!" I cry. "This is ridiculous. A total violation of privacy!"

"Leyla, I need to borrow you for a moment." We all jump. The harassed-sounding voice belongs to the chemistry teacher.

"I'll be right back," Leyla whispers and follows the teacher into the crowd. I take a steadying breath.

"She's wrong. She is, Olly."

"OK," he says. "You know him best."

I don't though, do I? Aaron's a stranger tonight. I can assert all I like that there's nothing in his car, but can I really be sure? How can I get through this evening, tomorrow, the weeks ahead, not knowing?

I look at Oliver. "Maybe…" The voice doesn't sound

like my own. "We could take a quick look. Just you and me. We don't need to mention it to Ley."

Oliver nods, straightening his bow tie. "Right. Let Operation Car Keys commence. I'm not dressed like a spy for nothing."

My laugh comes out sounding hysterical. Oliver disappears into the crowd. I move somewhere more discreet in case Leyla returns and concentrate on steadying my breathing as one minute turns to two, then five.

Finally Oliver reappears. He jingles a set of keys at me. We weave our way to the back doors and into the car park.

It's stopped raining, and the chill makes my skin break out in goosepimples. Aaron's Nissan is parked in the second row. The lock clicks as Oliver turns the key. I open the boot, my teeth beginning to chatter. The strong alkaline smell of cleaning products is almost overpowering. Aaron's usual crap – carrier bags, wrappers, empty cans of Coke – is gone. All that's left is a pair of trainers and a hoodie.

So Aaron had a clear out. Maybe his parents had been bugging him, and he finally got around to doing it. Heady relief rushes through me.

Then Oliver lifts the hoodie. Beneath it, on the upholstery, is a very faint but unmistakable rust-coloured stain.

Oliver and I gaze at the stain for what feels like ages.

"That is blood, isn't it?" He breaks the silence. "I mean, you wouldn't notice unless you were looking, but..."

"It's blood," I whisper. The words feel like a betrayal.

"Mia," Oliver says, his voice heavy. "Should we phone the police?"

The words send a jolt through me. "No! There'll be an explanation. There has to be. This doesn't mean Aaron hurt her, however bad it looks."

Oliver doesn't look convinced. I plough on, aware I'm desperately spitballing now. "We're going to go inside and find Aaron. We say what we found. Really pile on pressure.

He'll cave and tell us everything and how this got here. I bet it's nothing to do with Jade."

Oliver is silent. He's looking about as sick as I feel. Finally, he nods.

Inside, the foyer is buzzing. The ceremony is due to start in ten minutes and everyone is on a high. Oliver disappears to return the car keys. I'm about to follow when Leyla grabs me.

"Hey," she says. "Where did you go? Look, I know you're angry, but—"

I grab a canapé from a passing waiter so I don't have to answer. The little pancake is almost in my mouth when I catch the metallic whiff of smoked salmon. I chuck it in the closest bin, scrubbing my mouth and smearing my lip gloss.

A hand presents me with a napkin. Gratefully I dab my mouth – then freeze as I realize the hand belongs to Quin Farrell.

"Missed a bit," he says, tapping his chin.

"What are you doing here?" I ask, taken aback.

"I made that blini you just binned."

I take him in – stiff white shirt, black trousers, quiff combed to one side, empty tray in one hand. He looks far less intimidating than he did behind the Electric, threatening Aaron by the bins. "You're … at catering college?"

"Don't sound so surprised. What was wrong with the blini?"

"I'm vegan."

"Shame. Someone took the last pakora."

I stare at Quin. He stares back. Something in his eyes tells me he didn't come over to talk about canapés.

I picture him by the beach, his body wracked with sobs. Quietly, I say, "Surely no one expects you to work tonight."

"Cos I've got the perfect excuse? 'Sicko murdered my stepsister' is better than 'dog ate my homework', I s'pose."

Leyla takes my arm. I'm dimly aware of Oliver reappearing on my other side. "Leave him, Mia," Leyla says. "He isn't worth it."

"Not the first time I've heard that." Quin spins his tray on his fingertip like it's a football. His voice sounds a little slurred, and I wonder if he's downed a glass or two of wine himself. "Jade's secret boyfriend is definitely from Southaven High. I'm not gonna rest until I find him." He locks eyes with me again. "And you and I both know who I think he is. Where's Aaron?"

I don't answer. Neither do Leyla or Oliver. Quin frowns, instantly picking up on the vibe. "What's going on?"

"Nothing," I say quickly. "He's not here."

"Liar." Quin grabs my wrist. "You must know something. Was it him? There were pictures in Jade's room – did you two ever talk, or—"

I try to pull away. Quin doesn't let go.

Oliver's expression darkens. "Get off her."

"Or what, you'll punch my face in?" Quin gives Oliver

a dismissive up and down. "I'll let go once someone tells me what's going on."

"We're saying nothing, so get off me." I yank my arm downwards and Quin backs off.

"Fine," he says. "I'll find Aaron myself. I let him off too lightly last time. I can guess where he's hiding."

The next second he's gone, straight towards the staircase.

"Oh God!" I cry.

Oliver and Leyla are right behind me as I run after Quin, our shoes clattering on the steps. Quin's footfalls echo above us.

As we reach the third floor there's a shout and a thud. We skid into the gallery. Quin has Aaron pinned against the wall, exactly like outside the Electric Palace. One of Aaron's pictures lies nearby, its frame broken.

"Did you kill her?" snarls Quin. "*Did you?*"

Aaron makes a wheezing noise. He closes his eyes, not even attempting to fight back.

Quin thumps him against the wall. "Deny it. Go on. I dare you."

"Let him go!" I shout. "Do you want to get done for assault?"

Quin's grip eases for a second. That's all Aaron needs to wriggle away. I catch a glimpse of his eyes, wide with panic. The smooth soles of his brogues skid on the polished gallery floor as he dashes into the hallway.

Immediately, Quin's after him. Aaron makes a beeline for the fire escape, slamming the door shut behind him.

Quin yanks it open. I catch the door before it closes behind him — and then there's some heavy clattering, followed by a yell and a colossal thud.

I hurtle out on to the metal steps. There, lying on the concrete ten metres below, is Aaron.

The hum of the kitchen fans bores into my head as I take everything in. His leg is twisted. The position of his arms doesn't look natural either.

He isn't moving.

I career down the steps, kicking off my heels halfway and taking the rest barefoot, numb to the chilly metal kissing my soles. I jump the last three and fall to my knees by his side.

"Aaron! *Aaron*."

He doesn't respond. His eyes are closed. I pat his cheek, gently at first, then so wildly I'm practically slapping him.

"This isn't funny. Joke's over. You've scared me, well done."

No reaction. I press my trembling finger to his wrist, seeking a pulse.

Nothing.

He needs an ambulance — pronto. They'll do CPR or something, bring him back. A fantasy sequence runs through my head; a shout, "He's breathing!", paramedics appearing, a wild rush to get Aaron into the ambulance, to safety—

Someone else's finger is pressing against Aaron's neck: Leyla. Seconds stretch. Then, there's a low moan. Aaron's eyelids flutter.

"He's alive!" I cry.

"You had the wrong part of the wrist." Leyla leans closer to Aaron. "Can you move your arms and legs?"

Aaron's eyes have a dazed sheen as they move from Leyla to me. His face contorts and he howls. "It hurts."

"No shit, it hurts," says Leyla.

Aaron's left arm twitches. He flexes his fingers. My hand finds his before I've even realized it.

"Good job you're left-handed," I say. "You'll still be able to draw—"

Aaron makes a growling noise. Out of the corner of my eye I spot Oliver, phone pressed to his ear.

"Mia," Aaron rasps. "I'm so sorry."

"Don't talk now. Olly's phoning for an ambulance."

"No, listen. You should know the truth."

Fear gathers in my belly. I've been desperate to know why Aaron's been behaving so oddly for days, but suddenly I can't bear to hear it. "Shush. You don't need to say anything."

"Yes, I do. I can't live like this. It was me."

"What was?"

"Jade." He swallows. "I killed her."

8

What happens next takes on a dreamlike quality. A crowd grows outside and faces line the windows. A first aider elbows their way to the front. Aaron starts crying, blubbing incoherently about being sorry. His parents rush out, their faces chalk white. Then there are blue lights, paramedics and police. Everyone is herded away, the celebrations cut short.

After gathering a quick account of what happened, a police officer orders me, Leyla and Oliver to wait in the reception area. Quin is nowhere to be found. We sit side by side, barely moving. Mum stands nearby, speaking to Leyla's parents. She's outwardly composed, but I can tell from the tilt of her head just how bewildered she is. Oliver's parents are outside, having a massive argument about something.

It was me. I killed her. I'm so sorry. Even after finding the bloodstain, hearing those words from his own mouth has sent my head spinning. Surely Aaron confessed by mistake. It was a sick joke. I heard wrong. Yet I know I haven't.

Is the rest true too? Was Aaron also Jade's *secret boyfriend*? Jade received *love letters*. She might have sent some in return. Are they the letters I saw Aaron with, the ones he hid from me? Was everything I believed completely wrong?

Leyla's hair tickles my cheek as she leans close. "I'm really sorry, Mimi," she murmurs. "I know I hurt you, throwing accusations about. I never wanted tonight to end like this."

She looks close to tears. Any anger I felt towards her earlier has fizzled out. Even so, it takes a big effort to croak, "You were right. About the car."

"What? How do you—"

"Olly and I searched it secretly. I didn't want to give you the satisfaction of knowing you'd got under my skin." I draw breath and meet her eyes. "There was a bloodstain."

Leyla's hand flies to her mouth. "Oh, shit."

"Yep," I say flatly.

Leyla hesitates, then opens her arms. I gulp and go in for the hug.

"Are we good?" she whispers.

I squeeze before letting go. "Always."

After what feels like ages, DS Forster joins us. She takes me aside, her eyes kind as she asks what happened. I press closer to Mum and mumble my way through the events of this evening, feeling foolish, naive and a total child.

"Thanks, Mia," DS Forster says. "I'll need a formal statement tomorrow, but that's enough for now. Just to double check – Aaron definitely slipped? No one pushed him?"

I shake my head. "Quin wasn't close enough. He lost it, and Aaron bolted. Those steps were wet. Is he… Is Aaron OK?"

"I'm waiting for an update, but his injuries aren't life-threatening. We're getting a warrant to search his car and his home, and we'll take it from there."

Criminals have their homes searched. My insides turn to ice.

"Time we left," says Mum quietly.

As we walk to the revolving doors my eyes trail across the foyer. Only hours ago the place was buzzing, everyone swilling wine and gobbling disgusting salmon blinis. Now it's like a graveyard. A rubbish sack lies overturned, plastic glasses and scrunched-up napkins spilling out. Someone's cardigan is draped over one of the chairs and part-drunk juices are dotted everywhere. A puddle of red wine glistens under a table.

From here it looks a lot like blood.

The next day I sit in the police interview room beside Mum, DS Forster and DC West seated opposite us. I'm missing my first lesson, and Mum had to phone work to wrangle taking the morning off. God knows how she explained.

It's more comfortable here than I expected, modern and clean-smelling. To the left of me is what I guess is one-way glass. I wonder who's watching.

As I stumble through my statement again I get a nasty feeling that something has happened. Sure enough, DS Forster says, "My colleague has spoken to Aaron. He's repeated his confession that he killed Jade."

Mum squeezes my hand. Numbness swamps me. It feels as though I'm not really here.

"I'm going to ask you about Aaron now," DS Forster continues. "My questions might not be easy to answer, but we need the truth. Was Aaron ever violent towards you in any way, however minor?"

Our argument outside the cinema flits through my mind. Aaron's hand raised. Me backing away. That split-second thought: *he's going to hurt me*.

I imagined that, though. Didn't I?

"No," I mutter. "Never."

"What about other people?" asks DS Forster. "Does he get into fights?"

I'm a lover, not a fighter. Those were Aaron's words when he chased off the drunk guy. Even with Quin, he only acted in self-defence. I shake my head.

"Was Aaron angry with you that Saturday, Mia?"

Why is this relevant? "Um... Kind of, yeah. We argued."

"What about?"

I pause. "Do I have to answer?"

She nods. "Please."

Oh God. I can't lie, can I? I'm in a police station. I fix my eyes on the table. I can't bring myself to look at Mum, say the word sex, even though she already knows. "Aaron's parents were away. We were planning to ... go back to his, but I was too rattled because of my run-in with Jade, and I wasn't, uh, in the mood. If you know what I mean."

"I understand."

Thank goodness. My cheeks must already be the colour of cherries. "So, yeah, he got upset after that. Angry. Although..."

"Although what?"

I hesitate, piecing the evening together. "Now I think about it ... he was on edge before I even got there. Aaron had been receiving letters – he was secretive about them, but they really gave him the jitters. Did you – I mean, maybe you can't say, but were there any envelopes in Jade's room? Because she used to get love letters, and I thought she might've sent some to Aaron?"

DS Forster shakes her head. She asks more questions, mainly about Saturday, but also about Aaron generally. Unable to contain myself, I eventually blurt out, "Do you know why he did it? Because I don't understand—"

She holds up a hand. "I can't speculate. Right now, we have no evidence that Aaron and Jade ever spoke to each other."

Perhaps Aaron *wasn't* the secret boyfriend, then? My heart lifts slightly – but my head is also starting to throb.

If he and Jade had been seeing each other, I could imagine that an argument might have got out of hand. But if they weren't – maybe Jade did make the boyfriend up, like that year eleven girl thought – then why would Aaron hurt her? How did Aaron even come to meet her that night? And what the hell is in those letters?

DS Forster's phone rings. She excuses herself, leaving the room as she takes the call and asks whoever's on the line what the news is from Cedar. DC West shows us out. Behind us the door clicks shut. Something about the noise feels very final.

On the way to the exit, we pass a waiting area. Riyad is there, sitting bolt upright and clutching a polystyrene cup. His usual swagger is gone – it's odd to see him like this. Are they talking to him because he's Aaron's mate, or for some other reason? He's staring at the floor, and I'm too shaken to speak to him.

Mum waits until we're in the car to ask, "How are you feeling?"

I don't know how to even begin answering. How can Aaron have done this? My Aaron, who mispronounces the word falafel so adorably, and messages me updates on the cats that stray into his garden as though their activities are a soap opera?

It doesn't make any sense.

Mum seems to understand my silence. She offers me a sweet from the glove compartment. I shake my head.

"Not vegan."

Mum sighs and tosses the packet back. This must be hard for her to process too. It's like we're living in an alternate reality. Is she thinking of how she welcomed Aaron into our home, and cooked for him, and treated him like another member of the family? Or is she thinking about me – how I lied, hid things, planned on going all the way with my boyfriend despite her warnings for me to be cautious?

"We'll get through this, Mia," she says. It sounds like she's trying to reassure herself, too. "Everything will be OK."

Mum offers to take me home instead of back to school, but I'll only stew in my own head. There's too much of Aaron in my room, from the latest manga he lent me to the very first picture he ever drew of us, which is Blu-tacked by my bed. School will be hell, but part of me wants to hurt. It's better than the numbness.

Sure enough, the moment I walk through the gates, pressure mounts in my chest, building with every step. Aaron should be here. So should Jade. I don't know her timetable but he has double art; Wednesdays are the one day he never skives. There'll be an empty stool while other students clatter around with paint and pastels. An empty stool where a killer used to sit.

My self-control crumbles. Once inside, I stumble against the corridor wall and slide down to the floor, curling up into a ball. How long I sob into my hands I don't know. Someone kneels in front of me.

"Mia. Hey. Let's go somewhere more private, shall we?"

Mr Ellison helps me to my feet, and up two flights to the sociology office. It's no more than a box room, with chairs, a whiteboard and a desk with a laptop on it. The travel kettle on the window sill is guarded by a plastic T-Rex and a Lego spaceship I recognize as the Imperial Star Destroyer. Mr Ellison flips the kettle on and swivels his office chair round to open a cupboard.

"Cup of tea and a biscuit, I think," he says. "Coconut ring and camomile tea OK? The biscuits are vegan."

I perch on the chair by the door, trying to get a grip on myself. The biscuits he hands me are gooey and very sweet. I choke one down. The tea scalds my tongue, but I keep sipping, grateful for something to focus on.

Mr Ellison takes a biscuit himself. I didn't realize he was dairy free, or that he knew I was. "It's impossibly hard, isn't it?" he says. "Your mum called to ask us to keep a special eye on you. My friend was killed in a car accident when I was your age and that left me reeling, but this is on another level."

Dimly, it registers that I've stopped crying. I take another sip, not meeting his eyes.

"Let me know if you want to go home after this," says Mr Ellison. "If you stay, I'll open up my classroom so you've somewhere quiet to go at lunchtime. The canteen's brutal at the best of times. I don't want to know what goes into the soup of the day."

He's being nice. I should be nice back. I try a smile. It feels wrong.

Mr Ellison leans forward. "It's not my business," he says. "But was everything OK with Aaron, beforehand? You didn't ever feel in danger with him, or threatened?"

I blink. "What?"

"I was at the Electric Palace on Saturday and overheard you having words. Not what you said – I promise I didn't listen in – but it was clearly a fight. Perhaps I should have intervened."

Even though Mr Ellison doesn't know what we argued about, I still squirm at the idea we were seen. "Aaron isn't like that."

"Sure?" says Mr Ellison. "You can say no to boys if you're uncomfortable, you know. You don't need to be nice."

Something inside me flips. My cardboard cup flies across the room and thwacks the opposite wall. Tea explodes everywhere. Mr Ellison jumps up. It takes me a second to realize: I threw that cup.

My hands fly over my mouth. "I'm sorry! I don't know what came over me, I…"

I run out of words. Flipping out at a teacher? That isn't me! Mr Ellison squats down, inspecting the carpet, then plucks up my empty cup and tosses it into the bin.

"No harm done," he says calmly.

"Are you going to send me to the headteacher?" I ask in a small voice. I've no idea how school discipline works. The detentions I've been given have all been because of forgotten homework.

"It doesn't matter. It was only tea and this is hardly a normal day."

I can't believe he's being this cool. "I'm sorry I was rude."

"I only asked about Aaron because I was concerned. It's easy to get trapped in a bad relationship and not see it, however smart you are. And you are smart, Mia, even though I know you don't think it. A lot of highly intelligent people underachieve academically." Mr Ellison pauses. "Capital of Iceland?"

Mr Ellison's not seriously turning this into a practice Quiz Challenge session, is he? "Reykjavik. Sir, I—"

"Fabulous. What does 'Au' stand for on the periodic table?"

"Argon?"

"Gold. Learn the periodic table. Comes up without fail."

I went over elements two weeks ago. Proving myself mattered so much then. Aaron didn't get why I was bothering. "You and me aren't smart, what's the point in pretending otherwise?" he'd said. That stung. Oliver and Leyla were the ones who'd tested me on planets and Nobel Prize winners, building my confidence.

"I should drop out," I say. "I can't do it any more."

"We'll have this chat another time," Mr Ellison says. "Please keep going. In the worst times it helps to have distractions we can lose ourselves in, even if it is pointless trivia."

Oh. That's why he started the quizzing. Maybe he has a point... I've calmed down, haven't I?

Voices float in from outside.

"I'd better go to break," I say. "Thanks for the, er..."

I glance at the cup in the bin. Mr Ellison waves a dismissive hand.

"If you ever have any worries, please come to me. I'm happy to listen."

"OK. Thanks." I guess I'd rather chat to Mr Ellison than the school counsellor, who's retirement age.

"Any time, Mia." Suddenly Mr Ellison is in a hurry to get out of the office. He strides off, presumably to the staffroom.

As I turn towards the staircase, something occurs to me. Doesn't Mr Ellison live over the other side of Brighton? Another teacher mentioned it when he was held up in traffic and she covered our tutor group. There are loads of cinemas closer to home, including classic ones. I wonder why he came all the way to the Electric Palace on Saturday.

Leyla and Oliver are waiting at our usual meeting spot by the radiator outside the caretaker's cupboard, which luckily is quiet. We fold into a group hug.

"You look like crap, Mia," says Leyla, and that breaks the tension. She holds my pocket mirror so I can dab at my red eyes with the wet toilet paper Oliver fetches.

I tell them about my interview with the police. When I mention Riyad, Leyla hesitates. Then, reluctantly, she says,

"The police wanted to ask him a few questions. Aaron rang Riyad that night."

Immediately, I'm alert. Ringing his mates isn't something Aaron does – he's awkward on calls. "When did that happen? What did they talk about?"

"I don't know, Mia. The call was earlier rather than later – shortly after you argued, maybe. It doesn't mean Ri has anything to do with this."

I open my mouth to say that this is *the night of the murder* – whatever Aaron said to Riyad is important – then clock Leyla's defensive tone and stop. If Riyad was involved, or knows something, the police will get it out of him. Maybe he can throw light on a connection between Aaron and Jade. There's still so much we don't know – where Aaron went after our argument, how he and Jade came to meet, where she actually died…

I toss the tissue in the bin. It feels like I'm breaking. I simply can't shake my deep-seated conviction that this is all wrong, that Aaron, *my* Aaron, can't have done this – even though there isn't a shred of evidence he didn't.

9

Sticking out the entire day at school drains every drop of my strength. No one is unkind, not to my face, anyway. They go eerily quiet when I approach. Some narrow their eyes and whisper, but most look at me with pity. Every set of eyes boring into my back feels like it burns into my very being. When the shock wears off, the inevitable jibes and sneers will come.

Hey, Mia, did you know your boyfriend was a killer?

If he thwacked a girl round the head just imagine the kinky shit he and Mia got up to behind closed doors.

Not so perfect after all.

Mum texts to check I'm OK, and also rings at lunchtime.

"Can you bear to pick Felix up later?" she asks. "I'm back in the office and getting away will be tricky. Dad won't be back from London in time, and Noah's mum can't have him…"

It's hardly a big ask. Felix's school is close to mine. Mum doesn't caution me to be careful; with Jade's killer caught, I'm no longer in danger. That should make me feel better but it doesn't.

Felix pouts when I tell him we're going straight home.

"We always go to the playground when you pick me up," he says.

"No, Fe. I'm not in the mood."

"But why? I want playground!"

Screw it. I don't have it in me to deal with a meltdown. It's not like I can explain to Felix why I'm feeling crap. "Just half an hour then."

"Yahoo!" Felix's face lights up. He skips along, tapping lamp posts and walls with a stick he's named "Lord Sticky Stick", singing a song about the solar system.

Kids are swarming over the play equipment when we arrive, parents on benches with takeaway coffees. The massive climbing frame is shaped like a pirate ship, with different levels and lots of little hidey holes. Felix sprints off towards it.

How can the world carry on when the bottom has fallen out of mine? For these people, Jade is a face in the newspaper. Aaron isn't even that; he's a "seventeen-year-old boy being spoken to in connection with Jade's death." How long will it be before he's named?

The numb, leaden feeling returns. I search for somewhere to sit – then freeze. There, on a bench by the swings, is Quin. On his lap is a baby in a flower-print onesie. Her chin is shiny with drool. Quin wipes her with a cloth from the bag hanging off her pram, then folds it over his shoulder and plugs a bottle of milk into her mouth. The way he does it is so easy and natural that I can't help but stare.

Less than twenty-four hours ago, this guy was an out-of-control ball of rage. Now apparently he's the baby whisperer. Then two figures step between us: Riyad and Tyler, both carrying skateboards.

"Quinlan. Fancy seeing you here." Uh-oh. I know that tone on Riyad: fake charm, and underneath, a nasty edge. "How maternal you look."

Quin says nothing. Riyad glances at Tyler, who shrugs and lights a roll-up.

"Cookery school, now a baby," he says. "Turning into a lovely little housewife. Watching you cuddle your sweet daughter warms my heart. Where's the mum? Did you push her off the town hall fire escape too?" He pauses. "I hope you get done for that. Loser."

Quin stares into the middle distance. Riyad's expression darkens. Slowly and deliberately, he says, "I suppose we should express our condolences. RIP your stepsister. Sounded messy. But then you'd know. Violence is your thing. How long did it take the police to ask where you were that night?"

I suck in a breath. The skin around Quin's knuckles goes white where he clutches the bottle. "Fuck off."

"Free country," says Riyad. "I'm enjoying standing here." He accepts the cigarette Tyler passes him.

I can't let a fight break out here in front of these kids. I stalk over.

"Stop it, Riyad," I say. "Please."

Riyad scowls. "Me? I'm not the one at fault. Psycho here nearly killed your boyfriend. Lay into him!"

I hesitate. Then I position myself between Riyad and Quin. "He's grieving and he's with a baby and you're baiting him. That's not OK."

"Get you, Squidge, all assertive. What are you going to do, tell my mum?"

God, he's spoiling for a fight. I've never seen Riyad this way. I open my mouth to respond, then stop. "Is that a spliff?"

"Don't sound so disapproving," says Riyad. "This is tame stuff."

Aaron admitted smoking spliffs with Riyad a few times, so this is hardly news, but doing it in a playground is pretty low. "You're not going to help anyone by sticking around here."

Riyad takes a drag before returning the spliff to Tyler. "All right, Saint Squidge. I get it, it's easier if I leave. We all know you can't control yourself around me."

With that ridiculous attempt to gain the upper hand, he breezes off, a sniggering Tyler by his side.

"Tool," I mutter, turning to Quin. He's gripping the baby, his lips moving silently. I realize he's counting. When he gets to zero he releases a long breath.

"You didn't have to fight my corner," he says. "I can look after myself."

I take a moment to collect my thoughts. Why did I stick up for him? Sure, Riyad was being especially terrible, but Quin's hardly the good guy himself. Not that you'd know about his bad reputation from looking at him now. He's a mess – all tired, bloodshot eyes and pale skin – wearing the same hoodie as when I saw him crying. This boy is hurting, and badly. How can I not feel empathy for that?

Grief doesn't make last night OK, yet I can understand why he lost it. Gingerly, I perch on the bench. "I'm sorry. About Jade. How are you… Well. How are you doing?"

He narrows his eyes. "What's it to you?"

"Just asking."

"If you're here to give me an earful about last night, go ahead. I'm a sitting target." He pauses, then adds, "And if you're wondering why I'm here, this one needs fresh air, and I can't stick it at home any longer. We had this place to ourselves until ten minutes ago."

Is the baby really his daughter, or was Riyad messing? She's definitely got his pointy nose. "I'm not judging." I draw my knees to my chest, hugging them. "I don't understand any of this. The police told me they couldn't find a link between Aaron and Jade."

Quin balances the baby's half-drunk bottle on the bench, leaning her over his shoulder and rubbing her back. "Maybe he isn't the boyfriend, who knows. Jade was definitely meeting her guy when she left the house on Saturday, though. She was all dressed up."

"Have they found out who he is?"

Quin shrugs, which I assume means no. "She changed when he came on to the scene."

Again, I think of the bright-eyed girl I saw online, with her fun, vibrant life. "How did Jade seem when she left that night?"

"Mix of angry and nervous." I'm a bit surprised Quin's being so cooperative. He slides his phone from his pocket. A few taps and the screen is filled by the defiant photograph of Jade from the news websites. They only used her headshot, but this version goes to her knees. "She asked me to take this. Said she wanted to remember, whatever that meant."

The timestamp on the photo is five p.m. Jade must have found me immediately after arriving in Southaven. Was the confrontation what she wanted to remember?

Quin's manoeuvring the baby into a waterproof all-in-one, low-key impressive given how fiddly those things are. I decide to take the plunge. "I saw Jade not long after you took that photo. She said there was something important she needed to tell me. Do you know what that could be? She was scaring me, so I ran off without hearing her out."

Quin's looking at me with an intensity I don't like. "Jade isn't scary. She's just an insecure kid."

I pretend not to notice the slip into present tense. "Saturday wasn't the first time she followed me. You know that. You found those photos in her room."

"Big fucking deal. This isn't about your pain. You're here. You've got your life. Jade hasn't." Oh God, he's starting to look angry. "I don't know what those photos were, but Jade wouldn't stalk anyone. She could be a mouthy cow but creeping around? Nah. Not her."

"I'm sorry, but she absolutely did. I saw her."

"I don't care what you saw," he says, lowering the baby into the pram. "You have no idea what this is like. You can go home to your mum and dad and eat a nice dinner and whatever, but my family don't get that any more. Destroyed, for ever, because your sick boyfriend whacked her round the head and left her on that beach like a piece of rubbish."

He flips up the pram brake with his foot and storms off. My cheeks flood with colour. I wish I hadn't come across like I was accusing him, or trying to make Jade's death about me. What a mess.

Someone clears their throat. Oh great – Riyad's back, by himself this time. I unfold my legs, glaring at him.

"What?"

Riyad takes the spot Quin vacated. "Don't get at me. I was watching to check you were OK. Didn't want you to leave in an ambulance. Why were you even talking to Psycho Quin? After last night, really?"

"I don't have to explain myself to you. Do you know how offensive that nickname is?"

"Well, he is a psycho. Knocked four of my teeth out, remember? Killed my modelling career stone dead."

"You didn't have a modelling career. That person who DMed you wasn't a real scout."

"I'll never get a chance to find out, will I?"

He's still bitter about his replacement dentures not being good enough. I don't know why he's so fixed on modelling – like Leyla, Riyad gets top grades. In the future he'll be able to do any job he wants. "Riyad, do you think Aaron did it? I know he confessed but…"

Riyad shrugs. He becomes engrossed in flicking something off his skateboard. "Who really knows anyone?"

That's … curiously evasive. Even for Riyad. Especially as he was so angry with Quin minutes ago. "What did you and Aaron talk about that night? I know he rang you."

"That doesn't mean I picked up."

I'd have better luck getting jelly to stick to a wall. "Did you speak or not? Meet up, even? He left the cinema at half six. Leyla says the call was shortly after we argued, I'm guessing before Jade died—"

"I didn't see or speak to him. I was busy. As for that phone call, maybe he called to bitch about you holding out on him, Squidge, have you considered that?"

I blush. Riyad flicks his fake Ray-Bans off the top of his head and stands.

"Naturally I'd have told Aaron he was on to a good

thing and to kiss and make up. Anyway, I hate to love you and leave you, but I have places to go, people to see, things to do."

With that, Riyad strides off, his usual poise returning. Yet the way his jaw twitched betrayed that I'd hit a nerve.

Was he really watching out for me when I was talking to Quin? It's so hard to tell if Riyad cares, or in what way. He always brushed off our spin the bottle kiss, but sometimes I've wondered…

My mind slips back to Peyton Fletcher's party last October. I was outside trying to work out if the pressure behind my eyes was booze or an oncoming migraine when an arm snaked around my waist.

"You look so hot there, stargazing."

Riyad wore a tee, despite it being only five degrees. I stepped aside. "I'm getting fresh air, not stargazing."

"Oh? I thought you were into that kooky spiritualism shizzle. Cancer and Aquarius. That makes us compatible, yes?"

"Are you drunk?"

Riyad burst out laughing, then said how beautiful the night smelled. Assuming sarcasm – the nearby recycling boxes and wheelie bin were overflowing – I said, "I'm going back in."

He blocked me, hand over mine on the door handle. "C'mon, Squidgie, don't be a killjoy. Smile! I was your first kiss. I'm super sparkly unicorn special. I know you love unicorns."

I pulled away. "Hilarious."

"Don't tell me you don't think about it sometimes."

"I'm going to find Aaron."

"Forget lover boy. Come on. Let's dance. I'm a great dancer. Amazing moves. D'you think unicorns are good at dancing?"

"Riyad! Stop it. You're not funny."

"So you say."

"I wouldn't kiss you again if you were the last boy on Earth."

"Again, so you say."

The door crashed open. Someone blundered out and threw up all over the recycling. I caught the door and vanished into the house. Safely inside, with Aaron's arm around me, I soon forgot about Riyad. The look in his eyes when our hands had touched, though…

Ugh. I shake the memory away. Sometimes I can't believe Riyad shares genes with Leyla.

I didn't even get the chance to ask why he didn't come home on Saturday night. Before I can help myself, my phone is in my hand. Riyad hasn't posted any pictures from that evening, but Tyler has – lots of them. The whole crew were at one of the clubs by the station that aren't fussy about ID – except Aaron and Riyad. Could they have been together, despite what Riyad claims?

Riyad definitely knows something. He showed up at Aaron's when the news of the body broke – and took off the moment he spotted me and Leyla…

Suddenly, I realize that between Quin and Riyad, it's been ages since I last saw Felix.

I leap up.

"Fe?"

Felix doesn't appear. Not unusual – he often hides at home time. Last time we were here he gave me a real run around. I lodge my foot on the closest rope ladder and climb high enough to see the whole area.

"Felix! Where are you?" The words die in my mouth. None of the kids are curly-haired boys wearing navy jackets.

I swing round, expecting to see Felix behind me, grinning. He isn't. A sick feeling creeps into my belly. Felix must be up in the crow's nest. It's the only place I can't see properly. Once I'm the other side of this slide I'll have a better view...

The crow's nest is empty. Children swarm everywhere. None of them are my brother. Running now, I circle the frame. He must be here. He can't have vanished.

But Felix is gone.

10

Sweat beads on my forehead. Foolish Mia! I didn't once check that Felix was OK while I was talking to Quin and Riyad. It never crossed my mind that he'd run off.

Unless someone took him.

I dismiss the thought immediately. The play area isn't gated but there are parents everywhere. Tons of kids. Someone would have noticed. But all the mums and dads are chatting or on their phones. The few that aren't are watching their own children.

"Have you seen my brother?" I gasp. "He's five, wearing a blue coat."

Parents look up, shaking their heads. I want to smack

myself. In a moment I'll have to call Mum and Dad, admit I screwed up. What if Felix is hurt? Worse? My thoughts are spiralling, shooting towards the worst-case scenario. People do sick things to kids. What if—

A woman waves at me. "There's a boy in a blue coat at the back of the cafe, by the fish pond."

I race round – and there, watching the fish and clutching a Dairy Milk wrapper, is Felix.

A half-sob, half-cry rips out of me. I crush him into a hug.

Felix pulls away, his chocolate-smeared face one big smile. "Hello, Mia."

I grasp his shoulders. "If you wanted to see the fish you should've asked, not run away!"

Felix looks mutinous, as he always does when I tell him off. "I'm a big boy and I'm OK."

"I was scared! Really scared! I thought I'd lost you. Who gave you that chocolate?"

"A man."

I blink. "What man?"

"Just a man. He said 'your sister is pretty'."

My jaw drops. Felix crinkles the wrapper, completely unconcerned. "He comed when I was on the big slide. He had chocolate. He said you were busy talking to the other man."

The big slide is on the other side of the climbing frame, out of view from where I was sat.

"Fe." My voice is hoarse. "Did he touch you?"

119

"Nuh-uh," says Felix, and my shoulders sag in relief. "He said to give you this."

And Felix picks up a small bag I recognize.

My fingers tremble as I run them over the faux leather fabric. This is the clutch bag I noticed was missing when I searched my room. I was so buzzed when I found it on eBay – a lovely tan colour, barely used and vegan. Mum joked about handbags for dinner until I explained that meant that it had been made without any animal products or derivatives.

It doesn't smell of my mango spritz perfume any more. There are hints of something sharper, something alien. Someone else's scent.

It was stolen, just like the scarf and my other things. And now it's been returned – by a man who bribed my brother with chocolate and told him I was pretty.

Someone is watching me.

Only this time, it can't be Jade.

I drag Felix away, ignoring his wails about finding Lord Sticky Stick. The street outside is busy but that gives me zero comfort. Crowds mean it'll be easier for *the man* to hide. He's watching now, I'm sure of it. He's probably been watching all afternoon. Did he even follow us to the park?

By the time we reach home we're almost running. Inside I turn all the lights on and close the curtains. Through a crack in the living-room ones I watch the road.

"What are you doing?" Felix's voice sounds very small. "I don't like running. You hurt my arm."

I turn and give Felix a big hug. "If this guy ever speaks to you again, run and tell someone, OK? Are you sure you can't remember what he looked like? Have you seen him before, maybe?"

Felix frowns, then nods.

I lean forward. "Where, Fe? This is really important."

Felix looks confused and a little scared. "He was just a man."

"Do you mean a *man* man, like Dad? Or a boy, like Aaron? Can you remember the colour of his hair?"

A shrug. To Felix, anyone who isn't a kid is "man". "Can I watch *PAW Patrol*? Pleeease?"

And just like that, the park is forgotten. Fear lodges in my throat. My brother is all big eyes and long lashes and trusting innocence. I could have lost him back there. If someone really wanted to mess with me…

There are tears in my eyes. I blink them back. No crying in front of Felix, however frightened I am.

"Please don't tell Mum or Dad about any of this, Fe. They'll be really angry with me."

Felix looks uncertain. My cheeks flush; Mum and Dad often stress to Fe that honesty is important. I should confess. This is too big and too frightening for me to deal with alone…

But Mum and Dad have always impressed on me how important watching Felix is. I'm supposed to be trustworthy, responsible, almost a grown-up! I've let them down, big time. I've already brought the police and a boyfriend who's confessed to murder into their lives. How can I admit that I put my brother in danger?

Felix is hunting for the remote. I put on Netflix, then return to the window. I'm still shaking. How can I possibly have *another* stalker? Why is some *man* presenting me with a bag via my brother? Is it a message? Or a threat?

Think, Mia. Bag Man can't be Aaron. He's in hospital, and Felix would recognize him. Aaron wouldn't do something this creepy anyway.

And he wouldn't kill someone.

I curl my fingers round the bag, pressing it to my chest. That heavy gut feeling that Aaron's confession is all wrong returns. I *can't* believe it. Perhaps Aaron's been stitched up. Perhaps he's been backed into a corner, with no choice but to confess. Perhaps Bag Man is involved. Perhaps Bag Man even did it.

Whatever's going on, Jade's death isn't the end of it. I'm starting to fear it's only the beginning.

"Bag Man and Jade have to be connected," I say to Oliver the next day.

It's our free period after sociology, but class has left me too rattled to go to the library as we normally would. This term's module – ha bloody ha – is Crime and Deviance. Some horrible boy asked Mr Ellison whether people were born killers or turned into killers by society, and smirked at me as he said it.

Instead, we're in the old accessible toilet no one uses any more with the door locked. Oliver's powder-blue jeans are the wrong colour for sitting on grubby vinyl. Me a week ago would have cracked a joke about that.

Oliver pulls a face. He and Leyla know about yesterday. "Bag Man? Sounds like a not especially threatening *Doctor Who* alien."

"He felt pretty threatening yesterday."

Oliver looks chastened, and I regret sounding sharp. I carry on thinking out loud. "Aaron could have been manipulated. He's trusting, and he doesn't think things through."

"You think Bag Man killed Jade, not Aaron?"

"I don't know. But I need to find out what Aaron's hiding." I press my unicorn key ring into my palm. "DS Forster said something about 'news from Cedar' over the phone yesterday. The wards at the hospital are named after trees. I bet Cedar Ward is where Aaron is. After school I could sneak in…"

I wait for Oliver to tell me this is a terrible idea. Instead, he's quiet, thinking. Then he says, "OK, then. Let's go."

"What, now?"

"Sure. No time like the present."

The thought is both exciting and scary. "I don't know, Olly. Skipping school … I wouldn't even know how."

He smiles. "You just walk out. I did it loads at my old school. Aaron's not the only person who's mastered the art of truancy."

Ten minutes later we're on a hospital-bound bus full of

old people, parents with pre-schoolers and Kris Kowalski, year twelve's most hardcore computer nerd, who was also at the bus stop. He tells us he's visiting his grandparents during his free period. Up until a month ago, I'd barely spoken to Kris, but he's the quiz team reserve and always seems delighted whenever he bumps into me or Oliver. He sits across from us, delivering a monologue about his favourite online game.

"… and I've bought my character a new add-on cloak which makes her invisible," he finishes. "Anyway, this is my stop. Have fun wherever you're going."

He grins, gives us a mock salute and presses the stop button.

Oliver pulls a humorous expression as Kris leaves. "Did either of us say a single thing in that conversation? Or indicate that we were into gaming?"

"Kris is like that. But hey, for five minutes, life felt normal." Everything suddenly seems very funny, and I let out a nervous giggle. Oliver nudges me.

"See," he says. "Being bad feels good. We should do it more often." He pauses. "Do you know why humans laugh when we're on edge? It's a defence mechanism against emotions that make us weak and vulnerable. It helps us heal from trauma by distancing the threat."

"How do you know that?"

"I read a lot of shit online."

"You need to get out more, bro."

"That's what the bullies at my old school used to say.

Less nicely, while they were shoving my head in dustbins and calling me a gay boy, because apparently liking culture isn't straight. That's why I used to skive so much. Just in case you hadn't joined the dots."

Oliver's told me and Leyla about being picked on back in London, but I hadn't realized it was this brutal. I think he's been playing it down until now.

"I hope you know that if anyone messes with you here, I'll tear their heads off," I say.

"All five foot of you?"

"Yeah. 'Though she be but little she is fierce.' Ugh, if Mr Ellison was here he'd demand to know where that quote's from."

"Shakespeare, *A Midsummer Night's Dream*."

"How do you know this stuff?"

"Because I don't get out more."

My laugh is pathetic. Still, it's less nervous this time. Oliver laughs too, his eyes crinkling a little. They're grey, bluer round the edges. Why have I never noticed how nice his eyes are? He shares more random facts as the bus winds along and I lean my head on his shoulder. He tenses up slightly. For a second I wonder if this is too much, even for two friends who are normally tactile, but as he carries on talking I relax. He smells nice, like he's wearing cologne, and I allow myself to be distracted by the conversation.

Fifteen minutes later, we're inside the hospital, taking a rickety lift up to Cedar Ward. The reception desk is empty. Doing my best to project confident I'm-meant-to-be-here vibes, I turn down the corridor that leads to the ward proper – then stop because the first room we pass is Aaron's. He's lying in bed with his leg raised in a cast. He's alone. We slip inside.

When Aaron sees me and Oliver, he looks sickened. He's almost ghostlike in the white hospital gown. I keep my distance, not sure I'm brave enough for this. Then I square my shoulders, remind myself why I'm here and draw out the chair next to the bed.

"I'll be right outside." Oliver glances at Aaron – who looks away – then steps into the corridor, closing the door.

Aware we might only have minutes, I dive straight in. "You need to tell me everything. Where you went that night, who you were with, what happened. I don't believe you did it."

"There's nothing to tell," Aaron mutters. "And I did do it. When they get the lab results, the blood in my car will come back as hers."

There'll be an explanation for the car, even if I can't see it right now. "Then … you were set up. Or manipulated. You had no reason to hurt her."

"Did I need to have a reason?" Aaron shifts, his strapped-up leg wobbling.

"Does it hurt?" I ask.

"Not any more. I wish it did. I deserve to hurt. I'm sorry about blanking you all that time, Mia. I couldn't bear to see anyone. Weirdly, confessing is a relief. Hiding what I'd

126

done messed with my head, especially once I realized who she was."

I frown. "What? How could you not know?"

Aaron rubs his nose. Frustrated, I clasp then unclasp my hands. "I'm not leaving until you tell me everything. They'll have to drag me away, and I'll kick and scream."

"I don't want to hurt you more than I already have."

How can I get him talking? Pretty soon I'll be discovered and chucked out. The crime show Mum binge-watches pops into my head. What is it the detective says? Sometimes the most effective way of getting people to talk is to say nothing.

So I wait. Just as my last nerve is fraying, Aaron says, "What the hell. You deserve to know. This can't get any worse." He takes a deep breath. "People kept saying I'd feel better after Granddad's funeral, but I didn't. My head's a mess. Watching someone waste away from cancer is the worst. I feel weird and wrong most of the time, like there's no point doing anything. Sometimes I wake up and forget he's dead, just for a moment… There's other stuff, too. It feels too much sometimes."

I can't believe he never talked to me about this properly, or asked for help. I hadn't realized he still felt so low.

Aaron continues, "I was so frustrated with you on Saturday. We were going to have a great night. I bought you flowers, I had clean sheets, everything. It felt right." His eyes flicker downwards. "I didn't want to go home after we argued. I … drank. Then I hung about in the outdoor gym on the field near mine – and she showed up."

Jade.

"Marched straight over and started screaming, really furious. So I, you know. Pushed her away. Hard. I didn't realize how hard. The back of her head slammed against a metal bar, from the cross trainer, I think. I did it without thinking. There was blood everywhere."

I stare at him, speechless.

Aaron hangs his head. "When I realized she was dead … I panicked. No one would believe it was an accident. So I decided to hide her body."

This is making me feel queasy. So far it sounds surreal, but horrifyingly plausible. "So you, what, shoved her in your boot and drove to the nook? *Our* nook, Aaron. Why?"

"Isn't it kind of obvious?" mumbles Aaron.

"Not to me."

"I thought she was you."

I freeze.

"She was shouting at me. It was dark, I was … out of it, she had your coat and we'd argued. The nook felt like the right place to take you, somewhere special… A twisted romantic gesture. I wasn't thinking clearly."

Suddenly the small room with its bright lighting feels like a prison. "You wanted to hurt me. *I'm* the reason she died."

Misery is etched all over Aaron's face. He's a shell of the boy I've spent hours watching across classrooms and crafting messages to. "I'm sorry I was such a shit boyfriend in the end," he mumbles. "I tried so hard but I got everything wrong. I didn't mean to be pushy about sex, or dismiss you being afraid of Jade. When you think about me can you just … forget all this? Remember the good stuff? Like me drawing you pictures and sharing those brownies?"

My throat feels clogged. I swallow.

"I'm going to regret this for ever." Aaron's voice thickens. "I've ruined my life, my family's lives, her family's lives. I'm going to prison. I'm total scum."

He starts to cry. I watch his body heave with big, messy sobs. I remember how he wept at his granddad's funeral, and how I wrapped him in my arms and promised I'd always be there for him. It felt like his tears – his vulnerability – drew us closer.

Slowly, I say, "You've still not told me everything."

"What? I did it, Mia. How many times do I need to say so?"

"I came here because none of this makes sense. It still doesn't make sense. There's someone else involved. Maybe Jade's mysterious boyfriend." I lean forward. "You were scared of something. What was in those letters you kept reading?"

Immediately he's on his guard. "They're nothing to do with this."

"Why did Jade start shouting at you? Why did she seek you out?" My voice grows stronger. I'm right, I know I am. "A guy watched me at the park yesterday. He gave Felix a bag I thought Jade had stolen. He said I was *pretty*. So many weird things happening, all at once?

129

That's not a coincidence."

"Oh fuck," says Aaron. He's impossibly pale now.

A shiver dances up my spine at the recognition in his eyes. "You know what this means."

"I… I…" Aaron appears to be unable to speak.

I grasp his hand. "Tell me."

"I can't, I… You need to be careful, Mia. I'm sorry, I've made things worse…"

"How? Who is Bag Man?"

Aaron gulps. Frustration burns inside me.

"Aaron. *Please.*"

Wheels squeak outside, then stop by the door. Oliver says something and a female voice replies. We're out of time.

"Fine, then," I say fiercely. "I'll figure this out myself. Who this guy is, and how he's stitched you up."

Aaron's eyes widen. "No! Don't. You're not some plucky film girlfriend, going all out to prove her guy's innocence. It's dangerous. I'm telling you, Mia, *I did it.*"

"I'm not giving up on you," I hiss.

The door opens. A stern-looking nurse appears. I drop Aaron's hand and walk out, feeling as though I'm made of fire.

11

As the following week crawls by, I throw myself into digging out the truth. I trawl through Jade's social media, and through the accounts of those who frequently liked or commented on her posts. I check out the guys she follows and who follow her. I spend evenings by my bedroom window, peering through the crack in the curtains to see if anyone is lurking, watching me.

All that comes from my investigations is one tiny clue: a girl called Harper tagged Jade in a post on the last Saturday in January. The picture shows Jade's old friends laughing at a bowling alley. About ten comments down, Jade posts some heart emojis. Harper replies: I hope you know that when I fall in love I'll be blowing YOU off. Miss yooooou xx

It's a fair bet Jade was meeting her boyfriend instead of going bowling. And I know, having checked my own grid, that Aaron and I were together that day. That confirms it: he isn't her secret boyfriend. Even though I thought so already, it's reassuring to have proof.

If only everything else was as certain. All the loose ends eat me up at home, at school, and in bed at night, circling endlessly. Nothing else seems important. All my exercise books are filled with doodles and lists of questions I can't answer.

The biggest blow comes with the forensic results. The bloodstain in Aaron's car is a match for Jade. Also in the boot was a strand of her hair. Fibres from the T-shirt Aaron was wearing are identical to those under Jade's nails. Solid evidence *and* a confession. Case closed.

Aaron is moved from hospital to a young offender institution. He's on remand until his case goes to court. Thinking about him locked up, surrounded by dangerous criminals, breaks my heart. This will destroy him. I push what Aaron said about thinking Jade was me to the back of my mind. To even begin to process that he thought it was me he was shoving… I can't go there. All I know is this is still *Aaron*, and he's hiding something that fills him with fear.

I'm not smarter than the police, I know. I'm not even smart. But no one can stop me asking questions. I'm sure as hell not going to move on, like everyone keeps telling me.

"She's making herself ill," I hear Mum saying to Dad one evening when I'm lying in bed with a migraine, waiting for the triptans to kick in. "We're all in shock about Aaron, but denial isn't the way forward."

Dad sighs. "All we can do is be there for her. Shall I make those tempeh kebabs for dinner? I know the rest of us don't like them, but it might raise a smile."

"All right. I wish I could snap her out of it. Mia's never been headstrong or difficult like this."

No, because up until now I've been agreeable, and polite, and trusted other people's judgement rather than my own instincts. I roll over, pressing my nose into my pillow. My bedding smells different to usual, like lemons. Must be a new washing detergent.

Jade's funeral was today. I could barely look at the double-page spread in the local paper. Do her family feel like they have proper closure? There's no explanation for why Jade changed herself or why she stalked me. Or, as far as I know, for the secret boyfriend. He's probably been discounted as irrelevant. I wonder how Quin feels about the loose ends. They were clearly bothering him in the park.

I wonder. Would he help me?

DMing Quin about something so emotive feels too cold, so I head over to his college the day I have a free period last lesson. Even though it's light and busy outside, visiting a less familiar part of town alone makes me jumpy. Aaron and I came to this college once for an open evening. The eccentric art teacher bombarded us with his entire – very colourful – life story. My phone is in my hands before I remember the days of messaging Aaron are over.

Luck is on my side. Quin is leaning against a lamp post by the college bus stop, absorbed – or pretending to be – in his phone. He's wearing a grubby tee and grey jeans with no coat and his body language screams *go away*.

He glances up. Our eyes connect. For a moment, neither of us moves. Then Quin pockets the phone and strides over.

"I was hoping to run into you," he says. He doesn't smile. "A word?"

This is unexpected, but welcome. I was dreading approaching him. We duck down a quieter side road so we can hear ourselves over the traffic.

Quin clears his throat. "I'm sorry about the Talent Showcase. Not Aaron falling, he deserved that, but the stuff before. I made a bad situation worse, and it wasn't fair on you. Shouldn't have grabbed your wrist either, or cleared off after Aaron fell. That was shit of me. So yeah. Sorry."

His apology leaves me a little floored. "You've been feeling bad about that?"

"I do do them, you know. Feelings." He rubs his hand over his chin. "I was a bit pissed. I nicked a bottle of wine and drank most of it. Not that it's an excuse. I was angry and sad and looking for trouble. My dad was really disappointed. I was doing better with the self-control thing. I let him down. No one needs my crap right now."

The local hard guy is emotionally dumping on me. And

I'm a little hooked. "You were out of order, but like I said at the park, it's understandable."

"You don't need to be nice. I know I have a problem. Anyway. That's all I wanted to say. I'll get out of your face."

He turns.

"Quin, wait." His name feels odd on my tongue. "Don't you have … doubts?"

He turns back. His body language is guarded now. "About what?"

"Jade."

Quin looks me in the eyes, waiting. He hasn't told me I'm being ridiculous yet.

"We never found out what she was desperate to tell me the night she died," I say. "It definitely wasn't about Aaron."

I show Quin the Instagram post I found, and Harper's comment, then my own post proving that Aaron and I were together. Quin looks at both for what feels a long time, then nods.

"All right," he says. "It wasn't him. I remember Jade being out with her guy that night. She told her mum she was bowling. Which, obviously, was a lie."

Phew. I was half-expecting him to argue. I press on, "Then there's the photos, copying, stalking … what was that about? And, finally, Aaron. He's scared and holding something back. I think someone else was involved, probably the secret boyfriend. I'm guessing the police aren't interested in him now they believe they have their killer."

I wait. I've decided not to mention Bag Man just yet. I don't know if I can trust Quin. The bus I assume is his trundles by. Quin doesn't react. After a long silence, he says, "Also, why did Jade go to that outdoor gym and have a go at Aaron? From what I hear Aaron being there was random. He didn't call her or nothing. Her phone records show that."

He's taking me seriously. My body almost sags in relief. "Do they show anything else?"

"Nope. Only person Jade contacted that evening was Harper, her best mate from her old school. Jade sent her a WhatsApp saying 'Enjoy your takeaway'." He pauses. "Jade was acting weird. It was only us at home so when she got ready she didn't hide what she was wearing." Seeing my frown, he says, "My dad and her mum didn't know about the copycat gear. She only wore it outside the house."

More secrets. "Wasn't she close with her mum?"

"Used to be, but that changed when Zora was born. Jade resented her."

"Is Zora the baby? Your, er…"

"Half-sister?" Quin's tone is pointed. "Yeah."

Oh, crap. I can't believe I walked into that. I try to rise above the embarrassment. "Sorry! Just, Riyad—"

"Talks shit?"

"Well, yes, but—"

"Whatever. I hear worse rumours." Quin pauses, then says, "The police think Jade made the boyfriend up to impress people. There's no evidence he exists – no pictures, emails, messages, nothing. But I heard her on the phone to him once, after Dad and Demi were asleep, saying it was impossible for her to concentrate on classes knowing he was nearby. That's why I was sure he went to Southaven High. The police said I must've been mistaken."

So they've dropped that line of investigation completely. I get why – Jade would have communicated with her boyfriend somehow. I used to live for Aaron's messages, even mundane ones about what he was having for dinner. Something's pricking the edge of my mind here, something important…

I snap my fingers. "Jade had a second phone. I remember seeing it, in the library. It could have been a burner, one she used for messaging and calling him."

"The police never mentioned a second phone."

So it's missing. I open my mouth to say that's shady as – then freeze. "Quin, can you show me that photo of Jade again? The full-length version of the one they used on the news?"

He passes his phone over. I tap on the photo, magnifying the bag Jade's clutching. It's the same one Felix was given at the park! It looks generic, but the scuff at the bottom is identical. I can even see the edge of the distinctive leaf-print lining.

Jade had that bag in the CCTV picture DS Forster showed me too. Unless she lost it on the way to the outdoor gym where she died, the only place someone could have taken the bag from was there at the crime scene, or from the beach where her body was moved.

Someone other than Aaron *was* there when Jade died.

And that person was watching me at the park.

My instincts were spot on. There is more to this! I'm *not* being silly and stubborn. Exactly what this discovery means I don't know, but I'll pick my friends' brains before saying anything to Quin. They're straight-A students, they'll have ideas. We're meeting in a few hours at the Electric Palace after Leyla bugged me about needing an evening out.

I give Quin his phone back. "So. Jade's boyfriend. There must've been a big reason they needed to keep their relationship secret."

"Yeah, maybe, but if you're desperately searching for something to clear Aaron's name like a good little girlfriend, you ain't getting it from me."

Even though that's exactly what I'm doing, it stings. I glare at him. "All I want is the truth. And I think you want that too."

Quin's phone bleeps.

"I need to get home," he says without looking at it.

I tilt my chin. "Are Jade's friends hiding anything? Surely she confided in them?"

"Jade didn't have many mates since moving schools. The old ones drifted. Or maybe Jade distanced herself from them, I don't know."

"What about Harper?"

Quin presses his lips together. I wonder if he's regretting opening up. "They're still tight. Were, I mean. Harper claims to know nothing. That I don't buy. Jade was pissed off with her that Saturday. I assume the takeaway message was passive-aggressive."

For the first time, excitement sparks inside me. "I'd like to speak to Harper."

Quin narrows his eyes. I'm uncomfortably aware that I am intruding on what must be an unimaginably tragic time for his family, but I don't look away.

"All right," he says. "I'll help, but my family stays in the dark, OK?"

"Deal."

We trade numbers, then hover, not sure how to say goodbye. He probably wouldn't welcome a hug. In the end, we mumble see-you-laters, and I let Quin go, watching as he hurries off. Jeez, that denim's tight. Yeah, the jeans look good, but how does he even walk?

For the first time since Aaron confessed, I feel buoyed up and clear-headed. Quin is the first person who hasn't told me to let it go. He knew Jade, and I know Aaron. Surely between us we can unearth the truth?

12

By half six, it's pelting rain so Mum drops me at the cinema. Thankfully she's too nervous a driver to notice how keyed up I seem. At the door I'm greeted by Camille, looking smart in the scarlet usher's uniform.

She smiles at me. "Hey, Mia. You OK? I'm sorry about everything with Aaron. He always seemed so sweet and gentle. You must be reeling."

Most people find mentioning Aaron so uncomfortable that they avoid speaking to me – or, if they do, they don't make eye contact. Up until now, I'd thought of Camille as a bit of a princess type – the nice, sparkly Disney variety – but there's clearly more to her than being part of the popular crowd. It sounds like she was kind to Jade – and her life can't be perfect if she was ill enough to miss a month of school last year. "Reeling covers it pretty well."

Camille lowers her voice. "I know what it's like when a guy turns out to not be what you thought, and it hurts, so … if you ever need to chat, I'm here."

What a nice offer – but an odd one, too, from someone I've mostly chatted to in occasional Insta comments. Normally I'd linger, find out what her experience is of someone being false, but I'm impatient to see my friends so I just thank her before hurrying up the sweeping staircase.

Oliver and Leyla are waiting by one of the pillars, Oliver balancing a tray of drinks and a tower of brownies. Ivy must have let him help himself. She adores Olly, often joking he was born to upsell ice cream and cake to pensioners. Above them is the carriage clock – ten minutes until the screen opens.

I rush over and dive straight into an update about my chat with Quin and the significance of the bag. A little breathless, I finish, "I don't know when Bag Man picked the bag up, from the nook, gym, wherever, but it proves he was there when Jade died. If Aaron's holding back something this big, he could have lied about other things. Like pushing Jade, even!"

Leyla glances at Oliver. They're both frowning.

"I thought Jade was the one taking your stuff?" Oliver says.

"She was, but Bag Man took the bag from Jade to give to Felix."

Leyla's frown deepens. "Was it definitely the one Jade was carrying that day? The bag didn't have anything in it to prove that, right? No phone, or bus ticket, or purse?"

"It was empty, but definitely the same one. I saw it in the photo. Maybe Bag Man took her stuff – her second phone, too? Guys, this could change things, couldn't it?"

"I don't know, Mia…" Leyla's tone is wary now. "This is a lot of maybes. Aaron confessed, and they found evidence he did it. I get that the Bag Man thing was super creepy, but if the bag really was Jade's, wasn't it incredibly unwise of him to give it to Felix? It's basically an admission he was at the crime scene. Felix could have recognized him."

Oliver offers me a brownie. I shake my head. "Perhaps Bag Man was in disguise – a cap or hood, maybe a face mask too. Even for a five-year-old, Fe is spectacularly unobservant."

"I'm not sure the police would reopen the case based on this, Mia." Oliver's using his diplomatic voice. "We're behind you one hundred per cent, obviously, but Ley's right. It doesn't prove anything."

It's a real effort to hold back the frustration mounting inside me. "I'm going to text Quin. He'll get it."

Leyla sighs. "Ugh. Psycho Quin, Mia. Seriously?"

"I don't care about what he's done, not if it helps Aaron."

"What if I care?"

I meet her eyes. "Ley, I get that to you Quin is pond life, but he's my only way of finding out more about Jade. I'm not sure he's as horrible as everyone says, anyway."

"Mia, he attacked my brother! This isn't about that crush

142

you used to have on him, is it? If you're missing hooking up that badly, I can tell you for a fact you have way better options."

I gape at her, momentarily speechless. "That was out of order."

Leyla's cheeks are pink. "Sorry, but I don't trust the guy. Right now, I don't trust your judgement, either. What's in it for Quin? He's got what he wants: Jade's death solved. For all you know, he's Bag Man! He was at the park. He could've pretended to leave, then spoken to Felix."

"I can't drop this. It's not only about saving Aaron. I don't feel safe. Who's to say Bag Man won't do something else? And I need to know what Jade was trying to tell me that night!"

Oliver tries to speak, but Leyla raises her voice. "I get that, and I want you to feel safe, but you're burning yourself out. If what you say happened with Bag Man is true—"

"Are you saying I'm lying?" I demand.

"No! Of course not. I just think this has been a hell of a lot to deal with, and it's possible the bag isn't Jade's. What I was *going* to say is that Bag Man could be completely unconnected to her. We simply don't know. Yeah, he's a creepy weirdo, and if you want to report him to the police, I'll come with you. But does Bag Man being creepy prove that Aaron's been set up? No." She draws breath. "You need to get over Aaron. Sorry, Mia, but you do. He's nowhere near as special as you think."

My eyes widen. Even for Leyla, this is super blunt. "I love him! How can you say that?"

"Because it's true," says Leyla. "You think your relationship was perfect because of the shared interests and cute drawings, and because Aaron ticks eighteen out of twenty criteria on the 'ideal boyfriend' list you wrote when we were fourteen. But you guys only worked as well as you did because you compromised all the time."

"That's not true."

"He was pretty flaky, Mia. Skipping school and not telling you where he went, forgetting to reply to your messages? You cancelled on me and Olly without a second thought whenever Aaron wanted you, heaps of times. Aaron never did the old-school romantic stuff you love despite the billion hints you dropped. And you know what? If you were the one banged up, he wouldn't be fighting for you."

Leyla shoves her hands into her pockets, her face flushed. I bite my lip to stop myself ripping into her. It feels as though I've been slapped, repeatedly.

Oliver clears his throat. "Let's talk after the film, when you've both cooled off. This isn't worth falling out over."

Leyla makes a rude noise. "Forgive me for wanting my best friend to get her life back."

"Ley, you're being unfair." I've never heard Oliver sound this sharp. "Mia's upset and confused. I want her to 'get her life back' too, but have you thought this is something she might need to do?"

"Spoken like the hero of the cheesiest movie!" Leyla snaps, and Oliver scowls.

"Better cheesy than telling Mia she doesn't know her own mind."

"Oh, get you, Mr Sensitive! And that's *not* what I meant." Leyla turns to me. "I know what I said sounds mean but I love you, and I don't want you hurt. Aaron did this, Mia. You deserve better."

People are looking our way. I can't stand being here any longer. "Whatever. Enjoy the film."

Oliver calls after me, but I ignore him. Seconds later I'm outside in the driving rain, digging in my bag for the umbrella I already know isn't there. My suede pump plunges into a puddle and tears spring to my eyes. *Great.* I squelch towards the zebra crossing. How naive was I, thinking my friends might help me crack this? They want to get back to normal. But they're not the ones being handed belongings last used by dead girls.

A horn blasts. Someone yanks me backwards, out of the road. A car speeds past, the driver shouting "stupid cow!" out of the window.

I let out a choking noise. "Oh God. I didn't even look. Thanks."

"You were in a total daze. That driver should have stopped, though." An umbrella extends over my head. Mr Ellison is almost unrecognizable in contact lenses and a flat cap. "Is everything all right?"

He must have come out of the earlier screening. I wipe damp hair from my face. "I just want to go home."

"I can't let you walk away like this. Is there anyone you

can call for a lift?"

He guides me to a nearby bus shelter and I ring Mum. She's at the train station picking up Auntie Lou but can be with me in ten minutes.

"Good," says Mr Ellison when I tell him. "I'll wait with you until she gets here."

We perch on the metal seats. Mr Ellison unzips his jacket. The flannel shirt underneath is hipster cool. So are the cuffed jeans and shiny shoes. And he smells good, his cologne not dissimilar from the citrusy one loads of boys from school wear – I forget Mr Ellison isn't much older than we are, really. Was he on a date or something? This feels a bit personal, hanging out outside school.

"So," says Mr Ellison. "Do you want to talk about it? Maybe I can help."

I'm embarrassed. I can hardly tell him the full truth. Mr E will think I'm as delusional as Leyla clearly does. This is super pathetic, but it's flattering at school when he treats me like I'm cool. Reluctantly, I admit, "I wanted my friends' help with something important, but it turned into an argument. Ley said all this stuff about Aaron. Not about … what happened, but stuff like what we had together was bad, and I couldn't see it. I never realized she disliked him that much."

"Relationships are tricky. You can't always see clearly when you're in them, and sometimes it takes a wake-up call to see the truth of who's good for you and who isn't. You and Leyla will work it out."

I hope so. Bickering with her isn't new – our personalities

have always been different, and we make up quickly – but this feels serious.

Mr Ellison offers me a packet of chewing gum. I shake my head.

"I don't think that's vegan."

"Ah. Right." Mr Ellison drops the gum into his pocket without taking any. "Basically, what I'm saying is, it's complicated. 'Love makes fools of us all.' Where's that quote from?"

"Shakespeare?"

"Might be. I'll have to check. Anyway, you deserve to find someone who will treat you right. You've a lot going for you, Mia, even if you can't see it."

I blush. It feels weird to talk about my personal life with my teacher. "Thanks, sir."

"Don't mention it. Forget about boys for now. That's my advice."

My phone pings: Mum. She's waiting by the back of the Electric. Mr Ellison insists on walking me to the car with the umbrella, like a gentleman in a classic movie.

"I'll see you at school," he says as we near Mum's red Hyundai. "Everything will be OK, I…"

He trails off. I follow his gaze but all I can see is Mum gesturing for me to get in.

"Goodbye, Mia," Mr Ellison says quickly and hurries off. Caught in the rain again, I blink after him then dash to the car.

Mum swivels round as I climb into the back seat. "Was

147

that your teacher?"

"Yeah." I buckle up. "He waited with me."

"That's kind. Chivalry isn't dead, it seems. Why aren't you seeing the film?"

"Argued with Ley. I don't want to talk about it."

Auntie Lou smiles sympathetically from the passenger seat and says something about Ivy constantly falling out with friends when she was sixteen. Mum gives me a shrewd look in the interior mirror but doesn't push it. We pass Mr Ellison, walking quickly. I wave, but the umbrella is angled across his face and he doesn't see.

I wonder what made him take off so abruptly.

13

Saturday afternoon finds me on the rickety bus that connects Southaven and Wrabney, where Quin lives. The remote cliff road cuts through heathland. The sea is barely visible through mist and low clouds. It's like we've zipped from March to the darkest winter. *A bad omen*. The high wind is stronger out here because it's so open. I imagine it battering the bus off the road, over the cliff and into the water.

Ever since the penny dropped about the bag, I've been feeling spaced out and hyper alert at the same time. When I step outside, I feel like I'm being watched. Mum and Dad have picked up on my jumpiness. Whenever they ask if I'm

OK, I'm tempted to tell them. Then I remember Felix, and how I neglected him, and shame eats me up.

To distract myself I reread the message chain between me and Quin.

Quin:
Harper, 4.30
My house
Get 39

Mia:
39 what?

Quin:
Kitkats
I like them

Mia:
You can eat 39 kit kats?!

Quin:
Nah
Jokin
Bus

Mia:
Why didn't you just say get the 39 bus?
Is your house a good idea?

Maybe a park instead?
I don't want to bump into Jade's mum and
upset her

Quin:
Rain

I nearly typed *what* again. WhatsApping, it seems, is not Quin's thing, so I called instead. Quin told me his family would be out. And then he said, "Jade's room is fair game if you wanna look."

On the bus, I play with my unicorn key ring. Its rainbow mane is fading. I always seem to be fiddling with it now, a nervous tic I can't shake.

My other recent WhatsApp chain is with Tori, Aaron's mum. She's agreed to take me to visit him in the YOI tomorrow. Hopefully, I'll have news to share. At the very least, he should know I'm looking out for him like I promised.

When Mum found out, she looked like she'd swallowed bleach. "Mia, no," she cried. "Prisons are terrible places, full of the worst side of humanity. Sweetie, let Aaron go. First romances are special but this loyalty isn't healthy. I know you've found his actions hard to believe. We all have – Dad and I liked Aaron too. But he's been involved in something awful, and I want you to stay out of it."

Mum only wants to protect me but it's too late for that. I managed to persuade her that visiting Aaron would help me let go. She'd really lose it if she knew about today. Going to the house of the murdered girl who was obsessed with me is a colossally bad idea, but Harper might know something. Right now, *might* feels worth chasing. If I do find anything out, either from Harper or Aaron, then, I promise myself, I'll tell my parents everything, however much I'm dreading it.

Wrabney is grey and depressing, with shuttered shops, hoodie gangs hanging round smoking and a shingle beach overshadowed by humming wind turbines – the kind of place you can't ever imagine being nice, even without the drizzle. Quin lives on the outskirts, at the end of a close of houses that look like they've wound up together by accident. Mum would call it rough. She'd call Quin rough, too, and not just because he gets into fights. His house backs on to a wooded area which a sign claims is a nature reserve but seems to be an unofficial rubbish dump. An Aldi trolley lies on its side, weeds poking through the metal squares. Next to it is a bicycle wheel and a broken office chair. A kid's faded toy pokes out of a black sack.

I stand on the doorstep a moment before ringing the bell, trying to breathe through the nervous knot in my belly. Quin was OK the last time I saw him. There's no reason he'd hurt me. He's lost someone he cared about and that's what I need to focus on today, not his bad reputation. I ring the bell.

Quin opens the door, looking suspicious. His hands and lower arms are covered with flour.

"Hi." I might as well smile. "Is being early OK? I would've hung around town, but…"

"You can call it a dump. 'S true. Come in."

I take a deep breath and step inside. The air feels heavy and the hallway light is off. The copper-coloured carpet and woodchip walls are like something out of a time warp. A huge canvas wedding photo hangs to my left. A suited man who is basically Quin twenty years on beams into the eyes of Jade's mum. She holds Zora on her hip. Quin and Jade haven't been step-siblings long, then. Through the doorway is an untidy sitting room dominated by the largest TV I've ever seen. The blingy wallpaper is covered with family photos, including one of a younger Jade with lopsided pigtails, bright eyes and a gap-toothed grin.

I remind myself that this is my best bet for getting the answers I need and quash a strong urge to walk out again.

Quin goes through to the L-shaped kitchen and I follow. This room has been renovated recently, with French windows overlooking a lawn and the nature reserve beyond, and a dining table round the side. On the work surface are a can of tomatoes, herbs, oil, flour and a bowl of dough. Quin starts to knead, slamming the dough against the surface, gathering it up, repeating. He's wearing the tight jeans again and a snug-fitting T-shirt. I can't help but notice the way his biceps flex each time he smacks the dough down.

"Pizza," he says. "Gimme one minute."

"No rush. I don't mind watching."

He glances over his shoulder, raising his eyebrows. I unzip my mac, biting my lip to stop myself blurting out something about it being hot in here.

"Is, erm, the pizza a college assignment?"

"Nah." There go his arms again. "I've been making pizza for years. Home-made, it's dope."

"Did you always want to be a chef?"

"Never thought about it. My parents were crap cooks so I just took over. Catering's a classic place to shove bad lads so they learn how to behave."

"I thought that was the Army."

"Been there, done that."

"What?"

"Never mind." Is it my imagination, or does he smack the dough down extra hard? "The head chef at my placement is ex-Army. He's got a right temper."

"With all those sharp knives around? Grim."

"Not to mention the charcoal oven." He shows me his hands. Under the flour they're covered in tiny burns.

"Ouch. You know what they say, if you can't stand the heat, stay out of the kitchen…"

He laughs. The noise is startling, like it shouldn't be coming from him. He drops the dough into an oiled bowl and cling-films the top. When he turns to face me, he's unsmiling, all business again. "Wanna see Jade's room?"

Feeling grubby, I nod. Quin picks up a tin opener and tells me to go ahead. Even though no one else is here I tiptoe upstairs. Most of the first-floor doors are open. The place is cluttered in the sleep-deprived, parenting-a-young-baby way I remember from when Felix was tiny. The only exception is the room that has to be Quin's. Maybe tidiness is a chef thing – he had the pizza ingredients neatly lined up. In one corner of his room is a tall cage with straw at the bottom, though I can't see what lives there.

The only closed door is Jade's. I make myself open it and peek inside. Unlike the baby's nursery, which is decorated with woodland murals and fresh buttercup-yellow paint, this room has the dated vibe of the hallway: cream walls and moss green carpet clashing with Jade's pink and grey duvet set. The bed, wardrobe, desk and cabinet are crammed together. On her shelves are the usual trinkets – china animals, nail varnish collection, an old Barbie and photos, mainly of friends. One is a family shot taken at a restaurant, Quin leaning over the back of Jade's chair, his arm around her.

The air is stuffy. I imagine police officers with loud shoes and big hands turning the place upside down, rifling through private possessions, and feel sad.

If I linger I'll start over-thinking so I get to work. Hidden inside the wardrobe behind Jade's casual sports stuff is her new gear. I take out a peach-coloured dress. It's exactly my style, from an online shop I recognize. I shouldn't be surprised at the similarities any more but a shiver creeps up my spine.

The dress doesn't have pockets – massive fail – but in a cardigan that does there's a receipt. The address is a town twenty miles away. That's further than most people I know go. Does the boyfriend have a car? And I remember: Camille, in the library, asking Jade if her boyfriend could drive her home.

It's the tiniest clue – but it's something.

Quin's stirring tomato sauce when I go downstairs.

"Why do you think Jade was obsessed with me?" I ask.

He jumps, the spoon clattering against the pan. "Jesus! Don't creep up on me like that."

"Sorry. Did the police say anything about the pictures she took of me? Let me guess, silly teenage girls copy each other all the time, like following me wasn't immensely creepy?"

"If you're gonna answer your own questions, there's no point asking." Quin turns off the hob, covering the pan. "They never made much of it. Didn't feel relevant."

It felt a big deal when the police spoke to me. Their line of questioning must have varied depending on who they were interviewing. "But why would she stalk me?"

Quin folds his arms. "I told you before. She wouldn't do that."

The doorbell trills.

"Suppose you can ask Harper." Quin moves towards the front door then pauses. "Just so you know, she doesn't like me much. Good luck."

On the doorstep is a white girl with a pointy chin and big, curly hair who looks like she's stepped out of a Snapchat filter. I can't help but stare – postbox-red lipstick and full-on smokey eyes seem excessive for coming round here.

Harper tilts her head. "Got anything to drink? I'm thirsty."

"And hello to you too." Quin steps back to let Harper in. Her eyes lock on to me, and she goes still. Then she gives me a cool look that's almost challenging.

"Jade was prettier than you."

I purse my lips. I assume Quin told Harper at least a little about why I wanted to meet her, but I thought she'd be more thrown by my resemblance to Jade. Does this mean she already knew about the copying?

Quin rolls his eyes at me. "Did I mention Harper's a rude brat?"

"Speak for yourself," says Harper. "You didn't answer my question. What've you got to drink?"

"Juice, lemonade maybe. Are you coming in?"

She tosses her head. "We'll go to the cafe. Then you can buy me a Coke."

Quin gives me a look that says *told you so*. He grabs a hoodie and I retrieve my mac. Harper's already strutting away.

At the top of the road is a small parade of shops, including the old-school kind of cafe with chairs and tables bolted on to the sticky floor. Harper makes herself comfy at a table by the steamed-up front window. She looks like a wannabe rock star in her fluffy leopard-print coat and shiny leggings.

"I want a milkshake," she calls as Quin goes to the till. She's got guts, messing with him. I'm almost impressed.

I slide on to the seat opposite. "I thought you were gasping for a Coke."

"Changed my mind. Chips, too."

If Harper's set on being uncooperative this is going to drag. I try a smile, hoping to win her trust. "Thanks for coming. I don't know how much Quin told you, but I'm Mia, and I want to ask you about Jade."

"Well, duh. No one talks to me about anything else any more."

"Why was she stalking me?"

"She wasn't."

"The police found photos of me in her room. Hundreds of them."

"They're not Jade's."

Like hell they weren't. "You can't deny she made herself into me. Why?"

Harper inspects her nails.

I silently count to ten. I need to stay calm. This girl, annoying or not, lost her friend, and she's my best chance of understanding Jade. "She must've had a reason."

"Has Quin put you up to this?"

He joins us before I can answer, handing me a Coke and Harper a tall glass of frothy pink gunk. He places the steaming bowl of fries between us, then sits next to me.

Harper glowers, crossing her arms. Is it me, or has her body language tensed up?

I try a new angle. "Who was Jade seeing, then?"

"Jade's guy didn't kill her. Yours did."

"Oh, come on, Harper!" Quin slams his Coke on the table. "Can't you give a straight answer? If you're going to dick about why did you bother coming?"

"I don't know who Jade was dating," says Harper. "She never said."

Definitely lying now. "Fine, don't tell us. But why did Jade keep him secret? Was there something, like, taboo about their relationship?"

Harper's eyes flicker to Quin, then back to me. For the first time, there's vulnerability in her voice. "*He* wanted to keep things secret. That was part of the fun, Jade said. A Romeo and Juliet thing." I swallow the urge to point out that *Romeo and Juliet* is a tragedy. "I thought it was shady, but then…"

I prompt her. "But what?"

"Jade really liked him. He made her feel special. Driving her places and sending her sweet messages and buying her things…"

"What kinds of things?" I ask.

"Jewellery. A beret. Tights. Clothes, too."

"So she'd ask him to buy stuff, and he did?"

Harper hesitates, as though this is some kind of trick question. "I don't know if I should say."

"Please, Harper. This is really important."

"Yeah, go on," says Quin.

There's a long pause. Then Harper says, "The clothes were *his* idea. Jade wore them because he asked her to."

My breath catches.

All along, I assumed that copying me was Jade's choice. I took the confident girl with attitude from Instagram at face value. I saw her as dangerous, and assumed she wanted what I had.

I was wrong. Jade didn't make herself into me. Her secret boyfriend did.

He's the one who's obsessed.

14

Harper's still speaking. "I did ask Jade if she thought it was weird, but she'd never had a boyfriend and she wanted to make him happy. Said he was really kind and mature, listening to her venting about her mum's new marriage and the baby and feeling like her mum didn't care about her any more…"

In other words, Jade was vulnerable. Flatly, I say, "There's nothing romantic about changing another person."

"He wasn't changing her," says Harper defensively.

He was, though. And I have a horrible feeling that in Jade's position I would have gone along with this too. Girls are programmed to please, by everything we see.

Being wanted by someone – especially for the first time – is a powerful feeling. Especially when you're lonely and desperate to be seen.

How many small things did I change about myself to make Aaron happy? That's what Leyla was getting at the other day. I can see it clearly now. Shifting my regular bestie night with Leyla to Fridays so Aaron didn't have to change his plans. WhatsApping rather than FaceTiming. Even ditching most make-up because Aaron wasn't into it. He didn't make me do these things, and we genuinely did have shared interests, but I was happy to mould myself around him – while he stayed the same. I thought pleasing him was what I was supposed to do. What girls do, to keep relationships strong.

My brain feels fried, like a blown circuit. It's Quin who snaps, "You didn't think to tell the police this?"

Harper pouts. "Don't talk to me like I'm a silly kid."

"Don't act like one then. Why the fuck did you hold this back?"

"Cos all Jade's secrets are going to do is cause trouble." She stands, colour rising in her cheeks. "Get out of my face, Quinlan."

"Wait," I cry. "You said he sent Jade messages. The police didn't find anything on Jade's phone."

Harper goes rigid. "Everything was handwritten. She binned them."

"Bollocks." Quin's on his feet too now. "She had a second phone. Where is it?"

162

I scramble up. "Listen, Harper, I think this guy is obsessed with me, and maybe he's the real killer—"

Harper grabs the milkshake. The next second, cold, slimy liquid is dripping down my face and Harper is storming out. Quin chases her. They shout at each other outside before Harper jumps on a bus that's pulling up, giving Quin a rude hand gesture as the doors close.

He returns and hands me a wad of napkins. "You OK?"

"Ugh!" How has this crap got everywhere, over my face, hair, shoulders, even into my bra? "This stinks. Why did it have to be milk?"

"Sorry she flipped. Told you Harper was a brat."

Acting like a brat because she was afraid, more like. Perhaps she feels guilty. Didn't Quin say Harper and Jade fell out the day Jade died? I wish I'd asked about that.

"This second phone," I say. "The boyfriend must have it! Wouldn't be hard to swipe a phone no one knew existed. She was dressed up because she was meeting him, right? He took her bag. *He's* Bag Man."

Quin frowns. "How do you know he took her bag? That was never found. And what's Bag Man?"

Me and my big mouth. I'm weighing up whether to trust Quin when he says, "Come back to mine and wash that crap off. Then you can tell me."

At Quin's I sponge myself down in the bathroom and shampoo my hair in the sink. The shampoo is the same brand Aaron's family buy; it feels odd to see it here. As I'm towelling my hair dry, a message from Oliver arrives.

> Drama here, Zimmer frame lady fell over.
> Camille and I had to call an ambulance. On
> the plus side, I finished Honey and Clover vol
> 1 in my break. :-) You OK? Free now if you
> wanted a chat x

Oliver's been checking up on me all afternoon. I appreciate that he didn't tell me not to come, even though I'm sure he agrees with Leyla that it was a bad idea.

"Can't talk for long," I whisper when he picks up – a call rather than FaceTime, given I'm in my bra. "Would you believe it, I'm washing my hair in Quin's sink? Is Zimmer frame lady OK?"

"Fine," says Oliver. "She was more shaken than anything else. Though she kept gripping my hand and telling me I was a nice young man."

"Because you are, obviously."

"What happened to your hair?"

"Jade's friend chucked a milkshake at me. I can't tell you now, but loads more has happened."

"Yuck. You're OK, though? He's being OK?"

"Quin? Yeah. He's all right, actually."

Oliver goes quiet. Then he says, "The first time we met involved a chucked drink too. Remember?"

How could I forget? Right before sixth form started, the Electric was short-staffed so I was helping Ivy out here and there, and offering a sympathetic ear whenever she wanted to vent about Evil Ex Tom. One Sunday, I was sweeping the steps when I spotted Oliver over the road, wearing a suit that was total overkill for a minimum wage job interview. I knew who he was – Aaron had mentioned his parents' friends' son was starting at our school – but we hadn't yet spoken. The way Oliver paced told me he was nervous.

A car blasting chart music rolled past. It happened in slow motion. A jeer. Oliver's head snapping upwards. Dark liquid flying out of the back window. His pale-blue suit, splattered with Coke.

Man, I was raging! I strong-armed Olly into the Electric and explained everything to Ivy. She was disgusted and hired him on the spot. Oliver says if I hadn't been there he'd have bottled it. We joke that it was our meet cute.

"D'you want to borrow a T-shirt?" Quin calls from the other side of the door, and I snap out of the memory.

"Yes please. Just a sec." Into the phone, I whisper, "Got to go. Speak later."

I end the call. My face is inexplicably hot. Am I feeling … guilty? For what – cutting the call so abruptly? Or checking Quin out earlier? Oliver doesn't care. Why am I getting bothered about what Oliver thinks, anyway?

Hoping Quin didn't hear me whispering, I unlock the door. Quin's arm appears through it. The black T-shirt is his, and fits weirdly, baggy at the bottom but tight over my boobs. At least it smells of detergent rather than sour milk. I go downstairs to the kitchen, draping my rinsed shirt over a radiator.

"Thanks," I say.

"'S all right." Quin pointedly doesn't look my way. That means he's noticed how clingy this top is. My self-consciousness trebles. What was I thinking with that low-key flirting earlier? I look like his *dead stepsister*.

I lean against the counter, and tell Quin about the park, and what the bag means.

He looks horrified. "Wait, what? That's seriously creepy shit. Reeling your brother in with chocolate, Jesus. So what, you're saying the boyfriend was there when Jade was killed? Or just before, or just after?"

I nod. "Maybe they arranged to meet at the outdoor gym and that's why she went there. It's deserted in the evenings. Aaron and I used to mess around there sometimes." I shift, feeling uncomfortable. "At least I understand why Bag Man told Felix I was pretty now."

"Yeah." Then Quin seems to catch himself. "Not meaning to say there'd be no other reason. You are pretty. You know, just stating a fact. Not an opinion, necessarily."

My heart skips a beat. "What does that mean?"

"Nothing. Forget it." Quin rubs his jaw. "So … maybe Jade arrived before her boyfriend, and bumped into Aaron?"

"Aaron said she marched straight over and laid into him. I still don't get why, if they didn't know each other. Maybe the boyfriend turned up at some point, and Aaron's hiding it?"

"Or he arrived after Aaron moved Jade. The bag

could've been left behind. Actually, he could've got the bag from the beach later – we don't know. He and Aaron might not have met at all."

We go silent. This isn't fitting together very well.

"At least I know now that it wasn't Jade who took my stuff." I wet my lips. The words feel funny in my mouth, like they don't belong. "Her boyfriend likes me. A lot. It always seemed a little unlikely that a year eleven would sneak into the sixth form centre to break into a locker. He must have done it, not her. All the clothes and presents he gave to Jade, including my scarf... He was..."

Using Jade as some kind of twisted substitute for me. I can't complete the sentence, and Quin says nothing either. It's too hurtful, like Jade was unimportant, just a girl with the bad luck to resemble Mia Hawkins. *Disposable.*

Quin clears his throat. "Still believe Jade took those stalker photos?"

I shake my head, feeling ashamed. They're his. Maybe Jade got suspicious, went digging and found them. I wonder what she made of them, and how badly it must have hurt.

The police should know this. Jade's boyfriend is a disturbed stalker. But I'll hold off until I see Aaron tomorrow. Surely he'll share everything he knows if I tell him I'm vulnerable?

Quin pushes off the counter he was leaning against. "I'm gonna make them pizzas. Want one?"

I can't think about this any longer or my head will explode. I nod, watching Quin tip the dough on to the

167

floured counter and expertly roll it into two balls. He spins the dough above his head, catches it, stretches it and lays it on the baking tray.

"You're showing off," I say.

"It helps create a non-uniform crumb." He spoons tomato sauce on to the bases, then neatly dices dairy-free cheese. "This OK?" he asks, gesturing to the packet.

"You didn't get that in for me, did you?"

"Fancied trying it out." He checks the oven then slides both trays in, setting the timer. Ten minutes feels a long time to chat when the mood is so sombre. Was he hoping I'd stay? He certainly made enough dough.

Say something. "What's in the cage upstairs?"

"My rats."

"Rats are pets?"

"Domestic rats, yeah. Wanna look? They're friendly."

Upstairs Quin opens the cage and lifts out a grey rodent. "This is Aoife. Wanna hold her? She likes cuddles."

Cuddle is not a word I'd imagine coming out of this boy's mouth, like, ever. Gingerly I take Aoife, holding her against my chest as Quin did. Her fur is surprisingly soft.

I giggle. "I'm almost expecting her to start purring!"

"Probably helps that you smell like me right now, T-shirt and all." A white face with bright eyes pops out from the neck of Quin's hoodie and I jump.

He laughs. "This one's Saoirse. Aoife will sit on your shoulder if you like."

He gives her a gentle nudge. Aoife scuttles up and presses

herself to my neck. I catch our reflection in the window and giggle again.

"Cat person here, but this is cool."

"Do you have one?"

"A cat? Yeah, her name's Dotty."

"I like cats. All animals, really."

"Me too. My grades aren't good enough for me to be a vet, but I'd like to work with animals someday. Vet nurse, maybe."

Downstairs the timer buzzes. Quin lifts Saoirse back into the cage, and I hand him Aoife. In the kitchen, the pizzas – smelling divine, screaming EAT ME – are ready. We take them to the table. Quin asks me about "the vegan thing" and I explain how unethical and environmentally unfriendly the dairy industry is.

"There are loads of health benefits of being vegan, too," I finish. "I used to go to events when I had more free time. Sorry, more detail than you probably wanted."

"It's OK. I don't mind."

"I can send you links if you're interested."

He hesitates. "If you want. Not really a reader."

"Videos, then. This pizza is amazing. Totally dope, like you said."

"Yeah, well, I'm a pro."

I grin. "Not yet you're not."

"All right, all right." He smiles as he asks what my perfect restaurant dish is. As we finish eating, I enthuse about honey-fried aubergine and the amazing pumpkin-seed pesto I still have dreams about.

Then I remember where I am, and why, and the last crust of pizza turns dry in my mouth.

Quin's smile vanishes too.

"Shit," he says. "I forgot."

Silence. I stare at the plate, empty apart from a tomatoey smear. How messed up that for half an hour we were actually having fun! I wonder if Quin and Jade had pizza nights too. Maybe I'm even sitting in her chair.

"I should go."

"You'd better. Demi and my dad will be back soon. I don't have wheels but I'll walk you to the bus stop."

"You don't have to. I'll be OK."

Quin scowls. "That's what Jade said the last time I saw her. And you've got some creep obsessed with you. No bloody way."

Quietly I take my slightly damp shirt and slip into the downstairs toilet to change. When I come out he's pacing about, glowering again.

Outside the temperature has dropped. Without meaning to, I glance over my shoulder. The road is empty, but that's no surprise. Whoever's been following me knows how to blend into the shadows. We wait at the bus stop in silence. The computerized display is broken, but the timetable says there's a bus in five. Jade would have stood here the last night of her life, right where I am now. What was running through her head?

The bus arrives. This time I don't hesitate with a goodbye hug. Quin mutters something about not doing hugs, but he gives me a squeeze in return. He doesn't look happy. I half-think he's going to insist on coming too but instead he skulks off. The bus jolts just as it starts moving, and the doors open to admit a guy in a padded jacket and cap. He goes upstairs without looking my way.

My phone pings.

Quin: msg when u home

Is he worried about me? I can't believe how well we got on earlier. Not like me and Aaron, obviously, but there's more common ground than I imagined. If only there hadn't been a shadow hanging over us.

Someone is obsessed with me.

Not a model, or singer, or actress. Me. And it's not Jade.

Something occurs to me. Jade only realized I existed the afternoon of the teen screening. That's why her reaction to me was so strong! What a shock it must have been when the pieces fell into place. The guy she poured her heart out to, and trusted with her feelings, was using her in the cruellest way.

Her perfect boyfriend, and perfect relationship: a lie.

It's sick. Depraved. So … deliberately callous. What was running through his head on their dates? Was he picturing Jade as me? Did he accidentally call her Mia? He certainly knew how to make her fall for him. Did it give him a kick to see my scarf around her neck?

No wonder Jade hated me. It's so scarily easy for girls to see each other as the enemy – especially when boys want us. Maybe for the first time, it hits me how tragic her death really is. Jade was a kid struggling with friendships and changes at home. Unhappy and vulnerable and angry.

He must have been what Jade needed to tell me about that night. She was still angry, still hurt, but she'd faced up to the truth and decided I should know. The "important thing" wasn't a threat, as I assumed.

It was a warning.

Ping.

Expecting Quin, or maybe Oliver, I tap my phone – and suck in a breath.

Unknown: did you miss your bag?

My insides lurch, like the bus did moments ago.

Oh God.

It's him.

I grip the back of the seat in front with my free hand. How has he got my number? He gave me the bag a week and a half ago. Why is he messaging now?

I should ignore him. But … if I play this right, could I find out who he is? Nothing bad's going to happen on this bus, with people around.

With shaking fingers, I type. Why did you take it?

It takes me five minutes to gear myself up enough to press send.

The reply comes instantly.

Unknown: because it belonged to you lovely
mia

A pause.

Unknown: you have such beautiful long hair
those new hair clips suit it
i've imagined buying them for you before
but you chose them yourself <3
i know it's a message just for me

My fingers fly to the side of my head. They connect with the hard acetate of the clips I bought on impulse from the market craft stall I passed earlier.

He knows they're new. And he knows I'm wearing them.

That means one of two things.

He's been watching me today.

Or he's watching me right now.

I stay very, very still. Rain gleams on the window as an oncoming car dips its lights. It feels like hungry eyes are burning my back.

I slowly peer over my shoulder.

The only other people on the lower deck are women.

He's not down here. Phew.

Then I tense. The guy in the cap. He almost missed the bus. Could he have been lurking outside Quin's house, and tracked me here? My throat constricts. I force myself to send a new message: I want you to stop following me.

Unknown: how else will I know you're safe

I jam my finger on the stop button. Soon the bus shudders to a halt, and I rush to the exit and leap out. Cool air closes around me. The doors hiss shut. The bus trundles off, followed by the car behind it.

I'm alone.

My shoulders sag with relief.

I have another problem, though. So desperate was I to escape the bus that I didn't check where we were. This stop doesn't even have a shelter; it's just a sign by the two-mile heathland walk into town. Around me is thick darkness.

Great.

I button up my coat, wishing I'd kept my cool. I'll be OK – another bus will be along in half an hour – but that feels like a long time to wait. For a split second, I think of asking Aaron to come and pick me up, before remembering that's impossible. Should I ring Mum and Dad? Unless I can think of a convincing lie, I'd have to tell them everything. There's no way I'll be allowed to visit Aaron tomorrow if they know I'm being stalked – and I need to see him. And neither Leyla nor Oliver drive. No chance I'm asking Riyad. No one would get here much sooner than the bus anyway.

In the distance, further along the road towards home, headlights swing round. For a wild second I think it's the bus. Then I remember: the car, just behind the bus. It's turning back.

My stomach plummets.

Jade's boyfriend has a car.

175

He must have been tailing me, using a voice to text app. And now I'm out here, alone.

Totally vulnerable.

I launch into the heathland. Fear drives me forward. If I can find somewhere to hide, or put enough distance between us that I can vanish unseen—

My heel digs into mud and I stumble, stones skidding underfoot as the ground dips. I land by some kind of ledge. Instead of scrambling up, I crawl as deep as I can into the recess and curl up in the mud, trying to make myself as small as possible. My heart pounds so hard I'm scared it'll pop. Surely he won't trawl the heathland to find me?

Out here the wind's whistle is loud. There'll be no warning of anyone approaching. My phone is still in my hand, with just one tiny bar of 4G. Clumsily – my fingers are blocks of ice – I tap on the local bus app. Seconds tick by as it struggles to load. *Come on!* I swipe refresh once, twice, a third time. Finally the departure times pop up. I can make a bolt for it just before the next bus arrives...

The wind shifts, changing direction. Something cracks. Twigs? Are those footsteps? *Crack*. It's louder now – right above the ledge. I squeeze my eyes shut. Don't move. Don't breathe. Don't even think.

Everything goes silent above. Is he there, surveying the heathland? Waiting? Am I hidden, or will he spot me the moment he leaps on to lower ground?

Not thinking is impossible, so instead I focus on calm, comforting things, like the way sunshine glints on Dotty's fur when she snoozes on my window sill, and how soft her belly is to touch.

The next five minutes crawl by. My toes go cold in my boots. Ten minutes. Fifteen. At seventeen minutes I flex my arms and legs, psyching myself up. At eighteen, I scramble up and dash in the direction I came from. I skid on to the road. The bus stop is a couple of metres further up. Headlights swing round the far corner. *Please let that be the bus!*

It *is* the bus. I wave my arm frantically. The second the doors open I jump aboard, crashing down into the closest seat. Only then do I realize my entire body is trembling.

After a night dipping in and out of sleep I'm a total wreck. Each time I jerked awake, I padded over to the window and peeped out through the crack in my curtains at the pavement below. He wasn't there but he definitely has been. How else does he know where I go and who I see?

At least he can't follow me into the young offender institution.

My phone bleeps and I jump, but it's only Oliver asking how I am. He texted last night to check I'd got back from Quin's OK, but my head was too scrambled for me to type more than *yes*. Luck was on my side when I got home – I was able to slip straight upstairs and into the shower without my parents glimpsing my mud-streaked clothes. Even after a quarter of an hour standing under scalding water I still felt cold inside.

Dressing takes for ever. Before, I always chose clothes I knew Aaron liked, but that doesn't feel right today. I settle for a plaid dress I often wear for school. My hair – my *beautiful long hair* – I tie back. I can't bear to be reminded.

Mum appears at my doorway. "Are you sure about this, Mia?"

Yesterday it seemed so simple – question Harper, question Aaron. But yesterday I didn't know how obsessed this stalker was.

I lower my hairbrush, staring at my reflection. Is this my fault? He can't have got obsessed for *no reason*. I think of that conversation I overheard, where Mum bemoaned my interest in boys and attention-seeking clothes…

"Mia? Did you hear me?" There are dark circles under Mum's eyes. Guilt floods me. If I'd been the daughter she and Dad clearly want me to be, none of us would be going through this.

I feel small and ashamed. But I have to summon my courage. Frightened or not, seeing Aaron is more important than ever now I know I was right to be suspicious. "Yes."

"It's OK if you've had second thoughts." Softly, Mum says, "If you need closure, write Aaron a letter."

A lump forms in my throat. "I need to see him, Mum. Tori told him I was coming."

I thought Aaron might refuse to see me after our last conversation. That he hasn't gives me hope.

Mum's expression tells me she wants to argue, but she doesn't.

The young offender institution is grey, grim and businesslike. Barbed wire tops the walls. Mum's words come to me: *Prisons are terrible places, full of the worst side of humanity.* What have the other teenagers behind those walls done?

When Tori and I pass through the visitors' entrance we're ordered to stash our bags in a locker, then shown into a meeting room with strip lighting and a sad-looking artificial plant. It smells clean, like the police station did. We settle in plastic chairs on one side of a table.

I used to get on well with Aaron's mum, but I sense she'd rather I wasn't here. After she warned me Aaron was feeling down and it would be upsetting, we passed much of the long journey to Kent in an uncomfortable silence.

I jump as the door opens. Aaron swings in on crutches, accompanied by a guard. My eyes pop. He looks far worse than at the hospital, all slouching shoulders and unhealthy skin, and a brutally short haircut. A purple bruise circles one eye. The dark green tracksuit hangs off him.

He doesn't bother with hello. "Mum, are you OK? What about Soph, and Dad? Nothing bad's happened, has it?"

"We're fine," says Tori, and Aaron looks relieved. He lowers himself into the seat opposite us. His eyes flit to me, then away. I can barely look at him either. I'd convinced myself I was prepared to see him here, but I was wrong. This is the guy whose touch and smiles and messages I craved, who the romantic part of me once believed I would be with for ever – in prison.

Tori extends her arms across the table. "How are you today? Lessons going OK? Have you been able to draw?"

I find myself wanting Aaron to crack the obvious joke: firing questions without waiting for answers makes his mum sound like me. Instead he merely shrugs.

Say something. "You, um, spend time outside your room, then?" I manage.

"My cell, you mean," says Aaron flatly. "I leave it for class. There's a gym and a yard and a football pitch. Not that they're any use with a broken leg. I've a TV. Might get a games console, if I'm good."

I picture Aaron's boy-cave at home, with the large desk and graphics tablet and Apple Mac. All his talent that now goes nowhere. My lower lip quivers. None of this feels real.

"Who punched you?" asks Tori.

"Some nutter."

"Why?"

"No reason. That's what it's like here. Everyone wants to hurt each other, just because." He glares at me. "Why did you come, Mia? Stop bothering with me. Move on, all right?"

His words are a slap. Tori rubs her temples. "I'm sorry you can't talk in private, but there are no secrets between me and Aaron any more, Mia, so be as frank as you like."

To think I was naive enough to convince myself Aaron would be pleased I hadn't given up on him, and that he was missing me the way I've missed him! I've been living in a fairy tale.

But this is important. Before I can chicken out, I say, "Someone was with you the night she died. Jade's boyfriend."

If Aaron's surprised, he doesn't show it. "What makes you think that?"

It's not outright denial. I glance at Tori. Better keep my story vague. "I just know," I mumble. "She was meeting him. And I also know he's … followed me."

Aaron twitches at that.

"Do you know who he is?" I finish.

"No. Sorry."

"You weren't alone when Jade died though, were you?"

"Can't prove otherwise." Again, not denial.

Tori glances between us, frowning. "Aaron? Was someone else there?"

Aaron doesn't answer.

"Did you ever notice anyone following me before all this?" I ask. "Other than that night outside my house."

A beat passes. Then Aaron says, "Mia, please stop this."

The haunted look in his eyes has returned. The one he had in the hospital when I told him about Bag Man.

He knows.

"Ignoring it won't make it go away," I say.

"I wish I could help, but I can't." Aaron sounds pained, almost pleading.

"Aaron, if you know something—" Tori interrupts.

"What did Jade say the night she died?" I press. "She

was shouting at you."

"I don't remember. I was hearing things and I was—" He stops.

I frown. "What do you mean, hearing things?"

Aaron looks at his mum helplessly. Tori looks back, straight into his eyes.

He shrinks away. "Mum…"

"Aaron." Her tone is icy. "Why were you 'hearing things'?"

"I wasn't."

"I've asked before and I'm going to ask again. Were there drugs involved?"

He's shaking his head. And something slips to the front of my mind.

"You rang Riyad that night! Riyad could have joined you."

"I just rang him for a chat." The pitch of Aaron's voice rises.

"You never phone your mates to chat."

"Well, I did that night. Riyad has nothing to do with this."

What if he does, though?

I think of Riyad, smoking a spliff at the playground. Spliffs I know Aaron has tried before. Riyad, who calls weed "tame stuff" and acted so very strangely that time he hit on me at Peyton Fletcher's party.

"You weren't drunk," I say. "You were high. You can't remember!"

Tori and I stare at Aaron.

He goes as red as a tomato. Then he mumbles, "I took LSD."

16

"What?" barks Tori.

"I was in a bad place." Aaron sounds defensive. "I needed to get out of my head."

"So you decided to take *class A drugs*?"

"That was a terrible idea, Aaron!" I say.

"Don't lecture me," he snaps. "I'm not a druggie. I've only done stuff, like, a couple of times. Everyone does."

"I don't. Neither do Ley or Olly."

"Well, you lot are naive! It's no big deal."

Does he really believe that or is he acting hard? I can't believe he hid taking drugs from me!

Tori grasps his shoulder. "Words cannot express how

furious I am that you've held this back," she says. "LSD is a *hallucinogenic drug*. This could change everything. And if Riyad was there too…"

Aaron pulls back. "He wasn't! I told you. Some things are hazy but I remember killing her. There was blood on my hands, everywhere, and I didn't hallucinate that. It was in my car, remember?"

Tori pushes her hair from her face, blowing out a breath. "We have to notify the police."

"Please don't, Mum."

"Why on earth not?" demands Tori.

Aaron mumbles something. He doesn't look defiant any longer, just plain scared.

I know why he wants this kept secret. In Aaron's eyes, it doesn't change what happens to *him* — but it could drop his mates in it, if the police grill Aaron about where he got the drugs from. And they might. Last summer the police made a big noise about cracking down after some Southaven teenagers took bad drugs and were hospitalized. Aaron's call to Riyad was probably to get hold of the LSD; I don't believe Aaron would've had some stashed away. Even if Riyad's only involvement on the night of the murder was literally handing over drugs then leaving, that places him at risk of arrest.

I open my mouth, but Aaron gets there first.

"I'm not stupid," he says, looking at me. "If I care about people, I protect them. No matter what, Mia."

The way he says it is loaded. He's the old Aaron again, the one I fell for, who is loyal and kind. I reach under the table and grasp his good knee. The strangest feeling courses through me – not quite triumph, but something close. The police don't know everything. Aaron *was* keeping a secret, and I got it out of him. Everyone who told me to give up was wrong. Perhaps his whole story is a lie, or full of drugged up-uncertainties.

"Please tell me who was with you at the outdoor gym," I say. "Riyad? Another mate? Or am I going to need to find it out myself again?"

He pushes my hand away.

The guard clears his throat. "Five minutes."

"I'll be back soon, Aaron," says Tori, "and I'm going to need you to be honest if someone else was involved. Next time I'm bringing a lawyer."

"Aren't lawyers really expensive?" Aaron looks worried. "If you're using Granddad's money—"

"Granddad would want me to do everything I can. You didn't intend to hurt anyone. That's the key point. Even if you are convicted, you should get a light sentence. You can still have a life."

"Maybe I don't deserve one after what I did!" Aaron heaves himself up. The crutches wobble; he's trembling.

"We aren't giving up," I say. "I'm going to carry on fighting for you – however hard you fight back."

Aaron stares at me. I wait for him to tell me to let it go again. Instead, slowly and quietly, he says, "You really want to know what I'm hiding? Shall I tell you, even though you one hundred per cent won't like it?"

He's finally cracked. I've done it.

"It can't be worse than what you've told me already."

"It can. For you, anyway."

Tori says something, but I can't hear her over the alarm bells ringing in my head. The hard, precise way he's speaking… "What do you mean, Aaron?"

He draws a deep breath. "That Saturday. I slept with someone else."

The words are an electric bolt. I leap to my feet. "What?"

"I wanted to hurt you. I thought, if Mia doesn't want me then I'll find a girl who does. This was before the drugs, before I went to the gym. I knew exactly what I was doing."

I'm faintly aware of the buzz from the overhead light, of the guard in my peripheral vision and Tori laying a hand on my arm, but the room feels distant, as though I'm not really in it.

"Do you see?" Aaron says, still in that horrible tight voice. "You're holding on to a lie."

I want to say *I don't believe you*. Instead, what comes out of my mouth is, "Who?"

"Brooke. I bumped into her on the way home. I knew she liked me. It was easy."

Tyler's annoying cousin. I remember Brooke's tinkling laughter on the way to the Talent Showcase when I insisted Aaron and I were fine. The condescending way she called me Squidge. Way back, how she flirted with Aaron, making it very clear she liked what she saw.

"But… We're *us*. We're special, we're…" I choke on *I love you.*

Aaron looks at me with the same blue eyes I once couldn't resist staring into, but now they seem cold and distant. "Sorry. Stay safe, Mia."

I deflate, like a balloon that's been popped. Everything that's been spurring me on for weeks – the fierce hope and determination and love – dissipates. With it goes something else. Something deeper. The relationship I gave everything to was a lie.

I think Aaron's broken my heart.

By the time we pull up outside mine, I'm a dried-out shell. I've crumbled into two people. Before Mia, full of passion and fierceness, and After Mia, the blinkered, lovesick fool.

"I don't have any words that can make you feel better, Mia," says Tori softly. "I'm sorry."

I manage a nod. I'm too far gone to feel embarrassed for bawling in front of her. Flatly, I say, "I hope getting him to open up helps."

"I'm so disappointed in him. About everything."

"I don't understand," I say. "I trusted him completely."

Tori sighs. I feel bad for dumping this on her, when Aaron sleeping with Brooke is probably low down her worry list. "People aren't always everything they seem. Boys can be very … driven by sex. Rejection is a big deal, but you did nothing wrong."

If I stay I'm going to cry again. I open the car door. Tori

calls, "Mia? Please go to the police about being followed, OK? And tell your parents. I don't want you getting hurt."

I don't trust myself to speak, so instead I lean over and hug her. She hugs me back. Up close, I can see her eyes are glassy.

"Don't be a stranger," she murmurs. "For what it's worth, seeing you two together always made me smile."

As I'm hunting for my keys I catch a notification flashing up on my phone: my group chat with Oliver and Leyla. He's shared a selfie of them by the ancient shoot 'em up game in the pier arcade, him giving a thumbs up, her pulling an expression of pain. Jimmy's between them, ball in mouth, and fur wet from the sea.

> Oliver:
> Newsflash: @LeylaKazem is not unbeatable!
>
> Leyla:
> A fluke, Arrowsmith
> You're forgetting the million times I beat you before that
>
> Oliver:
> Some would call you a sore loser...
>
> Leyla:
> Some would tell you to shut up

Oliver:
Some would say that proves my point

Leyla:
Some would say this conversation was over
So @MiaHawkins ... how was it?
Sorry about the things I said. Wasn't trying
to upset you. Hope you're OK.

On another day them being mega goofs messaging each other when they're hanging out would make me smile. Suddenly all I want is to be with my friends. I go to tap the group call icon, then stop. I can't blurt out to Leyla that I think her brother gave Aaron drugs!

Instead I FaceTime Oliver. He picks up instantly. "Hey, Mia."

"Are you still with Leyla?"

"Nope, I'm on the train. Mum and Dad have tickets to an exhibition at the National Gallery." He frowns. "Hey, you've been crying."

I can't bring myself to care that he's seeing me looking such a mess. I sit on the doorstep and pour the whole sorry story out.

"He can't have really loved me if he cheated, can he?" I finish. "He doesn't even have any connection with Brooke, it was just sex. You said I was going to get hurt. I wish I'd listened."

"I didn't want to be right." Oliver sounds uncomfortable.

He's popped headphones in and moved down the carriage so we can talk more privately.

"I honestly thought I could clear his name, and things could eventually go back to the way they were before Jade. How naive was I!"

"I'm sorry, Mia," says Oliver. "Cheating is the worst."

Is this how Jade felt when she found out her "perfect" relationship was a lie? No wonder she was spitting rage when she spotted me at the Electric. It's a good thing Brooke goes to another school. Even though I blame Aaron most, she's part of this. I don't know how I'd react if I came face to face with her.

"It's unforgivable. Not that Aaron and I had any kind of future – another thing I've been in total denial about! Oh God, telling Ley's going to be awful. She never liked him, and she was right. I'm a complete fool…"

"Would you like me to tell her?"

It's tempting. But I shake my head. "She should hear it from me. Should I say something about Riyad?"

"I wouldn't unless you have evidence. All it'll do is cause trouble."

He's right, but keeping things from my best friend makes me feel uncomfortable. "I still can't believe Aaron took LSD – and kept it secret to protect his friends!"

"I can. Aaron likes to fit in." Oliver pauses. Then he says: "Remember that drink that got thrown on me?"

It takes me a second to realize he means our meet cute at the Electric – Oliver's interview suit, ruined by the

Coke flung from the passing car. "Don't tell me that was Aaron!"

"I don't know who threw it or had the idea, but Aaron was in that car with Riyad's crew. Clearly being the sad, overdressed new kid made me a prime target. Aaron apologized later, said they were joking around. For what it's worth, he did seem to feel bad."

Nowhere near as bad as Oliver felt — especially after being bullied so badly at his old school! I'm reeling. Aaron and Oliver aren't close like their parents, but they're friendly. Yet it fits. Aaron's never been secure being geeky. That makes him easily influenced. "Why didn't you say?"

"You wouldn't have wanted to hear it."

"I'd have told him he was a dick!"

"Would you?"

I have a nasty feeling I might not have, like the Nice, Agreeable Girlfriend I thought I needed to be. It's easy to make excuses for someone when they make you feel bright and bold and beautiful. "I really didn't know him at all. Perhaps..."

"Perhaps what?"

I take a moment. Do I mean what I'm about to say? Yes ... I think I genuinely do. "Perhaps the thing I liked most wasn't him, but the idea of us. The perfect couple." I feel myself deflate. "That doesn't mean I didn't genuinely love him, though."

"Oh no, Mia. I wish we were having this conversation in person. Don't cry. You deserve better."

His voice and expression are so kind. I think about that afternoon at the Electric, when Oliver brought me painkillers and plucked popcorn from my hair, and how he skipped school without complaint because I needed support and listened to me emoting about Aaron when everyone else had lost patience.

"Thank you," I whisper. "You're great."

"Well, thanks." Oliver pauses. "For what it's worth, I think you're pretty great too. Even and especially when you're crying down the phone at me."

"That's a proper movie line."

He laughs. "It's original, I promise."

A breeze blows my hair across my face. *My beautiful long hair.* I haven't even told Oliver about yesterday yet. He listens as I explain about Harper and the texts on the bus.

His face is full of concern. "And there I was taking ticket stubs while you were hiding in a bush!" he says. "You must have been really scared."

I draw my knees to my chest. "Yep."

Oliver goes quiet. "I know what it's like to be afraid," he says. "I dreaded leaving the house when we lived in London. It felt like the bullies were everywhere. I was a paranoid mess, just like they intended." Vulnerability creeps into his voice. "It was relentless. Once they threw my lunch on the concrete and forced me to eat it like an animal while they filmed it. My parents acted like it was my fault for not fitting in. Their way of helping was to buy me Jimmy 'as therapy'. Great in theory, but he can't discuss my feelings."

My hand flies to my mouth. "Olly! I didn't realize it was that bad."

"Things are much better now. Point is, I get it, and I hate that you feel unsafe. I don't want to come across as some douchey overprotective man, but... Will you let me help you? I don't mind walking you places, even if it means waiting around. I'll bring Jimmy. He'd never hurt anyone, but this guy doesn't know that."

"I can't ask you to do that."

"What else would I be doing? Brushing Jimmy's teeth? Hoovering up popcorn? Rewatching *Casablanca*? You being safe is more important than any of that. I was worried all day yesterday."

A horn honks. I give a start. A car pulls up outside the house, the driver's window winding down.

"Are you locked out, or are you sitting there looking tragic for fun?"

Oh God. Riyad. I don't know if I'm up to speaking to him – but it's a golden opportunity. I tell Oliver we'll speak later and drop the phone into my bag. Then I stalk to the pavement, hugging myself. "What do you want?"

Riyad peers at me. "Whoa, Squidge. What's with the red eyes? Have you been watching sad cat videos or something?"

"I asked you a question."

"I'm picking up Ley, then giving her an unofficial driving lesson. Wanna jump in?"

He's so casual. Doubt surfaces inside me. Was he at the

gym with Aaron that night? Oliver was right – that phone call isn't proof.

Maybe I can shock the truth out of him. "You gave Aaron LSD the night Jade died. You went to the outdoor gym."

Riyad mimes a pantomime "oh no". K-pop blares from my bag: my ringtone. I ignore it.

"Admit it," I say. "He wouldn't know how to get hold of hard stuff himself. I've seen you high."

"Bit of a leap of logic there, Squidge. Smoking a few spliffs does not a drug dealer make."

I frown. "I didn't call you a dealer."

"Whatever, Squidge. I didn't go near that gym."

"Where were you then? I know you didn't go home that night."

My phone rings again. I grab it and swipe to cut the call – then stop when I see Quin's name. Three missed calls, too?

"Popular Squidgie," says Riyad. His tone sounds different all of a sudden. Less jokey. He drives off with no goodbye.

A nasty feeling creeps into my belly.

I've strong reason to believe Riyad went to the gym. But what if he wasn't just there to drop off drugs? *Riyad could be Jade's boyfriend.* He used to date a lot, but there's been no one for months. He might still have been there when Jade appeared. Taking her bag would have been easy.

Maybe "Squidge" isn't a silly little joke. Maybe he meant

it when he called me *hot*. Maybe it isn't a coincidence he's driving past my house…

Is he my stalker?

And have I made a massive mistake confronting him and revealing what I know?

K-pop blares again. *Quin calling.* I want to curl up on my bed and shut everything out. But Quin wouldn't ring for a chat.

"We need to meet," he says when I pick up.

Instantly, I'm on red alert. "What's happened?"

"Can you grab your brother, get to the soft play centre on the pier?"

"Why there? You're scaring me."

"Safest place I can think of. People can't walk in without a kid. Frosted windows, too." He rings off.

I stare at the dead screen. What now?

17

Quin's in the soft play centre already when Felix and I squeeze through the turnstiles. He sits cross-legged in the baby pen, watching Zora play with a foam ball.

I take a moment to collect myself. After Quin's call, there was no time to waste. I put a cheery face on when my parents asked about visiting Aaron, and rushed out with Felix. But I can't go much longer without confiding in them.

Mum and Dad have been so supportive. Both have made time to talk when I've wanted to, never pushed it when I haven't. They've quietly cooked cheering vegan meals, coaxed me downstairs rather than letting me stew in my room, and Mum let me introduce her to *Sailor Moon* even though it's not her thing.

My original plan was: see Aaron, tell all – even if they're ashamed of me. And I will. Soon.

My heart is heavy as I guide Felix to the preschool section then join Quin. His expression is composed but his eyes tell me he's rattled.

"Quin. What happened?"

He draws folded paper from his pocket.

backoff from mia you delinnquent waste of space she might think your pathetic bad boy shit is edgy and yes maybe that pizzza tasted good but she belongs to me and noone is going to take her away when everythin is so close to being perfect she's in love with me the signs are all there she just doesn't realizeit you'll regret this

"Seems Mr Stalker was watching yesterday," says Quin. "He's not a happy bunny."

I sit down heavily on a large squishy cube. "This is… How can he know about the pizza? Could he see into the kitchen?"

"Wouldn't be impossible. The garden backs on to the nature reserve. Plenty of climbable trees. Big windows. Binoculars are probably a pretty essential bit of stalking kit, don't you think?"

I picture us at the table, chatting about pesto, no idea we weren't alone. "Nothing happened between us though!"

"He obviously thinks it could have." Quin looks me in the eye, and I blush.

"This note – when did it arrive?"

"It was on the doormat this morning with my name on it. You all right? Your eyes are red."

"I'm fine." My eyes trail across the brightly-coloured ball pits and well-loved plastic slides, taking in joyful faces and high-pitched laughter and cheesy eighties music. I check Felix is OK – I'm not making *that* mistake again – then reread the letter. Times New Roman, standard printer paper – no clues. Apart from all the typos. Did he type in a rage?

"Everything is *so close to being perfect*? He must think he's… Well. Nearly got me." I'm aware how horribly vague – sinister, even – "got" sounds. "Us hanging out has him rattled. He obviously has a temper."

"Wants to swing his dick, more like."

"Eww. Gross expression."

"It is what it is. He's not very smart, sending this."

"What makes you say that?"

"Cos the first thing I'm gonna do is tell you. Then we're both on our guard. Any idea who this is? Has anyone been trying it on? Riyad Kazem, maybe?" He waits a moment. "*Squidge.*"

I flinch. Quin peers at me, frowning. I tell him about the LSD and suspecting Riyad was at the gym, and even about the party where Riyad hit on me. Quin turns away, muttering under his breath.

"Right," he says. "Stating the obvious, but you'd better avoid him from now on."

"I can't," I say. "He's my best friend's brother, and we're on the quiz team together."

Quin scowls but says nothing. I thought he'd have a bigger reaction to Riyad and the drugs, given how much he dislikes Riyad, but he doesn't seem surprised. Before I can question it, a ball shoots out of the pit, bouncing off Quin's head.

He pulls a face at Zora. "Cheers, princess."

Zora gurgles. She really is very cute. Quin tosses the ball back. Then he frowns. "Hey. Mr Stalker giving you that bag. D'you think that happened cos he saw us chatting at the park, got jealous and decided to scare you? Maybe it wasn't something he thought through. Same with this dramatic crap." He waves the letter.

"How can it have been spontaneous?" I say. "He'd need to have had the bag on him."

"He's a creepy obsessed stalker. For all we know, he always has something of yours on him, for kicks."

Eww. I squirm. "But why scare me at all? Him creeping me out is only going to drive me away. A better tactic would be to be nice. You know, like a normal person."

"Yeah, but he ain't normal."

Fair point. And weren't we saying last night that giving me the bag didn't make any sense? Until now, I'd imagined my stalker as clever, calm and calculating. Dating Jade – grooming her, *ugh* – took charm, convincing her he was the perfect boyfriend. Avoiding being seen together is skilful too, as is following me undetected. He knew how to get into my locker, and he's been nicking my stuff for months.

Yet he's also done two rash, not-very-clever things. Is his patience running out?

Slowly, I say, "You might have something. He laid low after Jade died, scared of being suspected, maybe. With Aaron charged, he gained confidence … but then felt threatened because he saw me talking to you – or Riyad, I suppose – at the park. He had something of mine on him and decided to make a power play. Only it backfired, because it tipped me off about him being at the murder scene. He doesn't know you have that photo of Jade holding the bag. Basically, he screwed up."

Does it make me feel better or worse to know that my stalker has a temper? In theory, it's reassuring. He's not a genius. He makes mistakes. Then again…

What might he do when he gets really angry?

"Um, Quin?" I say. "We'd better stop hanging out. I don't want anything bad to happen to you because of me."

Quin's expression darkens. "He can fucking bring it on. He messes with me, he'll come off worse. Sick fucking bastard."

A nearby dad gives Quin a death glare. "Mind your language, son."

"Don't fucking 'son' me!" Quin grabs Zora's bag and bangs into the changing room with her.

I'm bundling a reluctant Felix into his coat when a more

calm-looking Quin reappears, carrying Zora on his hip. He clears his throat.

"D'you mind waiting?"

He goes over to the man who told him off. They exchange a few words, the dad's expression relaxing a touch. So Quin's apologizing. Good for him. Even so, seeing Quin mouthing off was unsettling. I'd kind of forgotten his self-control issues.

"Sorry 'bout that." Quin's back. "The not hanging out thing got under my skin."

I try an awkward smile. "I didn't realize you liked my company that much."

Quin shifts his hold on Zora. "You backing off won't fix anything. It's your choice, obviously, but it'll make him think he can control you, do whatever he likes. D'you feel OK about that?"

I feel less OK about people getting threatened because of me. I need to get out. This place is too hot, too loud, too happy. And we shouldn't be having this conversation in front of Felix. "Until I know who he is, there's not much I can do to stop him."

"That's why we need to keep him rattled, so he screws up again."

We. Quin has an intense look in his hazel eyes. "How?" I ask.

"We start going out. Not for real," he adds quickly. "We pretend. Post pictures. Faking stuff online is easy. He'll hate it. Might bring him out of the woodwork."

"I want ice cream," says Felix. I ignore him.

"If he loses it, you're the one he'll go for, Quin."

"So? I'm a big boy. Like I said, bring it on."

I don't understand why guys feel they need to act big, like they'll be judged for being anything other than fearless. "People will think it's weird if you start dating me. They'll say things."

"I don't care. They say things anyway."

Even if it's pretend, this screams bad idea. I'm reeling from Aaron cheating. Faking things with another guy — one I low-key flirted with, which he definitely picked up on — is going to smack home everything I thought I had and didn't. Quin's head is probably as much of a mess as mine at the moment. "Let's get out of here."

The fresh breeze outside is such a relief. As we cross the turnstiles at the end of the pier, Quin says, "It would take the power away from him. Get him scared for a change. This isn't me trying it on. I know you'd never be interested in someone like me. I won't touch you without permission. All I'm talking is a few posey photos. So we can nail this sicko."

Put that way, it's tempting. This is no longer about clearing Aaron's name. It's about me living my life unafraid — and justice for Jade. Doing nothing isn't an option.

But this shouldn't be a problem we have to solve ourselves.

Ten minutes later I'm inside the police station. Quin looked apprehensive when I asked if he'd come with me, but agreed to take Felix to a nearby cafe – I don't want Fe listening in on this.

The officer I speak to has a stain on his shirt and an unapproachable expression which makes me nervous. My suspicions sound so vague spoken out loud in this cool sterile room, like I've made everything up for attention.

"If you think you're being stalked, you need to keep a log," the officer says. "This leaflet has information and contact numbers."

Surely they're not going to palm me off with a leaflet. My heart sinks. "What about the bag, and the letter? Will you fingerprint those? I know officially Jade's case is closed, but…"

He gives me a brisk smile. "I'll pass that information on."

Disappointment trickles through me. Is this my life now? Freaking out on a daily basis. Feeling unsafe. Oliver offering to escort me places was sweet, but I'm so tired of being careful. Why should I be the one to change what I do, like I'm the problem?

When I enter the cafe, Felix is cosy on a sofa with Zora on his lap, and he and Quin are playing peekaboo and blowing raspberries at her. Two empty muffin wrappers are on the table in front of them.

Quin doesn't look surprised when I tell him what happened.

"They got their perp," he says. "Things that don't add up? They're not interested. Limited resources, other cases, all that crap. Sorry they can't help with the…" He glances at Felix. "Other thing."

I hesitate. Maybe Quin's idea to lure the stalker out isn't so bad. It could be our best shot at unmasking him. "What you said earlier…"

"Have a think as we walk home." Quin waves off my objection that my place is out of his way. "I want Zora to fall asleep in the pram. For all we know, he's watching. Wouldn't be much of a fake boyfriend if I left you stranded, would I?"

He smiles. Despite the heavy weight inside me, the side of my mouth twitches.

"Are you fake flirting with me?"

"Maybe."

We walk home in near silence. Dusk is creeping in, making familiar roads strange and shadowy. Wheelie bins sit on the pavements, ready for tomorrow's collection. Easy hiding places. I edge closer to Quin. Suddenly I'm glad Felix and I aren't alone. Something clatters and I jump.

"Jesus!"

"'S all right," says Quin. "Just kicked a bottle."

Is this me now, scared of random noises? As we near home, I decide I've had enough.

"Let's do it."

"Sure?" asks Quin.

I nod. "If it gets dangerous, we stop. We can meet later in the week, take photos then."

"After school you'll get me in chef's whites. But

maybe you like the idea of a fake boyfriend in uniform, I dunno."

I laugh. "Mmm. Maybe."

"Are you Mia's boyfriend?" asks Felix.

Quin says "yes" at the same time I say "no". There's an awkward pause. I roll my eyes at Quin, who mimes innocent whistling.

"He sort of is, Fe," I say. "No telling Mum and Dad, though."

Quin gives me a look.

"What?" I say. "If we really were dating I'd hide it from my parents."

"Cos I'm Psycho Quin?"

So he knows what we call him. "You've got a reputation. I'm being realistic."

Quin leans in and kisses the air by my cheek. "Bye, fake girlfriend."

Is he enjoying this? I rub my cheek where his lips were, watching him walk away.

His step is almost jaunty.

18

It feels bizarre to be back at school, like I was away a week, not a weekend. The call Quin overheard between Jade and her boyfriend plays on my mind: Jade saying it was impossible for her to concentrate knowing he was nearby. Each class I step into, each corridor I walk down, all I can think is *he's here*. Is he smiling about how "beautiful" my hair looks falling over my shoulder as I chew the tip of my biro, wishing I'd revised for this geography test? Does he believe my leaf print dress is a message for him, like the hair clips?

And for the first time in half a year, I'm not Aaron's girlfriend – I'm just Mia. I feel different. Not lesser, exactly – though I have lost some of myself in losing him – but more uncertain, like I don't quite know who I am. Everywhere I look are memories, like the time my new shoes were pinching and Aaron gave me a piggyback to lessons, pretending to be a horse. That feels tarnished and fake now.

After my last class, as I'm walking to our Quiz Challenge catch-up, my phone buzzes.

Unknown: you look stunning today

My skin prickles. I delete the text immediately. If only I could delete it from my head that easily.

"Hey, Mia. You OK?" Oliver catches up with me. "You look a bit…"

"I got another creepy message."

"From him?"

"Who else?"

Oliver glances round, as though expecting to see my stalker waving from down the corridor. It's an enormous effort not to bolt out of the nearest door.

"A hug would be nice," I mumble. Oliver puts his arms around me.

A cheery voice behind us says, "Nice to see some team bonding going on."

We jump apart. Mr Ellison grins. Today's tie is acid yellow with a pineapple print. "Bad joke, sorry. I come bearing pick-me-up coffees. Soya milk for you, Mia, of course."

He hands us cups from the cardboard drinks tray he's

carrying. Oliver pulls a face when he sips his; Mr E's forgotten that he's vegan, too. Hopefully this will be a short meeting so I can grab Leyla and explain the fake boyfriend plan. Call me paranoid, but I'd rather do it outside school.

"Good news," Oliver whispers as we follow Mr Ellison down the corridor. "My parents have agreed that I can have a birthday party."

"What? You turned seventeen months ago!"

He shrugs. "It's warm enough to host a party in the garden now. Mum didn't want the house getting trashed."

Typical Oliver's parents. Olly knows he comes low down their priority list. I feel anxious about a party – what if *he's* there? – but I keep that to myself and give Oliver a big smile instead.

Riyad is already seated in the sociology room, wearing his glasses, a pile of textbooks in front of him. I'm reminded of the old Riyad, before the spin the bottle kiss, who was actually fun to hang out with. He waves, as though our chat yesterday didn't happen, and I look away. Next to him is Kris Kowalski, looking sweaty and too nervous to monologue about gaming for a change.

Mr Ellison passes a packet of biscuits round and presents each of us with a booklet.

"So, A-Team," he says. "Battle commences on the Saturday after next, two o'clock, University of Brighton's theatre. I may or may not have pulled strings to get an afternoon slot, so you can sleep in, charge those turbo-powered brains."

Kris raises his hand. "Sir? Do I need to be there?"

"That is how being a reserve usually works…" Riyad deadpans.

Kris goes red. Mr Ellison rolls his eyes. "Sarcasm is the lowest form of wit, you know, Riyad. Who said that – anyone?"

"Oscar Wilde." Riyad bows his head at Kris. "Please accept my humblest apologies."

Mr Ellison groans. "I hope you're going to take the actual quiz seriously. Yes, Kris, you need to be there. The booklet has a filming consent form, so if you could get your parents to sign, that would be splendiferous. And a reminder that I'd like you to dress smartly."

Riyad groans. Mr Ellison stage-winks at me. Why is he acting as though we have some kind of shared joke? Smart isn't my thing either. Luckily Auntie Lou works for a fashion label and has offered to find something appropriate.

Oliver nudges me. On the booklet he's written, *Is it me, or is Ellison high today?*

Another time I'd doodle a kite in response, but this latte is sticking in my throat. I'd forgotten the quiz was going to be filmed. If I don't get my head into gear I'm going to totally embarrass myself.

After the meeting, we walk outside together, Mr Ellison swinging his car keys and shooting theories about who'll win a reality show none of us are watching. On the front steps I stop dead. Leaning on the wall opposite is Quin.

He straightens up when he sees me. "All right, Mia?"

Remembering what we agreed, I give him a quick hug.

"You never said you were going to show up here," I whisper.

"I finished early." Quin picks up a backpack from the tarmac, which must contain his chef's whites as he's in jeans and a jacket. The top underneath has a collar. He smells nice, too. "Up for taking them photos?"

Someone clears their throat.

"Is everything OK?" asks Oliver pointedly. Mr Ellison and Kris have disappeared, and Riyad is halfway across the car park, glancing back over his shoulder, eyes narrowed.

"This is what I wanted to speak to you about." Argh, why did Quin have to do this in front of Oliver? "Could you grab Ley from the library, and we'll go somewhere? Beach, maybe?"

Quin waits until Oliver's out of earshot. "You're telling your mates?"

"I won't lie to them," I say. "That's non-negotiable."

Quin shakes his head but doesn't argue.

The beach is lively this afternoon – amusement arcades pulsing, queues for ice creams and coffees growing by the minute, colourful bunting stretching between lamp posts, joggers and cyclists zipping along the parade. Without me noticing, spring has arrived. The four of us settle on the sand in a circle and I explain the plan. Oliver's eyes keep going to Quin, who leans nonchalantly back on his elbows.

"OK, this has escalated massively beyond Bag Man

being a creep," says Leyla. "Provoking this sicko is seriously dangerous, Mia. Was this his idea?"

She glares at Quin. He glares back. Ignoring her question, I touch Oliver's shoulder. "Olly? You've not said anything yet."

"What do you want me to say?" He doesn't look at me. "I agree with Ley. This is silly. We can protect you."

"I can't keep being a burden."

"Spending time with you is never a burden. How can you say that?"

I flinch. Oliver *never* raises his voice.

Leyla intervenes, asking if we can talk in private for a moment. She pulls me a few metres away to the beach huts.

"You can't do this, Mia," she says. "You don't need to be an Olly-level film nerd to know that fake dating is never a good idea – especially not when you're vulnerable."

My heart twinges. I'm more vulnerable than Leyla even realizes.

"What?" she says, narrowing her eyes.

I draw a deep breath. "Aaron cheated on me."

Leyla does a double take. "What? When—"

"With Brooke, the night we argued. He said so yesterday." I feel my eyes start to fill and blink the tears back. "I don't want to talk about it."

"Shit. I'm so sorry. Why didn't you tell me? I was hardly going to laugh and say I told you so!"

"Even though you were right?"

"I don't care about that." She throws her arms around me, and I relax. "You deserve so much better, Mimi."

"It's just so much, Ley," I whisper. "All of it."

"No shit. A month ago everything was normal." She draws back, squeezing my hand in hers. "This fake dating really isn't the answer, though – however good an idea distracting yourself might seem. Putting aside the fact that Quin's got serious issues, you look like Jade! How can he not be thinking of her when he's fake shoving his tongue down your throat? *Creepy*."

"We're not going to snog," I say. "It's photos only."

"I call bullshit. He's trying to get off with you."

"He isn't. He said so."

"Again, bullshit. And you were staring at his bum on the walk over. I'm scared you're on the rebound and you'll make a mistake. How do you know it's not him?"

"The stalker?" I give a start and drop Leyla's hand. She nods, unsmiling.

I glance towards Quin and Oliver, who are on their phones, ignoring each other.

"Not possible," I say. "The stalker is Jade's secret boyfriend."

"Who's to say that isn't him?"

"Eww, what? Quin wouldn't date his own stepsister."

"It'd explain why Jade kept her guy secret, wouldn't it? Maybe even why she was so bitter about her mum marrying Quin's dad."

I'm shaking my head before she's finished the sentence.

"The boyfriend sent Jade romantic messages. Quin's writing is … well, pretty basic. The texts I've received don't sound like him."

"Doesn't mean it isn't." Leyla's eyes are burning with growing intensity. "Maybe he can write better than he pretends. He could've faked that threatening note to make you trust him."

"But – but Quin was suspicious of Aaron from the start. And he's clearly grieving Jade—"

"He could've been setting Aaron up. Maybe guilt's why he's upset! For all we know, everything he's told you about Jade is a lie. Including that phone call he overheard, which apparently 'proves' the boyfriend goes to our school. What vibe did you get from Harper? How was she around Quin?"

"Uncomfortable," I admit. Leyla rakes a hand through her hair, looking anxious. Despite my words, my skin is prickling. I'm starting to doubt myself. So much of what I know about Jade has come from Quin.

"I have to do *something*, Leyla," I say. "I hate feeling like a victim, waiting for the next horrible thing to happen."

"Of course! I want you to be safe too. But the solution is not snogging Psycho Quin."

"We're not going to snog!"

"Tell him that. Actually, tell Olly that."

"What? What's Olly said?"

"Nothing. But I'm not blind. And neither are you."

The boys join us. Leyla looks at Oliver. "Fancy a walk

up the pier and back? Ten minutes should be enough for what Mia needs to do."

I grab Oliver's arm, but he pulls away.

"You can do what you want, Mia," he says. "Just so you know, the offer of walking you places still stands."

Leyla points V-sign fingers to her eyes, then at Quin, mouthing *I'll be watching*. My chest tightens as they leave.

"Crap."

Quin shrugs. "You were the one who decided to tell 'em."

"Well, you can't blame Ley for disliking you."

"Cos of what I did to Riyad? He deserved it."

I sigh. "Are we doing these photos or not?"

"For what it's worth, yeah."

"What's that supposed to mean?"

"Nothing," Quin says. "Only, if you're looking for someone with a hopeless crush on you, your mate over there fits the bill nicely."

I laugh at him. "Olly isn't my stalker!"

"How do you know that?"

"Because I do. Any … 'crush' is irrelevant. He's my *friend*."

"So? This nutjob could be anyone."

Including you, I think. Oliver and Leyla are halfway up the pier now. My heart starts to beat that bit faster. This is absurd. Completely out of order. I should bite Quin's head off for the very suggestion.

And yet… Oliver didn't react well to me fake-dating Quin. I trust him … but then I trusted Aaron, didn't I?

No. This is paranoia. Sick, horrible paranoia that my friend does not deserve.

"Let's get this over with," I mutter.

"All right," says Quin. "Tell me what to do. You're the expert."

Is that a dig at the loved-up selfies I used to post with Aaron? Quin's seen those. Is it creepy that he followed me online? *Argh*. I'm second-guessing everyone now.

I sit, motioning for Quin to join me on the sand, and lean in, angling my phone.

"You look pissed off," he says. "No one's gonna be fooled by this."

"You accused my friend. And you should've asked before showing up today."

I'm aware I sound like a spoilt child. Part of me wants Quin to get annoyed and abandon the whole plan.

Instead, he sighs. "I'm sorry. OK?"

"Leyla thinks this is a mistake."

"You can do things without her and fancy boy agreeing, Mia. They don't always know better."

His words strike a chord in me. He's got a point. My default is to believe Leyla and Oliver are right and I'm wrong, not only because they're my mates but because they get better grades than I do. Perhaps I've been too hung up on that. We won't be in school for ever. Quin's not academic and his life's nothing like mine, but that doesn't mean he's not worth listening to. Perhaps we all have different experiences to bring to the table, and our voices are equally valid.

Pretending to go out with someone for a week isn't a big deal.

"Put your arm around me," I tell Quin.

"You OK with that?"

I nod, shuffling closer. His arm settles across my shoulders. It feels weird to be held like this by a boy who isn't Aaron. His hands are criss-crossed with burns. One finger is plastered. This close, I can feel the rise and fall of his chest. It's rather quick. Do I make him nervous? I tilt my head so I can see him better. He smiles at me.

"Hi."

Despite everything, the corners of my mouth twitch. Using Quin's phone with its sharper camera, we try various poses – some serious, some jokey.

"Any good?" Quin asks, watching me scroll through his gallery. He hasn't moved his arm. I push away the strong urge to snuggle closer. One shot jumps out: spontaneous in feel, Quin's face part-hidden by my hair, me laughing.

"That's the one, yeah?" he says.

"Definitely." I give him a playful nudge. "You're more photogenic than expected."

"Cheers," Quin says dryly. "You're not bad yourself."

A WhatsApp pops up at the top of Quin's phone screen. I frown.

"Camille? I didn't know you were friends."

"We're not." Quin plucks his phone from my hand, swiping the message away. I remember Camille mentioning Quin in the library, and my surprise that they were in touch. She used to date Riyad. Why would she be on speaking terms with the guy who beat him up? My frown deepens as I remember Camille at the Electric, saying a guy had let her down, and offering to chat…

By the time Leyla and Oliver return we're sitting apart. Leyla huffs but says nothing. And this time it's me who won't meet Oliver's eyes, however hard he tries to catch mine.

Later that night, I'm in my room, clutching my phone. I've uploaded the picture. Reactions, seventy per cent shocked emojis and thirty per cent hearts, trickle in. I delete a *you desperate hun?!* and another comment that says *REBOUND ALERT*. I expected a reaction, but not this big. It's making me feel all hot and prickly, like I'm under a microscope. Tomorrow whispering and giggling will follow me around, like it did after Aaron was arrested. Oh God. What have I done? I didn't think this through – my judgement is all over the place.

There's no way *he* won't have seen this. I wonder if he's sitting there stewing, full of rage that another guy dares look my way when I'm supposed to be his.

I really hope I'm not playing with fire here.

Refresh. Two more likes. One is Camille. Might she have dirt on Riyad – dirt that might help me unearth what his game is?

I DM her.

Hey, I type. Can I ask something sensitive? It's about Riyad.

Camille takes a while to reply. Hi Mia. We didn't date for very long so I don't know if I can help. Saw your pic. Hope Quin makes you happy after Aaron! :)

Is she changing the subject? I wasn't expecting Camille to be cagey — she always seems so open. Perhaps she's decided offering to chat was a mistake.

Camille: I think he gave Aaron drugs, and I'm worried about the way he behaves around me. If there's anything you could tell me about him, that would really help.

I wait, tapping my fingers on the back of my phone. A moment passes.

Camille: Sorry, I don't want to talk about it.

And the chat falls dead.

Camille's guardedness rattles me. I go downstairs, fetch a drink and then refresh my post again. Another like: Aaron's sister. I can't believe Soph really likes this. Will she tell Aaron? What will he think? Nothing, probably. He doesn't care any more.

If I think about Aaron I'm going to spiral down an unhelpful rabbit hole. Instead I think about Quin. It felt good snuggled up earlier. In that photo it looks like he's kissing my head. I wonder what it would be like kissing him for real. Awkward? Hot? Unexpectedly romantic? How would it even work if Quin and I did date? Not well, probably. We're so different. I struggle to imagine us walking through town hand-in-hand or cuddling at the board game cafe. He's probably never picked up a manga.

Oliver has, though. Guilt wells up inside me. He's made it very clear he's there, without being pushy. That moment on the hospital bus, the call yesterday, all the check-up texts… It's almost started feeling like there's something between us. But I don't want to start something and risk hurting him unless I'm sure it's a good idea. And I'm not sure of anything right now – including who to trust.

There's an edgy, heavy atmosphere at school the next day. A couple of randomers ask if I'm really dating Psycho Quin then laugh like it's ridiculous. I get Leyla alone and ask if she's upset with me. She rolls her eyes.

"How many disagreements have we had in the eleven years we've been friends?" she asks. "I lost count ages ago. I still think this is dangerous, but I'm not going to be passive-aggressive about it. If Quin tries anything, he'll regret it. I don't know how yet, but he will."

Quin and I meet again after school, at The Green Leaf this time. We share one of their brownies, which of course he wants to know how to make. I keep looking at the photos after we say goodbye. You'd honestly assume we were together. How the camera lies. This time he kissed my cheek. Not a big deal, and it was my idea, but somehow it felt it.

As the week ticks on, there's no reaction from my stalker.

Have we made a mistake?

On Friday evening, I toy with asking Leyla over, but she has a hot date with her chemistry coursework. Oliver's probably free, but I'm not sure I want to see him alone. He rarely comes round mine anyway, I suspect because my quietly loved-up mum and dad make him feel awkward about his own parents' tension and arguments. I half-consider asking Quin before remembering he has evening service at his placement.

The doorbell rings. I freeze.

No one ever comes round in the evenings.

It's him.

No. He wouldn't be so obvious. But … if he's watching the house, he'll know that Dad's at a team-building day in London, and Mum's taken Felix to our grandparents'.

Breathe, Mia. You're being ridiculous. Even so, as I peer through the gap in the curtains, my heart is hammering. Whoever's on the doorstep is out of view – but a car is parked out front, its lights still on.

I edge downstairs, gripping the banister. I can see an unfamiliar outline through the glass. Opening up is a bad idea. But if it is him … I could find out who he is.

Am I brave enough?

I slide the safety chain on, count to three, then open the door.

Tori stands on the doorstep.

"Hi, Mia," she says. "I just had a phone call with Aaron. He wants you to have this."

She holds out one of Aaron's sketchpads.

I stare at it, then at her. "What?"

"I imagine it has something to do with these." Tori opens the cover. Hidden inside are two envelopes. "They fell out. I haven't looked."

A little stunned, I take them. Tori smiles sadly as she returns to the car. She must assume these are love letters. It's my kind of thing.

I race upstairs. Inside the first is a single A4 sheet.

it sickens me to see you with mia. she thinks she's in love with you because you sometimes say nice things and buy her cappuccinos (you don't even know she prefers lattes, what kind of boyfriend are you?) but you are not good enough. she deserves to be treated like a princess, by someone who'll treasure her. the only good thing you can do is to leave her. if you don't, i'll make you. you're nothing.

The second is even worse.

your mum is eating monkfish and talking about how much she wants to visit iceland. your dad enjoyed his medium rare steak but wishes there were more chips and he is annoyed because your mum said no to starters and he thinks they could do better than the mermaid inn for her birthday. his pet name for your mum is flower and he pulled out the chair for her before they sat down. your dad knows how to treat a lady, aaron, so i don't know why you don't.

their lovely evening will go downhill when they discover the tyres on their car are slashed. i could do a lot worse than that. maybe i will, soon. your mum walks home late from pilates on tuesdays. and your sister is careless about what she posts. i know all about where sophia goes and what she does. something might happen to her too.

i'm tired of you ignoring me. leave mia alone. it's very simple.

My hand flies to my mouth. These must be the letters that were bothering Aaron before Jade died!

I remember Aaron's parents' car tyres getting slashed — that happened during half-term. The pub car park didn't have CCTV so we assumed it was random vandalism. And

Aaron's sister – in January she fell down the stairs of her uni's bar. Soph was lucky not to be badly hurt. Aaron was scared her drink had been spiked, and wouldn't listen when I pointed out that Soph has a track record of boozy accidents. At the time I thought he was being cute and protective.

I never imagined he had good reason to be afraid.

I sink on to my bed, my legs shaky.

No wonder Aaron froze that time he spotted the letter in his rucksack – and no wonder he freaked out when we were photographed kissing. He knew exactly who was really watching. I bet there are tons of similar letters. Or were, rather – I'm guessing Aaron destroyed most of them. The two in this sketchbook must have somehow been missed when the police searched his belongings. Now I know why he acted so strangely – and why he didn't see Jade as the threat.

"If I care about people I protect them. No matter what." That's what he said in the YOI. He wasn't only talking about his mates.

A lump forms in my throat. Aaron kept these threats secret. He must have thought he could tough it out. That I was *worth* toughing it out for. He didn't dump me and take the easy way out, did he?

This is what he meant, the night we fought, when he said he'd stuck by me even when it would've been smarter to walk away. The "pressure" he was under.

Sending Tori round with these, too… He's still worried about me.

And yet he slept with Brooke. How can someone care so much and so little?

I lean against the wall. Presumably Aaron hasn't told the police about these letters – or, if he has, they've been dismissed as irrelevant.

My stalker's sicker than I thought. He must have stalked Aaron's family to know so much about them, right down to somehow hovering close enough to see their meal at The Mermaid Inn.

And this is the creep Quin and I have been baiting!

I sit very still, my pulse beginning to race.

This guy got to Aaron through his parents and sister.

Quin's not in danger. His family are. Specifically, his stepmum and Zora. He mentioned that his dad is in Belfast this week. Tonight Quin's not around either.

Shit.

I leap up and hit the phone icon next to Quin's name, tapping my foot as it rings. Voicemail. Crap. He must not be allowed his phone in the kitchen. I leave a message. Surely he'll take a break soon and see this.

What if he doesn't, though? I might be wrong about Demi and Zora being in danger. But if I wanted to make Quin pay, tonight's the night I'd do it. Finding out Quin's routine wouldn't be difficult. That's why my stalker's been so quiet!

Should I call the police? Will they even listen? I've zero proof.

There's another option, of course. Am I brave enough?

I try Quin's phone again. Nothing.

I've no choice.

I open the message chain with my stalker. An accusation isn't smart. If he's really angry it might encourage him. Better keep this simple, stall until Quin reads my messages.

Mia: Want to chat?

A minute passes.

Ping.

Unknown: of course my beautiful mia <3

I close my eyes in relief. He can't be doing something awful if he's texting me.

Mia: I saw the letters you sent Aaron. You slashed his parents' tyres.

Unknown: i didn't like spoiling his mum's birthday but i needed him to dump you

i did explain that we needed to be together

How the hell can he sound so reasonable about being utterly unreasonable?

Mia: You're lucky Aaron kept the letters secret. What about his sister falling? Did you spike her drink?

Unknown: no

but i could have done

aaron doesn't matter any more

you thought you were in love with him but you weren't really

It's like he can see into my head. Another message appears.

Unknown: just like you aren't in love with quin

Who *would* assume we were in love? This guy's nuts.
We've posted a couple of photos! At most you'd assume
we were dating.

Mia: You're right, I'm not

Unknown: :-)

i knew that already

but i like hearing you say it

Mia: So you don't need to scare him off

Unknown: oh i think i do

i don't like the way he looks at you

Mia: Leave him alone. Please. I'll tell him
to back off.

A pause. Then:

Unknown: i'm sorry beautiful mia but that
won't work

quin isn't good at doing what people tell him

i know a lot about quin you see

his family too

I check WhatsApp. Two grey ticks – Quin hasn't opened
my message. Come on! I don't know how much longer I
can do this.

I furiously type: Jade told you all about them,
didn't she? She really liked you. How could you
use her?

I add: I thought you were a romantic.

I mean to get under his skin and maybe I do, because
he goes silent. Then:

227

Unknown: i need to be with you mia
i can't control the way you make me feel
everything i do is for us
don't be angry with me about jade
aaron's the one who hurt her
Mia: You were there too. I know you were.
Unknown: let's talk about something else
i've been thinking about our perfect date
i can't decide if it would be cute and simple
like a secluded picnic under the blazing sunset
or splashy like a candlelit dinner where you
could wear a beautiful dress and a necklace i
brought you
you deserve to be romanced properly

This guy is a total fantasist. There's a sour taste in my
mouth now.

Admit it, you were there when Jade died, I type.

Another pause. This time, it stretches minutes. Then:

Unknown: demi is wearing a blue nightshirt
that says 'everybunny needs somebunny' on it
she made herself a hot drink then forgot
about it
between 6.01 and 6.15 she fell asleep on the
sofa while zora was on her play mat

Oh. God.

He's there. At Quin's house.

Right now.

Unknown: demi isn't a very good mother

zora is starting to crawl

she could easily have an accident

poor quin has already lost one sister

i would hate for something to happen to the other

My phone hits the carpet with a soft thump. For a second I feel faint. Then I grab it and dial 999.

20

"Police!" I shout when the operator asks which service I require. The second I'm transferred I blurt everything out. The person on the other end of the line stops me, asking where I'm calling from. I want to scream that this isn't important, that they need to get over to Wrabney, right now, but I do as I'm asked.

"Thank you," says the operator. "What's your emergency?"

"A guy who's been stalking me is threatening to hurt my friend's family. He's there now, watching them."

"Have you attempted to contact the people in the house?"

"I don't know their number."

"What's the address?"

I put the call on speaker, searching my WhatsApp chain with Quin. "Thirty West Road, Wrabney, Sussex."

"Is anyone injured?"

"Not yet."

"Are there weapons involved?"

Would he go that far? "I don't know."

"What's your name, address and phone number?" I tell her. "OK. I'll send somebody along."

I thank the operator and end the call, breathing heavily. Thank God. I was so afraid I wouldn't be taken seriously. I doubt the police will find anyone. He'll be off the second he sees flashing lights. At least they'll have a word with Demi and she'll be on her guard…

My stalker has a temper, though. When he doesn't get his own way he lashes out. What if he waits until the police leave and does something really wild?

Demi looked tiny in the picture I saw at Quin's house. She's sleep-deprived and battling grief. Will being on her guard be enough?

I call Quin again. Voicemail. I pace. I feel powerless – and guilty. Quin and I provoked this guy. I can't allow his family to be hurt because we made a bad call, I just can't.

Before I know it, my shoes are on and I'm out the door. Blood pounds in my ears as I sprint towards the nearby train station. If I'm lucky, there'll be taxis about to catch commuters – yes! A whole line of them. I yank open the door of the first, wheezing Quin's address. As we pull out it crosses my mind that this might be a really dangerous move. He doesn't know I'm coming, though. For once I know exactly where my stalker is, and that he's not watching me.

My phone buzzes: Quin.

"How sure are you that he's spying on Demi?" he demands.

"One hundred per cent," I gasp. "I've called the police, but I'm still scared. I'm going there now."

"I'm coming. Screw service."

"How close are you?"

"Half an hour away."

Something hoots on Quin's end of the line. An owl? This restaurant must be one of those village gastropubs, and he's round the back of the kitchen. Quin rings off. Five minutes later and I'm cobbling together the taxi fare from the coins in my purse, a quid short, which earns me an earful from the driver.

I creep from where I've been dropped off towards Number Thirty, thankful for the darkness. The road is very, very quiet. If the police have already been, they were quick. I inch around the side of the house and crouch behind the hedge. From here, I can see the dirt lane that leads to the nature reserve. Inside Quin's house there's a flickering glow in the front room. The TV? None of the other lights in the house are on.

TV.

My stalker said Demi was watching TV.

When I was at Quin's, he spied on us through the French windows. Foolishly – very foolishly – I assumed he was doing the same tonight.

But there isn't a TV in the kitchen.

He's watching from the front.

He can see me.

In slow motion, I turn around. Parked a couple of metres away is a dark car. At the wheel sits a shady figure.

Him.

The engine roars. Full beam headlights flood the road, blinding me.

For the briefest moment, I'm paralysed by searing fear. Then I bolt, down the track, over the stile and into the blackness of the nature reserve.

He didn't find me when I ran before. I've had a head start. If I can find somewhere to hide, or keep running, parallel to the backs of the houses—

My soles skid on pebbles. I lose my footing and fall. Pain explodes from my shoulder, then the back of my head. Everything goes black.

21

Something strokes my hair. Dotty, nuzzling me? I force my eyes open. Everything's dark. After a disorientated moment, I realize there's fabric obstructing my vision. Pebbles dig into my back. My shirt feels thin against cold air.

Why am I outside? Where's my coat? Am I blindfolded? I let out a low moan. The stroking stops.

Oh.

The thing in my hair is a *hand*.

Everything rushes back. Headlights. Running. Falling.

I sit up. Pain shoots up my left side and I cry out. A hand clasps mine. I pull away, snatching at the blindfold, but my stalker grabs my wrists. We grapple for a second before my injured arm gives out. He eases me back down. Convinced I'm going to die, I thrash about. My toes connect with something soft and there's a muffled exclamation. I kick harder. He – it's definitely a he – snarls. The next second his weight is on top of me. I wriggle, but his legs press my sides, pinning me down. He's strong. Too strong to fight.

Cold fingers brush my throat. They ease my top button loose before moving to the next. I go still.

Am I going to be raped?

My bad arm is free, but useless. I whimper as the shirt falls open. I hear his breath catch. His fingers trail across my stomach. His touch is light but it sends a horrible crawling sensation across my skin – *no, no, no.* I squirm as panic rises in my gut. He's not going to let me go. I can't fight this, fight *him*.

I squeeze my eyes shut under the blindfold, expecting his hands to move downwards. Instead, he undoes the button on my cuff. With great care, he manoeuvres the sleeve from my bad arm, then something wet and stinging presses against my skin. I catch a whiff of disinfectant.

He's … helping me?

I find my voice. "Am I badly hurt?"

No reply. From somewhere far away comes heavy trundling. A truck? Am I still at the nature reserve? Will anyone hear if I shout?

I try again. "Do I need to go to hospital?"

Nothing. He finishes cleaning the cut, then applies what feels like cotton wool and surgical tape. The back of my head throbs.

"I'm cold," I rasp. "I want my shirt on."

Arms snake round me, pulling my trembling body against his. Lips brush the tip of my ear, breath warm on my neck. I hear him inhale, as though my tea tree shampoo bar is the sweetest smell in the world.

Push him away. Fight. Scream. But my body won't move. I sit as limp as a doll while he strokes my hair tenderly.

After an age he pulls back. He slips my arm back into the sleeve and carefully buttons up my shirt. He helps me into my coat and to my feet, but I'm shaking so much I can barely stand. It feels like I've been deboned. Arm round my waist, he half-hoists, half-drags me along the path. Somehow he gets me over the stile. Hope soars inside me – *we're at the end of Quin's road, which means people, help* – then dies as I hear the click of a car unlocking. He's pulled right up, away from the road.

I try to resist as he settles me in the passenger seat, but my body still doesn't have any strength in it. He tugs the seat belt, checking it's secure. Is the gap at the bottom of the blindfold a little bigger now? Maybe if I can nudge it upwards unnoticed, I'll catch a glimpse of him. He'll be driving, his eyes on the road.

"Where are you taking me?"

A voice – his voice – says, "I'm trusting you not to take the blindfold off. Do you promise?"

His intonation is all wrong, the pitch gruff, with what sounds like a faked American accent. He's disguising his voice. Even so, it's familiar… If only I could think through the heavy fog in my head! I whisper a yes. The ignition roars and we bump slowly away. I'm itching to shift the blindfold but resist, my heart hammering. A gravelly male voice croons out of the speakers. Some love song – I can't place the artist. The car's movement feels smoother than it did moments ago. We haven't slowed for lights or junctions. We must be on the heath road heading back to Southaven. If I can hold my nerve until the end of this song and the next, we'll be at the edge of town. If I can somehow escape I can raise the alarm…

A third song begins. The car slows, indicator ticking. I'm tempted to rip off the blindfold, but he could hurt me. Kill me, even. *No. Be cautious.* I raise my hand, as though pressing my palm to my head. My fingers tremble as I tweak the blindfold. A strip of vision opens up. A dark hoodie. Jeans. Cap. Something over his face—

His head snaps round. I jerk the blindfold down but too late. *Screech.* He slams on the brakes. I'm thrown forward, my face almost whacking the glove compartment. His hand smacks my shoulder, right over the wound. Pain explodes like a firework. I cry out and double over, sucking in my breath. Seconds later he's outside the passenger door, unclicking the belt, pulling me from my seat and hurling me into the night. My knees and palms smack wet grass. I roll on to my side in agony.

An engine roars, and he's gone.

It takes a while to steady my breathing, both adrenaline and relief coursing through me. Blindfold discarded, I see that the front garden he pushed me into is a couple of roads from Leyla's – the route home from Wrabney. Was he really taking me home, or were we heading somewhere else?

Phone. I need to call for help, and check Demi and Zora are OK. I grope around, but either I dropped my bag in the nature reserve or he has it.

Cradling my throbbing arm, I clamber up and stagger away.

Leyla opens the front door, barefoot and wearing PJs. Her eyes widen when she sees me.

"Mia! What happened?"

A telly blares from the sitting room – that cooking show that Ley's parents love. And then I freeze. I'm so used to seeing Leyla's house as safe that I didn't think…

"Where's Riyad?" I whisper urgently. "He's not here, is he? Please tell me he's not here."

"He's out. Mia, you're scaring me."

I look over my shoulder to the driveway. Leyla's parents' car, the one Riyad uses, is gone. Was he the one leaning over me?

"I don't think I should come in," I mumble, backing away. Leyla catches my good arm.

"I'm not letting you walk off like this. Come inside. I'll get Mum and Dad – they can help."

"No. I don't want your parents involved." If Mr and Mrs Kazem see me this way, I won't be able to hold back blurting out that their son could be responsible for it.

Leyla gives me a hard look then guides me inside, whispering that she'll be right with me.

In Leyla's room, I catch sight of myself in her mirror. I look like I've emerged from the apocalypse – dirty face, wild hair, laddered tights. Under my jacket a red "O" of blood covers my arm and shoulder. I start unbuttoning my shirt before nausea envelops me. His cold fingers, working downwards, lips on my ear...

The reality of what happened hits me and I sink heavily on to Leyla's bed. By the time she returns with painkillers, water and clean clothes, I'm trembling. She has to hold the glass to my lips so I can swallow, and help me change. Tears of pain trickle down my cheeks as she peels off my top. Underneath the bandage a layer of skin the size of a bottle cap is missing. The cotton pad is soaked.

"Tell me everything," Leyla says.

Her expression shifts from fearful to deadly serious as I describe my evening. Somehow, I can't make eye contact, so instead I focus on her pin board. The photo booth reel of us pulling faces on GCSE results day peeps out from under a revision timetable. We look so carefree.

"OK," Leyla says. "You're going to the police again. No arguing. They'll have to help. Your stalker basically kidnapped you!"

I hug my knees to my chest with my good arm, relieved I've managed to stop shaking and that the T-shirt Leyla gave me to wear is soft and clean. "I'm scared of telling Mum and Dad. They'll be so ... ashamed."

"Erm, why?"

"Because … I must have done something to make this happen. He seems to believe I love him. Mum thinks I'm silly around boys. She'll blame me, say I gave him ideas, that this wouldn't have happened if I was more sensible…"

"Your mum will not say that. This isn't your fault, Mimi!"

Why does it feel like it is? "I'll do it tomorrow. Tonight, I'm too… I can't."

"But you promise you will? I can come with you."

"I promise."

"Did you notice anything about him? Like, skin or hair or eye colour, or any stubble, or…?"

I bite my lip, trying to remember. "It was dark and I only saw him for a split second. He was hiding his face. I suppose he was slim build, or average, I guess? I knew his voice, I think, but he was disguising it. Honestly… All I could focus on was fear."

Leyla picks up her phone, saying she wants to look up stalking. I lean back, a little more comfortable now the painkillers are kicking in. It's quiet tonight. Normally Riyad's crappy music thumps from the other side of the wall – he and Leyla share the top floor extension and a bathroom.

I wonder where he is. Driving around, in a rage? Or somewhere totally innocent? I'm hopeless with cars but my stalker's is a dark colour, mid-sized. Riyad's fits that description. It could be him. It really could be. I rejected him at Peyton Fletcher's party, didn't I? Didn't Tori say what a big deal rejection can be for guys? That kiss years ago could have been the start of something twisted…

I stifle a sob. I wish my stalker was an outsider, from a town far away. We all get lectured about stranger danger. Yet the person whose lips brushed my ear tonight is someone I know. Someone I've partnered with at school, or shared a joke with. Even someone I like. Someone who seems normal.

That's far more chilling than a stranger in the dark.

Leyla inflates the air-bed on her floor, telling me I can stay over. I call home on her mobile. Mum sounds suspicious but calms down when Leyla gets her mum on the line to confirm I'm actually here. Leyla's patched me up enough for it to not be obvious I'm hurt. I want to hug her for thinking of everything, as usual, but the thought of pressing my body against another person's, even Leyla's, makes me queasy. Instead I crawl under the covers. Leyla gets ready for bed, then turns off the light. I insist on us locking her bedroom door.

I try to concentrate on the soft tick of the clock or buzz from the bathroom fan. My mind's having none of it. It propels me back to the nature reserve: blind, wobbly and helpless. His weight presses against me, and his nose is there, inhaling.

You have such beautiful long hair.

How will I ever sleep if every time I close my eyes I feel his presence?

Something buzzes at the back of my brain. Something to do with how he half-dragged me into the car. It feels important. If only I was sharper!

Leyla's breathing is hushed and regular. I shift on to my good side but anxiety is making me sweat. Quietly, I rise, unlock the door and slip into the bathroom.

As I splash cool water on my face there's a sound downstairs. My hands freeze under the running tap. Creaking. Footsteps creeping upstairs. It can only be Riyad.

Oh God. Do something, Mia. Run back to Ley's room.

Yet for the second time tonight I can't make my body move. In the mirror over the sink I see the back of his head come into view, then his shoulders. He turns at the top of the stairs. He sees me and stops.

Riyad's hair is mussed, eyes tired, expression stony. He looks me up and down, head tilting. My bare legs and arms break out in goose pimples. Leyla's T-shirt feels like no protection at all.

"Mia," he says.

My legs come back to life. I bolt into Leyla's room, lock the door and slide down it, curling into a ball. I stay there long after Riyad's bedroom door closes, my eyes squeezed shut.

I can't stay here.

I find my shoes, tuck Leyla's T-shirt into my skirt and tiptoe downstairs, taking my coat from the banister. The Kazems have a little blackboard by the front door. I scribble a note to say I've gone. Then I step outside, closing the door behind me.

Leyla's road is still, lit by the dull gleam of the street lights. Trees and hedges and bins cast contorted shadows across the pavement.

Something bursts from the hedge. I jump backwards but it's only a fox. Of course it is. The streets of two a.m. belong to them. All normal people are tucked up under duvets, asleep.

I wonder if he is too, and if he's dreaming about me.

Like a drunk I stumble along, my arms and legs leaden. Then, as if by magic, I'm home.

It's only as I raise the clasp on the gate that I remember: no keys.

Then I see my bag, waiting on the doorstep.

I wheel round, expecting to see him over the road, watching. He isn't. Even stalkers need their sleep.

I fumble inside my bag. Phone, purse, manga – nothing is missing. It takes several attempts to slide my key in the lock.

Inside, warmth and familiar clutter envelop me. Dotty races down the stairs, eyes shining huge in the darkness. I cuddle her so tightly she mews in protest.

"Sorry, baby," I whisper, letting her down. I'm not sure my legs will get me all the way upstairs so I crash on the sofa. I turn on my phone.

"Oh my God."

My home screen wallpaper should be Dotty. Instead, it's an image of a picnic blanket and hamper underneath a blazing sunset, two plates and glasses ready and waiting.

My stalker's perfect date.

He knows my pass code. He's been in my phone.

All my private messages, apps, photos. Violated.

I tap the gallery icon. Immediately I see fewer photos. Every single shot with Aaron in it has gone. So have our WhatsApps and emails. On Instagram it's like I never had a boyfriend.

Six months of my life, an entire person, wiped.

Maybe one day I'd have deleted Aaron, but that would have been my choice. Not *his*. I feel naked, vulnerable. Invaded.

Leyla can say it's not my fault, but this guy *can't* have developed such strong feelings over nothing.

Again I feel his face in my hair, inhaling me. How could I have ever believed Jade was the threat? Poor Jade didn't deserve to be used as a pawn in someone else's sick love story. If there was no stalker, no Mia, she'd still be alive.

I picture the garden fence that wouldn't be so hard to climb over if he wanted to come right up to the sitting room window, to drink me in. This is my life now. Being watched. Being preyed upon. Being scared.

You have such beautiful long hair.

My lip trembles.

Half in a trance, I go to the kitchen and pluck the scissors from where they hang by the hobs. Moonlight pours through the skylight, glinting on the shiny blades.

I gather my hair in one hand, raise the scissors in the other.

Snip.

22

"Mia!"

I rocket upwards out of my slumber. For a moment I can't place where I am, what the hysterical voice that woke me is saying, why I'm wearing my coat. Then everything snaps into focus. I'm on the lounge sofa; Mum's at the door, face wild. She waves a rope of hair.

My hair.

"What have you done?" Mum's voice is so shrill it could shatter glass. "I thought you stayed at Leyla's?"

Last night comes thundering back. My hand flies to my head. "Does it look awful?"

"Worse than awful! You look like a Charles Dickens urchin. Your beautiful long hair! Why, love, why?"

"I didn't want to have beautiful long hair any more." I burst into tears. Mum's expression changes. She sits next to me on the sofa, unzipping my coat. I hear a sharp intake of breath.

"You're hurt."

I'm crying too hard to explain. Mum inspects my wound. It doesn't look as bad as it did last night, although my entire left side aches. Dad and Felix arrive in their pyjamas. Everything spills out in a choky, incoherent mess — that Jade's boyfriend has been stalking me, that he's obsessed, that he all but kidnapped me. I skip over the details of how Quin and I have been investigating — it's too complex for now. The relief I feel to have everything out in the open crushes any sense of shame. Why have I put this off so long?

As the seriousness of it all sinks in, Dad's expression becomes guarded. Mum is shaking her head, repeating over and over that Aaron is on remand, as though Jade's murder is the only bad thing her brain has space for. Felix is in the kitchen watching something on Mum's tablet, but he keeps glancing up, sensing that something isn't right.

"Why would this man stalk you?" Mum whispers. "You're an ordinary girl. Stalking happens to actresses, or models."

She's wrong. Stalking can happen to anyone.

"And now you know I messed up watching Felix," I sob.

Mum puts her arm around me. She's trembling. "Oh, Mia, you should have told us all this straight away. Forgetting to watch Felix wasn't a good enough reason to keep this hidden – we can talk about that another time, when you're less upset."

Dad grabs a notebook from the coffee table, adjusting his glasses the way he does on work calls. He asks me to go through everything again. His notes cover four whole sides. By the time Dad lays down the biro, he's gone the colour of putty. So has Mum.

"I think," says Dad, "that we'd better ring the police."

It's midday by the time an officer arrives. He's young, a little twitchy. Thank God for Dad's notes, because a third time round I'm struggling to explain and distracted by the burnt smell of the leek and potato soup that Mum somehow managed to prep, then forgot. The officer listens, asks questions, then breaks the news that even though things have escalated, there's not a lot the police can do.

"Like my colleague explained the other day, you must make a note of every time you think you're being watched, or followed, and screenshot any texts," he says. "The more information we have, the more likely it is we can find this person. Then we can have a word."

"Is that it?" demands Mum. She and Dad are holding hands, as though drawing strength from each other. "My daughter's in danger! A girl who looked exactly like Mia died not long ago. This monster groomed her. Doesn't that mean anything?"

The officer is tight-lipped about any connection to Jade's death, repeating several times that it'll be looked into.

"I appreciate this is a stressful situation, but at the moment, the most helpful thing Mia can do is keep a log and report anything suspicious."

"A log isn't going to keep Mia safe. And what about these?" Mum waves Aaron's letters. "They're threatening!"

"We'll look into this, I promise. For now, Mia will have to be very careful."

"That won't stop him." Everyone looks at me, surprised, as though they'd forgotten I could speak. "This guy dated Jade. Her stepbrother overheard them talking, and he clearly goes to my school. He's there, every day. He's been all over my phone. He knows where I go, where my friends live. Everything. Why is it on me to be careful, while he does as he pleases? Stalks and scares me as he pleases, even?"

Afraid I'm going to cry again, I lean forward, put my head between my legs. Am I concussed? This morning feels all blurry round the edges. Dad shows the officer out. The sofa dips as Mum sits next to me.

"You should rescue the soup," I mumble.

"I've lost my appetite."

"Sorry I've ruined things for you."

"What things? Soup? Don't be silly."

"I have, though. You and Dad hate fuss."

"Mia, please— Yes, your dad and I are finding this tough. We're anxious and stressed, but only because we love you, and want you safe! I wish you had told us sooner."

"Mum..." The words stick in my mouth. "Do you think I brought this on myself?"

"What? No!"

"Be honest. I know you think I'm a flirt. I've heard you say so to Auntie Lou. You didn't like me having a boyfriend at first. You gave me that talk about how to behave, and dress, and how I shouldn't be in a rush to … you know. You called my clothes 'attention seeking'."

She groans. "Oh, Mia… You're so young still, that's all. Friends and school are far more important than boys … and the world isn't a safe place for girls. All I want is to protect you. I was worried about teen pregnancy, stuff like that. But of course this isn't your fault! Boys aren't entitled to stalk girls, even if there has been a bit of flirting."

"Then you do think I've encouraged it."

"I didn't say that—"

"You did! You implied this happened because I flirted with him, and I haven't."

"All I meant was, you're a kind and friendly girl who presents herself nicely, and boys get ideas…"

And there she goes again. "So I should be unkind and unfriendly, just in case someone turns stalker?"

"Of course not. I'm sorry, sweetheart. I'm using all the wrong words. I know you're not to blame… I'm trying to understand how this has happened, that's all. There must be a trigger."

Maybe there isn't. Maybe he's a psychopath. He thinks I wore hair clips to send him a secret message. I slump back on the cushions.

"If I made you feel like you had to keep this to

yourself" – Mum's voice wobbles – "then I'm the one who should feel ashamed. I'm sorry."

"I just wanted to be good enough," I choke. "Sometimes it feels like everything I do is wrong."

She hugs me tightly. "We'll get through this, darling, I promise. This man isn't superhuman. We'll find out who he is."

He feels pretty superhuman. Mum glances at my hair, lying on the coffee table.

"I'll get you a hairdressing appointment. You can't go to school like this."

At the word school, my belly flip-flops. *He's* there. "Can't I stay home?"

"In an empty house?" Mum says gently. "Dad and I will be at work. You'll be safer around people. We can sort something out so you aren't walking between school and home alone."

I still feel sick. Everyone laughing at how awful I look will destroy me. I didn't even cut straight – it's shoulder length on my left side and only just tucks behind my ears on my right. I google how to donate my hair. If someone gets a wig out of this that's a tiny silver lining.

At lunch I manage only four spoonfuls of soup. As we're clearing up, the doorbell rings. Mum answers and I hear Leyla's voice asking how I am. I stick my head out of the kitchen door.

"I'm sorry I vanished on you, Ley— Oh."

With Leyla is Oliver, dressed in the usher's uniform

we take the mick out of — crimson waistcoat with shiny gold buttons, bow tie, the kind of stiff trousers that make a funny shape when you sit down. He's pale, fidgeting with the button on his cuff. "Mia!" he says when he spots me. "Are you OK? Ley told me everything."

"We're here to set up a council of war," says Leyla. "Olly and I figure if we put our heads together we must be able to work out who this sicko could be. Would've been here earlier but this one" — she elbows Oliver — "insisted on being extra and buying you cake, and we missed the bus."

"Just wanted to cheer you up," mumbles Oliver, colouring. The paper bag in his hand no doubt contains Green Leaf brownies. Ley was joking but she's right. Oliver is extra. He's always buying little presents. I'd dismissed it as insecurity — if I'd been bullied, I'd be grateful for friends who weren't my dog, too — but maybe it's suspicious.

Mum doesn't notice I've frozen. "Talk to your friends, love. I'll clear up."

Bile rises in my throat. "Don't you need to get to the Electric?"

Oliver blinks. "Me? Not yet."

Rather unwillingly, I take them to my room, pulling the bobble hat I've been wearing all morning lower around my ears. Oliver hesitates at the doorway. Suddenly I'm very aware that he's a boy, and there's a heap of dirty clothes on the floor including — cringe — pants and bras.

We settle down, me and Leyla on the bed, Oliver on

the beanbag. Dotty's claimed my desk chair. Before we can start, Dad sticks his head through the door.

"Sorry to interrupt, but there's a boy on the doorstep who says he needs to see you. Eyebrow piercing. Seems agitated. Is this someone you know, or…?"

Dad's voice is heavy with suspicion. Feeling fragile isn't a good enough reason to turn Quin away, so I tell Dad he's a friend and to send him up. Dad doesn't look too happy but does as I say. Quin appears a minute later.

I speak before he can. "Are Demi and Zora OK?"

"Fine. Police checked everything out. No one around." Quin hesitates, glancing at Leyla and Oliver before locking eyes on me. "I did ring you, last night. There something wrong with your phone, or are you blanking me?"

For the fourth time today, I run through what happened. Quin looks angry, then, maybe clocking that going apeshit isn't helpful, shuts his mouth.

"… and if you want to join the council of war, be my guest." I'm sort of hoping he'll go, but he shoves the dirty clothes to one side and sits on the floor, holding out his hand for Dotty to say hello. For a moment the only sound is her rhythmic purr.

Oliver clears his throat. "Mia … what's the hat for?"

I mentally count to ten. Off comes the hat. All three go wide-eyed.

Leyla recovers first. "Oh, shit!"

Oliver's staring. When he realizes, he gives himself a shake. "Sorry! Bit shocked. It's…"

"Awful?" I whisper. "I just grabbed the kitchen scissors – cut it off in a daze…"

"I'm going to kill this bastard!" cries Leyla. "Even when we were kids you could sit on your hair. It's your identity, your … everything."

"I think you look punk," says Quin. "It's cool."

My cheeks flood with colour. "Liar."

"I mean it. Hot look. You should dye it too. Look even more punk."

Oh God, that little smile. "Can we stop talking about it, please?"

"Then let's kick off the council of war." We all look Leyla's way. She takes a deep breath. "I wasn't going to tell you this, Mia, but I think you should know. It's about Mr Ellison. Remember the test he set to select the Quiz Challenge team?"

My mind flies back to January, and the half-hour general knowledge paper we sat after school. I still can't believe I made the team. "What about it?"

"I overheard Mr Ellison chatting to Miss Dawson the next day while I was on library duty. When he said he'd chosen you, she was surprised. Said you weren't the academic type."

I wince at the same time Leyla does.

"Ugh, too blunt," she says. "Story of my life. Sorry. Mr E laughed and said being academic wasn't everything. Told her that actually Peyton and Erikah had done best, but he wanted to give you a chance. The way he was smiling … I don't know how to describe it."

"Why didn't you say?"

"I didn't want to knock your confidence. I knew how much the quiz mattered." Leyla tries a smile. "Not that you need to prove you're smart, not to us, anyway. It never occurred to me until now that Mr E was being anything other than kind."

I open my mouth to ask what she means. Then I picture Mr E protecting me with his umbrella outside the Electric, saying I had a lot going for me. Inviting me to go to him rather than the school counsellor. The dairy-free biscuits and lattes. Those coincidentally overheard conversations…

"You think … Mr E is the stalker?" I say.

"I'm not saying he is," says Leyla. "Just, he's a person of interest."

"This isn't a cop show! He… He can't be. No. Without make-up I look about twelve… Him putting me on the team doesn't mean, you know. *That*."

"What does it mean then?" demands Quin.

"I don't know." I feel small. "Maybe he's just really nice."

"Yeah, well, he would be nice. That's what grooming is, innit. He knows how to get people to like him."

I shift, feeling uncomfortable. "I guess the boyfriend being a teacher would be a reason for Jade to keep the relationship secret."

"How old's Ellison?" asks Quin.

"Young."

"Fit?"

I swallow. "Kind of, yeah. Would Jade really date a

teacher, though? She was only fifteen, Quin."

"Last summer we visited my grandparents in Belfast. It pissed it down all month. Not Jade's idea of a holiday. Spent most of it hanging out with my cousin and his uni mates. They gave her loads of attention. She loved it. Didn't care that they were older. Ellison? No different."

This conversation is sucking the oxygen from the room. I want them to be wrong. This is my form tutor, my teacher, a man I trust. But I can see the logic. Harper said the secret boyfriend was *mature*. The receipt I found in Jade's cardigan is from a town near where Mr Ellison lives. I've seen him parking a car. It's black, I think, about the same size as the stalker's. He covers GCSE geography as well as sociology. Although…

"Quin, did Jade take GCSE geography?"

Quin shakes his head.

"He didn't teach her, then," I say. "Would he even have known she existed?"

We fall silent. Then Oliver says, "He's helping with the new school prospectus, isn't he? I picked up the school camera from him once and he was telling me about dipping into main-school classes and societies."

"Jade did try out dance club for a couple of weeks," says Quin.

Perhaps that's the link. "Can we look at the school camera?" I ask Oliver. "On the off chance there's a clue…"

"I'll get hold of it ASAP."

My sick feeling returns. God. How on earth am I going

to be able to look Mr Ellison in the eye on Monday?

"What about you-know-who?" asks Quin.

I think of last night, and how I froze when I heard Riyad's footsteps on the stairs. "Stop it."

Leyla shoots Quin a dirty look. "What are we, five years old? I do know who you're talking about. Discuss Riyad if you want. *I* know he couldn't have done this. If my brother likes girls, he hits on them."

"What about girls he's already hit on, who said no?" Quin fires back.

Leyla rolls her eyes at him. Oliver shoots a glance at Ley, then says, "Riyad does watch you an awful lot in Quiz Challenge meetings, Mia. Not to cast shade, but … he does."

I give a start. "What? Really?"

"Yep. I've noticed."

"I bet you have," says Quin.

"What's that supposed to mean?" Oliver snaps.

"Nothing." Quin smiles, but this time it's not entirely nice. "I hate thinking about Riyad with Jade, but it could be him. He's a total dickhead."

If Riyad did secretly date Jade, perhaps Quin's the reason they kept it secret. He'd have been furious!

There's a knock at the door. This time it's Mum. "Mia, Ivy's offered to tidy up your hair first thing on Monday. I know she never finished her hairdressing course, but I thought you'd be more comfortable with her than a salon? It'll mean missing your first lesson, though."

Mum really must feel sorry for me if she's proposing

missing school. I say yes and Mum leaves.

Oliver sighs. "Speaking of Ivy, I do need to get to the Electric now. Camille's got a bug so we're short-staffed. Unless you want me to stay? I will if you need me. Ivy can manage somehow."

I shake my head. "Don't lose your job. Go."

"I should be done by eight." He looks at me. "We could finally stream *Sunset Boulevard* together, maybe? Or something naff and take the mick out of it?"

Like we did in normal times, before I started suspecting everyone. I make a noise that could mean yes or no. There's silence after Oliver leaves. Quin fidgets, glancing at Leyla, who's glaring at him.

"I should go too," he says.

"You don't have to," I say.

Quin mumbles about prepping a family dinner. The tops of his ears have reddened. Was he hoping to get me alone?

When he's gone, Leyla says, "Do you think Riyad did this, Mia?" Her voice is low, not combative. Is she having doubts? "What Quin said about Riyad hitting on you … he was talking about Peyton's party, right? But that was nothing."

I downplayed it to Leyla at the time. "I don't know, Ley."

Leyla shifts. "I'm not denying my brother can be an arrogant douche, but he's a good guy really. You know what my dad's side of the family is like. They don't approve of anything I do. Not just the maybe liking girls thing, but all my choices. Riyad always says the right thing to get them off my back."

Being nice to Leyla doesn't mean Riyad's nice to everyone. People are complicated, with many layers, some contradictory. When I don't reply, Leyla says, "Watch yourself with Quin, Mia – however much you like him. We can't be sure it's not him. He could've been pointing the finger at Ri there to throw you off the scent."

So much for this council of war. There's no evidence. Just paranoia, maybes and he-was- looking-at-you-funnies.

Problem is, when you're scared every little thing takes on a dark slant.

You even start to doubt your friends.

23

On Monday at school I visualize myself as a horse with blinkers, shielded from all the whispers and nudges. Ivy kept my hair asymmetrical, but now it looks neat and intentional instead of nightmarish. She was way too chirpy for nine in the morning, which maybe had something to do with the pair of boxers I noticed under her sofa. Good for her, moving on from the evil ex. But I still don't feel like myself.

It doesn't help that Mr Ellison does a double take when he strides into class, and exclaims, "Whoa, Mia. What a change. Everything all right?" He keeps glancing my way. Even though going short wasn't entirely my choice, it needles me that everyone sees girls cutting their hair as the sign of some kind of breakdown.

My phone sits in my bag. I've blocked my stalker's number, but once he figures that out he'll no doubt buy a burner. Is he fuming that I've cut my hair? Or is he enjoying the power his words had over me?

I start to sweat.

What will he do next?

By the time we hit half three I'm desperate to escape. Outside school a familiar figure is waiting. Quin gestures towards the road. "Wanna get out of here?"

I nod, hurrying out of the gates. A couple of year ten boys snigger as I pass.

"What're you looking at?" Quin demands, and they scuttle off.

We head in the direction of the town centre – I'm walking quickly to put distance between myself and school. The tight feeling in my chest eases a touch as we hit the high street.

"Feeling better?" asks Quin.

"Not much," I say. "What if I've pissed him off? The way he was with my hair… He'll be angry. What if he…"

"What?"

"Does something." Maybe he won't go for me. Maybe it'll be Felix. He took him easily enough at the park. That's his MO, getting to people through their families…

Hands settle on my shoulders.

"You having a panic attack?" asks Quin.

Am I? I feel funny and floaty and tight. My lungs feel like they're collapsing in on themselves, all the breath squeezing out, and my heart, oh my God, my heart is pounding...

"He's watching," I gasp. "I know it."

Quin glances round. "I don't see anyone."

"He's always there. Oh God."

Quin steers me to a nearby bench. I sink on to it, the cold metal bars pressing into the backs of my thighs. Quin squats in front of me, close enough to block out everything else.

"Concentrate on your breathing," he says. "Breathe in, count to five, blow out, then repeat."

"I can't."

"Yeah, you can. I'm here. This is gonna pass."

I screw up my eyes and take a deep, shaky breath. How many times I go through the process I don't know, but after a while, my pulse slows. The world comes back into focus.

Quin smiles at me. "Better?"

"Better."

"They taught me to do that in therapy, to manage my anger. So. Talk to me. What's upsetting you? Him? Or the hair?"

"Both. It's only hair, I know it'll grow back, but it's like who I am has been taken. When he pinned me to the ground... I'd never felt so tiny. You won't get it. You're

261

a guy. You don't know what it's like to feel vulnerable by default… I think I should go home."

"You go home, he wins. Come on. I've got an idea." He offers a hand, pulls me up and leads me into Boots. I find myself in the hair care aisle, perfect women smiling at me from dozens of packets.

"Pink, right?" says Quin. "That's the colour you'd go, if you were to choose."

"How do you know that?"

"You said so."

Not to him. He must've been on my Insta. "School wouldn't allow it."

"Screw school. Show this bastard who's boss and own it – do something with your look that *you* want."

"I don't know if I'm brave enough."

He makes a rude noise. "You went to watch over my family knowing he was there. That's pretty nails. So don't give me that shit."

I didn't feel brave. And this is a bad idea. So why am I still looking at the dye packets?

"Look." Quin's voice softens. "How about I do it too? You choose. I don't care."

"You're seriously going to dye your hair to make me feel better?"

"Looks like it." He picks up a box with a laughing blue-haired woman on the front. "I assume this isn't magic fairy dust? It does work on blokes?"

"Quin, no. This is sweet, but you don't have to."

"Can't stop me. Once in a lifetime opportunity to see what I look like…" He squints at the packet in his hand. "Shocking Blue."

A smile tugs at the sides of my mouth. "I don't think that's your colour."

"What is, then?"

He's being so kind. I take one deep breath, then another. Let's be brave.

Fifteen minutes later we're at mine, shut in the bathroom. I check the instructions on the box we bought for Quin, then mix the powder and the developer. It feels unexpectedly intimate, standing close to him and rubbing the yoghurt-like mixture into his hair. He does the same for me with the rose pink I chose. A nervous giggle comes out of my mouth. Now we're here, hidden from the world with gloop plastered to our heads, this seems funny. And almost romantic, too. My heart starts to race – this time in a good way.

"Your dad's going to think I'm a bad influence," I say.

"Nah. Dad's chill. He'll be happy I hung out with an actual person." Quin flexes his arms. "What about your parents, they going to freak?"

"No more than they did when I cut it off, probably." I giggle again. "I'm going to be in so much trouble at school tomorrow. I've never done anything against the rules."

"Bet you a quid you get away with it."

"You're on." We settle down on the vinyl flooring,

our backs to the bathtub. I study his strange, angular face, noticing for the first time how long his eyelashes are. They soften his tough-guy image.

Quin raises his eyebrows. "Enjoying the view?"

"I was thinking about how horrible I used to think you were."

"I am horrible. Just not to you."

"When did I become special?"

"When you put your neck on the line for my stepmum and sister." A pause. "That's why I was waiting for you today. I wanted to say before, but your mates were there and… Family's important to me. For years home wasn't all that. Things got better, but now Jade's gone and nothing's the same." He heaves a sigh. "I was such an arrogant dickhead for pushing that fake dating idea on you like those threats were nothing. I put Demi and Zora at risk, you at risk…"

"You couldn't have predicted what happened. If I was a hard guy I'd have been arrogant too. You are pretty nails."

I meant to lighten the mood by using his words, but it seems to make Quin uncomfortable. "I'm not hard," he mumbles. "Really… I'm not. I just lash out when I'm angry and make bad decisions. It's not big or clever. I let them down, and if you hadn't gone to check they were OK, that thing in the nature reserve would never have happened. I hate seeing you messed up cos of me."

"Erm, I went along with it, remember? Quin, honestly, this isn't your fault."

"Yeah, you're right. I'm making this about my wangst,

and it isn't. Point is, Mia, I owe you. Big time. I know I've not got a lot to offer, but if you ever need me, I'm here."

Quin's eyes flicker away. Suddenly he seems shy. I get it. Talking about how you feel is never easy, especially when you're someone – as I suspect Quin is – that has got used to hiding it. What did he mean about home not being all that? I'm buzzing with curiosity but I sense he doesn't want to be pushed. Instead I change the subject to some butternut squash ravioli I want to make, and he relaxes. The timer on my phone makes us both jump.

"You first." Quin waits for me to lean over the sink and wash out the dye, then does the same himself, getting as much water on the floor as down the plughole. I slip a towel round my shoulders and fetch my hairdryer. Minutes later, we're staring at the new us.

"Wow." I run my fingers through my rose-coloured hair. "I look like Sakura!"

"Who?"

"She's a character from an anime called *Naruto*. She actually cuts her hair too, because it makes her vulnerable in combat and she wants to be a strong kunoichi, but never mind. This is cool. You know what else is cool, Quin? You!"

Quin pulls a face, running his hand through the quiff of his newly platinum hair. I knew it would suit him. It makes him look edgy. Very himself, somehow. "So it's all right?"

"More than all right. When it grows out a little and you get darker roots, that'll look even cooler."

He shuffles awkwardly, as though he doesn't know what to do with the compliment.

I nudge him, smiling more broadly. "Say it to the mirror. *I look dead cool.*"

"You should be a therapist." He smiles back. "If you like it, I like it. At least I dodged the Shocking Blue."

Yet he would have gone through with it to make me feel better. I gaze at him a second longer. He looks right back. Are we having a moment? In the mirror I catch a glimpse of myself out of the corner of my eye.

I've never looked less like Jade.

Quin must see that too.

We mess about downstairs for a bit playing with Dotty, but after Quin asks for the second time when my parents are due back, I realize it might be better to carry on chatting later, over FaceTime. I watch him lace up his trainers, thinking how sad it is that everyone dismisses him as the angry thug he maybe once was. If people could only see how much more there is to him, maybe they'd change their minds...

"Hey, Quin?" I say. "Olly's having a party on Friday. D'you want to come?"

He goes still. "I don't think that's a good idea."

"You don't have to be there long. Obviously it's your choice, but listen..." I try a smile. "Your course is three years, right? You're stuck here awhile. Might be more fun if you made friends? I bet your dad would be pleased."

"He'd be over the bloody moon."

"So come." I fiddle with my bracelet. "I'd like you to be there."

"I doubt fancy boy would."

"Olly won't mind."

Quin grunts. "This wasn't what I meant about owing you." He double knots the lace. "I'll think about it. OK?"

Quin wins that quid because I totally get away with the new hair. My head of year, Ms Worthing, gives me the softest telling-off, but, following a call with Mum, she's more interested in discussing what could be done to make me feel safer at school. The answer is basically nothing, as part of her solution is "speak to Mr Ellison if you feel stressed or worried". I toy with telling Ms Worthing why there's no way in hell I'll be doing this, but I'm scared I'll sound silly. If Mr Ellison's innocent, accusing him might ruin his career.

Instead, I concentrate on my classes. As Tuesday and then Wednesday morning pass with no word from my stalker, I begin to feel hopeful. Has cutting my hair killed the attraction?

And then my phone buzzes.

Unknown: hi

How can I be so spooked by a single word? I rattle through the afternoon on high alert. The urge to skip our Quiz Challenge meeting after school is enormous, but it's the last one before our match on Saturday. If we win, we'll progress to the next round, but if not, we're out of the competition. Luckily, Mr Ellison seems distracted and pays me no special attention. By the time I escape, the corridors are quiet, the only sound the hum of the cleaners' hoovers.

"Mia! Wait up," Oliver calls.

Reluctantly, I slow. "I thought you were talking to Kris."

"For thirty seconds, yeah. You didn't need to race off." He lowers his voice. "I've got the camera. Want to go through it?"

Oliver offered earlier and I said no, pretending I wasn't OK doing this at school. The truth was Leyla had a violin lesson and leaving the busy canteen to find an empty classroom with Oliver made me uncomfortable.

"Tomorrow," I say. "I'm in a hurry."

"OK," he says after a pause. "Where are you off to?"

"Just home. See you."

I clear the gates, picking up pace. Other than some year thirteens laughing at something on a phone, no one's around. I'm at the end of the road when Oliver catches up. "Mia, hey. I thought you weren't supposed to walk by yourself?"

I'm not, but my parents can't pick me up today. They think I'm walking with Olly. I mumble something, turning into the alleyway that shortcuts home. Oliver falls into step beside me.

"Are you annoyed with me?" he asks. "I know stuff is weird, but this feels personal."

I knew this conversation was coming, but even so, my stomach flips.

"Is it because I kicked off about that fake dating last week?" Oliver presses. "If I upset you, I'm sorry. You know I support you one hundred per cent."

"You don't have to apologize for disagreeing with me. Ley disagrees with me, all the time. I'm used to it."

"You're not blocking Ley out, though."

Something clatters behind us.

I whip round. A phone skids across the pavement at the entrance to the alleyway. Someone reaches to pick it up. A guy, his hood pulled up and his face hidden by a mask and cap.

Him.

24

I'm frozen, rooted in place. Then words rip out of my mouth.

"Leave me alone!"

He runs. Oliver moves too, tearing back down the alleyway and vanishing round the corner. Someone shouts.

Move, Mia. Help Olly! But again, I'm frozen. I screw my eyes shut, gulping air. Everything goes fuzzy.

The next thing I know, someone's helping me to my feet. Dazed, I realize I was sitting on the pavement.

Oliver's face swims into focus. His hair is mussed. Blood trickles from his nose.

I clutch his arm. "What happened?"

"I caught him and he lashed out. I hit him back. Then he ran."

"Did you see who it was?"

He shakes his head. "It all happened so quickly. Maybe I should have chased him, but he was fast and I was more worried about you. Are you OK?"

Did I have another panic attack? I've gone all shaky. Oliver loops his arm around my waist.

"Come on," he says. "Let's get out of here."

Somehow we make it to my house and crash on to the sofa. Silence answers when I call; we're alone.

I pass Oliver some tissues from the coffee table so he can dab his nose. "Does it hurt?"

"A bit." He smiles, rather shyly. "Can I say 'just a scratch', or is that too cliché?"

Guilt floods me. I grasp his free hand. "Olly…"

"It's all right," he says.

"It isn't, though. I…"

Thought it could be you. How ridiculous. Suspecting my friend, just because Quin made an offhand comment and Olly happens to be a guy? He hasn't even learned to drive yet!

Oliver's hand squeezes mine. I sense that, somehow, he knows what I was thinking. "It doesn't matter."

I look into his eyes. There's a warmth inside me as I squeeze his hand back. Dotty vaults on to my lap with a delighted *meow*. Oliver and I jump, breaking apart.

"Jeez, cat!" Flustered, I move Dotty on to a cushion. "Sorry, she does that. So, er, the camera. Do you, um…"

"Want to look at it now? Yep." Oliver turns to open his messenger bag. Is he flustered too?

I get us some juice and the peanut granola squares I made yesterday, while he connects the camera to my laptop so we can see the photos on a bigger screen. He glances at me as he takes the cup and smiles, but doesn't say anything.

The screen floods with thumbnails. Relieved for something else to concentrate on, I click on the first. I'm not seriously expecting there to be anything relating to Jade and, sure enough, a hundred-odd snapshots later, I'm losing hope. I'm about to close the folder when something jumps out at me.

"Hang on. Is that the teen screening at the Electric?"

The event where Jade had my scarf.

Oliver frowns. "Oh, yeah, that's right. Mr E let me borrow the camera. I thought he'd deleted everything."

"He must've missed these." Two of the three photos are general, but Jade pops up in the third. With her is Harper – and Quin. Jade is laughing. So is Quin. Their heads are close, his face practically in her hair, his hand on her shoulder.

Quin never pretended he wasn't close to Jade. All the same, seeing them like this…

"Huh," I say. "I didn't realize they went to the screening together."

"Maybe he gave her a lift?"

"He doesn't drive."

"Pretty sure he does. I saw him getting into the driver's seat of a car the other night. We were eating at that gastropub my parents like." Olly downs the last of his juice. The gastropub must be Quin's placement. "Funny to think he might've cooked my dinner."

"Are there more of these?" I ask. "I'm guessing Ivy copied them on to her laptop at the Electric before they were deleted."

Oliver shrugs. "No idea. Ivy's got really sloppy with admin." The rest of the photos are probably gone, then. Annoying – but at least I've seen this one.

"She's started leaving early a lot, too. Not that I mind locking up." He grins. "Don't tell anyone, but after she's gone I pretend it's my cinema."

"You're a funny boy, bro."

"Got to get my kicks somehow, Mia. I've had long chats with that cardboard cut-out of James Stewart. He's very flattered I named my dog after him."

I giggle. "I never did get around to watching *Vertigo*. We'll have to do it sometime. You have better taste in films than books. That again, seriously?"

I nod at his open bag, which reveals a lurid red and black spine. Oliver pulls a humorous face.

"Gothic horror is no more melodramatic than *Honey and Clover*."

"A hell of a lot more gory."

"*The Monk* isn't gory. It's pretty tame by today's standards."

Oliver launches into a detailed plot summary. Normally this is a habit of his that Leyla and I take the mick out of, but today it comes across as endearing.

On Friday, Leyla and I get to Oliver's house early to help set up his party. Mum gives us a lift over. She was a bit twitchy about tonight, but she knows I'll be surrounded by my friends, and Oliver's dad will be driving me home afterwards.

We arrive to find that his parents have done most of the work already – picnic blankets on the lawn, the garden gazebo open and dusted, speakers plugged into Oliver's phone with YouTube playlists selected. No K-pop, but I bet I can sneak some in later. Oliver's mum and dad are eating out with friends. Once upon a time those friends would have been Aaron's parents. Yet more relationships ruined by what's happened.

"We'll be back at midnight sharp, Oliver," says Mrs Arrowsmith, rather curtly. I get the impression if it was only down to her, this party wouldn't be happening. "Everywhere apart from the kitchen and downstairs toilet is out of bounds, remember. I'm sure your harem can help you keep everything in check."

"We're not a harem," I say before I can stop myself. "And Olly can keep stuff in check perfectly well himself."

Mrs Arrowsmith barely acknowledges me, just struts out in a mist of Chanel. A few minutes later, she's swinging her long legs into the brand-new BMW on the drive.

Mr Arrowsmith opens and closes the door for her. A few months ago, I thought the way the Arrowsmiths acted was dead romantic, but it seems kind of hollow now I know how much they argue.

Oliver is watching too, looking a little sad as he strokes Jimmy. I touch his shoulder. "Sorry if that was out of order," I say. "I didn't like her dismissing you like that."

"I'm used to it. Thanks, though."

"Is stuff OK with your parents at the moment? I'm here for you, you know."

"I want to forget all that tonight. If you guys can make people stay in the garden, that'd be good. My life won't be worth living if anything gets broken." He opens the fridge. "Fancy a drink before people arrive? Dad put a couple of bottles of prosecco in."

"Ooh! Très sophisticated! Yes please."

Leyla shakes her head, asking for something non-alcoholic.

"Sorry, I forgot you don't drink." Oliver opens an orange juice. Booze being haram doesn't stop Riyad, but I won't be mean and bring him up. We clink our plastic flutes, then laugh at the disappointingly flat clink.

"Don't let me drink too much," I say to Oliver as we drift out on to the lawn. Jimmy races ahead, his tail wagging. "We need our beauty sleep for tomorrow."

He smiles. "You don't need any of that."

I giggle. "Ooh, smooth. You neither, Mr Secretly-Been-Working-Out."

I couldn't believe it yesterday when he arrived at school wearing a T-shirt – when the hell did those arms happen? "I've been lifting Dad's weights. It isn't a secret, I just didn't mention it because it's boring."

"Same thing, oh man of mystery."

"Man of Mystery? I like it."

"You do look a bit James Bond tonight. Is that the tux from the Talent Showcase?"

"Well spotted. No thanks to the James Bond comparison, though. He's a massive misogynist. Rick Blaine, maybe, or Roger Thornhill, though arguably they're problematic too— Hi! Come in."

I smile after him as he leaves to greet guests – then catch myself. Was I just flirting with Olly? And was he … flirting back? I try to work out what this means. It hasn't come out of nowhere, but does it make any sense, given how close I feel to Quin?

Over the next half hour guests trickle in. It's a fifty-fifty split between those who've taken Oliver's "classic Hollywood" dress code with good humour and those who've ignored it completely. Jimmy is even wearing an adorable dog bow tie attached to his collar, which is totally worth the fiver I paid for it on Etsy.

I can't imagine Quin will play along – though I'd quite like to see him in a suit. Each time footsteps sound from the side path leading to the garden gate my heart leaps. But Quin doesn't appear. The ages I spent perfecting cat-eye make-up isn't wasted – it's so good to be able to enjoy make-up without worrying about Aaron not liking it – but I'm still disappointed. Quin made no promises, but I thought he liked me. Maybe more than liked me.

Well, whatever. I don't need a boy to make me feel good. I down my prosecco and channel my inner Strong Independent Woman. Tonight, I'm determined to forget my stalker. I feel safe here and I'm going to enjoy myself. I'm wearing a flouncy white and sage sundress with a lace overlay, which doesn't strictly fit the theme but I couldn't resist. It arrived this morning from Auntie Lou. It hardly meets the "smart" brief for the quiz but is still gorgeous.

Kris makes a beeline for me across the lawn. "Lovely teammate! Hello!"

Drunk Kris. Wonderful. He follows me into the kitchen, jabbering about how he was sceptical about partying the night before the quiz, but he's now decided it's an excellent way to unwind, and hey, he's uncovered a simulated Japanese game from the nineties called *Princess Maker 2* that I'd like because it has manga artwork. I brace myself for a bombardment, but after picking up a fresh bottle of beer Kris stumbles away.

"Was he bugging you?" asks Oliver, filling the cocktail shaker.

"I suppose he was being nice, in his own way," I say. "Did you invite him? I've never seen Kris at a party. He hasn't got many friends."

"I felt sorry for him. Oh, crap." The cocktail shaker slips from Oliver's hands and rolls under the table. We both duck to pick it up, bumping arms.

Someone clears their throat behind us. "Evening."

My face lights up and I forget the cocktail shaker. "You came!"

"Seems so." Quin's wearing ripped jeans and a white tee. Maybe it's the prosecco, but the platinum hair looks even cooler than it did on Monday. He nods at Oliver. "All right? Sorry for ignoring the theme. Ain't got that kind of gear. This OK on the counter?"

He has a box of beer under his arm. I lean on tiptoes and give him a big hug. "That doesn't matter. Between you and me, smart isn't my thing either."

"You sound a bit pissed."

"No, just happy you're here." I let the hug linger before pulling back.

Oliver asks Quin what he wants to drink. He sounds a little off. Is he annoyed I invited Quin? I didn't intend to make things awkward. People are already looking our way, nudging and whispering. Quin turns his back but I know he's noticed.

Feeling protective, I slide my arm through his.

An hour and a half later, people are a lot more relaxed, lounging on picnic blankets, a few even dancing. Whoever scrapped Oliver's carefully selected playlists in favour of blasting chart bangers on repeat has done a good thing. Jimmy's the centre of attention and loving it. From the smile on Oliver's face as he moves from group to group offering to make cocktails, he's enjoying himself too.

Quin has stuck to me like glue, barely speaking or sipping his Coke. Even for him, this is intense. It's making it hard for me to enjoy myself. Now everyone has loosened up, they're openly staring, even giggling. I pick up "Aaron" and "d'you think she likes it rough". Even though I expected gossip, I go pink. If Quin would only relax he wouldn't stand out in the wrong way!

When, feeling self-conscious, I snap that he shouldn't have come if all he's going to do is stand there scowling, he says, "You asked."

That gets under my skin, and I escape to the upstairs bathroom. I sit on the closed toilet seat, fanning myself. Inviting Quin was a mistake. What was I expecting to happen? Quin to forget his issues, hug everyone, then sweep me off my feet in a movie kiss?

Ridiculous mind, racing ahead as usual. And now I'm fixating on the couple I bumped into at the end of the garden earlier. Coiled round each other, she stroked his cheek as he gazed into her eyes.

Aaron used to look at me like that. I *lived* for those touches and kisses. I felt special and seen. Friend hugs are good, but they don't cut it, not in the way I'm craving tonight. Aaron would have found this party hilarious, and he'd probably have insisted on talking like a fifties actor all evening. He's a good mimic. God, I really miss him sometimes.

Knock knock. "Hello? Mia? Are you OK?"

Peering into the bathroom is Camille, looking like a

nineteen twenties goddess in a yellow dress that's amazing against her black skin.

"Oh, you're fine," she says. "Just checking you weren't throwing up."

"I'm not drunk," I say, even though I think I might be.

"Actually, Mia, I was wondering if we could chat…"

Mindful that we aren't supposed to be upstairs, I take her down into the sitting room and perch on the suede cream sofa. Camille looks around appreciatively.

"Oh, wow, this is gorgeous. No wonder Oliver always looks so smart. So … are you still dating Quin?"

I can't explain to her that we were never dating in the first place. I shrug, ignoring the funny pang inside. The WhatsApp from Camille on Quin's phone pops into my head. "Is he your ex?"

Camille's eyes widen. "Me and Quin? God, no! You're thinking of Riyad."

Her face goes blank a moment. Quin beat Riyad up around the time Camille and Riyad split, now I think about it. Could a love triangle be the reason?

"You're friends, though." Somehow, I can't let this go. "You message him."

"Only a tiny bit." Is she protesting too much? It's hard to tell. "I've always tried to be kind to Quin, that's all. My mum used to work with his. There were problems at home, like, major mess-your-head-up problems, and he couldn't hack school. He's dyslexic, and they diagnosed it really late so he didn't get much support. The drama teacher used to rave about how good he was when he could be arsed participating, but … anyway, I felt sorry for him."

Does this story have a point? "OK?"

"So I was curious about how things were going. I'm happy Quin's here."

"Not happy enough to talk to him." Oh crap – where is my filter?

Camille gives a shaky laugh. "I was going to, but my friends were being silly… They have this joke about Quin crushing on me."

Is she baiting me? I open my mouth to ask why, then close it. If I wait, Camille will tell me anyway. She clearly wants to. Sure enough, her smile wobbles.

"You know I was off school for a while, last year?"

I lean forward, nodding.

"I was … ill. Quin…" She plays with a dreadlock. "Well. He visited me in hospital. It was weird. Didn't say much, and he was only there, like, five minutes, but the nurse said he'd really pressured them to let him in. After that he started messaging me. Nothing specific, just general chat, but a lot… That's why my friends call him clingy. Maybe you should be careful."

Is that a warning? I sit upright, narrowing my eyes at her. Camille holds up her hands.

"I'm not stirring," she says quickly. "I just thought you should know he can be intense, and Quin's head is probably a mess right now. He obviously *adored* Jade. My mum works in Wrabney. She saw them out together all the time. Said he walked with his arm around her, all protective. Mum actually thought they were together! Can you imagine—"

A thunderous shattering noise cuts her off. It's like hundreds of glasses are exploding all at once. Someone screams. Camille and I rush into the kitchen.

Riyad is sprawled face down on the tiled floor in a pool of blood. It's everywhere – the floor, the units, up the walls. And the person pummelling him is Quin.

Quin's fist slams into Riyad's nose. He too is covered in blood. There's so much of it – surely one person can't bleed that much!

"Quin, no!" I cry. "You'll kill him."

"Not bloody likely," Quin snarls. He buries his trainer into Riyad's side then storms out, pushing his way through the growing crowd. I fly to where Riyad is groaning.

"Can you speak? Where are you injured? Someone call an ambulance!"

"Careful." Oliver squats next to me. He holds out a wad of napkins and I realize the red liquid splashed everywhere isn't blood, it's wine. The bottle unit which

Oliver's parents keep by the door is overturned, glass everywhere.

"I didn't know you cared." Riyad leans on me as he sits up. "What the hell? He decked me for no reason!"

Around me witnesses are nodding. I catch whispers: *Psycho. Out of control. Looked like he wanted to kill him.*

I leave Riyad and race after Quin. He's halfway down the road. By the time I catch up I'm panting.

"Quin! What the hell was that about?"

He wheels round, his fists clenched. "Why didn't you tell me he was gonna be there?"

"He wasn't supposed to be! He must have invited himself."

"Are they laughing? Calling me names? I've seen the way everyone's looking at me, like I'm a joke."

"*I* don't think you're a joke. But I do think that was out of order."

"Well, you shouldn't have asked me to come, then!"

The words are a blow. "What? Don't blame me. You could've refused. Why did you go for Riyad anyway – because of Camille?"

"Leave her out of this. There isn't a reason. This is who I am. *No good.*"

"I think you're laying into me because you're angry at yourself."

"Don't psychoanalyse me!" shouts Quin.

"You know why I invited you tonight?" My breathing is shallow. "I like you. I thought we could have a nice evening, forget about the stalker for a few hours. I thought you were better than your bad reputation. But you're not. You're out of control. Stay out of my life, *Psycho* Quin!"

I march away, tilting my chin defiantly. I'm not going to cry. If he's hurt I fired out the horrible nickname, good. He hurt me. Maybe he only spends time with me because he can't have Camille. The one he's *clingy* with.

Or maybe all he really likes is hanging out with someone he can pretend is Jade. Maybe he even sat with her while she dyed her hair, too.

Back in the garden, Oliver is herding people away.

Leyla comes up to me. "I hate to leave but I need to get Ri home. He's OK, just shaken."

"Of course," I say. "I mean, shit… I'm so sorry."

Leyla walks Riyad to the garden gate with the help of one of his friends. He's hunched over, his usual cockiness gone. An unfamiliar song pumps forlornly out of the speakers. I turn it off and join Oliver. He's surveying the mess, his hands in his hair.

"I don't even know where to begin," he says.

The entire kitchen is white. *Was* white. Wine has even dribbled into the hallway and under the crack of the cupboard door where the Arrowsmiths keep coats and shoes.

I roll up my sleeves. "We'd better get started."

Oliver shakes his head. "Don't. You'll ruin your clothes."

"Why don't you give me something old of yours? I'm not leaving."

Oliver fetches pyjama shorts and a T-shirt, turning his back as I change. Olly's clothes fit better than Quin's did after Harper's assault-by-milkshake. *Don't think about Quin.* I arm myself with a bucket and mop.

Twenty minutes later the kitchen is looking less horrifying, but chunks of glass keep sticking in the soles of my shoes, and even after two rounds of Vanish the fabric seats of the dining room chairs are stained.

"There's no way we can hide this from your parents," I say. "How bad d'you think the freak-out will be?"

"Nuclear." Oliver's on his hands and knees with a dustpan and brush, sweeping glass. Overwhelmed by the urge to hug him, I squat at his side and bury my face into his shoulder.

"I'm so sorry your party was ruined. I should never have invited Quin."

He tenses. "I don't want to talk about him."

I flinch and let go. "OK."

Oliver empties the dustpan with a clang against the side of the bin. "Do you want to know something sad? This is the first birthday party I've ever had. As a kid my parents took me fine-dining even though all I wanted was a trashy play party like everyone else. I finally bent their arm when I was fourteen, and had a thing in the bowling alley. Only one kid showed up and he was even less popular than me. To have tonight, and for people to come and have a good time meant so much… Oh, Mia, don't look like that. I'm not angry with you."

He scoots around and bear-hugs me. I press my face into his chest.

"I hate seeing you hurt. I'll help explain everything to your parents."

"They'll be furious no matter what you say. But please stay."

We break apart. "You should have changed too," I say. "That shirt looked so good and now it's ruined. Does that stain remover work on clothes?"

Oliver glances down at himself. "I can try."

He unbuttons his shirt and chucks it in the washing machine. My eyes pop – I can't help it. Those are actual abs. Were they always there? He catches me staring and my insides flutter.

Oliver looks away first. "I'll get something on."

I swallow a *you don't have to*. By the time he returns I'm perched on the sofa. Oliver places a bottle and two glasses on the table in front of us.

"Let's finish that prosecco. You liked it, right?"

Maybe more booze will drive Quin out of my head. I sip the drink he pours, then hiccup. "I don't think I'm classy enough for this."

"You're plenty classy." Oliver settles down next to me. There's something intimate about the darkness, the late hour, the two flutes, Jimmy snoozing by the curtains. I don't want to talk any more so I ask if we can put something on. The film he brings up is a Grace Kelly one. I lean against him and rest my head on his shoulder, unable to quite focus on the screen. He draws his arms around me. This doesn't feel like the comfort-hug earlier, or even the time we sat close on the bus. This feels … new. And exciting. I push away thoughts of Quin and snuggle closer, savouring his warmth and solidity. It's been so long since anyone held me like this.

"I'm sorry tonight went wrong," I murmur. Everything's starting to feel cosily warm and blurry. "Like, really. Next year I'll throw you a really epic party. I don't know how it'll be epic, but it will."

"People could come in togas?"

I giggle, and he smiles, his eyes crinkling a little at the side. Such nice eyes. *He's* nice. Even when I'm difficult or annoying he doesn't complain. He always helps and never lets me down.

He has a fit body, too. *What if…?* I pull back. His eyes move to my lips before locking with my eyes.

The belly flutter returns.

I kiss him. His lips are cool and taste of prosecco. I wait for him to kiss me back. Instead he takes my shoulders, lightly pushing me away.

My face burns. "Oh God. I'm sorry. I thought you wanted—"

"I need to check." His voice is hushed. "You're not too drunk for this? You really do want me to kiss you?"

"I really do want you to kiss me."

He makes a sighing noise. Our lips meet; little, delicate, closed-mouth kisses. When I try to kiss harder, he murmurs something about going slow. His face has gone fuzzy, so I close my eyes and go along with it, letting myself enjoy the gentle way his hand cups my cheek, his thumb stroking my cheekbone as though I'm something precious. When we kiss again he lets me deepen it. Now the warmth I've been missing courses through me.

Thump. The noise comes from outside. Jimmy leaps up, barking. I pull away from Oliver, my heart in my mouth.

"Someone's there."

"Jimmy! Shush," Oliver calls. The dog immediately quietens. Oliver kisses my forehead. "It's not him. Relax. Our neighbour often leaves for her shift around this time." He gets up and pulls the curtains closed. "Better?"

I glance at Jimmy. He's settled down, his head on his paws. Oliver returns to the sofa, drawing me close.

"I won't let anything happen to you," he whispers. "I think you're wonderful, Mia. I like you so much." And he brushes his lips against my neck.

Oh. Wow. Aaron used to do this. It feels weird that this time it's Oliver, but … I forgot how much I liked it. I move my hands downwards and slide them under his top. When I tug it, Oliver stops.

"Mia. No. This is enough for now. Really."

I pull a sad face. "Said no boy ever."

"Says me."

"You're not like the other boys then. Is that a trope? Or is it only girls who are not like the other … boys?"

"What?" His eyebrows draw together. "You are drunk."

"I'm not! Promise. I know what I'm doing."

We kiss again. I throw myself into it, wanting to forget all the bad things that have happened.

Gravel crunches outside, followed by the click of a car engine turning off. Oliver's parents. Jimmy goes wild again, but this time in delight. We break apart. Oliver's fingers thread through mine, pressing our palms together.

Then we face the music together.

26

Oliver: Morning
Hope you're not feeling too fuzzy-headed
You made me really happy last night :-)
See you later
Xxx

I squint at my phone, shielding my eyes from the too-bright morning light. My sluggish brain adjusts to being awake. Last night I dreamed I was a lemon and someone baked me in a cake, whole. That new detergent – something about it is really bothering me.

I made Oliver happy? What the—

Oh. I raise a finger to my lips. They feel tender. How much snogging was there? *Oh, help.* I tried to push it, didn't I? It was only as Oliver's quietly furious dad dropped me home that I realized how tipsy I was. I didn't throw up and ruin the lovely cream interior of the BMW, but it was a close call.

And today is Quiz Challenge. *Craaaaaaap.* I launch myself out of bed, then groan at the weight in my head.

Mum's waiting outside the bathroom door when I emerge from the shower. Under her arm is a parcel. She wears a resigned expression.

"Can you stomach toast?"

I nod. The shower has perked me up. "What's that?"

"The outfit from Auntie Lou, I imagine."

Frowning, I perch on my bed and rip the parcel open. Inside is a pale pink blouse with a pussy bow and a black A-line skirt. The label tells me it's from the company Auntie Lou works for.

"That's perfect, Mia," says Mum. "Nice and neutral. I knew Lou would come up trumps."

If this is from Auntie Lou, who sent me yesterday's dress?

I clatter downstairs and into the cupboard where we keep our recycling bags. Paper and card fly everywhere as I tip them upside down, my other hand clutching my towel. There it is – the slip that came with the dress. Definitely addressed to me. Attached to it is a scrap of paper I missed.

i saw this and thought of you <3

A sour taste seeps into my mouth. Was my stalker at Olly's party? Did he watch me dance, feeling like I was his, that his dress claimed me?

Even though my long hair is gone, I feel his nose at my ear, inhaling me.

I'm too shaken to do much beyond get dressed before we're in the car, heading to Quiz Challenge. I couldn't bring myself to say a word to Mum about the dress. Leyla's messaged to wish me luck. So has Ivy, even though she normally doesn't give two hoots about school stuff.

Quiz. Think quiz. Members of the cabinet, number one albums, kings and queens. But every time I try to redirect my brain it slides back to him. I keep glancing in the wing mirror. That black car has been on our tail since we left Southaven. It's a coincidence, surely. My stalker has no reason to tail us. He must know exactly where Quiz Challenge is. Even so…

My phone pings. I jump and drop it, and have to fish it out from the footwell.

Oliver: Capital city of Pakistan? :-) #LastMinuteCramming xxx

Three kisses. Oliver only ever puts one. What am I going to do about him? Last night felt good, but I don't know if that was prosecco brain. Was the snogging about Olly, or about snogging someone? Quin was the one I couldn't wait to see.

HELP

I kissed Olly and I don't know what to do

After a minute, I remember Riyad being hurt, and add a quick **Hope Riyad's OK.**

Last night in the chaos, I forgot my suspicions of him. Now, though … the thought of having to sit next to Riyad – work together, even – makes my insides crawl. Mr Ellison will be watching too. My other prime suspect. Oh God. How can I sit and smile like everything's normal? I'm going to throw that toast up in a moment.

Minutes pass. Nothing from Leyla. She should be in the car with Riyad and her parents heading to Quiz Challenge too. Has something happened?

Quin hasn't messaged either – of course he hasn't – but I don't want to think about him.

"Here we are!" Mum sounds cheery as we park. Dad hunts for a ticket machine while Mum helps Felix into his coat and I stand there shivering. I always imagined I'd feel powerful and smart when this day came, but I feel anything but.

Oliver is already in the theatre foyer when I arrive, talking to Kris. When he sees me, he beams. My stomach somersaults.

I join them. Oliver leans in with a hello hug, kissing my cheek. Over his shoulder I catch Kris's bloodshot eyes bulge. Then he gives Oliver a big grin and a thumbs up. Before any of us can say anything, Mr Ellison strides over, all smiles and smart-casual in jeans and a print shirt.

"A-Team! Today's the day!"

He holds up his hand for high fives. None of us give him one.

"All right." Mr Ellison drops his arm. "I'll stop being cringe. Anyone seen Riyad?"

We shake our heads.

"Stuck in traffic?" Oliver offers.

Mr Ellison nods. "Probably. How are you feeling, Mia? You look a little peaky."

"Fine," I mumble.

Oliver leans in close. "Seriously, how are you feeling? You didn't reply to my message."

"No, because…" The rest of the sentence turns to bile as Oliver's hand finds mine. "Um, Olly, we need a word."

"Anything wrong?" asks Mr Ellison.

"It's a private word."

Mr Ellison looks taken aback by my sharp tone, but doesn't call me out. Oliver and I find a quiet spot by the fire doors.

"Sorry," he says. "Too much touching. Next time I'll ask first."

I wish he'd stop being so nice! Of course Oliver's clued up on consent and respect. He's doing all the right things – only I don't know if I'm the right girl.

He speaks again before I can. "I don't want you to think it was booze making me kiss you last night. I've wanted to for a long time but you had Aaron, and then it never seemed OK, with the stalker and everything… We can take things as slowly as you like. I don't want Ley to feel pushed out either. Basically, whatever you want, we'll do. I like you so much."

He smiles, looking relieved to have delivered what was clearly a pre-planned speech. I start to sweat. This goes beyond a crush! He has actual feelings. Deep down, I think I've always known, even when I was with Aaron. The brownies he saved from the Electric, borrowing my manga so we could chat about it, escorting me places…

I will myself to see the boy whose face I wanted to snog off yesterday. Surely the dawning realization that I've unknowingly loved him all along is coming.

But all I see is Oliver. And all I feel is panic.

I force myself to hold eye contact because, damn it, I am not going to do this any way other than properly. "Olly, last night I was in a really funny place. The kissing was great, you're great, but… I'm not sure us getting together is a good idea."

Oliver stares at me, unblinking.

I plough on. "It's not that I don't like you. You'd be an amazing boyfriend. But I'm confused, and feeling vulnerable, and until last night I really liked Quin, and I was quite drunk. I don't think it's fair to date anyone until I'm in a better place. I'm sorry I didn't explain this last night." Another silence. "Olly? Can you say something please? I'm really nervous I've screwed our friendship up."

A long moment passes. Then Oliver looks away. He adjusts his collar. "It's fine."

"You don't have to pretend. You're allowed to feel hurt."

"I said it's fine. I was drunk anyway."

We both know that's not true. I reach out. "Oliver…"

He moves away. "No, don't. You can't reject me one moment then expect to hold my hand the next. Boys aren't toys. We have feelings too."

I flinch, but let it slide. "I won't touch you if you don't want me to."

"I don't even want to talk any more. I need to concentrate. My parents are here. I need to impress them." He paces, then pivots round to look at me again. "Is this a definite no? Or is this a no right now? I would never have made a move last night if you hadn't first. I've tried so hard to respect and support you, but sometimes you give really mixed messages."

I swallow. "Sorry. I never meant to."

"Were you faking being into it? If I hadn't stopped you, how far would things have gone?"

He hasn't raised his voice. I'd almost rather he shouted.

"I wasn't faking," I say. "But that doesn't make it right—"

"It felt right to me." His cheeks flush. "Why did you kiss me then? Just because you were drunk?"

"No, no! I felt attracted to you and you were *there*, and—"

"So I could have been anyone?"

"Not at all! I care about you. Look, I know I behaved badly and I'm sorry. You're the nicest guy ever—"

"And nice guys always finish last. Crappy trope, right there."

He stomps away, but not before I see the pain in his eyes. The pain I put there.

Have I broken his heart?

Twenty minutes later, I'm sitting behind a desk staring up at the packed auditorium. My focus is shot to pieces. I've never felt less in the zone.

Mr Ellison strides over. "Change of plan." His voice is terse. "Mia, captain's chair, please. Riyad can't make it."

"What?" I splutter. "Why?"

"I don't know the details." Mr Ellison ushers a rattled-looking Kris into the chair I vacate.

What the hell is going on? Is Riyad ill? This can't be because of last night. He wasn't badly hurt. Unless something happened after Ley took him home…

No. Quin wouldn't. We argued, he was furious, but that doesn't mean he'd do anything really extreme … right?

The other team take their seats. They're in smart grey uniforms and look horribly competitive. I search the audience as the camera person runs through the final checks. In the fourth row I spot my family. Felix gives me a big toothy grin and Ivy blows a kiss. Next to her are three empty seats. Leyla's family. None of them have made it.

Ley never replied to my message.

My back and palms go clammy as the lights swivel to face us and the camera whirs.

The host, a university-age guy whose team won a few years back, introduces the competition.

"The school that triumphs today will proceed to the next round," he says. "The other will sadly be eliminated." No pressure there, then. "Let's meet the teams. First up, Southaven High."

The spotlight turns on us. It's so hot! I'm conscious of the many eyes watching me, of being the only girl. "Hi, I'm Mia Hawkins, and I'm team captain."

There – that sounded confident enough. Perhaps I can muddle through. Captaining is a curveball, but Mr Ellison's been saying for months I should believe in myself more. Mum and Dad think the same.

"First question," announces the host. "Whichever team gets this will receive the three bonus questions. What is the fifth planet in the solar system?"

Kris smacks the buzzer. "Jupiter."

"Correct! Your bonuses are on film."

Film! I try to catch Oliver's eye. This is his turn to shine.

"Name two actors who've won multiple Oscars. You can confer."

"Olly?" I ask, but he looks blank, even though he must know the answer.

"I need an answer, team," says the host.

I guess, incorrectly. The next question is about *Star Wars*, the third about a director. We score on neither. The other team grabs the next bonuses.

By the time we hit the halfway point I want to die. We're thirty points behind. Kris did a good job getting bonuses to start with, but his confidence nosedived when he made a silly mistake over which type of dog Lassie is and the audience tittered. I got a few questions right, but they were dead easy, and I blanked on another I should have known. Oliver's frozen up completely. I catch sight of his dad in the audience, holding his head in his hands.

The other team swoop in for the kill. Their lead surges. Unless we fight back soon we'll be in total embarrassment territory. I grit my teeth.

"Which fictional character lives at 221B Baker Street?"

I smack the buzzer. "Sherlock Holmes!"

"Correct!" says the host. "Your bonus questions are on the London Underground. Which line has the most stations?"

I look at Kris. He shakes his head. Under the desk I nudge Oliver's foot with mine.

"We need you, Olly," I whisper. "You're from London. You know this."

Oliver doesn't respond. My blouse is plastered to my back now. Everyone must be able to see the sweat gleaming on my forehead.

"Answer please, team."

Time to guess again. I open my mouth.

"District." The voice is Oliver's.

The host tuts. "I'll allow it, but answers from the captain only next time. Which station has the longest escalator?"

"Angel." Oliver meets my eyes, giving me a tiny nod.

Angel is correct, and we get the third question right, too. Buoyed up, we grab the next bonuses. The lead closes. But the other team aren't going to be steamrolled. They buzz a split second before us and ace a round on the periodic table. Mr Ellison was right, it did come up. The gap is thirty points now. Can we stage a comeback? We claw back ten on star signs — something I do know — but this only fires the other team up more. Forty points. Fifty. Sixty. And five minutes to go.

I slump in my chair. It's over. We've lost.

After the cameras stop, we're shown into the room where we stowed our bags and coats. Mr Ellison runs over.

"A-Team, what was that wobbly start about?" He sounds wounded. "I know losing Riyad wasn't the plan, but you are so much better than that."

Oliver walks out without a word. Mr Ellison's eyebrows shoot upwards. "What's up with Olly?"

I clear my throat. "That chat we had before we went in. I think it … um … put his form off."

The winning team stroll past, all smiles.

"Bad luck," says their captain. "At least you gave the audience a laugh. Can you imagine if Lassie had been a Cockapoo?"

They swagger off, laughing. Kris glares daggers at me, as though it's my fault our opponents are jerks, then walks out. Mr Ellison clenches his jaw. Then he turns and smacks his hand against the wall.

"Bloody hell. What an embarrassment. This is my fault."

I hang my head, and will a hole to open up and swallow

me. I escape by hiding in the toilet. Mum and Dad will be waiting in the foyer, but I can't face them right now. They'll be comforting and kind but I know the truth: I've let everyone down – including myself.

I turn my phone back on. I need to check Leyla's OK. *Oh.* I suck in a breath.

> Leyla: Riyad's been charged with dealing drugs

27

"The police have known there were drugs going around school for a while."

Leyla sounds hollow. I can't see too well over FaceTime because her room is only lit by her Anglepoise lamp, but she looks terrible, all slumped shoulders and ashen skin. I called her as soon as I got home. "An anonymous tip-off led them to Riyad. They showed up as we were leaving for the quiz. He had class A drugs hidden in his room! Not loads, and he swears he's not a crackhead himself, but he's definitely been dealing them. Says it was easy cash and he needs new dentures, cos the ones our parents paid for look crap in photos. Can you believe it?"

She dabs her eyes. I wish I could give her a hug.

"You had no idea?"

"Did you?"

I pinch the top of my nose, wishing I didn't feel so tired. "Yes," I admit. "He seemed high at Peyton's party. I thought he probably gave the LSD to Aaron. I didn't have any proof, otherwise I'd have told you."

"Sure?"

"What, you think I rang the police?"

"No." A pause. "But Riyad does."

"Are you kidding me?"

"He's frothing at the mouth. Raging that this is your revenge for Aaron."

I've never seen Riyad angry before. The idea is surprisingly chilling. "How are your parents taking it?"

"Badly. They're so proud of Ri and have such high hopes for him. They're hurt, too. Maybe those dentures aren't the greatest, but it was still money we didn't have. Dad keeps repeating 'you dealt drugs because of selfies' like he can't believe it."

I can. Riyad's used to being looked up to, a big fish in a small pond. From his social media you'd assume he was a reality star or even a model. Looking perfect – not just good – matters. "What about you?"

"I'm furious! He lied to me. He's been doing it for almost a year! I knew he smoked a bit of weed, but dealing… Wasn't there that article last year about some Sussex teen being hospitalized from a bad batch of something? Drugs ruin lives."

"What will happen to him?"

"He's got no criminal record and they didn't find loads on him, so if he's lucky he'll get a fine and a warning. If not…" She sighs. "He's better than this, Mia. It's unreal… But what's all this about snogging Olly?"

I feel ashamed making a fuss when Leyla's world has been rocked, but I need to talk to someone. I explain about last night, and bombing the quiz. When I'm done, she says, "Well, shit."

I nod miserably. "That sums it up."

"Do you not like Olly that way?"

I scratch Dotty behind the ears. She stretches out, displaying her belly. "I don't know. Last night I think I just wanted someone. Maybe if Quin wasn't around I'd feel differently…"

"Clear as mud, then."

I don't answer, concentrating on Dotty.

"If you're confused, why don't you ask Olly if he'll wait?" says Leyla. "There are times I've literally had to bite my tongue to stop myself shouting how great you'd be together. If you want a good guy who's going to treat you well, hello! He's right there."

"He might not want me any more. I've hurt him. Humiliated him, too, because I did it just before the quiz. Oh God. I just want to hug him and take the pain away, only I can't. I am the pain."

"Now you're being dramatic. Let the quiz go. If Mr E carries on being all emo, that's his fault for being over-invested."

"I don't care about Mr E. I care about Olly. Ugh, sorry. You don't need my drama. Do you want me to come over?"

At the corner of my screen Leyla's mum appears. Leyla mutes me while they speak, then returns sounding stressed.

"Riyad and Dad are having a blazing row in the garden. Woo-hoo, a show for the neighbours! This day keeps delivering. Thanks for the offer, but you'd better stay out of it." She moves to end the call, then pauses. "Shit. I didn't even ask. The stalker – has anything happened with him today?"

On instinct, I glance out of the window. "He's been quiet." I don't add that this might be – if the stalker is Riyad, or even Mr Ellison – because he's had a busy day. "Nothing happened yesterday either, apart from him sending me that dress."

She shudders. "Why does that not reassure me?"

I know what she means. It feels like he could be planning something. Leyla ends the call. Poor Ley. I wish I could help more. Under the breezy dark humour, I can tell how hard this has hit her.

I scroll to Oliver's name in my contacts. His profile picture is one I took. He's holding the upturned collar of his vampire coat, smiling a little apologetically over the cheesy pose. We *can't* let today ruin everything. At the very least we need a proper conversation, even if it eats me up with shame.

I take a deep breath and press call. Oliver's phone rings, then goes dead.

He's cut me off.

The next week is the first of the Easter holidays. The weather is beautiful. I think longingly of the beach, and the woods where Aaron once did a gorgeous photoshoot of me as a forest girl, and all the places I used to visit, completely carefree. But the more hours that pass with nothing from my stalker, the more my anxiety cranks up. Surely this is some kind of mind game, even a trap, lulling me into a false sense of security. And he will be watching. He always is. Going to school – which I had no choice over – was one thing. Choosing to go out is another.

Unfortunately, Mum and Dad are working most of the first week of the holidays, so it falls to me to look after Felix. After a day of watching TV and playing in the garden, he's bored and grumpy, so the next day I call Leyla, and together we brave the park. I keep a constant, crushing grip on Felix's hand, glancing backwards every few seconds. It's a struggle to focus on Leyla talking, or to count and calm myself the way Quin taught me. I can't even relax enough to sit on a bench. I hover by the climbing frame instead, tracking Felix.

"I hate that he's done this to you, Mia." Leyla sounds tearful, which is unlike her. "He's squeezed your world smaller and smaller. We used to come here without a second thought."

The memory of not being afraid feels like such a luxury. Leyla carries on talking, distracting me by shooting theories about where the anonymous tip-off came from.

Riyad's still adamant I did it. I can tell he's furious from what he's been posting online: dark quotes about karma and defiant selfies with braggy captions. It was freaking me out, so I blocked him.

That evening, at home, I try messaging Oliver again. A couple of days later he finally replies, but only to say he wants space. Twice I get Dad to drive me to his house, but Mrs Arrowsmith snootily turns me away. Leyla's not getting much out of him either. Mum, who I confide in, advises me to leave him be.

Quin's vanished too. Is he angry? Hurt I called him by his horrible nickname? I tell myself that life is easier without his issues, but it's hard not to feel stung – and even harder to turn off everything I was beginning to feel.

"Let's have a family day out," Mum says on Thursday evening, after I've been drifting round the house. "Dad and I are both off tomorrow. How about we pop up to London and visit the zoo?"

Felix shrieks in delight. I bite my lip. "I don't know."

Mum pats my shoulder. "Don't worry, Mia. London is busy. We'll buy advance tickets, and go straight through the turnstiles."

Even if he does follow us to the zoo, we'll lose him on arrival. I don't know how much longer I can stick living like this. Weighing up everything I do is exhausting.

The next day I feel sick the entire train journey. Once in the crowded zoo, however, I perk up. We watch penguins gobble fish, pull faces at the gorillas and coo over the otters – my favourites. In the gift shop Felix goes into an excitable frenzy before eventually choosing a stuffed flamingo. As Dad queues to pay, Mum says, "I'm proud of you for coming out today. I know it was difficult. I'm proud of you for the quiz too."

"Mum, I bombed the quiz."

"You tried. I never had the confidence to do anything like that at school. Too afraid of failing."

I sigh. "I wanted to prove myself. Seems silly now."

"You don't need to prove anything to us." She squeezes my shoulder. "You've had such a hard time. You've been brave and resilient. That says more about you than grades, sweetheart."

It's approaching five o'clock by the time we get home. Felix dances impatiently by the door, shouting that he needs a poo and his flamingo wants to watch him, and I laugh. Mum jokes that most people like to use the toilet in private and Dad scrolls through today's photos on his phone. It feels nice and normal – for the first time in far too long.

Felix shoots into the downstairs toilet. I kick off my pumps and go upstairs to charge my phone. If I ask nicely maybe we can get takeaway from the mezze place…

At the top of the stairs I freeze.

The warmth and laughter of the past few hours turn to ice in my stomach.

Through the banisters I can see that the door to my room is ajar. The wardrobe hangs open, empty apart from a couple of hangers. Drawers have been pulled from my cabinet, my desk swept clear, the chair tipped over. On the carpet is a mountain of clothing.

And there, dangling from the light fitting, is a clothes hanger. On it is my favourite dress.

Around the neck is rope tied into a noose.

My throat constricts. "Mum?" The word comes out as a whimper.

She appears at the bottom of the stairs, still in her jacket. "What's wrong?"

"Someone's been in my room."

Quietly, Mum joins me. When she sees, the colour falls from her face. She holds me back, placing a finger to her lips, and we listen. From the kitchen, Dad's calling, "Dotty! Dinner!" and Felix is singing a nonsense song about toilets.

"I don't think anyone's there," Mum whispers after what seems like ages. "Wait here, Mia." She retreats to the bottom of the stairs, where Dad dumped his sports bag last night. My eyes widen as she arms herself with his cricket bat.

Together we creep towards the door of my room. It's like a whirlwind's swept through it. Everything has been turned upside down – my jewellery box, make-up, even my school pencil case.

"Don't touch." Mum's voice is sharp. "The police need to see this. It's evidence. And that" – she nods to the noose – "is a threat."

A chill creeps up my spine. Mum's right. This destructive behaviour is new. My stalker is obsessive *and* angry.

Last weekend was a car crash. A lot of people are raging at me right now.

Including everyone I've ever suspected.

I don't even know where to look. My things don't feel like mine any longer. The china giraffe money box I've had for ever lies in pieces, and my clock's face is smashed. The outfit my stalker sent lies by my foot. I pick it up. Mum's admonishment dies as the dress falls apart in my hand. It's been slashed neck to waist. The cardigan next to it has been shredded and so has the plaid skirt I wore to the Talent Showcase.

"Is Dotty there?" Dad's voice seems very loud, and we jump. "She's not showed up for dinner."

Mum and I lock eyes. A gaping hole opens inside me.

My room being evidence goes out of the window. Garbling panicked explanations, we show Dad the carnage, and search under clothes, books, the bed, frantically calling Dotty's name. Dotty is an indoor cat. There are only so many places she can be. Dad immediately checks that Felix is safe and together they warm her Whiskas in the microwave, hoping the smell will draw her out. But there's no meow, or jingle from the bell on her collar.

Dad returns from searching downstairs and in the garden. He stands in the doorway, where he can keep an eye on Felix, who's introducing his flamingo to the toys in his bedroom. "I don't think whoever did this is still around,"

Dad says. "He must have used the front door. Nothing's broken or forced. This person can't have a key, can he?"

"I haven't lost mine," I say.

"We must have forgotten to lock up," says Mum. "Maybe Dotty got out while he was here..."

"How? Surely he wouldn't have left the front door open for long. Even if he spooked Dotty, she'd have hidden, not escaped." I gulp. "He's hurt her. I know it. Dotty's so placid. She lets anyone pick her up. Doing something horrible would be easy..."

Mum goes ashen. "Oh God."

"I'll call the police," says Dad.

I start to sob. "I can't bear it. Oh, please, please let Dotty be OK!"

"She'll turn up soon." Mum tries to sound reassuring. "She's probably had a little explore, that's all."

Not Dotty. She isn't curious. Too fond of curling up on beds, or by toasty radiators. Mum hugs me. "Mia, I know you said you haven't lost your key, but is there any way this guy could have got hold of it? It doesn't take long to copy a key, then replace it." Mum lets go, but I can sense her trembling. "How many things have you lost since this started? Try to remember if anything in your room has ever been out of place. This is important, Mia."

My jaw drops as I realize what she's thinking. "No way."

"The police are on their way," Dad calls.

"Good." Mum's eyes don't leave mine. "Now call a locksmith."

28

A police officer arrives. His visit passes in a blur. He inspects my room, asks questions and listens with a serious expression on his face. His colleagues will be back later to collect evidence.

My phone shrills as the officer leaves.

Oliver calling.

My stomach flip-flops. I pick up, trying to sound normal. "Hi."

I hear him take a deep breath. "Hi. We should talk."

"Yeah. We should."

"You don't sound like you want to."

"It's … not a great time right now."

"What's wrong?"

The concern in Oliver's voice almost sets me off again. Oh, *why* did I mess up our friendship? "He's been in my house. Trashed my room. And I think … I think he's killed Dotty."

Oliver appears ten minutes later, looking like he ran the whole way. He opens his arms. I gulp and go to him. It should feel awkward, but it doesn't.

"Thanks for coming." My voice is muffled by his jumper. "I'm not sure there's much you can do, but…"

"We can look for Dotty. She could be trapped in a shed or garage. How about we knock on a few doors?"

"Do you mind?"

"Of course not. I know you love her. If anything ever happened to Jimmy… Not that anything has happened to Dotty. We'll find her."

Forty-five minutes later, we've covered my road and the one our house backs on to. Dotty is still MIA.

"Three houses didn't open up," says Oliver, when we meet back at mine. "We can try again later. I doubt Dotty's gone far, honestly, Mia. Even outdoor cats stick pretty close to their food source."

"We're not Dotty's food source. We're her home." I'm going to cry again. Dad gives my shoulders a squeeze.

"Cheer up, sunshine. We didn't find her hurt, did we? I doubt this stalker took Dotty with him. It's more likely she's simply lost."

"How about we make posters?" suggests Oliver.

"Can you help?" I ask. "You're good at design."

"Sure."

I fetch my laptop and Oliver knocks up a missing poster, pulling a picture from my social media. Dotty's yellow-green eyes gaze out mournfully from the screen. I choke back the lump that forms in my throat. I won't find her by falling apart.

By the time the posters are printed it's dark. Oliver lights the way with his phone torch while I tape them to lamp posts. Back home, the locksmith is scribbling an invoice. A delivery driver arrives after he leaves.

"Order from The Golden Lantern?"

Mum looks puzzled. "Not ours."

"That was me," says Oliver. "Sorry, I would have asked, but you were busy. I guessed no one fancied cooking."

Only Oliver could apologize for doing something like this. He firmly turns down Mum when she tries to pay him back, joking that he's basically lived at the Electric over Easter. I want to hug him as Dad opens up steaming boxes of noodles in the kitchen, but I don't know where we stand so I hold back. No one says much as we eat, even though the kung pao tofu and bao buns are really good. Mum gets Felix to bed while Dad clears up. Oliver and I go on to the patio.

"I'm so sorry, Olly," I say softly.

He sighs. "When I said I liked you a lot … I meant it."

"I know."

"You definitely don't see me that way?"

I trace circles in the air with my toe. "I don't know."

"Don't know isn't yes. And if it isn't yes…"

"Are we still friends?"

He gives me a tiny smile, though his eyes are sad. "Always. Sorry I went off in a sulk. I needed some space."

The back door opens.

"Mia." It's Dad. "That boy is here again."

Quin? "What does he want?"

"I didn't ask." Dad pauses. "Are you sure he's a friend? Because…"

The sentence hangs in the air unfinished, Dad's meaning obvious. My stalker's got into my parents' heads now, making them as paranoid as I am. "It's OK."

Dad doesn't look entirely convinced as he goes back in. I glance at Oliver. He picks up his messenger bag.

"Night, then."

"You don't have to go. I'm going to tell Quin to leave me alone."

Oliver shakes his head, saying he has stuff to do. Outside the front door Quin is pacing about. I glare at him over Oliver's shoulder as we hug goodbye.

"Thanks for being awesome, Olly," I say.

"Let me know the second you hear anything about Dotty."

I let him go. Quin watches Oliver walk down the road, then turns back to me. "Just so you know, I apologized to him and his parents, and paid for the damage. Well,

Dad did, but I gotta pay him back. I'm sorry I ruined the party."

He shoves his hands in his pockets. Once upon a time I'd have mistaken his attitude for defiant when really it's defensive. "OK," I say.

A pause. "That's it? OK?"

"Quin, I don't care, all right? I was wrong to invite you. Let's forget it."

His eyebrows draw together. "What's going on?"

Letting Quin in again is a bad idea but I don't have the energy not to. Keeping it brief, I explain.

"Shit," says Quin. "Are you OK? Silly question, course you're not. You done a knock around? I used to have a cat. She got trapped in—"

"Done that, thanks. I don't want to talk about it."

He twiddles the cord on his hoodie. "I'll go, then. Mind if I wait by the hedge? My old man said he'd pick me up here in half an hour and my phone's dead. Sorry about the quiz, by the way. Hope what I did at the party didn't put you off your game."

And now he's being nice and reasonable and reminding me why I liked him so much. I sit on the doorstep, gesturing for him to join me.

"I take it you heard about Riyad?" I ask.

He picks up a pebble and becomes engrossed in it. "Uh-huh."

"Did you know he was dealing?"

"I had some idea."

"Is that why you punched him?"

"Yes and no. I'm glad he got done. He had it coming."

"Leyla said there was a tip-off. Was it you?"

"You're asking too many questions." He tosses the pebble away. Is that a confession? "That party was a bad idea. I knew I'd get triggered. School was a hard place for me."

"Why did you go then?"

"I said before. You asked."

"And you have to do what I say?"

He rakes his hand through his hair, not making eye contact. Our arms brush as I shift to face him.

"I don't get it, Quin. Who's the real you? The guy I thought I was getting to know or the angry one who beats people up?"

"I'm not proud of all that. I'm better at dealing with my issues now."

"What were your issues?"

Silence stretches. As I'm thinking I've overstepped the mark, Quin says, "My parents were splitting up and I didn't like it. Sorry if you were expecting something less cliché."

"That sucks. I'm sorry. How bad was it?"

"Off the scale. They absolutely hated each other. Blazing rows and slammed doors. House was a tip. Then they were fighting over custody of me." His lip curls. "Like I was some kind of point to score. I'm glad Dad won. Mum cheated on him, more than once. Really shitty blokes, too."

I think of Aaron cheating on me, and wince.

"Mum and I don't speak much any more," Quin carries on. "It's better that way. School wasn't any escape. Being" – he hesitates – "dyslexic makes keeping up really hard. Feeling thick all day when you already feel shit, it's, well…"

"Extra shit?"

"Pretty much. I hated being around happy normal kids with their happy normal lives. I hated them. I hated my parents. Most of all I hated myself. There was this hot ball of rage inside me, every day, and the tiniest thing made it explode. Once I lost it, I couldn't stop. I wanted to break things. People. Dad calls it 'my demon'. Like I'm possessed."

He makes horns either side of his head with his fingers. "Didn't take long for everyone to decide I was bad news. But I liked people staying away. If you're not close to anyone, they can't hurt you. The downside is that being an angry knob gets pretty lonely. So yeah. That's the sob story." A pause. "Don't share this, all right? I'm only telling you because … well, I want to."

"Of course I won't. It must've been awful."

A shrug. "Mum and Dad always brought out the worst in each other. Toxic relationship. It's taken me years to get that. Dad's better with Demi. I was happy when they got together. It felt good to have a proper family, a home where it was nice to be, two sisters. I was doing all right with self-control, and the chef course. I'd failed at everything I'd ever tried before that. Life was looking up. Now Jade's gone, everything's spiralling. But I don't want to be demon boy again, Mia."

I gaze at him. "You're really ... self-aware. I don't know many people who can look at themselves from the outside like that."

"I'll tell Dad. He'll be delighted therapy was good for something. Apparently I have 'low self-esteem' as well as a foul temper."

There he goes again, mocking himself. Now I know what it's masking, it no longer puts me off. I take his hand.

"Well, I think you're all right, Quin Farrell, so maybe you should kick that low self-esteem where it hurts."

"You still think that even after I decked Riyad?"

I frown. "Why is he such a trigger for you? If you know something about him, Quin, you should really tell me."

Quin hesitates. "He just is. I really am sorry I lost it. I was on edge anyway, and seeing him made me snap."

Opening up to me only goes so far, then. "Sorry I called you ... that name. I was upset, and saying stuff I didn't mean. Well. Some of it I did mean. The nicer stuff. So... Um, yeah."

He looks at our hands, linked together, his with two plastered fingers, mine with chipped sage-green nail varnish. He gives mine a firm squeeze. We only break apart when a dark car pounding rap music draws up. Quin gets to his feet.

"That's the old man. Call if you get lonely." He gives me a hasty hug, and then he's gone.

By the time the police finish going through my room it's late. They've swabbed for fingerprints but warn us that unless my stalker is on file there won't be a match. He definitely had a key – one of the neighbours saw a guy at the door, but all she can remember was that he was wearing a hoodie.

I survey the mess and try to imagine who could do this. Riyad always seems unflappable, but is it a front? Dealing drugs doesn't mean he hasn't also been stalking me. Leyla said he was furious over me supposedly dobbing him in. Could he really take this sort of revenge? What about Mr Ellison? What would have provoked him? He was weirdly invested in the quiz but surely this couldn't be because I screwed that up. Of course, whoever it is might be in a jealous rage about me kissing Oliver. The curtains were open. It might not have been a neighbour Jimmy barked at.

Despite the time, none of us feel settled enough for bed, so Mum, Dad and I sort my clothes into piles – those that are untouched, those that can be repaired, and those that are only good for the bin. It took years to build an image that made me feel good. How long did it take him to ruin it – ten minutes?

"He's even gone through your underwear," Mum says in a wobbly voice. "We'd better buy you some basics tomorrow."

Under a skirt I find the first drawing Aaron did of the pair of us, the special one I Blu-tacked on the wall. Somehow I couldn't quite bring myself to take it down, even after he confessed to killing Jade and sleeping with Brooke. This drawing felt like a reminder of a simpler, happier time when I was falling for a guy I thought was wonderful, and everything and everyone around me made sense. It's been torn in half, across our necks. It feels like another threat.

I gulp back the lump in my throat and pick up my pillow, hugging it. The pillow smells strongly of that lemon detergent—

Hang on.

This bedding isn't fresh. I put it through the wash myself days ago – using our usual cotton-scented powder.

So why does it smell of lemons?

"Mum? You haven't changed our detergent recently, have you? Or started using spray, or diffusers, or…"

Mum looks at me like I've lost it. "No."

I press my nose to the pillow again. Not cotton, not shampoo. Definitely lemon.

What does it remind me of? Something I smell frequently. Something from school…

The citrus cologne loads of the boys wear.

Every part of my body goes cold.

The pillow falls from my arms with a soft thud.

"Mum." I have to force the words out. "I don't think this is the first time he's been in my room." I swallow. "He's been coming in here for weeks and lying on my bed."

My parents don't argue when I ask to sleep on the sofa bed in the home office. This bedding smells reassuringly normal, but whichever way I turn I can't settle. I keep picturing a male body stretched out on my duvet, his face pressed to the pillow, inhaling like he inhaled the scent of my shampoo. How many times did he sneak in? What did he think about as he lay there, surrounded by my old stuffed toys? Did he fantasize about us together, the same way I used to dream of being romanced?

I wish the lemon cologne was a clue but it isn't. It's super common. Hell, I even remember Mr Ellison wearing something similar. I'm shaking again. I can't stop. Going through my things was bad enough, but something this intimate… I don't know if I'll ever be able to sleep there again. Even once it's washed, to me that bed will always smell of him.

I try Quin's breathing trick, and reclaim a little calm. The office is tucked away at the back of the house, and crammed full of Dad's work stuff, but I still don't feel fully safe. If Dotty was here her small, comforting body would be nestled close to mine. Is she in the cold and dark, confused and scared? Hurt? She'll be hungry and thirsty. Cats can't last long without water.

Will the police be able to trace my stalker from the fingerprints, or the messages he sent? That was on their to-do list, but this guy was smart enough to buy Jade a burner and dispose of it. He won't leave an obvious trail.

My fingers hover over the screen of my phone.

What have I got to lose?

Have you hurt my cat?

The message sits there. One minute, two, five. Ten. Nothing.

323

If I've upset you, I'm sorry. But Dotty hasn't done anything wrong. Please tell me what you've done with her.

Another minute. Then:

Unknown: why should i

Mia: What do you want from me?

Unknown: nothing any more

i'm glad you're hurt

you deserve to hurt like i have

bitch

your cat is dead

sweet dreams

29

"You find Dotty?" Quin sounds sleepy when he answers my video call.

"He says he killed her," I say.

The soft hum of TV in the background goes silent. Quin moves his phone into a better position. It's a comfort to see his face. One of the rats is curled up on his chest. "Tell me exactly what he said."

I do. Quin makes an angry noise.

"Dramatic piece of shit, isn't he? He's bluffing. If he'd really hurt Dotty, he'd leave her somewhere you'd see."

"Surely we'd have found her by now, though?"

"Not if she's trapped. Mia, he's messing with you, all right?"

"Did I wake you up?"

"Nah. I was watching a thing about whales. Turns out certain types can live for two hundred years, who knew. Police any help?"

"Not much. Do you genuinely think Dotty is OK?"

"Yeah."

"Sorry, you already said. It's just I'm spooked, and... If you don't want to chat, just say. I used to embarrass Aaron by getting worked up and being needy—"

"Mia, shut up," says Quin. "One, if I didn't want you to call I wouldn't have offered. Two, I ain't Aaron. Three, stop apologizing. You're upset, not needy."

He's right. Aaron not knowing how to deal with me being emotional doesn't mean I was wrong to seek comfort. "Thanks."

"Aoife says hi." Quin lifts her up to the screen.

I smile slightly. "Hi, Aoife. Your dad is wise."

"Dad?"

"It's a saying when you have pets. You know, that you're their parent."

"Right. Father of Rats. Not in the same league as Mother of Dragons."

I shift. "I hate feeling this helpless."

"How about we focus on what we know, rather than what we don't?"

"OK." Conscious of my flimsy pyjama top, I pull the

326

duvet higher. "This guy was there the night Jade died. He took the bag. Aaron knows more but won't say."

"Why would Aaron protect someone?"

"I think he's scared. My stalker was threatening him. Remember those letters?"

"I still don't buy that Aaron and Mr Stalker were both in that outdoor gym by coincidence."

A tiny head with big ears pops up on Quin's other shoulder. He strokes Saoirse absently.

"Only Aaron knows the truth," I say. "He got his mum to give me the letters so he does want to help, but I can't visit him without an adult. I've checked. Mum or Dad might take me, I guess."

"Do I count as an adult? I'm eighteen. Not by much, but whatever."

"Oh! Late happy birthday. I didn't know."

"'S all right. It wasn't a big thing. What do you think, then?"

"Let's do it." The tiniest hope sparks inside me.

"Hang on a sec," says Quin. "Dad wants something."

I wait while Quin speaks to his dad. He returns to the phone after about a minute.

"Dad's just qualified as a self-defence instructor," he says. "Since Jade died it's been his new thing. Says that if it stops even one family losing a kid it'll be worth it. Dad wants to know if you think it's something people – mostly girls, but boys too – would be interested in."

I think of how helpless I felt at the nature reserve. "Definitely."

"Dad's happy to give you a class this holiday, if you want."

"He'd do that for me?"

"Uh-huh." Quin rubs the side of his nose. "Think he wants to meet you, too."

I wonder what Quin's said about me. "Thanks, Quin. I'm so glad we made up."

"Yeah." He sounds gruff. "Night then."

The next day Mum and I spend the morning repairing some of my clothes before going shopping. I let Mum buy neutral basics without complaint, even though they aren't really my style.

She insists on stopping at the retail park Costa afterwards. "We deserve coffee and cake. Grab a table while I order."

The armchairs by the window are free. Bea Eaton from my geography class is clearing empty cups. I didn't realize she worked here.

Bea smiles when she sees me. "Hey, Mia. What d'you make of Riyad dealing? I heard his parents are raging."

"Pretty much," I say. "Did you know?"

"Nope, but a lot of things make sense now, that's all I'm saying."

It's obviously not all she's saying, because Bea is a massive gossip. My new tactic of silence works yet again, and Bea leans closer.

"Remember the *incident* last spring? Bad drugs? Girl being hospitalized?"

"Oh no – that wasn't because of him, was it?"

"I reckon so," says Bea. "There was a party that weekend and he was acting shady. The timing fits. And we all know who took a month off school afterwards, don't we?"

My jaw drops as I piece everything together.

Sunday afternoon is when Quin and I are due to visit Aaron. I'm at our meeting spot outside the train station first. I rock from my heels to my toes, glancing at my watch. Quin is cutting it fine. Potentially missing our train isn't the only thing making me nervous, either.

"Oi! Mia."

I do a double take. Quin is waving from a mint-green Fiat a couple of metres away.

"I got wheels today." He leans over and opens the passenger door. "Proper girl car this, innit? Kills my street cred."

"You told me you didn't drive."

"I never."

"You did. After we met Harper, I'm sure of it."

"This matters because...?" Quin sounds impatient. "Maybe I said I didn't have a car. Until I got insured on this that was true enough. It's Demi's. Dad never liked me borrowing his."

I hesitate. My mind slips to the feeling of being blindfolded in my stalker's car before I pull it back. I get in beside him.

"You free tomorrow evening?" he asks, releasing the

handbrake. "Dad has an hour spare for that self-defence class."

"Sure. Thanks. That's really kind of him."

"Still no Dotty?"

I shake my head. "Quin … did you beat Riyad up because he gave Camille bad drugs?"

The car lurches as Quin brakes.

"Jesus, Mia! Could've said that before I pulled out. Let me park again, we got time."

I wait for him to drive into a bay. "Is it true, then?"

"Who told you – Camille?"

"I worked it out. You could have said."

"Not my secret." He looks at me. "It means a lot that you always believed I had a reason for going for Riyad and didn't just write me off as no good like everyone else."

"So what's the story?"

Quin leans back. "Camille was the only person who was ever kind to me at school. Riyad was her boyfriend then. He should've looked after her, not given her dodgy shit. It made me see red, him getting away scot-free when Camille was so ill and having to drop out of that tennis competition she could've won. I knew the bad dope came from him. I overheard Riyad bugging her to try it."

I turn this over in my head. "So you got kicked out of school and let everyone believe all these terrible rumours to … get revenge for a girl who was sometimes kind to you? Why get involved?"

"Why not? I didn't care, Mia. Getting a bad rep, hated

on – big deal. No one liked me anyway. Me included. Now, yeah, I can see I should've handled it differently."

"Did Camille know you did it for her?"

"Not at the time, nah."

"Why did you change your mind and tip the police off?"

"I didn't."

"Then who— Oh." My eyes widen. "That was Camille?"

He nods. "She called me the morning after your mate's party. Everything came out. She said she almost reported Riyad after word got out about Aaron being high, but she was scared. Wanted to put that chapter behind her. But this time she realized the truth would help."

"God, Quin. I can't work out whether you've been honourable in the wrong way or made really bad decisions."

"Bit of column A and bit of column B?"

Am I going to go there? Yeah, apparently I am. "So you and Camille never had a thing going?"

He blinks. "That's what you think?"

"You visited her in hospital." I can't help remembering how Camille described Quin: clingy. "She said you started messaging her a lot afterwards. You still message now."

"Not very often." Quin drums his fingers on the steering wheel then turns to me. "Do you remember me not being around much for a few months last year?"

That was when all the rumours about Quin having been in prison started circulating. "Sure."

"I signed up."

I stare at him. "You mean … the Army? You're kidding. You're too young!"

"Not for basic training. You said it yourself once – the Army's where they shove bad lads. Tames their aggression. I hated it. Homesickness is no joke. So I dropped out. Told you I fail at everything I try."

Now I feel grubby for even listening to the rumours. Quin's just a messed-up kid trying to find his way. Same as me, same as everyone. "Oh."

"Turns out I belong in the kitchen." Quin's voice lightens. "Still got the Army uniform somewhere. You know, in case that's of interest."

I roll my eyes. "All right, Quinlan."

"I'm telling you this cos that's why I messaged Camille so much. The barracks were a lonely place. I didn't have other friends."

"That makes sense. It's just, Camille said you were … clingy."

"What, cos I pestered the nurses to let me see her in hospital? I wanted to check she was all right." Quin fidgets. "Look. Maybe I did fancy her. Can't blame me for that. Popular girl and loser. Another cliché. I never harassed her, though. Please tell me she didn't take the messages that way?"

I shake my head, making a mental note to check with Camille just in case. Maybe I still appear disbelieving, because Quin suddenly looks amused – and pleased.

"Were you jealous?" he says.

"No! Of course not. I was curious. That's all."

"Well, as you're so *curious*, yeah, Camille's nice, but that's it." He smiles. "She's not my type any more."

"What is your type?"

"That'd be telling."

I smile back. "Shall we hit the road?"

An hour later we're parking outside the young offender institution. The comfortable atmosphere that built up in the car evaporates. After going through security, we're shown to the meeting room. The fake plant is gone. I wonder if someone broke it. Quin shuffles closer. Is he thinking this could easily have been him? I squeeze his hand.

A squeak from the door at the other end of the room announces Aaron's arrival. This time I'm prepared for how awful he looks. The guard points us towards a table. Aaron slouches on the plastic chair opposite us, leaning his crutches to one side. He gives my new hair a quick once-over but doesn't comment.

"I said I didn't want to see you again," he says.

"Could've turned me away," I say.

Aaron hesitates, then drops the attitude. "Are you OK, Mia? Did something bad happen?"

So he does care. I knew it. "Do you mind Quin being here? I know he's not someone you want to see, but we're friends now."

Aaron bites his lip. Quin folds his arms, mirroring Aaron. He doesn't speak, letting me take the lead.

"Tell me about those letters," I say.

"There isn't much to tell," says Aaron quietly. "They started a couple of weeks before everything went to shit. There were more I didn't keep. I wish I'd done what he said."

"Why didn't you tell anyone you were being threatened?"

"I didn't like being told what to do. I thought I could tough it out."

Typical Aaron. "I wouldn't have thought you were a wuss for being scared. Honestly. I liked it when you opened up to me."

Aaron glances again at Quin, his expression wary. "Are you still … you know?"

"Being stalked?"

He nods. I tell him about the break-in and Dotty.

Aaron pales. "Poor Dotty. I'm sorry, Mia. How do you think I can help?"

"By telling me who was with you when Jade died."

"I can't."

"Why not? This person is the stalker, the guy who groomed Jade! He's terrifying, Aaron!"

Misery is all over his face. "I'm sorry, Mia. It's… I want to help, but this is really difficult for me."

I dig my nails into my palms. "So you're going to lie in court and say you were alone? Why?"

"What's the point of dragging someone else into this? My trial's in two weeks. Pretty soon it'll all be over."

My stalker must have something on Aaron. I can't see another reason why he's being so difficult. And there's fear in his eyes. I swallow my anger and change tack. "How do you feel about that?"

A shrug. "Scared shitless. It's my mum and dad and Soph I really worry about, though."

For the first time Quin speaks. "Go through what happened that night again."

"No."

Quin holds up his hands. "I'm not gonna lose it. Promise."

Aaron gives me the *really?* look he used whenever Oliver brought up some especially obscure film. For a second it's like the old days.

"If that's what you want," he says. "Mia and I met at the Electric. I came home just before seven."

"With Brooke," I add, so I don't have to hear him say it first. Aaron hesitates then nods.

"Yeah. Brooke." I look away. "After she left I felt like shit. I thought, screw that, I want to get out of my head. So I went to the outdoor gym."

"Where you called Riyad and asked for the LSD?"

Aaron nods again. "Mum told me he's been caught so there's no point protecting him any more. We did LSD once before. I was surprised, Riyad dealing. He's the golden boy. He said forbidden things gave him a kick, but I reckon he was talking big. He's not as confident as he acts. Dunno why I looked up to him, really."

I wonder if to Riyad I'm a forbidden thing, too… "Did he join you at the outdoor gym?"

"Yeah. He brought the stuff, but he didn't stay."

I purse my lips. It's so hard to know whether to believe Aaron or not. "Why were you hanging out there anyway?"

"No real reason. Didn't want to be inside, I guess."

"My stalker. When did he show up? Did you invite him to hang out, or was it a coincidence?"

Aaron hesitates again. "He just appeared. To be honest, I half-thought he was a hallucination, you know, part of the trip… We talked about you. That I remember. Then she showed up. She was angry and laid into me."

Quin's fist thumps the table, making both of us jump. "Her name was Jade. Use it, all right?"

Aaron swallows. I nudge his foot with mine. "Go on. What was Jade angry about?"

"From what I remember, relationship stuff. Part of why I mistook her for you, I guess. Jade raised her hand to hit me."

This is new. I exchange a glance with Quin. The room has gone deadly quiet.

"And she was talking to you?" I ask.

"Yeah."

"But why would she? Don't you think Jade might really have been having a go at the guy with you? Her boyfriend, who she'd found out was obsessed with me?"

"I don't know. It's a blur. How is this helping, Mia? I killed Jade. I don't want to talk about it any more."

"I do. We're getting somewhere." I visualize the scene – the outdoor gym on the field, path running parallel, gardens from the houses at the edge of the estate backing on to it. "How did you get Jade to your car?"

"I carried her."

"All the way to your house without anyone seeing? Are you sure you didn't go home, grab the car and drive it closer?"

He doesn't answer.

"Aaron, please," I say. "Why did you move her?"

"I wasn't thinking clearly. I panicked. Probably I brought the car to the gym, I don't know."

I feel the stalker's arms around me at the nature reserve, hefting me to his car. He's not weak, and that was hard work. I turn to Quin. "Were there any signs on Jade's body of her having been dragged?"

He shakes his head. I smack the table. "That's it, then. He helped you carry her. He's the one who drove the car to the beach. All that rubbish about managing yourself! That's when he nicked the bag."

Aaron's forehead glistens with sweat. "Maybe you're right. But it doesn't change what happened!"

"What if it does, though?" My voice is quiet but my thoughts are racing and by God I've never felt so sharp. "You said it yourself. It's a blur. Aaron, this guy helped you cover up Jade's death. Don't you think that's pretty sick?"

"Mia, *I remember killing her.*" The guard on the other side of the room glances up. Aaron lowers his voice. "Two hands on her shoulders, shove. Blood all over the bar. Can we stop now?"

Beside me, Quin tenses. I sit very still. Thump thump thump goes my heart. "You don't, though."

"Don't what?"

"Remember killing her."

"I do."

"No. You remember pushing her."

Aaron leans forwards. "Blunt force trauma to the back of the head. That's what killed Jade. I saw her hit her head. She was dead."

Out of the corner of my eye I catch Quin watching us closely. "When you fell from the fire escape I thought you were dead," I say. "You looked it. I couldn't find your pulse, and for thirty seconds I was out of my mind. How did you know Jade was dead?"

"There was blood. She wasn't moving."

"Neither of those things mean she was dead. Tell me exactly what you remember."

"When I saw the blood, I threw up, OK? When I looked at her again, her eyes were … staring."

"What did the other guy do while you were throwing up? Or don't you know?"

Aaron is silent. I put myself in my stalker's shoes. Desperately loved up, using Jade as a substitute for me. Jade, who'd realized I existed. Jade, furious about being used.

Jade, a threat.

I look Aaron square in the eyes. "You've been set up."

30

Aaron keeps saying no, it's not possible. He's started to shake. The guard clears his throat, tapping his watch.

I clutch his hands. "Aaron, you don't want to go to prison. What do you have to lose? Tell me this sicko's name. I'll do all I can to prove what really happened, before you go to court."

"I can't." Aaron speaks through gritted teeth. "Even if there's a chance that you're right and he did this, I can't."

"Why not?" My grip tightens. "I'm in danger. Breaking into my house, killing my cat? How long before he goes for Felix, my parents? Maybe it doesn't bother you, but—"

"Don't say that," Aaron hisses. "Of course it bothers me."

"So give me a name."

"Two minutes," says the guard.

"There's a way out of this," I say. "Don't give up. Fight."

Do Aaron's eyes flicker to Quin? He beckons me closer. I lean in. Breath warm against my ear, Aaron murmurs, "Your stalker's still sending me letters."

"What – like the others?"

"These are chatty, innocent sounding. Our mail gets read here so they have to be. But I can read between the lines and it's very clear. If I tell, he'll hurt my family. I've put them through hell already. I love them. I can't risk their safety."

I draw back an inch. "Not even if it means getting out of here?"

He shakes his head. "Be careful, Mia. Thanks for trying to save me, but it's hopeless."

"Of course I'm trying. I love you, silly."

Aaron goes rigid. My hands are still curled around his. I look at them, then up at him, blinking. Aaron gulps. His eyes have gone glassy.

"I didn't do it, Mia," he says.

I sit up straighter, alert. "Kill Jade? I knew—"

"Not that. Brooke."

What?

"I lied about sleeping with her," he says. "I'm really sorry, Mia. I needed to push you away."

340

I recoil. "You… Why would you—"

"You were so determined to clear my name. I loved that, but I knew it was so dangerous. Pretending I'd cheated was the only thing I could think of to get you to stop." He wipes his eyes. "I was trying to protect you."

I stare at him, barely able to process this. Everything I felt – the betrayal and the confusion, the relationship I mourned – flashes before me.

"I should've known you still wouldn't give up," says Aaron. He's choked up now, and a tear trickles down his cheek. "And people go on about me being stubborn."

"You hurt me," I croak. "Badly, Aaron."

"I know. I hated doing it. I'm sorry."

The guard comes over. "Time's up."

I give his hands a fierce squeeze before dropping them. "I'm going to get you out of here. That's a promise."

Aaron looks over his shoulder as he's led away. His eyes are wide with wonder – as though he's finally seeing me properly.

"I take it that whispering wasn't Aaron giving you a name." Quin breaks the silence. I lean back in the passenger seat of Demi's car, blowing out a long breath.

"No."

"Sure?"

"If he'd said, I'd tell you."

He turns the key in the ignition. "Yeah?"

"How can you be so unemotional?" I burst out. "Aaron

didn't do this, Quin! I'm certain Jade was only hurt after he pushed her. My stalker must've killed her while Aaron was throwing up. He sure as hell has a motive – and he groomed your sister. Why aren't you gunning for him?"

"I am. I want to find him and make him pay. That hasn't changed. I still think Aaron's a knob, though." His eyes meet mine in the interior mirror. "But if him being set up makes you happy, good. Maybe he'll get off and you can fall into his arms and ride off into the sunset."

I frown. "I didn't say I wanted that."

"You didn't need to. You're going to forgive him, aren't you? Even though he's completely left you in the shit. Keeping his family safe, yeah, I get that, but what about your safety? And as for 'I broke your heart to protect you'?" He pulls a face. "How is that OK? Not that you ever told me about him cheating."

I stare at him. "Why are you being like this?"

"You work it out."

We crawl out of the car park. I push my hair from my face, taking a moment to process everything. Am I going to forgive Aaron? Might there be a future for us – and do I even want that? With a start, I realize that Quin's wrong: Aaron didn't break my heart. For a while I was lost, hurt, confused, but other things – other people – filled the hole Aaron left. People like Quin, who make me feel strong, and fierce, and secure in myself. The things I thought mattered, like common interests and shared references, haven't been so important after all. And I don't fret over Quin's approval like I did Aaron's. The circumstances are the worst, but good has grown from the bad.

Without consciously being aware of it, I've finished grieving Aaron. We had something special, and it mattered – but he wasn't the right guy for me.

Quin brakes at some lights. Slowly, I say, "I don't want to get back together with Aaron. I started out unable to let go, but it's not like that any more. I do still want to help him, though. I care. And I don't want my stalker to win. Is that so bad?"

"Yeah? That's all the L-bomb was about?"

So he heard. I take a breath. "Saying that felt natural. There are lots of kinds of love, Quin. Telling my friends I love them is something I do. But I'm not *in* love with Aaron. There's a difference. Are you the jealous one now?"

"Lemme drive, all right?" Quin snaps.

I flinch. Why is Quin acting up? Only moments ago I was thinking how good it was to have him in my life. Should I apologize? No. I'm not at fault. I've explained what I meant, and he should accept that, not act like a child.

We drive in silence. Two weeks until the trial. A ticking clock. If I can only find some evidence, Aaron can still have a life. And this bastard can face the consequences of everything he's done.

The next morning BITCH is sprayed across the garage door in bright red. Learning how to defend myself from the stalker has never felt so critical. That evening I find myself in a sweaty, mirror-lined fitness studio with Quin and his dad, Cormac, who's cheerful and chatty and immediately puts me at ease. One of the tattoos on his arms says *Quinlan* in enormous letters, which in other circumstances would make me giggle. Cormac's teaching a Muay Thai class in an hour, but assures me that's enough time to run through the basics of self-defence. They turn out to be surprisingly … basic. If attacked I should always go for what Cormac calls 'vulnerable areas'. Unsurprisingly, the eyes and groin are two of them, but the throat and nose can also cause a lot of pain.

"How you strike depends on how you're attacked," says Cormac. I did know he was from Northern Ireland, but I still can't get over how different his accent is to Quin's. "From behind is common, so we'll cover that first. Quinlan?"

Quin walks over and folds his arms around my waist. I do my best not to be distracted by how his body feels pressed to mine as Cormac shows me how to shift my weight, then swing my elbow round. The first time, I accidentally use too much force and Quin drops his hold with an exclamation.

"That's what we want to happen!" Cormac holds up his palm for a high five. "You all right, son?"

"I'll live," Quin mutters. "Don't you dare do that when he shows you how to kick someone in the balls."

We practise escapes when attacked from the front, side and pinned up against a wall. This last involves squatting, then jumping up and aiming for Quin's jaw with my forehead. I can't get my balance right, and I'm at a real height disadvantage. Cormac tells me to keep practising on Quin, smirking at the death glare his son sends him.

"Final simple tip is keys," he says. "Used correctly, they're an excellent weapon. Contrary to popular culture, don't hold them between your knuckles. Your best options are a knife grip and a hammer grip." He demonstrates with his house keys, then passes them over.

I curl my fingers round a key and mime a downwards stab. "Nasty."

"That's the aim. I won't get you to experiment on Quinlan. Don't want to ruin his good looks, do we?"

I cover my embarrassment with a cough. We run through everything again before people start arriving at the other studio for Muay Thai. Cormac offers to drive me home if I'm happy to wait an hour, and, not fancying the bus, I accept. The door swings shut behind him, muting the voices outside.

I look at Quin. The studio feels very large for just the two of us. "Can we practise those moves again?"

"If you like. How d'you want to be attacked first?"

I glare at him. "Don't be a dick. I get that your dad's a bit cringe, but it's really nice of him to help me. I wish all girls knew self-defence."

I also wish we didn't have to. Quin kicks his heel against the wall.

"OK, that was a dick thing to say," he mutters. "Sorry. Obviously I want you to learn this stuff and be safe."

345

"But…? You've been acting funny since yesterday."

"I'm not acting funny."

I rest my hands on my hips. "You are. Is this about the L-bomb again? I told you, I'm not *in* love with Aaron, so if you're upset—"

"I'm not upset," he snaps. "I don't care, all right?"

That stings. Quin's not meeting my eyes any more. Is he saving face or does he mean it? He didn't reply to the message I sent earlier. Maybe he doesn't like me any more. The silence grows until I can't bear it any longer.

"Let's just practise, OK?"

"Fine." Quin steps behind me, looping one arm round my neck and the other across my upper arm. I grab his wrists – stop the choke-hold – turn, squat down. I lose my balance and almost topple.

"Again, please."

His arms move across my shoulders, as before. They hover, then drop and close around my waist. I can feel the tension in his muscles. He presses his face into my shoulder. I stare at our reflection in the wall mirrors. This is definitely a hug and not a potential assault.

"I can't do this," he mumbles.

My breathing quickens. In the mirror he closes his eyes. Then he lets go and stalks off. The doors swing closed behind him.

Cormac drops me home in his black Ford, waiting until I'm inside the house before driving off. Quin doesn't even wave. He said nothing the whole drive, only grunting in response to his dad's chatter. I hate how guarded he's become, like those moments of warmth and closeness didn't happen.

"I can't do this." Perhaps tonight was weird for him. Seeing me learn to defend myself in ways Jade couldn't – I can understand how that might mess with his head.

Whatever the reason, Quin definitely wants emotional distance between us.

Feeling deflated, I go to grab a drink before FaceTiming my friends. As I open the fridge, there's scuffling from the back door, followed by a soft thud.

I go still. There it is again.

Something's in the garden.

I open my mouth to call my parents. Then I stop. If it's him, this is a massive mistake. A metre away is a switch that will flood the patio with light. The kitchen's still dark. He can't know I'm here.

Sliding out a knife from the block by the cooker, I edge towards the French windows.

Scuffle, scuffle. Crash.

My finger flips the switch.

31

On the patio sits Dotty, an overturned flowerpot next to her.

My heart leaps. "Baby!"

She paces, then claws the glass. I swipe the keys from the clay pot on the window sill. The second the door is open I drop the knife and scoop her into my arms, pressing my nose into her cold fur.

"Mum! Dad!"

My parents hurry into the hallway. When they see Dotty they gasp. She gives a pathetic mew, her skinny body vibrating with a strong purr. I set her down on the kitchen table, feeling for injuries.

"She seems fine." I wipe my eyes. "Oh, Dotty! I thought you were dead."

"She must have been trapped after all." Dad scratches Dotty under the chin. "Do you want dinner, puss?"

Dotty mews. We all laugh nervously. Dad empties a sachet of Whiskas into her bowl and she wolfs it down.

Mum glances my way. "So he lied."

"I guess it was too good an opportunity to scare me," I say. "She probably did slip out after all."

That night Dotty cuddles up with me on the spare bed as though nothing happened. I feel the tiniest bit emboldened.

Two weeks. Time for Aaron is running out. How can I get this guy to slip up? Could I set a trap? Even with help, that screams danger. Are there any leads I can chase? The only one I can think of is finding the rest of the photos from the teen screening, if they even still exist, but that's so tenuous. Actually, what about Harper? She was hardly cooperative the first time, but if I explain that Jade's boyfriend might be the killer, maybe she'll spill?

Harper ignores the two DMs I send. I toy with asking Quin to set up a meeting then decide not to. Harper wasn't his greatest fan, and Quin's retreated into his shell anyway. So I message again, stressing how important it is. This time, she replies.

Ok we can chat. Wednesday afternoon. Only you though.

I purse my lips. Going alone isn't ideal, but it's worth the risk. My friends are busy on Wednesday anyway, Oliver

349

at the Electric, and Leyla at a violin lesson. Perhaps I can arrange to meet Quin after seeing Harper and hopefully patch things up between us. If she does tell me what she knows, that might break the ice.

Harper and I agreed to meet at a park close to where she lives. I spot her enormous curls as soon as I enter. She eyes me suspiciously as I approach.

Without the make-up, Harper looks younger. Less abrasive. "I didn't recognize you at first," she says. "You changed your hair. Is he here?"

"Who? Quin? No. I came alone, like you asked."

"All right then." We sit on a bench shaded by evergreen trees. Harper inspects a scab on her knee, miming nonchalance. I glance around, paranoid I've been followed, but the only people around are young families.

Here goes.

"Harper, I need you to tell me absolutely everything you know." And I explain that I think Jade's boyfriend killed her.

Harper pales. In a small voice, she says, "Jade was mad at him. Her boyfriend, I mean. She was going to dump him the night she died."

"What? You never said."

"Look, I only agreed to even speak to you before because her stepbrother went on and on until I couldn't say no. He's so intense."

Quin's definitely that.

"I get you being angry. You knew the boyfriend had made Jade into me. Not saying I appreciated the milkshake attack, mind."

Harper doesn't apologize, just shrugs. But she's confirmed one theory – it was almost certainly not Aaron Jade was shouting at.

"Jade figured out her guy's game, didn't she?" I say. "That screening at the Electric Palace – she and I were in the same place, for the first time. The penny dropped."

Harper nods. "She was going to march over and demand to know what was going on, but he was there."

How sick that both of us could be in the same room and my stalker knew Jade wouldn't say anything! I wonder if it gave him a kick, to see how totally under his thumb she was...

Only he got that wrong, because later Jade went digging.

"What happened next?"

"Jade was heartbroken. She thought he was so perfect, that they were perfect together." Harper's words make me shift uncomfortably. I know who that sounds like. "Jade had a hard shell but she was soft inside, once you knew her. She felt a fool for being so easily played. Angry, too. Jade wasn't one for sitting around crying. We scrolled all through your social media, piecing it together. We even followed you once."

"What, in person? Jade stalked me?"

"Not for long. It felt too creepy. The photos in Jade's room genuinely weren't hers."

Maybe Jade went snooping and found them in my stalker's car, or house, if she ever went there. I can see a distraught girlfriend doing something like that.

"She wanted to give him a chance to explain," Harper carries on. "That's what meeting him the night she died was about, why she glammed up. I dunno whether the idea was to get him to realize it was her he really wanted, or if she was power-dressing. It's what we do when we're nervous."

I think of Harper rocking up at Quin's with her killer make-up on. She certainly intimidated me. Perhaps I'll try power-dressing myself. I'm getting a sneaking admiration for Jade. She was fierce. It's taken me longer to realize my worth, but she knew hers straight away.

Harper picks at her scab again. "Maybe I should've told the police everything, but I don't trust them. Then your boyfriend confessed and I didn't need to." She pauses. "Jade wanted me to go with her, you know. I said no. It was cold, and far, and my dad had promised us a takeaway. We literally never argued, me and Jade. That was the first time ever."

Now Jade's passive-aggressive WhatsApp to Harper makes sense. I wince. "You can't blame yourself, Harper."

"What if I'd been there, though? Maybe she'd still be alive."

"It's not your fault. It's his."

"Doesn't feel that way. And I don't need your sympathy." She shrugs off the arm I put around her shoulder.

"Please talk to someone, Harper," I say. "This is going

to be with you for ever."

"Thanks for reminding me." But Harper's words have no bite. I feel so bad for her, but I know when to back off.

I turn the conversation back to the boyfriend. "If I showed you photos, do you think you'd be able to pick him out?"

"I never saw him. I told you, Jade was ultra-secretive."

"Is there anything specific you remember? What they talked about, or where they went?"

Harper shakes her head. "It was all Romantic Date 101 stuff. Almost from a manual. Even the love letters and messages — I thought they were classy, but now they seem kind of, I dunno, copy and paste? He could've found everything online."

"There must be something. I'm desperate, Harper. Think."

She goes quiet. Then: "There was one thing. Jade said mostly he listened to her talking, but there was something he went on about once, when they met up. Something he was into. A computer game, maybe." She wrinkles her nose. "Don't remember. Jade WhatsApped me about it, though."

"Can you check now?"

Harper shakes her head. "Jade's messages are on my old phone. Seeing her name everywhere, and photos… It was too much." She's choking up. "I wish I could get a new brain too. Every day, she's here. Sometimes I wish I could forget her. Then I feel terrible. I miss her so, so much."

I really want to hug her again. "Will you please message me whatever the thing was when you get home?"

Harper somewhat unwillingly lets me type my number into her phone. She gets up, straightening her skirt. "You're not going to tell her stepbrother about this, are you?"

It bothers me that she won't say Quin's name. "What's your problem with Quin?"

"I don't trust him."

"Why not?"

"Just don't." And she hurries off.

On the bus home I check my phone constantly but there's nothing from Harper. All I can do is wait.

Maybe I should stop by the Electric and chase up those photos, long shot or not. Harper stressed that seeing me there was a pivotal moment for Jade – I should at least rule them out. Quin can meet me there rather than The Green Leaf.

Oliver is sweeping the foyer when I arrive. He gives me a big smile. "Hey, Mia. I wasn't expecting you."

"I wanted to see Ivy. Is she in the office?"

"For what it's worth. I doubt she's actually working."

Ivy's reapplying her make-up in a compact mirror when I stick my head round the door. She looks glamorous in a cherry-print wiggle dress, a flower pinned in her hair.

"Hey, you," she says. "What's up?"

"Do you have the photos from the teen screening? I was wondering if I could see them."

"Sure, hon…" Ivy flicks through a towering pile of paperwork on her desk and pulls out a pink file. "Here you go. Hard copies. We're closing in ten, though."

I forgot the Electric shut at five on Wednesdays. Good job I rushed over. Inside the folder are maybe thirty prints. Grateful that for once Ivy was organized, I leaf through them. The fifth shot is one I remember posing for. I'm in the centre, presenting a cone of popcorn with a smile. Jade's face jumps out from the background. She hovers by the stairs with Harper and Quin, but she isn't joining in their conversation. Instead, she glares straight down the lens.

That look must be directed at my back. Or…

Is it directed at the person I was serving, out of shot? I remember exactly who was there, because he was making a joke about the cheesy words photographers say to get people to smile.

It was Mr Ellison.

The door clicks as Ivy breezes out, saying something about the loo. I flick through the rest. Mr Ellison's only in one other shot. I almost miss him because he's crouched behind the cut-out of James Stewart.

He's hiding. Why?

I photograph the shots on my phone, then stuff them back into the file. As I replace the file my eyes are drawn to the window.

Someone is lurking behind the advertising panel of the bus stop on the other side of the road. The town hall clock chimes five in the distance, and they step out. It's Mr Ellison. As he crosses the road, he glances up.

Right at the window where I'm standing.

I duck down. Oh God. He knows I'm here. Why else

would he be hiding nearby? At the bus stop I used minutes ago, no less! Did he tail me?

He'll know the building is almost empty, too.

I grab the file and dash into the foyer, almost crashing into Oliver.

"Oh, thank God!" I gasp. "I thought you might've left. Olly, it's Mr E." I whip the photos out. "Look. Jade's glaring at him. She realizes she's being played! No wonder he deleted these from the camera. He's out there right now, and—"

The main doors at the bottom of the sweeping staircase rattle. My heart leaps into my mouth.

Oliver places a reassuring hand on my arm. "They're locked. He can't hurt you."

More rattling. Then nothing.

He's gone.

"Shit, Mia, you're shaking," says Oliver. "Do you need a glass of water?"

I nod, leaning against a pillar as Oliver fills a cardboard cup from the tap on the other side of the refreshments counter.

Clang.

I rocket upright. This time the noise is behind us. "Did you lock the other door?"

Oliver freezes. I rush along the corridor where the screens are and yank open the back exit, leaning over the metal banister. Mr Ellison is at the bottom of the staircase.

He has Ivy pinned against the wall.

32

"Get away from her!" I shout, barrelling down the stairs. Mr Ellison jumps back as though he's been shot.

His mouth is covered in lipstick.

"Mia?" Ivy's ruby-red lips are smudged. My jaw drops as her hand settles on Mr Ellison's arm.

"I thought…" *You were hurting her.*

Mr Ellison runs a hand through his hair, glancing at Ivy. "Well. This isn't embarrassing at all. Should we, er…"

"Upstairs, Mia." Ivy waves me backwards. I stumble back into the foyer. Oliver gives me a WTF look. I mouth *I don't know* at him.

Ivy's grinning. "Mia, meet my ex, Evil Tom."

"What?" I gape at Mr Ellison. "That's not Tom! I saw pictures before you deleted everything. He had a beard, and long hair, and tattoos, and—"

"That look wasn't professional," says Ivy. "Shame. Obviously, I don't think he's evil any more. Well, only in good ways."

She winks. Oh God. The boxers I saw on Ivy's floor. I'm pretty certain I know whose those are now. "Please don't."

"Seconded," says Mr Ellison.

Ivy laughs. "Tom has been gradually winning me back. He's had quite the game plan. Taking a job nearby, encouraging a certain little cousin of mine to aim high…"

"This is why you've been so nice?" I demand.

Mr Ellison looks even more embarrassed. "I like to think I'm nice to all my students, but, in a nutshell, yes. When we were backpacking, Ivy said you were smart but didn't believe it. I agree with her. I hoped the quiz would give you confidence—"

"I thought you were perving on me!"

Ivy hoots with laughter. I scowl at her.

"It's not funny, Ivy. It made me really uncomfortable. Fine, it was about scoring brownie points with you, but he dialled being 'nice' up to, I don't know, a thousand! I could've landed him in real trouble if I'd said something."

Mr Ellison's scarlet. "I may have misjudged things. That's why I backed off. I'm very sorry, Mia. I was so desperate to make things right with Ivy, I tried too hard."

I think back over the weird things about Mr Ellison,

and groan. Outside school I only ever crossed paths with him at the cinema, didn't I? Ivy's tried going dairy-free recently. That explains Mr E's vegan biscuits. Looking out for me has been about Ivy the whole time! God, he really has it bad.

Mr Ellison looks worried. Love doesn't make the way he acted OK, but at least he realizes he screwed up.

Ivy touches my arm. "Do you mind keeping this secret, squirt? It's going to take a while for my parents to accept Tom. I'd like to tell them we're together again on my own terms."

"Whatever." Mr Ellison must've been hiding from Ivy's mum in that photo – Auntie Lou showed up halfway through the event. It explains why he took off that time Mum picked me up in the rain, too. Grudgingly, I add, "I'm glad you're happy again, Ivy."

"Cheers, hon. People deserve second chances."

Without meaning to, I glance at Oliver, who's doing a terrible job of pretending he isn't listening. Ivy and Mr Ellison leave, Ivy calling to Oliver to finish locking up. I watch them out of the window, walking hand in hand through the car park. They pass Quin. Of course – I asked him to meet me here.

I glance at Oliver.

"Guess we know why Ivy's been distracted now," he says.

"I hope she's doing the right thing. Mr E broke her heart."

There's a loaded pause. Oliver becomes fascinated by an

imaginary speck on the counter.

Quin's arrival breaks the silence.

"Hey," he says. "Could've told me to use the back door."

"Sorry. It's been a weird afternoon. Olly, is it OK if we stay a moment? Unless you urgently need to get home, of course…"

Oliver shrugs. He tosses the cloth into the bin and heads towards the staffroom. I sink into one of the foyer sofas. Now the shock is wearing off, I feel empty.

If it's not Mr Ellison, who is it?

Quin settles next to me. He's wearing a jacket I've not seen before, a roomy camo-print thing that's ninety per cent pockets. Are the shiny white trainers new too? I itch to cuddle up next to him, but hold myself back; it probably wouldn't be welcome.

"What's up?" he asks.

"I thought I had evidence it was Mr E, but that's blown out. This is hopeless. Aaron's going to get convicted if we don't work this out."

Quin grunts.

I sigh. "I forget how hard it is for you. The case was closed. Then I came along and turned everything on its head."

"Yeah. You did that all right. In more ways than one."

He gives me a sideways look. He seems … different today. His manner is purposeful. As though he means business.

Nerves flutter in my belly. "Whatever happens with the

verdict we can still hang out, if you want to be friends. But if I remind you too much of Jade, and you'd rather not, I under—"

"Why would you say that?" His jaw clenches.

"What?"

"That you remind me of Jade." Is he angry?

"We look alike. Not much now, but it must be something that goes through your head."

"Stop, all right? This is pissing me off."

"I was trying to be understanding—"

"Yeah? For someone so tuned into feelings, you're pretty bloody clueless. Or are you playing a game with me?"

"What do you mean?"

He makes an exasperated noise. I don't like the way he's looking at me. Harper's right, he is intense. Too intense, even?

I get up. "I'm OK to go now."

"No, hear me out. I need to say something." He's by my side in an instant. I step away, putting distance between us.

"Quin, I don't want an argument. I need to focus—"

"So do I." Quin's hands clench, then unclench. "And the way things are right now, I can't."

My back bumps the wall. Without realizing, I've crossed the foyer. I'm not scared of Quin, am I?

Harper is. But she doesn't know him like I do.

Or think I do.

Quin stops just in front of me. Not quite touching but almost. His chest rises, then falls. Quick, shallow breathing.

Eyes on my lips. He leans closer.

He's going to kiss me.

If this had happened a few days ago, I'd have grabbed his cheeks and snogged his face off. But all I can think about is one thing.

He smells of lemon cologne.

33

My hand snakes into the side pocket of my bag, closing around my unicorn key ring. I step to the side, plastering what I hope is a nice smile on my face. My mind races, connecting dots.

Way back, out of the blue, Quin followed me online.

He was the one who suggested the fake dating.

Camille said he was good at acting. Harper said the letters to Jade were copy-paste jobs. After that argument at Oliver's party, Quin went funny.

So did my stalker.

He and Jade were close…

And what could be more taboo than dating your own stepsister?

I need to keep him talking. Oliver's nearby. Surely he'll come to find me soon. "Why did you lie about Jade?"

Quin's cheeks flare. "What?"

"Camille's mum saw you out together. You had your arm round her. You looked like a couple in a photo I saw, too."

"Of course we weren't. For fuck's sake, Mia! She was my *stepsister*." He steps closer. My fist shoots out and connects with his jaw, key first. Quin cries out. I make a break for the stairs, then remember the doors are locked and swerve towards the back of the building.

"Olly!" I shout. "Help!"

"What the fuck?!" Quin roars. I rattle the side door – *locked too, shit* – then stumble as he grabs my shoulder. I lash out, aiming for his face. The key's jagged edge slices his forehead, buying me time to cannon into the corridor, shouting Oliver's name. The screens are locked. I tumble into Ivy's office and duck behind a row of filing cabinets.

The door swings open.

"What the hell's going on?" Quin's voice is loud. "You nearly had my eye."

"Don't you dare come closer." I grip my key tightly. "I know you did it, Quin, everything! This whole time you've been acting and lying. I only ever had your word that Jade was dating someone from school. You were the one who found the stalker photos in her room. Not difficult to plant when you live in the same house!"

364

"Are you serious?"

"You were really good at playing me, just like you played Jade. I liked you, a lot. Never saw all the little things that didn't add up."

"What things?"

Is he coming closer? I think he's stopped by Ivy's desk, just out of view. We're making a lot of noise. Please let Oliver have heard!

Keep him talking. "The night Demi and Zora were threatened was staged. Those messages convinced me the stalker was someone else, just like that threatening letter you faked. You were even outdoors when we spoke on the phone. I heard an owl hoot."

"This is bollocks."

He's angry. Good. Quin screws up when he's rattled. Maybe he'll admit everything. I grapple for my phone. If I can somehow record this…

"It brought us closer, didn't it?" I'm spitballing now, but it's making a horrible kind of sense. "Coincidentally turning up the night my room was trashed – you didn't come to apologize; you wanted to see me upset, then spilled your sob story to seem all nice and innocent. No wonder Aaron couldn't speak frankly in the YOI with you there! And that shit about helping me dye my hair 'for me' – did you get some kind of kick from seeing your power over me, is that it? Did you hope investigating together would make me fall for you, *Mr Stalker*?"

There's a heavy, smacking noise, then an almighty

crash. Another thump. A cabinet falls, files spilling across the floor.

A hand reaches for mine. "Mia, come on!"

I let Oliver pull me to the doorway, leaping over Quin. He's sprawled on the floor by an overturned chair, groaning and clutching his head. His hands are bloody.

Outside the office, Oliver slams the door, locks it, then rams the bolts in top and bottom. I fling my arms round him.

He hugs me tight. "Are you OK? He didn't hurt you?"

"I'm fine. Quin's the stalker, Olly. I attacked him – I—" The edge of my key is crimson. My legs turn to putty. Oliver helps me to the staffroom, easing me on to the sofa.

I'm shaking uncontrollably now. "How badly was he hurt? I didn't hit an artery or anything?"

Oliver shakes his head. "If anyone's getting done for assault, it's me. I conked him over the head with a film reel."

"Did you suspect it was Quin? You never liked him."

Oliver hesitates. "Not exactly. He kept coming up with reasons to get close to you, but, you know. Couldn't blame the guy for that. I thought me not liking him was just sour grapes."

"Everyone kept telling me he was a dangerous guy with a ton of issues, but I didn't want to believe it. You and Leyla warned me. I invented excuses. Ignored Camille when she as good as told me he was obsessive! Everyone else was right, and I was wrong." I bark out a laugh. "I have terrible taste in guys."

"It isn't the best, I'll be honest. But, you know. Biased."

I lean against him. "Quin can't break that door down, can he? I mean, assuming he's in a state to try and escape?"

"I doubt it. The doors here are pretty sturdy."

I close my eyes in relief. "There were so many red flags I never noticed. Throwing shade on you, lying about being able to drive. His dad's car could easily have been my stalker's. Even the night Aaron's parents' tyres were slashed – that was at The Mermaid Inn, where Quin's placement is! No wonder he knew what they ate. He cooked it."

"So Quin and Jade were secretly together? Wouldn't their parents have noticed?"

"Not if they kept it outside the house. We should phone the police, shouldn't we?"

"I'll do it once I've made you a sugary tea. That's what they give people for shock in films."

He smiles. I smile back, feeling guilty for the way I've treated him.

"Thank you for saving me, Olly. You were like a film hero. I'm sorry I've messed you about. No more bad boys. Nice guys all the way."

Oliver goes to fill the kettle, taking a clean mug from the cupboard. From what seems far away my phone bleeps. The screen shows a text from an unknown number.

It was some book called The Monk that he wouldn't stop going on about. Harper.

I frown. That sounds familiar. Did I learn about it for Quiz Challenge maybe?

"Here." Oliver hands me a steaming mug.

I take a sip, still frowning. I've definitely heard *The Monk* mentioned recently. Someone read it, only I can't remember…

And then it comes to me.

The mug slips from my hands. Tea splatters up my leg, across the carpet.

Oliver leaps up. "It's OK. I'll get a cloth."

I message Leyla what I've realized and where I am. My breathing is shallow. I think I'm going to pass out. She needs to have the photos from the teen screening I took earlier too. They're evidence…

Out of the corner of my eye I catch movement. Oliver has silently crept behind me. I blank the screen but it's too late. Slowly – very slowly – he folds the cloth and lays it over the back of the sofa.

"Shit," he says. "I really thought I was going to get away with it."

34

Tea drips down my shin. I search Oliver's familiar, lovely, kind face for a sign I'm wrong. He looks at me, his expression level.

"It's you," I say. "The photo from the screening – Jade's not glaring at me. She's glaring at you. The photographer. You're the one who deleted everything from the camera, not Mr E – you left that shot of Quin and Jade looking close on purpose and made out the other photos were lost."

"You've got tea all over my trousers." Oliver tilts one leg, a crease between his eyebrows. "I could deny everything but there's no point, is there? You won't buy it."

"I don't want it to be you," I whisper.

"Five minutes ago you were convinced it was Quin."
Contempt creeps into his voice. "I was surprised, but I was
happy to roll with it."

"*You* were with Aaron the night Jade died. I thought
you were…"

"Doing my homework like a good boy? Watching
Casablanca for the hundredth time? You never asked."

I swallow, my mind suddenly blank. Oliver sits next to
me.

"I'm not convinced Aaron's going to go down quietly
any more. He wrote me a letter after your most recent visit.
Very worked up about your safety. So." He smiles an empty
kind of smile. "I think I'm cornered."

It's a confession. A genuine IT WAS ME confession.
"Oh God."

"Poor Quin." His smile widens before vanishing. "I hit
him pretty hard. Lots of blood. You can die from a blow
to the temple, you know. Under the weakest part of the
skull is the middle meningeal artery. If it's damaged, that's
game over. Nasty things, film reels." A pause. "Yep, I'm
definitely done for. This is it. The end."

He dives forward and snatches my phone before I can
stop him, then strides out. He shuts the door and I hear the
key turn in the lock.

"Olly!" I jump up. "Come back. I want to hear how you
did it, how clever you've been, everything—"

"Not falling for that!" he calls. "You're trying to be a
film heroine, keeping the baddie talking until help comes.

But you're not the hero, Mia. I am. Don't worry. I'll return soon."

His feet pad away. I gaze around the cluttered staffroom – the oh-so-normal lockers, the enormous wooden bookshelf that fits nowhere else, breakfast bar, microwave, dishwasher and sink. This isn't happening. It can't be Oliver. He's kind, thoughtful and respectful. A nice guy. He believes in old school romance.

Yet he's admitted it. Everything – trashing my room in a malicious frenzy, spraying BITCH across the garage, the menacing messages, pressing close to me while I was blindfolded, smelling my hair, throwing me from the car – was him.

No wonder he knew my phone pass code and where I lived. His parents were probably with Aaron's in The Mermaid Inn, and told Oliver what Aaron's mum and dad ate and talked about! And the turning point in the stalker's behaviour came after I rejected him. The noise from outside while we were kissing really was his neighbour.

Why Oliver helped me search for Dotty, why he was still acting like my friend … well, that I don't understand, but I can't waste time figuring it out.

I drag a chair to the sink and clamber on to the draining board, but the high-up window's tiny, even for someone my size. It's dead out there. Screaming for help is pointless.

Panic builds in my belly. This Oliver, the real Oliver, isn't my friend. He won't let me out alive. If he was going to buy my silence he'd have already tried. No one even knows I'm still here – apart from Leyla.

Hope shoots through me. She'll read my message, realize I'm in danger, and call the police. And Quin's here too. He could break down the office door and come to save me. That Army training must be good for something.

Who am I kidding? Quin's injured, badly. He might even be dead. And Oliver will have deleted the messages I sent Leyla, probably before she read them.

I don't have a phone. There are no police racing along with flashing lights, no strong guy to play the hero, no Leyla to figure out a smart plan.

It's just me.

In the dishwasher there are blunt knives and cheap forks. Useless. I could unplug the microwave and chuck it at Oliver, I suppose, but I don't fancy my chances.

Click. Oliver reappears. He looks flushed, a spark in his eyes I don't like.

"Sorry that took a while."

He closes the door and leans against it. I jump down and go right up to him, forcing myself to lay my palm on his chest even though touching him makes my skin crawl. "Let me go. Please. Whatever you're planning, it doesn't have to be this way. If it's about rejection" – I try to smile – "maybe I was wrong."

He swats my hand away. "Don't touch me. It's too late to flirt your way out of this. You made it very clear I'm only a boring nice guy."

372

I step away, changing tack. "What really happened the night Jade died?"

Oliver sighs, running a hand through his hair. "I saw Aaron messing about in the gym from my bedroom window. It overlooks the field. Riyad was there too, but he didn't stick around. I knew you had plans with Aaron that night, so realized you two must have argued. I had an hour before meeting Jade, so I thought I'd go and find out what happened."

He's too calm. I wish he'd step away from the door.

"Jade's death wasn't planned," he continues. "It was instinct. I was going to dump her that night. She'd been acting funny. I had a speech all prepared; I was going to be kind… We were supposed to meet further up the field, where no one would see. I wasn't expecting her to be early. She found me talking to Aaron and started raging at me. Raised her hand. Then Aaron gave her this almighty shove, right into the cross trainer."

He winces. "So much blood. I would have called an ambulance, but Jade knew the real reason I was dating her. It wasn't great, both of you showing up for that screening. I did tell her not to come. I was really angry that she'd disobeyed me. And when she stole my photos of you, well. That was game over. I couldn't have you finding out I loved you, not like that. I knew you wouldn't understand. I was scared…"

He goes quiet a moment. "I didn't give it much thought, just grabbed her shoulders and thumped her head again, hard. Aaron didn't see. He was throwing up. He thought he'd killed her. I didn't correct him. I'm not proud of what I did, but I had no choice."

"Of course you had a choice!" I cry. "So what if I found out about your sick crush?"

"You'd never have wanted me if you knew about Jade – or the following, or the photos. But I did those things because I *loved you*, Mia. I *adored* you, and I couldn't have you, so I tried to get as close to you as I could while I worked out how you could be mine for real. Love trumps everything. Nobody else matters. You're a romantic – I thought you believed that too."

"Don't. Just don't." I can't bear him dismissing Jade like that. "Jade was a human being, and you treated her like she was nothing. Did you convince Aaron to move her body? To … what, set him up?"

"Aaron was the one who panicked, started babbling about needing to get 'you' to the nook. Drugged-up idiot. He was making so much noise. Wouldn't take no for an answer. I drove his car but I barely touched her body. I'm not a fool."

"What about when you killed her?"

"It was cold. I was wearing gloves. Could you pass my tea, please?"

"Get it yourself."

"And move from the door? Nice try. I made sure her blood got in his car boot. Considering I was thinking on my feet, you have to admit it was neat. Poetic, almost.

374

My girlfriend, your boyfriend, two obstacles gone in one night. Aaron was so grateful I helped him that he promised to swear I wasn't there. He's loyal, I'll give him that. Not very bright, though. It took him for ever to realize I wrote those letters."

He checks his watch. My arms prickle with goose pimples. Is there a funny smell coming from under the door?

"How could you do this? Any of this?" I cry. "You're supposed to be my friend!"

Oliver grabs my hands. His grip is crushing. "I needed to be more than your friend. You remember our meet cute? I fell for you so hard that day, Mia. It was a sign." His eyes bore into mine. "You were beautiful and fierce. No one had ever treated me like I mattered before. You made me see that life really could be like a movie. Seeing you with immature, ordinary Aaron broke my heart. I was so much better than him! More intelligent, more caring, more romantic, better dressed… I'm good at art. Maybe not as sporty, but I was working on that. If you'd been mine, I would have worshipped you."

My hands are burning now. He's so strong!

"Deep down, you knew we belonged together too," he says. "Passing notes in school, our in-jokes, the way you'd started to sit close to me and touch me…"

Finally he lets go, and his expression is cold. "I can talk about this dispassionately now, because I don't care about you any more. You rejected my love in the cruellest possible way."

I massage my palms, wincing. "I was thoughtless and drunk and kissed you when I shouldn't have. I'll admit that. But that was all."

"No, you rejected my love in the cruellest possible way. Say it."

"No. I won't. You've been creeping into my house. Taking my stuff. Lying in my bed. You're sick!"

"Not sick, Mia. Lovesick. I needed to be close to you." He tilts his head. "How do you know I lay on your bed?"

"My pillow didn't smell right." Talking of smells, whatever's out there's stronger now. "You didn't need to do any of this. Jade really liked you, Olly. Using her as a plaything... I thought you respected girls."

"I do. I was the perfect gentleman with Jade."

"Until you *killed her*?" My voice goes higher. "Are you a total psychopath, Olly? Why date Jade at all?"

He looks away, adjusting his collar. "I didn't have any experience with girls. I needed some so I'd know how to be a good boyfriend to you. Mr Ellison asked me to photograph the year eleven dance auditions. Jade was there. I couldn't get her face out of my head. I knew that with the right look, I could almost pretend she was you. Rather like how Scottie asks Judy to make herself into Madeleine in *Vertigo*. Judy does it because she's in love with him – dyes her hair and changes her clothes – but the one Scottie really wants is Madeleine."

"We're talking about real life, not your precious films! Jade just went along with your sick plan, did she?"

"Jade made it easy for me," says Oliver. "She was so unhappy. Just wanted attention. I listened and told her what she needed to hear. A bit like I always did with you. Jade was so keen to please. Never even questioned us keeping it secret. And she loved being bought stuff and driven around."

"But you don't have a car. You haven't even passed your test."

"There's a lot in my life you don't pay attention to, Mia. I took intensive lessons over Christmas. Dad gave me his hatchback when he bought the BMW. I was planning on doing a big reveal about the car when we finally got together."

I press my palm to my forehead. I don't know how much more I can take. "Oliver, you and I were already close. I liked you. Why would you send such creepy, threatening messages?" My voice catches. "I was terrified. How could any of that make me want you?"

"Don't you get it? That was a persona. I was trying to push you into my arms. Waiting for you to notice me wasn't working. Only you fell into Quin's instead, the bad boy – the most clichéd trope ever! So much for wanting a sensitive guy who respects you. Quin probably can't even spell the word romance."

Pressing up against me in the nature reserve when I was injured wasn't part of the persona, though. Oliver did that because he wanted to – couldn't resist, even.

Something occurs to me. "The guy you chased in the

alleyway. Did you … get someone to follow us so you could play hero? Someone like…" I take a guess. "Kris?"

Oliver nods. "Kris wanted to be invited to my party. He was happy to help."

So desperate for friends he didn't care how weird it was, more likely. "Was trashing my room part of the persona too? If me rejecting you was such a turning point, I don't understand why you carried on being nice afterwards."

"Ever heard the saying 'keep your friends close and your enemies closer'? As your 'friend', I could better enjoy watching you suffer. Why else do you think I called to 'make up' that night, and came to help you search for Dotty?"

"Oliver. I want to go. Please."

"It's too late for that." Oliver strokes my cheek. "I wish things could have worked out between us. We'd have been perfect together."

I place the smell.

Smoke.

I reel back. "What have you done?"

"I'm not getting out of this. I don't see why you should either. If you hadn't made me love you, none of this would have happened." Oliver's smile is shaky. "We're still going to be together for ever, Mia. That's always been how our story ends. Only, in this version, the credits roll in" – he checks his watch – "probably about five minutes. Very flammable, film reels."

I shove him. Caught by surprise, Oliver topples over. I

yank open the door and run into the smoke, slamming it shut behind me. The foyer is billowing with toxic black fumes. Coughing, I rip off my cardigan and press it to my face, dropping low as I stumble to the main staircase. Flames lick the lower steps, the right banister alight.

Shit.

I half-fall, half-jump down. Using the cardigan to protect my hands from the heat, I grab the metal bar across the doors, pulling downwards.

It doesn't shift.

I rattle the bar. Locked. How did I forget?

And Oliver has the keys.

I hurl myself forward, like I've seen in films. My shoulder smacks wood and I suck in pain. I can barely see. The smoke is choking, my lungs straining. I try again. It doesn't budge. I pound on the doors. Coughing overpowers me when I try screaming.

Surely somebody will have called the fire brigade. Quin, maybe. There's a landline in the office. Oh God. Please let Quin have somehow got out!

I give the door a final, hopeless whack. The flames are devouring the staircase. In a minute it'll be gone.

I crash back into the staffroom. Oliver looks up from where he's sitting, clutching his tea. His face is pale but resolute. Filthy tendrils of darkness curl under the door and snake around his legs, but compared to outside, the air is sweet and delicious. I double over, gasping as it fills my screaming lungs.

"Give – me – the keys!"

"I don't have them any more," says Oliver.

"Liar!" I scream. "I don't want to be burned alive and you don't either!"

"We won't be. Smoke inhalation will knock us unconscious first. It's relatively painless. I researched it, in case I needed a way out. It's a shame to destroy this beautiful place, but it feels fitting to die somewhere I love."

Oliver holds up his phone. "I've posted that we've decided to die together. I've chosen a nice picture of us, see? You'd think we were in love. Our names will be entwined for ever. Whether you like it or not."

He gets up and throws his phone out of the window before I can grab it.

"*No!*" I cry.

I spring at him. We crash on to the floor, grappling. Oliver rolls on top of me, straddling and pinning my body exactly as he did in the nature reserve. I swing my hips, tipping him off-balance enough to rip an arm free and slam my palm against his nose. He falls away. I scramble to my feet. He dodges when I fly at him again. I smash against the wall, turning, ducking and bringing the full force of my head up against his jaw, just like Cormac showed me. Oliver lets out a bellow of pain.

"Keys!" I shout. "Now!"

"No!" Oliver snarls. "You don't get to tell me what to do! I've wasted my life on you. Even went fucking vegan!"

He lunges at me. I bring up my knee at exactly the right

moment, hitting him bang between his legs. He crashes back into the bookcase. It teeters, then falls – right on top of him.

I clutch my chest, gasping with the exertion. Oliver's lying on his front, not moving. The full weight of the bookshelf presses down on his body.

I've killed him.

Then he lets out a growl. He tries to move but the bookshelf only wobbles. I squat by his side, slipping my hand through the gap and into his pocket. My fingers close around keys.

"Help me," rasps Oliver.

The room is rapidly filling with smoke. Sweat rolls into my stinging eyes. How far have the flames spread? To the door? Or do I still have a chance? And Quin. I have to find Quin. He needs me. If he's even alive.

"Bye, Olly," I whisper. Grabbing the wet cloth, I press it to my face and plunge into the foyer. Heat sears my skin and my mouth fills with a rancid burning taste. Where the steps were is a wall of fire. It roars with might and fury. No air. Just smoke. Thick, suffocating and deadly.

I stagger to the office, keeping myself low. My hand hits a wall, then the door. I loosen the bolts. The second key I try fits. Inside I can't even see the desk in front of me. A faint voice crackles from deep within: "Stay on the line, Quin, the fire engines are two minutes away…"

I try to call Quin's name but only splutter. I crawl forward. My hand knocks something. A foot. He's lying on the carpet, motionless. I grab Quin's ankle and shake. He stirs, coughing.

I find his hands and help him up. He's unsteady, his breath rattling. Blood covers one side of his head. How long does he have before he passes out again? Minutes? Or seconds?

I loop my arm around his waist and guide him to the doorway. Which way now? Towards the side or back exit? The side's closest. But the back steps are made of stone and railing. My vision is fading and my skin is peeling. This heat... So overpowering... I can't think...

With the last ounce of my strength, I tug Quin left, into the corridor. If I've made the wrong choice, we'll die. The floor feels springy. Is it about to give way?

A door. The back entrance. I grasp the handle, pull. Locked. Of course. My body screams as I stretch upwards with the keys. My lungs are burning. *I'm* burning. This key's wrong. So is the second. The third. Quin slumps on to the floor. The fourth slides in. My hands shake. I can't grip the key properly, can't get it to turn, can't breathe—

The door swings open just as something collapses with a thud behind us. Fresher, cooler air hits me. I force myself upright and grasp Quin's wrists. Using the entire weight of my body, I drag him on to the concrete, my muscles screaming.

Footsteps echo below. Figures in protective gear appear. Someone prises me from Quin. I wheeze out about Olly, the staffroom.

Then darkness closes around me.

35

I'm only aware of snatches of what happens next. Something closes over my nose and mouth. Faces loom above me. Lights. Voices. Then I'm rattling through a corridor, and it's all bright – so bright...

I must black out, because when I'm next conscious, the voices are familiar ones.

"Mum?" I croak.

"Oh, Mia!" Cool hands squeeze mine. "Try opening your eyes."

I don't want to. I'm scared. My head throbs and my mouth tastes bitter. But the air is sweet, and if Mum is here I must be safe. Cautiously, I open one eye, then the other. The lights of the hospital ward are dimmed. Mum sits on one side of my bed, Dad the other. Standing nearby is a nurse, a blue curtain surrounding us. I take a deep, experimental breath. It rattles.

"Don't talk too much, Mia," says the nurse. "You're recovering from smoke inhalation."

"Is Quin OK?" I whisper.

"Your friend's being looked after."

I close my eyes, dizzy with relief.

The next few days blur together. I feel weak, with a headache that doesn't shift. Apparently I've been lucky. Another minute and I'd have passed out. When I think of what could have happened if I'd spent that minute trying to save Oliver, I have to stop myself. It's too much.

When I get to see Quin, we match again: like when we dyed our hair, but this time in our hospital gowns. Quin sports a bandage on his head and a deep cut stretching from his forehead to his lip. He mumbles about complaining to my lawyer but stops when I burst into tears.

"I'm sorry," I manage. "I hope it doesn't scar."

"I could rock a scar. Fits the hard guy image." He starts crying too. "I thought I was gonna die. The operator kept telling me to stay awake. Every time I close my eyes, I'm scared I won't wake up. Why did you flip out at me, Mia?"

"I thought it was you. Stuff didn't make sense. Like you following me online—"

"That was Jade. I let her use my account to look you up."

"Sometimes it seemed like you were a couple…"

"We were just close." Quin wipes his eyes. "I always wanted a sister. Having one was great. Jade didn't care about the bad stuff I'd done. She was funny and spiky and kind… I'd have done anything for her. How much I miss her hurts."

"And Harper?"

"She doesn't like me. Her cousins go to Southaven High. She's heard the stories."

"What about the cologne? My stalker wore that. I thought—"

"I wanted to impress you, all right? I was making an effort. I like you, Mia. A lot. I thought you liked me too, only then we visited Aaron and you obviously had this connection. It made me insecure, so I got defensive. Feelings… I'm not great at them. If you admit how much you care about people, you're vulnerable. I've got used to protecting myself." He's stumbling over the words, but he keeps going. "At the cinema, I was determined to apologize and explain why I'd been acting up, even if it meant getting hurt, but I went about it wrong. I was scared to say I liked you before then in case you told me it was fucked up, cos I'm Psycho Quin the demon boy, and who wants him?"

I reach for his hand before he's even finished speaking. "I don't see you like that, Quin. It's OK."

He cries harder. "It's not OK. I was unfair to you. I'm sorry. I'm trying to be a better person but it's hard. I keep fucking up."

I take his other hand, repeating that it's OK.

Then the nurse appears and tells me the police are here.

It's not an easy interview. There's so much to cover, and talking hurts my throat. At the end I ask, "Will any of this make a difference for Aaron?"

"His case will be postponed," says DS Forster. "We'll speak to Aaron, see if he's prepared to talk. Then when Oliver is in a position to interview, we'll see what he says, too."

I don't know how I feel knowing that, somewhere not too far away, the boy who killed Jade and tried to kill me and Quin is recovering. Oliver was unconscious when the firefighters reached him and his heart stopped in the ambulance, but the paramedics brought him back. If I hadn't told them where to go, he'd be dead.

I don't know how I feel about that, either. Oliver won't get the cinematic climax he planned, but the Electric burning to the ground and his twisted suicide post have catapulted Southaven into the national headlines. It doesn't feel right. All Jade's death got was the local front page. The part of Olly that is – in Quin's words – *a dramatic piece of shit* will love this.

The suicide post has been removed at the police's request, but not before it was shared thousands of times. Leyla screen-shotted it. She – and Mum, and Dad, everyone, in fact – reassures me his obsession was not my fault.

"I think Olly was at rock bottom when he moved here," says Leyla.

I'm at home now, and we're huddled on the sofa with Dotty snoozing between us.

"The bullying at his old school was hardcore and his parents acted like it was his fault. Maybe this would have happened with any girl who was kind to him." She clears her throat. "This is my amateur psychology, but I'm guessing he's suffering from some kind of serious delusional disorder. I read about something called erotomania online. It's a condition where you believe another person's wildly in love with you."

Or maybe Oliver is a psychopath who genuinely believes that obsession is love. For a long time, it's just been him, the dog and films. Movies don't exactly present a very healthy image of relationships a lot of the time – and his parents aren't a shining example, either.

"I thought he was such a nice guy," I say bitterly. "He played me and Jade totally."

"And me," says Leyla. "I liked him too. I'm questioning whether anything about him was real, or whether he just moulded himself into the person he thought we'd like."

"Did you hear Aaron finally talked? He's allowed to wait for a new court date at home."

"Good." Leyla pauses, fiddling with a cushion tassel. "I don't know if his lawyer will be able to prove Oliver killed Jade. This doesn't mean Aaron will be OK."

Of course it doesn't. There are no guarantees, no neat, easy, happy ending.

Three months pass. Three long months, during which I hide from the media buzz and do nice, normal things. Like schoolwork. My grades become more consistent – not A grades, but good for me. Mr Ellison – who I do not feel OK seeing Ivy snog, and am never, ever going to call Tom – was right: I'm a smart girl. I just needed to believe it.

Outside of school, it's back to being me and Leyla again. I didn't realize how much I'd missed it. We talk lots, not just about Oliver, but Riyad too. He's been very lucky – as it was a first offense, he's only been fined for drug dealing. He's subdued, all his swagger gone, but he'll be OK – maybe this will be a wake-up call. Leyla's crushed, though. I'm so glad I'm here to support her.

Sometimes I see Quin. We're very slowly feeling our friendship out. Neither of us is in the right headspace for anything more. He's having trouble sleeping, and sometimes panics while cooking because the flames of the stove bring back his near-death experience. I hate that Oliver did that to him.

For me, it's having been stalked by my friend that's most haunting. It took a month to feel OK sleeping in my own bed. I still look over my shoulder and grip my keys. Sometimes the sadness is so suffocating it's unbearable. I'll see a silly thing like a badly photoshopped film poster, or an obscure fact, and be halfway to messaging Olly before remembering. Twisted as it is, I miss him – or who I thought he was. I keep thinking about poor Jimmy, and how confused he must be that Oliver's vanished. That dog loved him so much. It breaks my heart. We made a great trio, me, Olly and Ley, or so I thought. I really believed we'd be friends for ever.

The next time I meet Aaron, just for a walk round the park, he looks almost his old self, with floppy hair and his crutches gone.

"My lawyer's optimistic the case will collapse," he tells me. "If I get a sentence, it'll hopefully be a light one, including time served."

"You didn't kill Jade. Oliver did. He should be the one who gets punished for it."

"Yeah, but there's no evidence he was even there, let alone that he did anything to her. Them dating is irrelevant. My lawyer thinks he'll deny everything. It's my word against his."

"So Oliver will walk free."

"For Jade, yeah, probably."

Not if I can help it. My testimony of Oliver's confession has to count for something – and the police might yet gain leads from the appeal they've launched for witnesses of Oliver's whereabouts the night Jade died. Ivy will testify he wasn't at the Electric, which is where everyone believed he was.

Aaron adjusts his glasses, looking sombre. "I still can't

believe he actually did it. You must wonder why I protected Olly, before I realized he was the one threatening me in those letters… I thought he was helping me. It's pathetic, but I felt really guilty about chucking Coke at him the day of his job interview. I was supposed to look after Olly when he started at our school, but he wasn't cool, so I didn't. This felt like my chance to make it up to him."

I groan. "You're a total fool, Aaron."

He spreads his hands apologetically. "For ages I couldn't believe that he might be the one obsessed with you. I thought he was gay. He isn't, I know, but he told me he was, which is pretty sick. Guess he didn't want me getting suspicious when he fished for info. I might've told him private stuff, sorry." Like where I enjoyed being kissed, no doubt. I think of Oliver's cool lips on my neck and shudder. "He's a good listener."

"Good liar, more like. I don't know for sure if he'll get a sentence for stalking either." Even basking in the summer sun, I feel cold. "Guess I should be glad he burned the Electric to the ground and tried to kill me and Quin. Can't deny he did that. Not with the suicide post biting him in the bum."

Aaron looks uncertain, as though not sure whether I'm being sarcastic. "My lawyer reckons he'll get maybe three years for that. Two, if he makes a good impression in court."

Which no doubt he will. Oliver's MO is telling people what they need to hear. It's so unbelievably wrong that his sentence will be basically nothing. I thought the law was supposed to protect people, to serve justice. Instead, Oliver will be out before I finish university. He'll have a restraining order, but that's a hollow victory.

It's so broken. It's not only me, either. So many women and girls suffer like this. The stories I've started reading online are horrifying. Stuff needs to change. I can't solve it alone. My voice is tiny, but it isn't insignificant. When I feel stronger, I'm determined to use it – however hard that might be.

"Mia?" Aaron asks. I must've gone silent. "I'm never going to stop regretting the crappy choices I've made. I know I've screwed my future up. Granddad would be so disappointed. He always said I didn't think. I thought loyalty was a good trait, but it isn't when you protect the wrong people. All I can do is be better." He shifts. "I know that doesn't bring Jade back. I'll never stop regretting what I did. If I'd trusted you – or anyone, really – when I first received those letters, rather than playing the tough guy, it could've been so different."

I clear my throat. "We'll never know. You did what you could to keep me safe, even if it was in the wrong way. It's not OK, and I don't know if I forgive you, but you're not a bad guy."

"Just a really foolish one most of the time." Aaron touches my arm. I look him in the eyes. The eyes, once upon a time, I couldn't get enough of looking into. They're pretty ordinary, really.

"I think it's better if we don't see each other for a while," I say. "I'm still clearing my head when it comes to you. Maybe later we can watch some anime. As friends."

He nods. "That sounds good. No *Sailor Moon*, though."

"What? You like *Sailor Moon*."

"Nope. That was a lie to keep you happy. Can't stand *Miss Kobayashi's Dragon Maid* either."

And I thought I was the only one making compromises to keep our relationship strong.

Aaron takes a deep breath. In a rush, he says, "I thought about us a lot in my cell, Mia. All those people who told us we were perfect and going to be together for ever created really unhelpful pressure. It made you not being sure about us having sex such a big deal. I didn't mean to be pushy. I mean, I wanted it, obviously, but I guess I also wanted to stick two fingers up to the person sending the letters."

I sigh. "I put pressure on us too. I had silly, romantic ideas and so badly wanted us to work that I couldn't see that perfect on paper doesn't mean right. What even is the perfect couple, anyway?"

There isn't much else to say. For the first time in a while, Aaron and I are on exactly the same page.

"Bye then, Mia," says Aaron. "Thanks for not giving up on me. You've been brilliant."

He kisses me on the cheek. And I feel absolutely nothing.

That Saturday is my birthday. It's tempting to let it pass, but I'll only turn seventeen once. I'm not going to allow

Oliver Arrowsmith take that from me, too. Leyla and I bum around in London (our arms burn carting home the ton of manga I buy from Forbidden Planet), and the next day Quin invites me to his and cooks the most amazing vegan three-course lunch. Maybe I'm weird but I can't get enough of watching him cook. There's something so hot about how he owns the kitchen. Cormac leaves us a bottle of wine with a Post-it on it saying *This was never here! ;-)*.

Predictably, seeing the effort he's gone to makes me happy-cry. Quin looks bemused and gives me a hug.

"Was that pumpkin-seed pesto as good as the stuff you have dreams about?" he asks.

"Better, honestly," I say. "I can't believe you remembered that! I'm so glad you're getting your cooking mojo back."

"The therapist is helping. I've had worse knocks. Here, got your books to return."

I take the manga volumes he hands me. Quin isn't the keenest reader, but he's enjoyed everything I've lent him so far, and it means a lot that he wants to share. We chat about it on the bus back to Southaven, and the conversation continues as we amble down the pier to walk off our food bellies. It's heaving, the heat baking. There's something comforting in seeing kids splashing through the waves, all the sunbathers and queues for ice creams. Life going on. Quin mentions Jade a few times. It's good that he feels able to talk about her normally, and keep her memory alive. In a weird way, I feel a responsibility to understand who she was, too. I'm not sure we'd have got on, but she's a real person to me now – not just a victim.

393

We lean on the railing at the pier end, looking out to sea. Even not speaking with Quin feels comfortable. Neither of us has mentioned the looming court case. Today, it has no place.

Quin gives me a smile. His still-platinum hair is shiny in the late afternoon sunshine. "All right?"

I smile back. "Very all right. The way to my heart may be through my stomach."

"That's good news for me."

"Very. *Quinlan*." I nudge his leg with my foot.

He raises his eyebrows. "What's this about?"

"Me saying I think you're cool."

"With your toes?"

"Uh-huh." I nudge him again. Quin hesitates then extends his arm. I cuddle up against him and he puts it round me.

He clears his throat then doesn't say anything. I watch the waves, thinking. Then, softly, I say, "Just so you know, demon boy, I fancy the hell out of you and your skin-tight jeans."

He goes tense.

"And if we can carry on hanging out, only with, like, some added more-than-friends stuff, then that would make me happy. Assuming what you said in the hospital wasn't the painkillers talking, obviously."

He relaxes. "It wasn't." A pause. "That sounds pathetic. Wish I was better with words. I fancy the hell out of you right back? And I think you're amazing, brave and super smart, and you saved my life, and I can't believe something this good is happening to me. That less pathetic?"

"Who are you and what've you done with Quin?" I giggle, and he smiles. A proper, big smile.

"You sure you want this? You know, after…"

I look him in the eye. "He doesn't get to control my life any more."

I tilt my face upwards, making it very clear what I want him to do. A little shyly, Quin places his hands on my hips and pulls me close. Our mouths meet. And after that first, nervous moment, all the magic I remember from those early kisses with Aaron rushes through me. Only better.

So much better.

I draw back, beam at Quin, then lean in again and lose myself in the kiss.

This feels right. We're not perfect together, but I'm so over perfect. I'm into him, he's into me, and we've taken time to figure out what we want us to be. We trust each other, we talk, and I'm sure there's going to be more pumpkin-seed pesto. Maybe on paper we don't fit the way I did with Aaron, or even Oliver, and Quin is definitely not red roses and love poems, but none of our differences matter. It's him I want, not the gestures I once thought I was supposed to. He's a work in progress, but then I am too.

I like where I'm headed now. I think I'm finally figuring this love thing out.

Acknowledgements

Every book goes on a journey, and this one started out with apps, bodies in amusement arcades and a convoluted plot strand involving a cat allergy – yes, really. Thankfully, we've come a long way since then, guided by some very talented and astute people.

Huge thanks to my agent, Lydia Silver, for being a brilliant advocate. Thank you to Yasmin Morrissey for commissioning this book, to Julia Sanderson for all her editorial fabulousness, to Jamie Gregory for a beautiful front cover, to Emma Young for a sharp copyedit, to Sarah Dutton for her proofread, to my publicist Kiran Khanom, and everyone else at Scholastic.

This book's direction has also been steered by wonderful friends and beta readers: Grace Carroll, Heather Chavez, Tyler Koke, Valerie Ward, Annette Dodd, Luke Blaxill and Rebecca Anderson. Thank you! The YA Discord chatters have also been a brilliant support and so have the good folk of #WritingCommunity Twitter, who, with their hive mind, have helped me with many things from minor character names to pets to part-time jobs.

Thanks, as ever, to my parents, who always support me, and especially to Hugh, who on this one has been my primary collaborator. Lastly, thanks to the booksellers who've championed my stories, and to YOU, my readers. Thank you for picking *Love You to Death* up!